EVERYMAN,

I WILL GO WITH THEE,

AND BE THY GUIDE,

IN THY MOST NEED

TO GO BY THY SIDE

EVERYMAN'S POCKET CLASSICS

THE BEST
MEDICINE

STORIES OF HEALING

EDITED BY THEODORE DALRYMPLE

EVERYMAN'S POCKET CLASSICS
Alfred A. Knopf New York London Toronto

THIS IS A BORZOI BOOK
PUBLISHED BY ALFRED A. KNOPF

This selection by Theodore Dalrymple first published in
Everyman's Library 2021
Copyright © 2021 by Everyman's Library

A list of acknowledgments to copyright owners appears at
the back of this volume.

All rights reserved. Published in the United States by Alfred A. Knopf,
a division of Penguin Random House LLC, New York, and in
Canada by Penguin Random House Canada Limited, Toronto.
Distributed by Penguin Random House LLC, New York. Published
in the United Kingdom by Everyman's Library, 50 Albemarle Street,
London W1S 4BD and distributed by Penguin Random House UK,
20 Vauxhall Bridge Road, London SW1V 2SA.

www.randomhouse.com/everymans
www.everymanslibrary.co.uk

ISBN 978-0-593-31858-4 (US)
978-1-84159-629-7 (UK)

A CIP catalogue reference for this book is available from the
British Library

Library of Congress Cataloging-in-Publication Data

Names: Dalrymple, Theodore, editor.
Title: The best medicine: stories of healing / edited by Theodore Dalrymple.
Description: New York: Alfred A. Knopf, 2021. | Series: Everyman's Library
pocket classics | Summary: "An anthology of short stories about physical
and psychological illness, healing, and healers–featuring an array of
classic and contemporary writers, from Anton Chekhov to Lorrie Moore"–
Provided by publisher.
Identifiers: LCCN 2020039573 | ISBN 9780593318584 (hardcover; US) |
ISBN 9781841596297 (hardcover; UK)
Subjects: LCSH: Diseases–Fiction. | Short stories, English. | Short stories,
American. | Healing–Fiction.
Classification: LCC PR1309.D57 B47 2021 | DDC 823.008/03561–dc23
LC record available at https://lccn.loc.gov/2020039573

Typography by Peter B. Willberg

Typeset in the UK by Input Data Services Ltd, Isle Abbotts, Somerset

Printed and bound in Germany by GGP Media GmbH, Pössneck

THE BEST
MEDICINE

Contents

7

PREFACE

Most people have experience of illness and everyone dies, so it is hardly surprising that matters of medical interest or concern are frequently to be found in literature. Many doctors have been writers, and many writers were the children of doctors: Flaubert, Dostoevsky and Proust spring to mind, but there have been others. Whole shelves full of books have been written about the relationship of Shakespeare to illness and medicine.

Somerset Maugham, who trained as a doctor and whose first book recounts his experiences as a medical student delivering babies in the slums of London (he retained his licence to practise for decades after he gave up medicine so that he could continue to prescribe for himself), believed that a medical training was excellent for a writer because a doctor both enters the most intimate details of a patient's life and yet keeps at a distance, the observing eye never sleeping. The combination of empathic intimacy with distance – or ice in the heart, if you prefer – is just what a writer needs.

But if doctors observe patients, patients observe doctors – which they, the doctors, are sometimes inclined to forget. The doctor is therefore an important figure in many stories, and though I have done no scientific survey, I suspect that more portrayals of doctors are critical than admiring. The more-or-less useless doctor is a frequent figure in Chekhov, perhaps the greatest of all short-story writers. An active member of the profession himself, he was a close and not uncritical observer of his colleagues. ('Medicine is my lawful wedded wife and literature is my mistress,' he once wrote. 'When I tire of one, I fly to the other.')

Then, of course, there is illness itself. In the recent epidemic of Covid-19, many were the recommendations that, in our idleness, we should read Boccaccio, Defoe, Manzoni, Giono, Camus, among others, who made of epidemic disease the occasion of their work. Illness and mortality are made the moral teacher of humanity: we know that the deathbed is the only place in which Ivan Ilyich would ever survey his life.

Many writers had prolonged struggles with disease ('this long disease, my life' wrote Alexander Pope, which was not a whine of self-pity, but rather a pithy summing-up of his experience on earth). In the twentieth century, writers such as D. H. Lawrence, Katherine Mansfield and George Orwell were lost to tuberculosis at a young age: perhaps the intensity or urgency of what they wrote was in part a consequence of their chronic illness that kept mortality before their eyes.

Whether illness has any message for us is an open question. Some say yes, others say no: illness is just what it is, the working out of a pathological process in the human body, with no more moral lessons than the force of gravity has.

Nevertheless, as an essential experience of human existence, illness and the response to illness has been, and will always be, an important stimulus to reflection on what, in shorthand, is called the meaning of life, as I hope the following stories amply demonstrate.

Theodore Dalrymple

THE DOCTOR'S
EXPERIENCE

ANTON CHEKHOV

A DOCTOR'S VISIT

Translated by Constance Garnett

THE PROFESSOR RECEIVED a telegram from the Lyali-kovs' factory; he was asked to come as quickly as possible. The daughter of some Madame Lyalikov, apparently the owner of the factory, was ill, and that was all that one could make out of the long, incoherent telegram. And the Professor did not go himself, but sent instead his assistant, Korolyov.

It was two stations from Moscow, and there was a drive of three miles from the station. A carriage with three horses had been sent to the station to meet Korolyov; the coachman wore a hat with a peacock's feather in it, and answered every question in a loud voice like a soldier: 'No, sir!' 'Certainly, sir!'

It was Saturday evening; the sun was setting, the work-people were coming in crowds from the factory to the station, and they bowed to the carriage in which Korolyov was driving. And he was charmed with the evening, the farmhouses and villas on the road, and the birch-trees, and the quiet atmosphere all around, when the fields and woods and the sun seemed preparing, like the workpeople now on the eve of the holiday, to rest, and perhaps to pray. . . .

He was born and had grown up in Moscow; he did not know the country, and he had never taken any interest in factories, or been inside one, but he had happened to read about factories, and had been in the houses of manufacturers and had talked to them; and whenever he saw a factory far or near, he always thought how quiet and peaceable it was outside, but within there was always sure to be impenetrable ignorance and dull egoism on the side of the owners, wearisome, unhealthy toil on the side of the workpeople, squabbling, vermin, vodka. And now when the workpeople timidly and respectfully made way for the carriage, in their faces, their caps, their walk, he read physical impurity, drunkenness, nervous exhaustion, bewilderment.

They drove in at the factory gates. On each side he caught glimpses of the little houses of workpeople, of the faces of women, of quilts and linen on the railings. 'Look out!' shouted the coachman, not pulling up the horses. It was a wide courtyard without grass, with five immense blocks of buildings with tall chimneys a little distance one from another, warehouses and barracks, and over everything a sort of grey powder as though from dust. Here and there, like oases in the desert, there were pitiful gardens, and the green and red roofs of the houses in which the managers and clerks lived. The coachman suddenly pulled up the horses, and the carriage stopped at the house, which had been newly painted grey; here was a flower garden, with a lilac bush covered with dust, and on the yellow steps at the front door there was a strong smell of paint.

'Please come in, doctor,' said women's voices in the passage and the entry, and at the same time he heard sighs and whisperings. 'Pray walk in. . . . We've been expecting you so long . . . we're in real trouble. Here, this way.'

Madame Lyalikov – a stout elderly lady wearing a black silk dress with fashionable sleeves, but, judging from her face, a simple uneducated woman – looked at the doctor in a flutter, and could not bring herself to hold out her hand to him; she did not dare. Beside her stood a personage with short hair and a pince-nez; she was wearing a blouse of many colours, and was very thin and no longer young.

18

The servants called her Christina Dmitryevna, and Korolyov guessed that this was the governess. Probably, as the person of most education in the house, she had been charged to meet and receive the doctor, for she began immediately, in great haste, stating the causes of the illness, giving trivial and tiresome details, but without saying who was ill or what was the matter.

The doctor and the governess were sitting talking while the lady of the house stood motionless at the door, waiting. From the conversation Korolyov learned that the patient was Madame Lyalikov's only daughter and heiress, a girl of twenty, called Liza; she had been ill for a long time, and had consulted various doctors, and the previous night she had suffered till morning from such violent palpitations of the heart, that no one in the house had slept, and they had been afraid she might die.

'She has been, one may say, ailing from a child,' said Christina Dmitryevna in a sing-song voice, continually wiping her lips with her hand. 'The doctors say it is nerves; when she was a little girl she was scrofulous, and the doctors drove it inwards, so I think it may be due to that.'

They went to see the invalid. Fully grown up, big and tall, but ugly like her mother, with the same little eyes and disproportionate breadth of the lower part of the face, lying with her hair in disorder, muffled up to the chin, she made upon Korolyov at the first minute the impression of a poor, destitute creature, sheltered and cared for here out of charity, and he could hardly believe that this was the heiress of the five huge buildings.

'I am the doctor come to see you,' said Korolyov. 'Good-evening.'

He mentioned his name and pressed her hand, a large, cold, ugly hand; she sat up, and, evidently accustomed to doctors, let herself be sounded, without showing the least concern that her shoulders and chest were uncovered.

'I have palpitations of the heart,' she said. 'It was so awful all night. . . . I almost died of fright! Do give me something.'

'I will, I will; don't worry yourself.'

Korolyov examined her and shrugged his shoulders.

'The heart is all right,' he said; 'it's all going on satisfactorily; everything is in good order. Your nerves must have been playing pranks a little, but that's so common. The attack is over by now, one must suppose; lie down and go to sleep.'

At that moment a lamp was brought into the bedroom. The patient screwed up her eyes at the light, then suddenly put her hands to her head and broke into sobs. And the impression of a destitute, ugly creature vanished, and Korolyov no longer noticed the little eyes or the heavy development of the lower part of the face. He saw a soft, suffering expression which was intelligent and touching: she seemed to him altogether graceful, feminine, and simple; and he longed to soothe her, not with drugs, not with advice, but with simple, kindly words. Her mother put her arms round her head and hugged her. What despair, what grief was in the old woman's face! She, her mother, had reared her and brought her up, spared nothing, and devoted her whole life to having her daughter taught French, dancing, music: had engaged a dozen teachers for her; had consulted the best doctors, kept a governess. And now she could not make out the reason of these tears, why there was all this misery, she could not understand, and was bewildered; and she had a guilty, agitated, despairing expression, as though she had omitted something very important, had left something undone, had neglected to call in somebody – and whom, she did not know.

'Lizanka, you are crying again . . . again,' she said, hugging her daughter to her. 'My own, my darling, my child, tell me what it is! Have pity on me! Tell me.'

Both wept bitterly. Korolyov sat down on the side of the bed and took Liza's hand.

'Come, give over; it's no use crying,' he said kindly. 'Why, there is nothing in the world that is worth those tears. Come, we won't cry; that's no good. . . .'

And inwardly he thought:

'It's high time she was married. . . .'

'Our doctor at the factory gave her kalibromati,' said the governess, 'but I notice it only makes her worse. I should have thought that if she is given anything for the heart it ought to be drops. . . . I forget the name. . . . Convallaria, isn't it?'

And there followed all sorts of details. She interrupted the doctor, preventing his speaking, and there was a look of effort on her face, as though she supposed that, as the woman of most education in the house, she was duty bound to keep up a conversation with the doctor, and on no other subject but medicine.

Korolyov felt bored.

'I find nothing special the matter,' he said, addressing the mother as he went out of the bedroom. 'If your daughter is being attended by the factory doctor, let him go on attending her. The treatment so far has been perfectly correct, and I see no reason for changing your doctor. Why change? It's such an ordinary trouble; there's nothing seriously wrong.'

He spoke deliberately as he put on his gloves, while Madame Lyalikov stood without moving, and looked at him with her tearful eyes.

'I have half an hour to catch the ten o'clock train,' he said. 'I hope I am not too late.'

'And can't you stay?' she asked, and tears trickled down

21

her cheeks again. 'I am ashamed to trouble you, but if you would be so good. . . . For God's sake,' she went on in an undertone, glancing towards the door, 'do stay to-night with us! She is all I have . . . my only daughter. . . . She frightened me last night; I can't get over it. . . . Don't go away, for goodness' sake! . . .'

He wanted to tell her that he had a great deal of work in Moscow, that his family were expecting him home; it was disagreeable to him to spend the evening and the whole night in a strange house quite needlessly; but he looked at her face, heaved a sigh, and began taking off his gloves without a word.

All the lamps and candles were lighted in his honour in the drawing-room and the dining-room. He sat down at the piano and began turning over the music. Then he looked at the pictures on the walls, at the portraits. The pictures, oil-paintings in gold frames, were views of the Crimea – a stormy sea with a ship, a Catholic monk with a wine-glass; they were all dull, smooth daubs, with no trace of talent in them. There was not a single good-looking face among the portraits, nothing but broad cheekbones and astonished-looking eyes. Lyalikov, Liza's father, had a low forehead and a self-satisfied expression; his uniform sat like a sack on his bulky plebeian figure; on his breast was a medal and a Red Cross Badge. There was little sign of culture, and the luxury was senseless and haphazard, and was as uncomfortable as that uniform. The floors irritated him with their brilliant polish, the lustres on the chandelier irritated him, and he was reminded for some reason of the story of the merchant who used to go to the baths with a medal on his neck. . . .

He heard a whispering in the entry; someone was softly snoring. And suddenly from outside came harsh, abrupt, metallic sounds, such as Korolyov had never heard before, and which he did not understand now; they roused strange, unpleasant echoes in his soul.

'I believe nothing would induce me to remain here to live . . .' he thought, and went back to the music-books again.

'Doctor, please come to supper!' the governess called him in a low voice.

He went in to supper. The table was large and laid with a vast number of dishes and wines, but there were only two to supper: himself and Christina Dmitryevna. She drank Madeira, ate rapidly, and talked, looking at him through her pince-nez:

'Our workpeople are very contented. We have perform-ances at the factory every winter; the workpeople act themselves. They have lectures with a magic lantern, a splendid tea-room, and everything they want. They are very much attached to us, and when they heard that Lizanka was worse they had a service sung for her. Though they have no education, they have their feelings, too.'

'It looks as though you have no man in the house at all,' said Korolyov.

'Not one. Pyotr Nikanoritch died a year and a half ago, and left us alone. And so there are the three of us. In the summer we live here, and in winter we live in Moscow, in Polianka. I have been living with them for eleven years – as one of the family.'

At supper they served sterlet, chicken rissoles, and stewed fruit; the wines were expensive French wines.

'Please don't stand on ceremony, doctor,' said Christina Dmitryevna, eating and wiping her mouth with her fist, and it was evident she found her life here exceedingly pleasant. 'Please have some more.'

After supper the doctor was shown to his room, where a bed had been made up for him, but he did not feel sleepy.

The room was stuffy and it smelt of paint; he put on his coat and went out.

It was cool in the open air; there was already a glimmer of dawn, and all the five blocks of buildings, with their tall chimneys, barracks, and warehouses, were distinctly outlined against the damp air. As it was a holiday, they were not working, and the windows were dark, and in only one of the buildings was there a furnace burning; two windows were crimson, and fire mixed with smoke came from time to time from the chimney. Far away beyond the yard the frogs were croaking and the nightingales singing.

Looking at the factory buildings and the barracks, where the workpeople were asleep, he thought again what he always thought when he saw a factory. They may have performances for the workpeople, magic lanterns, factory doctors, and improvements of all sorts, but, all the same, the workpeople he had met that day on his way from the station did not look in any way different from those he had known long ago in his childhood, before there were factory performances and improvements. As a doctor accustomed to judging correctly of chronic complaints, the radical cause of which was incomprehensible and incurable, he looked upon factories as something baffling, the cause of which also was obscure and not removable, and all the improvements in the life of the factory hands he looked upon not as superfluous, but as comparable with the treatment of incurable illnesses.

'There is something baffling in it, of course . . .' he thought, looking at the crimson windows. 'Fifteen hundred or two thousand workpeople are working without rest in unhealthy surroundings, making bad cotton goods, living on the verge of starvation, and only waking from this nightmare at rare intervals in the tavern; a hundred people act as overseers, and the whole life of that hundred is spent in imposing fines, in abuse, in injustice, and only two or three so-called owners enjoy the profits, though they don't work at all, and despise the wretched cotton. But what are the profits, and how do they enjoy them? Madame Lyalikov and her daughter are unhappy – it makes one wretched to look at them; the only one who enjoys her life is Christina Dmitryevna, a stupid, middle-aged maiden lady in pince-nez. And so it appears that all these five blocks of buildings are at work, and inferior cotton is sold in the Eastern markets, simply that Christina Dmitryevna may eat sterlet and drink Madeira.'

Suddenly there came a strange noise, the same sound Korolyov had heard before supper. Someone was striking on a sheet of metal near one of the buildings; he struck a note, and then at once checked the vibrations, so that short, abrupt, discordant sounds were produced, rather like 'Dair . . . dair . . . dair. . . .' Then there was half a minute of stillness, and from another building there came sounds equally abrupt and unpleasant, lower bass notes: 'Drin . . . drin . . . drin. . . .' Eleven times. Evidently it was the watchman striking the hour.

Near the third building he heard: 'Zhuk . . . zhuk . . . zhuk. . . .' And so near all the buildings, and then behind the barracks and beyond the gates. And in the stillness of the night it seemed as though these sounds were uttered by a monster with crimson eyes – the devil himself, who controlled the owners and the workpeople alike, and was deceiving both.

Korolyov went out of the yard into the open country.

'Who goes there?' someone called to him at the gates in an abrupt voice.

'It's just like being in prison,' he thought, and made no answer.

Here the nightingales and the frogs could be heard more

distinctly, and one could feel it was a night in May. From the station came the noise of a train; somewhere in the distance drowsy cocks were crowing; but, all the same, the night was still, the world was sleeping tranquilly. In a field not far from the factory there could be seen the framework of a house and heaps of building material: Korolyov sat down on the planks and went on thinking.

'The only person who feels happy here is the governess, and the factory hands are working for her gratification. But that's only apparent: she is only the figurehead. The real person, for whom everything is being done, is the devil.'

And he thought about the devil, in whom he did not believe, and he looked round at the two windows where the fires were gleaming. It seemed to him that out of those crimson eyes the devil himself was looking at him – that unknown force that had created the mutual relation of the strong and the weak, that coarse blunder which one could never correct. The strong must hinder the weak from living – such was the law of Nature; but only in a newspaper article or in a school book was that intelligible and easily accepted. In the hotchpotch which was everyday life, in the tangle of trivialities out of which human relations were woven, it was no longer a law, but a logical absurdity, when the strong and the weak were both equally victims of their mutual relations, unwillingly submitting to some directing force, unknown, standing outside life, apart from man.

So thought Korolyov, sitting on the planks, and little by little he was possessed by a feeling that this unknown and mysterious force was really close by and looking at him. Meanwhile the east was growing paler, time passed rapidly; when there was not a soul anywhere near, as though everything were dead, the five buildings and their chimneys against the grey background of the dawn had a peculiar look – not the same as by day; one forgot altogether that inside there were steam motors, electricity, telephones, and kept thinking of lake-dwellings, of the Stone Age, feeling the presence of a crude, unconscious force. . . .

And again there came the sound: 'Dair . . . dair . . . dair . . . dair . . .' twelve times. Then there was stillness, stillness for half a minute, and at the other end of the yard there rang out:

'Drin . . . drin . . . drin. . . .'

'Horribly disagreeable,' thought Korolyov.

'Zhuk . . . zhuk . . .' there resounded from a third place, abruptly, sharply, as though with annoyance – 'Zhuk . . . zhuk. . . .'

And it took four minutes to strike twelve. Then there was a hush; and again it seemed as though everything were dead.

Korolyov sat a little longer, then went to the house, but sat up for a good while longer. In the adjoining rooms there was whispering, there was a sound of shuffling slippers and bare feet.

'Is she having another attack?' thought Korolyov.

He went out to have a look at the patient. By now it was quite light in the rooms, and a faint glimmer of sunlight, piercing through the morning mist, quivered on the floor and on the wall of the drawing-room. The door of Liza's room was open, and she was sitting in a low chair beside her bed, with her hair down, wearing a dressing-gown and wrapped in a shawl. The blinds were down on the windows.

'How do you feel?' asked Korolyov.

'Well, thank you.'

He touched her pulse, then straightened her hair, that had fallen over her forehead.

'You are not asleep,' he said. 'It's beautiful weather outside.

27

It's spring. The nightingales are singing, and you sit in the dark and think of something.'

She listened and looked into his face; her eyes were sorrowful and intelligent, and it was evident she wanted to say something to him.

'Does this happen to you often?' he said.

She moved her lips, and answered:

'Often, I feel wretched almost every night.'

At that moment the watchman in the yard began striking two o'clock. They heard: 'Dair . . . dair . . .' and she shuddered.

'Do those knockings worry you?' he asked.

'I don't know. Everything here worries me,' she answered, and pondered. 'Everything worries me. I hear sympathy in your voice; it seemed to me as soon as I saw you that I could tell you all about it.'

'Tell me, I beg you.'

'I want to tell you of my opinion. It seems to me that I have no illness, but that I am weary and frightened, because it is bound to be so and cannot be otherwise. Even the healthiest person can't help being uneasy if, for instance, a robber is moving about under his window. I am constantly being doctored,' she went on, looking at her knees, and she gave a shy smile. 'I am very grateful, of course, and I do not deny that the treatment is a benefit; but I should like to talk, not with a doctor, but with some intimate friend who would understand me and would convince me that I was right or wrong.'

'Have you no friends?' asked Korolyov.

'I am lonely. I have a mother; I love her, but, all the same, I am lonely. That's how it happens to be. . . . Lonely people read a great deal, but say little and hear little. Life for them is mysterious; they are mystics and often see the devil where

28

he is not. Lermontov's Tamara was lonely and she saw the devil.'

'Do you read a great deal?'

'Yes. You see, my whole time is free from morning till night. I read by day, and by night my head is empty; instead of thoughts there are shadows in it.'

'Do you see anything at night?' asked Korolyov.

'No, but I feel. . . .'

She smiled again, raised her eyes to the doctor, and looked at him so sorrowfully, so intelligently; and it seemed to him that she trusted him, and that she wanted to speak frankly to him, and that she thought the same as he did. But she was silent, perhaps waiting for him to speak.

And he knew what to say to her. It was clear to him that she needed as quickly as possible to give up the five buildings and the million if she had it – to leave that devil that looked out at night; it was clear to him, too, that she thought so herself, and was only waiting for someone she trusted to confirm her.

But he did not know how to say it. How? One is shy of asking men under sentence what they have been sentenced for; and in the same way it is awkward to ask very rich people what they want so much money for, why they make such a poor use of their wealth, why they don't give it up, even when they see in it their unhappiness; and if they begin a conversation about it themselves, it is usually embarrassing, awkward, and long.

'How is one to say it?' Korolyov wondered. 'And is it necessary to speak?'

And he said what he meant in a roundabout way:

'You in the position of a factory owner and a wealthy heiress are dissatisfied; you don't believe in your right to it; and here now you can't sleep. That, of course, is better than if you were satisfied, slept soundly, and thought everything was satisfactory. Your sleeplessness does you credit; in any case, it is a good sign. In reality, such a conversation as this between us now would have been unthinkable for our parents. At night they did not talk, but slept sound; we, our generation, sleep badly, are restless, but talk a great deal, and are always trying to settle whether we are right or not. For our children or grandchildren that question – whether they are right or not – will have been settled. Things will be clearer for them than for us. Life will be good in fifty years' time; it's only a pity we shall not last out till then. It would be interesting to have a peep at it.'

'What will our children and grandchildren do?' asked Liza.

'I don't know. . . . I suppose they will throw it all up and go away.'

'Go where?'

'Where? . . . Why, where they like,' said Korolyov; and he laughed. 'There are lots of places a good, intelligent person can go to.'

He glanced at his watch.

'The sun has risen, though,' he said. 'It is time you were asleep. Undress and sleep soundly. Very glad to have made your acquaintance,' he went on, pressing her hand. 'You are a good, interesting woman. Good-night!'

He went to his room and went to bed.

In the morning when the carriage was brought round they all came out on to the steps to see him off. Liza, pale and exhausted, was in a white dress as though for a holiday, with a flower in her hair; she looked at him, as yesterday, sorrowfully and intelligently, smiled and talked, and all with an expression as though she wanted to tell him something special, important – him alone. They could hear the larks trilling and the church bells pealing. The windows in the factory buildings were sparkling gaily, and, driving across the yard and afterwards along the road to the station, Korolyov thought neither of the workpeople nor of lake dwellings, nor of the devil, but thought of the time, perhaps close at hand, when life would be as bright and joyous as that still Sunday morning; and he thought how pleasant it was on such a morning in the spring to drive with three horses in a good carriage, and to bask in the sunshine.

SAMUEL WARREN

THE FORGER

CHAPTER XL

A GROOM, IN plain livery, left a card at my house, one afternoon during my absence, on which was the name, 'MR GLOUCESTER, NO. ——, REGENT STREET;' and, in pencil, the words, 'Will thank Dr —— to call this evening.' As my red book was lying on the table at the time, I looked in it, from mere casual curiosity, to see whether the name of 'Gloucester' appeared there – but it did not. I concluded, therefore, that my new patient must be a recent comer. About six o'clock that evening, I drove to Regent Street, sent in my card, and was presently ushered by the man-servant into a spacious apartment, somewhat showily furnished. The mild retiring sunlight of a July evening was diffused over the room; and ample crimson window-curtains, half drawn, mitigated the glare of the gilded picture-frames which hung in great numbers round the walls. There was a large round table in the middle of the room, covered with papers, magazines, books, cards, &c.; and, in a word, the whole aspect of things indicated the residence of a person of some fashion and fortune. On a side-table lay several pairs of boxing-gloves, foils, &c. The object of my visit, Mr Gloucester, was seated on an elegant ottoman, in a pensive posture, with his head leaning on his hand, which rested on the table. He was engaged with the newspaper when I was announced. He rose, as I entered, politely – I should rather say obsequiously – handed me to a chair, and then resumed his seat on the ottoman. His countenance was rather pleasing, fresh-coloured, with regular features, and very light auburn hair, which was adjusted with a sort of careless fashionable negligence. I may perhaps be laughed at by some for noticing such an apparently insignificant circumstance; but the observant humour of my profession must sufficiently account for my detecting the fact that his *hands* were not those of a *born and bred* gentleman – of one who, as the phrase is, 'has never *done anything*' in his life; but they were coarse, large, and clumsy-looking. As for his demeanour also, there was a constrained and over-anxious display of politeness – an assumption of fashionable ease and indifference, that sat ill on him, like a court dress fastened on a vulgar fellow. He spoke with a would-be jaunty, free-and-easy, small-swagger sort of air, and changed at times the tones of his voice to an offensive cringing softness, which, I daresay, he took to be vastly insinuating. All these little circumstances put together, prepossessed me with a sudden feeling of dislike to the man. These sort of people are a great nuisance to one, since there is no knowing exactly how to treat them. After some hurried expressions of civility, Mr Gloucester informed me that he had sent for me on account of a deep depression of spirits, to which he was latterly subject. He proceeded to detail many of the symptoms of a disordered nervous system. He was tormented with vague apprehensions of impending calamity; could not divest himself of an unaccountable trepidation of manner, which, by attracting observation, seriously disconcerted him on many occasions; felt incessantly tempted to the commission of suicide; loathed society; disrelished his former scenes of amusement; had lost his appetite; passed restless nights; and was disturbed with appalling dreams. His pulse, tongue, countenance, &c., corroborated the above statement of his symptoms. I asked him whether anything unpleasant had occurred in his family? – Nothing of the kind. Disappointment in an *affaire du cœur*? – Oh, no. Unsuccessful at play? – By no means – he did not play. Well – had he *any* source of secret annoyance which could account for his present depression? He coloured, seemed embarrassed, and apparently hesitating whether or not he should communicate to me what weighed on his spirits. He, however, seemed determined to keep me in ignorance; and with some alteration of manner, said suddenly, that it was only a constitutional nervousness – his family were all so; and he wished to know whether it was in the power of medicine to relieve him. I replied that I would certainly do all that lay in my power, but that he must not expect any sudden or miraculous effect from the medicines I might prescribe; that I saw clearly he had something on his mind which oppressed his spirits; that he ought to go into cheerful society – he sighed; seek change of air – that, he said, was, under circumstances, impossible. I rose to go. He gave me two guineas, and begged me to call the next evening. I left, not knowing what to make of him. To tell the plain truth, I began to suspect that he was neither more nor less than a systematic London sharper – a gamester – a hanger-on about town – and that he had sent for me in consequence of some of those sudden alternations of fortune to which the lives of such men are subject. I was by no means anxious for a prolonged attendance on him.

About the same time next evening I paid him a second visit. He was stretched on the ottoman, enveloped in a gaudy dressing-gown, with his arms folded on his breast, and his right foot hanging over the side of the ottoman, and dangling about, as if in search of a stray slipper. I did not like this elaborately careless and conceited posture. A decanter or two, with some wine-glasses, stood on the table. He did not rise on my entering, but, with a languid air, begged me to be seated in a chair opposite to him. 'Good evening, doctor – good evening,' said he, in a low and hurried tone; 'I'm glad you are come; for if you had not, I'm sure I don't know what I should have done. I'm deucedly low to-night.'

'Have you taken the medicines I prescribed, Mr Gloucester?' I inquired, feeling his pulse, which fluttered irregularly, indicating a high degree of nervous excitement. He had taken most of the physic I had ordered, he said, but without perceiving any effect from it. 'In fact, doctor,' he continued, starting from his recumbent position to his feet, and walking rapidly three or four paces to and fro – 'd—n me if I know what's come to me, I feel as if I could cut my throat.' I insinuated some questions, for the purpose of ascertaining whether there was any hereditary tendency to *insanity* in his family; but it would not do. 'He saw,' he said, 'what I was *driving at*,' but I was 'on a wrong scent.'

'Come, come, doctor! after all, there's nothing like *wine* for low spirits, is there? D—e, doctor, drink, drink. Only taste that claret;' and, after pouring out a glass for me, which ran over the brim on the table – his hand was so unsteady – he instantly gulped down two glasses himself. There was a vulgar offensive familiarity in his manner, from which I felt inclined to stand off; but I thought it better to conceal my feelings. I was removing my glove from my right hand, and putting my hat and stick on the table, when, seeing a thin slip of paper lying on the spot where I intended to place them – apparently a bill or promissory-note – I was going to hand it over to Mr Gloucester; but, to my astonishment, he suddenly sprang towards me, snatched from me the paper, with an air of ill-disguised alarm, and crumpled it up into his pocket, saying hurriedly – 'Ha, ha, doctor! – this same little bit of paper – didn't see the *name*, eh? 'Tis the bill of an extravagant young friend of mine, whom I've just come down a cool hundred or two for; and it wouldn't be the handsome thing to let his name appear – ha – you understand?' He stammered confusedly, directing to me as anxious, sudden, and penetrating a glance as I ever encountered. I felt excessively uneasy, and inclined to take my departure instantly. My suspicions were now confirmed – I was sitting familiarly with a swindler – a gambler – and the bill he was so anxious to conceal was evidently wrung from one of his ruined dupes. My demeanour was instantly frozen over with the most distant and frigid civility. I begged him to be reseated, and allow me to put a very few more questions to him, as I was in great haste. I was thus engaged, when a heavy knock was heard at the outer door. Though there was nothing particular in it, Mr Gloucester started and turned pale. In a few moments I heard the sound of altercation – the door of the room in which we sat was presently opened, and two men entered. Recollecting suddenly a similar scene in my own early history, I felt faint. There was no mistaking the character or errand of the two fellows, who now walked up to where we were sitting; they were two sullen Newgate myrmidons, and – gracious God! – had a warrant to arrest Mr Gloucester for FORGERY! I rose from my chair, and staggered a few paces, I knew not whither. I could scarcely preserve myself from falling on the floor. Mr Gloucester, as soon as he caught sight of the officers, fell back on the ottoman – suddenly pressed his hand to his heart – turned pale as death, and gasped, breathless with horror.

'Gentlemen – what – what do you want here?'

'Isn't your name E—— T—— ?' asked the elder of the two, coolly and unconcernedly.

'N—o – my name is Glou–ces–ter,' stammered the wretched young man, almost inaudibly.

'*Gloucester*, eh? – oh, ho! – none of that there sort of

blarney! Come, my kiddy – caged at last, eh? We've been long arter you, and now you must be off with us directly. Here's your passport,' said one of the officers, pointing to the warrant. The young man uttered a deep groan, and sank senseless on the sofa. One of the officers, I cannot conceive how, was acquainted with my person; and, taking off his hat, said, in a respectful tone – 'Doctor, you'll bring him to his wits again, a'n't please you – we *must* have him off directly!' Though myself but a trifle removed from the state in which he lay stretched before me, I did what I could to restore him, and succeeded at length. I unbuttoned his shirt-collar, dashed in his face some water brought by his man-servant, who now stood looking on, shivering with affright – and endeavoured to calm his agitation by such soothing expressions as I could command.

'Oh, doctor, doctor! what a horrid dream it was! – Are they gone? – are they?' he inquired, without opening his eyes, and clasping my hand in his, which was cold as that of a corpse.

'Come, come – none of these here tantrums – you must *off* at once – that's the long and short of it,' said an officer approaching, and taking from his coat-pocket a pair of handcuffs, at sight of which, and of a large horse-pistol projecting from his breast-pocket, my very soul sickened.

'Oh, doctor, doctor! – save me! save me!' groaned their prisoner, clasping my hands with convulsive energy.

'Come – curse your cowardly snivelling! – Why can't you behave like a man, now, eh? – Come! – off with this peacock's covering of yours – it was never made for the like of *you*, I'm sure – and put on a plain coat, and off to cage like a sensible bird,' said one of the two, proceeding to remove the dressing-gown very roughly.

'Oh! my God! – oh! my God – have mercy on me! – Oh,

strike me dead at once!' nearly shrieked their prisoner, falling on his knees on the floor, and glaring towards the ceiling with an almost maniac eye.

'I hope you'll not treat your prisoner with unnecessary severity,' said I, seeing them disposed to be very unceremonious.

'No – not by no manner of means, if as how he behaves himself,' replied one of the men respectfully. Mr Gloucester's dressing-gown was quickly removed, and his body-coat – himself perfectly passive the while – drawn on by his bewildered servant, assisted by one of the officers. It was nearly a new coat, cut in the very extreme of the latest fashion, and contrasted strangely with the disordered and affrighted air of its wearer. His servant placed his hat on his head, and endeavoured to draw on his gloves – showy sky-coloured kid. He was standing with a stupefied air, gazing vacantly at the officers, when he started suddenly to the window, manifestly with the intention of leaping out.

'Ha, ha! *that's* your game, my lad, is it?' coolly exclaimed one of the officers, as he snatched him back again with a vicelike grasp of the collar. 'Now, since *that's* the sport you're for, why, you must be content to wear these little bracelets for the rest of your journey. It's your own seeking, my lad; for I didn't mean to have used them, if as you'd only behaved peaceably;' and in an instant the young man's hands were locked together in the handcuffs. It was sickening to see the frantic efforts – as if he would have severed his hands from the wrists – he made to burst the handcuffs.

'Take me – to *Hell*, if you choose!' he gasped, in a hoarse, hollow tone, sinking into a chair utterly exhausted, while one of the officers was busily engaged rummaging the drawers, desks, &c., in search of papers. When he had concluded his search, filled his pockets, and buttoned his coat, the two approached, and told him to rise and accompany them.

'Now, covey! are you for a rough or a quiet passage, eh?' said one of them, seizing him not very gently by the collar. He received no answer. The wretched prisoner was more dead than alive.

'I hope you have a hackney-coach in waiting, and don't intend to drag the young man through the streets on foot?' I inquired.

'Why, true, true, doctor – it might be as well for us all; but who's to *stump up* for it?'* replied one of the officers. I gave him five shillings, and the servant was instantly despatched for a hackney-coach. While they were waiting its arrival, conceiving I could not be of any use to Mr Gloucester, and not choosing to be seen leaving the house with two police officers and a handcuffed prisoner, I took my departure, and drove home in such a state of agitation as I have never experienced before or since. The papers of the next morning explained all. The young man 'living in Regent Street, in first-rate style,' who had summoned me to visit him, had committed a series of forgeries, for the last eighteen months, to a great amount, and with so much secrecy and dexterity as to have, till then, escaped detection; and had, for the last few months, been enjoying the produce of his skilful villany in the style I witnessed, passing himself off, in the circles where he associated, under the assumed name of *Gloucester*. The immediate cause of his arrest was forging the acceptance of an eminent mercantile house, to a bill of exchange for £45. Poor fellow! it was short work with him afterwards. He was arraigned at the next September sessions of the Old

* ' "Oui, c'est très bien," repondit le recors; "mais qui *bouchera le trou?*" ' says the French translator; and adds in a note – 'Ang. to *stump up* – Terme d'Argot?' (The forger is called *Edward Werney!*)

Bailey – the case clearly proved against him – he offered no defence – was found guilty, and sentenced to death. Shortly after this, while reading the papers one Saturday morning at breakfast, my eye lit on the usual gloomy annunciation of the Recorder's visit to Windsor, and report to the King in Council of the prisoners found guilty at the last Old Bailey Sessions – 'all of whom,' the paragraph concluded, 'his Majesty was graciously pleased to respite during his royal pleasure, except E—— T——, on whom the law is left to take its course next Tuesday morning.'

Transient and anything but agreeable as had been my intimacy with this miserable young man, I could not read this intelligence with indifference. He whom I had so very lately seen surrounded with the life-bought luxuries of a man of wealth and fashion, was now shivering the few remaining hours of his life in the condemned cells of Newgate! The next day (Sunday) I entertained a party of friends at my house to dinner; to which I was just sitting down when one of the servants put a note into my hand, of which the following is a copy: –

'The Chaplain of Newgate has been earnestly requested by E—— T—— (the young man sentenced to suffer for forgery next Tuesday morning), to present his humble respects to Dr——, and solicit the favour of a visit from him in the course of to-morrow, (Monday). The unhappy convict, Mr—— believes, has something on his mind which he is anxious to communicate to Dr——.

'*Newgate, Sept.* 28, 18—.'

I felt it impossible, after perusing this note, to enjoy the company I had invited. What on earth could the culprit have to say to me? – what unreasonable request might he put me to the pain of refusing? – ought I to see him at all? – were questions which I incessantly proposed to myself during the evening, but felt unable to answer. I resolved, however, at last, to afford him the desired interview, and be at the cell of Newgate in the course of the next evening, unless my professional engagements prevented me. About six o'clock therefore, on Monday, after fortifying myself with a few extra glasses of wine – for why should I hesitate to acknowledge that I apprehended much distress and agitation from witnessing so unusual a scene? – I drove to the Old Bailey, drew up opposite the Governor's house, and was received by him very politely. He despatched a turnkey to lead me to the cell where my late patient, the *soi-disant* Mr Gloucester, was immured in chilling expectancy of his fate.

Surely horror has appropriated these gloomy regions for her peculiar dwelling-place! Who that has passed through them once, can ever forget the long, narrow, lamp-lit passages – the sepulchral silence, save where the ear is startled with the clangour of iron doors closing harshly before and behind – the dimly-seen spectral figure of the prison patrol gliding along with loaded blunderbuss – and the chilling consciousness of being surrounded by so many fiends in human shape – inhaling the foul atmosphere of all the concentrated misery and guilt of the metropolis! My heart leaped within me to listen even to my own echoing footfalls; and I felt several times inclined to return without fulfilling the purpose of my visit. My vacillation, however, was abruptly put an end to by my guide exclaiming, 'Here we are, sir!' While he was unbarring the cell door, I begged him to continue at the outside during the few moments of my interview with the convict.

'Holloa! young man! – Within there! – Here's Dr—— come to see you!' said the turnkey hoarsely, as he ushered me in. The cell was small and gloomy; and a little lamp, lying on the table, barely sufficed to show me the person of the culprit, and an elderly, respectable-looking man, muffled in drab greatcoat, and sitting gazing in stupefied silence on the prisoner. Great God, it was his FATHER! He did not seem conscious of my entrance; but his son rose, and feebly asked me how I was, muttered a few words of thanks, sank again – apparently overpowered by his feelings – into a seat, and fixed his eyes on a page of the Bible, which was lying open before him. A long silence ensued; for none of us seemed either able or inclined to talk. I contemplated the two with feelings of lively interest. How altered was the young culprit before me, from the gay 'Mr Gloucester,' whom I had visited in Regent Street! His face had now a ghastly, cadaverous hue; his hair was matted with perspiration over his sallow forehead; his eyes were sunk and bloodshot, and seemed incapable of distinguishing the print to which they were directed. He was dressed in a plain suit of mourning, and wore a simple black stock round his neck. How I shuddered, when I thought on the rude hands which were soon to unloose it! Beside him, on the table, lay a white pocket-handkerchief, completely saturated, either with tears, or wiping the perspiration from his forehead, and a glass of water, with which he occasion-ally moistened his parched lips. I knew not whether he was more to be pitied than his wretched, heart-broken father. The latter seemed a worthy, respectable person (he was an industrious tradesman in the country), with a few thin grey hairs scattered over his otherwise bald head, and sat with his hands closed together, resting on his knees, gazing on his doomed son with a lack-lustre eye, which, together with his anguish-worn features, told eloquently of his sufferings!

'Well, doctor!' exclaimed the young man, at length, closing the Bible, 'I have now read that blessed chapter to the end; and, I thank God, I think I *feel* it. But now, let me thank you, doctor, for your good and kind attention to my request. I have something particular to say to you, but it must be in private,' he continued, looking significantly at his father, as though he wished him to take the hint, and withdraw for a few moments. Alas! the heart-broken parent understood him not, but continued with his eyes riveted, vacantly as before.

'We *must* be left alone for a moment,' said the young man, rising and stepping to the door. He knocked, and when it was opened, whispered the turnkey to remove his father gently, and let him wait outside for an instant or two. The man entered for that purpose, and the prisoner took hold tenderly of his father's hand, and said, 'Dear – dear father! you must leave me for a moment, while I speak in private to this gentleman;' at the same time endeavouring to raise him from the chair.

'Oh! yes – yes – What? – Of course,' stammered the old man, with a bewildered air, rising; and then, as it were with a sudden gush of full returning consciousness, flung his arms round his son, folded him convulsively to his breast, and groaned – 'Oh, my son, my poor son!' Even the iron visage of the turnkey seemed darkened with a transient emotion at this heart-breaking scene. The next moment we were left alone; but it was some time before the culprit recovered from the agitation occasioned by the sudden ebullition of his father's feelings.

'Doctor,' he gasped at length, 'we've but a few – very few moments, and I have much to say. God Almighty bless you,' squeezing my hands convulsively, 'for this kindness to a guilty unworthy wretch like me; and the business I wanted to see you about is sad, but short. I have heard so much of your goodness, doctor, that I'm sure you won't deny me the only favour I shall ask.'

'Whatever is reasonable and proper, if it lie in my way, I

shall certainly' – said I, anxiously waiting to see the nature of the communication he seemed to have to make to me.

'Thank you, doctor; thank you. It is only this – in a word – guilty wretch that I am! – I have' – he trembled violently – 'seduced a lovely, but poor girl! – God forgive me! – And – and – she is now – nearly on the verge of her *confinement*!' He suddenly covered his face with his handkerchief, and sobbed bitterly for some moments. Presently he resumed – 'Alas! she knows me not by my real name; so that when she reads the account of – of – my execution in the papers of Wednesday – she won't know it is *her* Edward! Nor does she know me by the name I bore in Regent Street. She is not at all acquainted with my frightful situation; but she *must* be, when all is over! Now, dear, kind good doctor,' he continued, shaking from head to foot, and grasping my hand, 'do, for the love of God, and the peace of my dying moments, promise me that you will see her (she lives at ——); visit her in her confinement, and gradually break the news of my death to her, and say my last prayers will be for her, and that my Maker may forgive me for her ruin. You will find in this little bag a sum of thirty pounds, – the last I have on earth. I beg you will take five guineas for your own fee, and give the rest to my precious – my ruined Mary!' He fell down on his knees, and folded his arms round mine, in a supplicating attitude. My tears fell on him, as he looked up at me. 'Oh, God be thanked for these blessed tears! – they assure me you will do what I ask – may I believe you will?'

'Yes – yes – yes, young man,' I replied, with a quivering lip; 'it is a painful task; but I will do it – give her the money, and add ten pounds to the thirty, should it be necessary.'

'Oh, doctor, depend on it, God will bless you and yours for ever, for this noble conduct! – And now, I have *one* thing more to ask – yes – one thing' – he seemed choked – 'Doctor, your skill will enable you to inform me – I wished to know – is – the death I must die to-morrow' – he put his hand to his neck, and, shaking like an aspen leaf, sank down again into the chair from which he had risen – 'is hanging – a painful – a tedious'—He could utter no more, nor could I answer him.

'Do not,' I replied, after a pause, 'do not put me to the torture of listening to questions like these. Pray to your merciful God; and, rely on it, no one ever prayed sincerely in vain. The thief on the cross' – I faltered; then feeling that, if I continued in the cell a moment longer, I should faint, I rose and shook the young man's cold hands; he could not speak, but sobbed and gasped convulsively – and in a few moments I was driving home. As soon as I was seated in my carriage, I could restrain my feelings no longer, but burst into a flood of tears. I prayed to God I might never be called to pass through such a bitter and afflicting scene again, to the latest hour I breathed! I ought to have visited several patients that evening; but, finding myself utterly unfit, I sent apologies and went home. My sleep in the night was troubled; the distorted image of the convict I had been visiting, flitted in horrible shapes round my bed all night long. An irresistible and most morbid restlessness and curiosity took possession of me, to witness the end of this young man. The first time the idea presented itself, it sickened me; I revolted from it. How my feelings changed, I know not; but I rose at seven o'clock, and, without hinting it to any one, put on a greatcoat, slouched my hat over my eyes, and directed my hurried steps towards the Old Bailey. I got into one of the houses immediately opposite the gloomy gallows, and took my station, with several other visitors, at the window. They were conversing on the subject of the execution, and unanimously execrated the sanguinary severity of the laws which could deprive a young man, such as they said E——T—— was, of his life, for an offence of merely civil criminality. Of course, I did not speak. It was a wretched morning; a drizzling shower fell incessantly. The crowd was not great, but conducted themselves most indecorously. Even the female portion – by far the greater – occasionally vociferated joyously and boisterously, as they recognised their acquaintance among the crowd. At length, St Sepulchre's bell tolled the hour of eight – gloomy herald of many a sinner's entrance into eternity; and as the last chimes died away on the ear, and were succeeded by the muffled tolling of the prison-bell, which I could hear with agonising distinctness, I caught a glimpse of the glistening gold-tipped wands of the two under-sheriffs, as they took their station under the shed at the foot of the gallows. In a few moments, the Ordinary, and another grey-haired gentleman, made their appearance; and between them was the unfortunate criminal. He ascended the steps with considerable firmness. His arms were pinioned before and behind; and, when he stood on the gallows, I could hear the exclamations of the crowd – 'Lord, Lord! what a fine young man! Poor fellow!' He was dressed in a suit of respectable mourning, and wore black kid gloves. His light hair had evidently been adjusted with some care, and fell in loose curls over each side of his temples. His countenance was much as I saw it on the preceding evening – fearfully pale; and his demeanour was much more composed than I had expected, from what I had witnessed of his agitation in the condemned cell. He bowed twice very low, and rather formally, to the crowd around – gave a sudden and ghastly glance at the beam over his head, from which the rope was suspended, and then suffered the executioner to place him on the precise spot which he was to occupy, and prepare him for death. I was shocked at the air of sullen, brutal indifference, with which the hangman loosed and removed his neckerchief, which was white, and tied with neatness and precision – dropped the accursed noose over his head, and adjusted it round the bare – the creeping neck – and could stand it no longer. I staggered from my place at the window to a distant part of the room, dropped into a chair, shut my eyes, closed my tingling ears with my fingers, and, with a hurried aspiration for God's mercy towards the wretched young criminal, who, within a very few yards of me, was perhaps that instant surrendering his life into the hands which gave it, continued motionless for some minutes, till the noise made by the persons at the window, in leaving, convinced me all was over. I rose and followed them down stairs; worked my way through the crowd, without daring to elevate my eyes lest they should encounter the suspended corpse; threw myself into a coach, and hurried home. I did not recover the agitation produced by this scene for several days. – This was the end of a FORGER!

In conclusion, I may just inform the reader, that I faithfully executed the commission with which he had intrusted me, and a bitter, heart-rending business it was!

ELIZABETH BERRIDGE

THE HARD AND THE HUMAN

THE DOCTOR WATCHED the green charabanc emerge from among the yews flanking the drive and draw up in front of the wide stone porch.

They were late. From habit she glanced at her watch. That meant she would be late examining them. As she looked the door of the charabanc opened and the women dropped heavily, one by one, on to the snow-buried gravel. For a moment she was reminded of the blundering honey bees of summer, over-weighted with pollen. But the image passed as they clustered together before the house, gazing about, their faces cold, movements distrustful. Swiftly she counted them. Two missing. That always happened: a husband or mother insisting on the child being born at home, raid or no raid. Turning from the window she caught a glimpse of a scarlet coat. Startled by the colour, she looked closer. She saw a girl standing apart, as in denial, and something about the arrogant head with its swathes of rich hair disturbed her. The others would be no trouble, but – with a definite feeling of unrest the doctor drew back into the room as Sister Matthews stepped out from the porch to welcome them.

The women looked hardly more at ease when they gathered for their examination. The doctor glanced swiftly at them as the nurse set up the screens at the far end of the room. They looked strange and pathetic, most of them in their early twenties, schoolgirl faces peaked with cold and the unaccustomed surroundings. They seemed unable to believe that the journey was over: the cold journey started early that morning from among familiar streets, bombed buildings looking like half-destroyed snow-castles; the long journey during which each had time to realise that before she could return there would be pain and a new experience, to be borne alone. And at last the flat, frost-bitten country, which bewildered even the driver, had yielded them up to shelter – no, they could not quite believe it.

It seemed to the doctor that pregnancy had given back to each of them an innocence which sat hauntingly behind her eyes. It mixed with the flame of fear that gathered up and exposed each separate strand of emotion, weighting more finely the balance between reason and hysteria. She felt this fear reach out to claim her as she started the examinations, bending over each full-formed belly, placed so incongruously between a girl's face and slender legs, she felt the full flood of power take possession of her hands, giving out calmness and strength, guiding her to the living child. Confidence was the first essential. Something had to replace the loss of home, the cosseting of friends. Here one made the first move towards a successful delivery.

She was fully absorbed when the girl she had seen from the window walked round the screen. She recognised her thick hair and upright carriage. The doctor saw her eyes were large, the pupils dilated, dark, with green lights, as if she continually strained to focus attention away from her heavy body. She sat on the couch and drew away from the nurse's hands, pulling off her clothes. The doctor felt her shock of interest deepen and realised for the first time that Sister Matthews' actions were repellent – impersonal as a brothel-keeper's, partially undressing a girl for a client's appraisal. 'That will do, sister,' she said, and the tone of her voice made the nurse withdraw, hurt, to the table, where she made a show of checking names.

What lay behind those painfully wide eyes? wondered the doctor as she carried on the examination. 'Relax,' she said. 'Relax.' But the girl's muscles seemed locked. That would mean trouble later. 'Relax,' she said again. 'You must let yourself go loose. There's nothing to be afraid of. I won't hurt you.'

That touched something in the still face and a flare of colour covered the cheeks. 'I'm not afraid,' said the girl, 'this is just a process, like anything else . . .' but she relaxed and smiled slightly. The doctor nodded approval.

'That's better,' she said. What a voice the girl had. After the hesitancy of the others, their frayed enunciation, its clearness was astounding. It was like her own voice, decisive, entirely under control. Sister Matthews handed her a slip of paper, and she frowned slightly, motioning the girl to dress. 'We'll be keeping you in here for a few days,' she said, 'then we'll see about billeting you out.'

The girl sat up and pulled on her clothes. 'Oh!' she said, 'I expected that. My blood-pressure's always been erratic.' She laughed, as if here she was on the doctor's ground and could claim equality.

The doctor looked at her sharply. 'Then you'll know how to take care of yourself. No smoking, no alcohol.'

'Alcohol? In this wilderness?' the girl raised her eyebrows. 'All right to go now?' she asked.

'Lady touch-me-not,' murmured the sister as she re-adjusted the screens. She was angry and her eyes were unkind. 'She'll soon find her level here.'

In the days that followed the doctor and each one of the staff saw Theresa Jenkins moving silently among the other women, accepting no mien of behaviour. Hers was a dark dress where the others wore flowered smocks, full, but not full enough to disguise the bouncing burdens which governed their every movement. She walked erect and lightly in contrast to the lurching tread of those around her. She did not knit or sew to patterns, she very seldom read. But every day she walked the two miles into the nearest market town and brought back silks or wools or books for the others.

It was here the doctor next encountered her; on a day of blizzard when the snow drove horizontally across the heath, lying flat as a footprint between the hall and Airton. She was leaning against the low wall on the bridge, the wind whipping the scarlet coat around her. Below, the waterfall was frozen. She did not look round when the car drew up until the doctor's voice, sharp with command, came through the blinding flakes. The door was opened and she climbed in, shutting it behind her with dead fingers. 'A little exercise I said, not a cross-country run . . .' Firmly the doctor rubbed the windscreen and adjusted the wipers. They moved forward as a camouflaged army lorry passed them in a white cloud.

'Yes, it was a bit too much to-day,' said the girl; she was blue round the lips. 'But I'm well ballasted.'

'Well, I'm putting you and your ballast to bed when we get back, and you're staying there.'

Theresa looked coolly at the determined face beside her and shrugged. 'But not in one of those great communal bedrooms – there's no fire, and the beds are awful, filled with chicken-food. . . .'

They entered the drive. There was a tensed sparring atmosphere between them. The doctor fell back on her power of position. She said, 'I'm putting you into solitary confinement. You're in for an attack of 'flu.'

As she drove the car round to the back of the house she thought: She upsets me, makes me feel – oh, I don't know.

In the nursery on the ground floor there was never complete silence. Nurse Griffith, standing by the weighing machine, looked with sudden exasperation along the rows of baskets. From nearly each one came a thin gasping cry or a long effortless wail. 'If they'd only stop. Just for a moment. All together,' she said aloud. But as if in defiance a quacking gurgle joined in. 'Well, you'll be gone to-morrow, glory be,' she observed, 'and I wish your mother joy of you.'

The door opened and two other nurses came in, carrying bundles under their arms, bundles done up in striped blankets and shaped like paper twists for sweets.

'Bullying them again, Griffith?' said one of them and, laying one of her burdens in a basket she sat down and unwrapped the other, revealing a tiny crumpled face and one red fist. She started to change its napkin.

'I was just telling Donald Duck how glad I shall be when he goes.'

'Poor little Donald, I shall miss him. Such an *individualist*,' said the other nurse. Her eyes were dark and moist. She looked as if she overflowed with love for each baby there.

Nurse Griffith grunted. She was Scottish and spared her emotion. 'Have you seen the doctor?' she inquired, 'I want her to look at young Rolly – he'll have to be circumcised, I think.'

'She's due any minute.' The dark-eyed nurse was frowning at the child she had unwrapped and who now lay screaming on the scales. She checked the weight, then whisked the child off. 'Not enough food. I thought her milk was going off. Come along, chicken.' She took up a bottle warming by the fire and settled herself in a chair. The child's face uncrumpled as its mouth found the teat. 'I can give a guess where she is, though. In Ward 12, and there's nothing wrong with Mrs. Jenkins now.'

'Nothing apart from having a baby,' said Nurse Griffith, 'I said to her the other day, "Soon be over, Mrs. Jenkins. Next week for you." And she gave me such a look. Sat up and said, "No doubt you're looking forward to it. Well. I'm not." So I said, "One baby more or less makes no difference to me, my girl. I've brought enough into the world."'

'Doctor seems to get on well with her, though,' said the other nurse.

'Get on well!' Nurse Griffith sniffed. 'There *was* an atmosphere when I went in this morning. Cut it with a knife, you could.' She broke off as the door opened and the doctor came in with the matron, who was in her outdoor clothes. She was frowning slightly, and Nurse Griffith looked keenly at her. It seemed that the wailing of the babies affected her more than usual this morning; her frown had deepened as they walked down the rows together. Carefully she asked questions and conducted examinations in her usual capable manner, but it seemed to the nurse that her eyes were preoccupied.

'You're quite right, nurse,' she said, 'Baby Rolly needs to be circumcised. I'll see his mother.' Turning to the matron she said, 'I think I'll leave those vaccinations now, and do all three together later.' With a nod she left them and walked quickly from the nursery.

'Perhaps she's a little tired,' said the matron, 'she *does* work hard.'

But the doctor was not feeling tired as she walked across the cold stone hall and down the passage opposite to where the narrow wooden stairs ran up from just past the dining-room door. As she went slowly up to the next floor and passed along the narrow corridor of closed doors she thought, a little shakily: That was a strange thing for a patient to say to me. It's never happened before. She had passed through the width of the house and now stood on the first main landing. The huge polished space of floor with the broad and shining staircase curving down to the hall below and up to the labour ward on the next floor quietened her. As always its familiarity was startling; she might have been born here. The wide windows framed the winter and for a moment she stopped, undecided. She's no right to speak to me like that, she thought, and made to go to her own room, with the comforting china procession along the mantelpiece; ducks, elephants, donkeys – but the pricking unease forbade her the comfort of a fire or even the absorption of study. No right?

She had said, going into Ward 12 that morning, 'You'll be having your baby very soon, Mrs. Jenkins. I like to tell the more intelligent mothers exactly what happens, it makes it easier . . .' but had been unable to go on, seeing the irony on the other's face. The girl sat there in bed, a little flushed, the eyes mocking her, openly mocking the whole procedure of birth, the diet, the routine, the urine tests.

'I expect I shall find out for myself, thanks,' she said. Her voice was casual as if she were turning away an itinerant salesman. The doctor went white, but forced herself to say, as if she had heard nothing, 'And if there's anything worrying you, preventing you from sleeping, you'll tell me, won't you? It's important not to have anything on your mind.' She turned from the bed and walked over to the fireplace as she spoke, and standing in the attitude of her father, with legs apart and hands clasped loosely, she felt some of his strength flow into her.

'Yes, people seem to hate you having anything on your mind,' came the voice from the bed. 'Calm motherhood, that's the idea, isn't it? The most beautiful time of a woman's life, preparing for the little stranger—' her whole face twisted

59

suddenly, but whether with pain or disgust the doctor could not make out.

'That wasn't my idea at all,' she said. 'Some people think that way, others don't. Nurse Barnes tells me you're not sleeping. I want to know why.' She had accepted the challenge flung out by the mocking face, but immediately regretted it. For the girl had sent her a glance meaning: Is it really your business? The door opened then and Nurse Griffith had come in.

Now, standing in the faint chilled sunlight, she thought: Of course it's my business. Did the girl think that having a baby was as easy as that? Did she think that at such a time she could remain private and apart? Where would you be in medicine without method and routine? I won't let her bother me, she thought, and shrugging, turned to go up the stairs past the labour ward. I must see Mrs. Rolly.

The visit to the quiet ward with its rows of docile women knitting or talking was curiously soothing. Here was her defence, among the soft-eyed women, soft as if milk flowed through every vein. No complications. No questioning of her authority and importance. They were gentle as cattle in good pasture. I must go back to Ireland, she thought as she left the ward in a small stir behind her. That's what's wrong. I need a holiday. Whenever things were too difficult – examinations near, her mind caught at the low green image of the land near her home.

She looked in at the dispensary on her way down.

'Oh, Nurse Barnes,' she said, 'give Mrs. Jenkins a sleeping draught to-night.'

From below, distantly, came the ring of the telephone. 'I'll go,' she said, 'Matron's out.' But as she ran down the main staircase the bell stopped abruptly. Opening the door of the matron's sitting-room she saw Theresa Jenkins at the desk, a blue dressing-gown clasped round her, and holding the receiver tightly to her ear.

The girl looked up.

'Long distance,' she said, her hand over the mouthpiece, 'for me.'

It was annoying how composed, how *right*, she looked, sitting there in the matron's room, at the matron's desk. The doctor let her feelings out in a sentence she knew with all her being would hurt. 'You know you women are not allowed in here,' she said, leaning deliberately against the door, eyebrows raised. She saw the deep flush spread over the girl's face, and knew she had scored. But next moment the girl was speaking into the phone. Her voice was hurried, a little shaken. 'Hallo, yes darling, it's me.' The doctor could hear nothing of the voice at the other end of the line, but it spoke at length and the girl listened, her colour ebbing to normal. Then, 'Of course,' she said.

The doctor walked towards the wide white fireplace where the matron's cat, grey as the ash falling from the logs, arched itself for a caress. What can I say to her, she thought, automatically smoothing the quick ears. The quiet of the pale walls, the cat's electric purring, the soft private answers of the girl at the telephone helped the doctor to define the feelings which had disturbed her since that first glimpse of the scarlet coat through the window. Odd how she had felt there would be trouble from her. She was always right in these things. She remembered the old man who had said he could see the power about her: 'You could heal by a touch, dear young lady,' and the sweat was ridged above his eyebrows, caught in the bushiness of them. He had died the next day. Shaking herself free of that Dublin slum she looked into the fire. The girl was different, outside her power. It was like being faced by a new and hostile world. She heard footsteps and laughter go past the door and felt again the tremendous difference between the girl at the desk and those others. They had accepted life in the hospital as a logical conclusion to the months of carrying the child; putting behind them their private lives. At this time everything was swamped in the expectation of birth; husbands were unreal, the newspapers not important. They were the childbearers.

The doctor pushed a log in place with her foot and watched the sudden sparks showering. The cat jumped a little. That attitude makes it much easier for us, she thought. Biological, impersonal. The nurses must feel the same.

The girl at the desk was speaking now, purposefully, with a hint of impatience.

She mightn't be having a child at all, thought the doctor with indignation. She goes on exactly as if she were at home, or on a visit. Perhaps her own life is too exciting. As this thought passed through her mind a sudden envy attacked her. It came as unexpectedly as the sound of the clock outside the door, striking with the ponderous hesitation of old age.

Snaking over the countryside went the wire connecting Theresa's life with Rowley Hall. Somewhere out in the snow, in a city, a man was sitting, or maybe standing, one leg up on a chair, watching his cigarette spiral in smoke as he spoke into the receiver. Other worlds, other relationships; the whole organisation of Rowley Hall meaning nothing beside them. She, the doctor, of as little significance as an obliging bus-conductor, a helpful policeman. She felt enclosed in this smooth-running house, its babies across the hall, its mothers above. Yet they all depend on me. The thought brought no pride, only a sense of suffocation and a sudden, I would give it all up for a telephone call from a city . . .

The receiver was hung up with a small metallic noise.

For a moment both women stared at it. The line was dead now: over snow wastes ran the slack wires.

'Come and get warm before you go upstairs,' said the doctor, and the girl moved slowly, heavily towards the fireplace. Her face was like stone.

'Cats are so magnificently selfish,' she said, staring down.

The doctor knew it was her moment; the girl looked drained, as if contact with the vital world outside had been too much for her. She was lost between the two existences; a word and she would be shattered. As a woman, cunning, before the fire, the doctor could spin a web of words – she could capture that world, suck it from the girl. But she said, 'I'll walk upstairs with you,' and put a hand on her elbow. 'You'd better get into bed and rest.' Without a word they left the room and went up the shallow stairs in silence. Something has happened, thought the doctor. I do hope . . . but her fear was a vague thing, scarcely yet known to her intuition.

As they turned in to Ward 12 the girl said: 'Matron knew I was expecting a call.' She sat on the bed and knocked off her blue slippers. As she settled against the pillows the doctor pulled the clothes round her. She felt at ease doing these things, her brain working, Does she need sal volatile, a cup of tea? A glance at her watch told her tea would be brought round within ten minutes. She sat down.

'Do you really want your baby?' she asked.

They looked at each other. The distance between them was so vast, so wearying, that it had to be accepted, could never be crossed.

'You'd like me to want it, wouldn't you?' said Theresa, exhaustion seemed to edge her voice, and increase the hidden store of rancour. Or was it bitterness, torment,

63

sorrow? 'You'd like to feel it meant everything to me, and I was relying on you to get me through.'

'What nonsense,' said the doctor. Despite her reason she felt suddenly malicious. 'You're just one patient, and I don't want any trouble. You're the sort of person to cause it . . .'

'Trouble?' Theresa laughed outright. 'No, you're not used to that, are you? The only people you can deal with are weaklings – the world's temporary throw-outs. The world's too sharp a place for you . . .'

The doctor was stung to anger. Almost with relief she let hatred take possession of her. 'And you,' she said, 'and you? What do you do to face the world – what do you do for it?'

But the girl turned away; her face suddenly dulled.

'I?' she asked, and dropped her hand on the sheet. 'I?' Glancing at the doctor, still white and taut by the fire, she smiled, almost kindly. 'I am the pincushion you sit on by mistake, or perhaps a rash between the shoulder-blades you cannot reach. A very special function. And very necessary. Look how I have roused you.'

The doctor turned away with a gesture. Lack of sleep, nerves. She didn't like it. Futile to waste the energy of anger on her.

The door opened and a nurse brought in the tea.

'Mrs. Stimpson is up in the labour ward, doctor,' she said, placing the tray in front of the girl in bed, on to her flattened knees. 'Run it pretty close,' she moved over to the windows and hauled the black-out into position. 'Went into town this afternoon to have her hair set. What will they do next?'

'I'll go up,' said the doctor. As she went from the room she saw a letter lying on the tray. 'I was expecting this,' she heard Theresa say to the nurse, and as she walked away up the corridor it was as if some other world had brushed against her own, brushed past and was gone forever.

The next afternoon Mrs. Stimpson lay in the smaller post-natal ward, which was on the ground floor next to the nursery. Centuries back it had been a refectory, built on to the side of the house with its own fine pointed roof, all timber. Later, as sunroom, the roof had been cut off and sheets of glass laid across, so that now, lying flat in bed and gazing up, it was as if the sky itself domed the room.

Red Cross nurses stood on chairs pulling the cords which operated a complicated system of black-out.

'Good-bye to the evening star,' said one of them as the black canvas was slowly manoeuvred across the darkening sky. Mrs. Stimpson glanced at the empty bed beside her.

'Still worrying, Stimmy?' said the woman in the bed opposite. 'She'll be all right, you'll see.' She broke off as one of the regular nurses entered the ward. 'Any news, nurse?'

'Doctor's still up there. She looks worn out.' The little nurse, trim and young, was concerned. 'Mrs. Jenkins will be down sometime this evening . . .'

'Boy or girl?' asked the woman eagerly.

The nurse turned away. They would know later.

'She lost it. A boy,' she said, and to calm the sudden gasp quickly went on, 'Now, Sister will be round in a minute. What shall it be? Liquid paraffin or cascara?'

Mrs. Stimpson lay still. She remembered the hurry and shock of the matron, brought at midnight to the labour ward; the quiet sobs of pain, the sudden high note in the doctor's voice. Then silence and they had quickly carried her down here.

There was another empty bed in the ward, and the occupant was moving uncertainly about. The other women watched her. The floor seemed ominous as a stage, an empty dance floor; too big, too shiny to cross. They had seen her dressing, shared the pleasure in pulling on the narrow elastic belt, the slim skirt. With the putting on of normal clothes she had stepped out of the circle of their small world; already she was apart from them. She had become once more the wife, the mother with a home of her own. In a day or two she would be gone, in a week forgotten: they would never meet again. She moved across to put more coal on the fire, then sat down, grave. Fancy losing your baby, she thought, shocked. To-morrow at nine she was to bath hers. In a month, in a week, it would be a common thing, but now it was terrifying. The experience upstairs would be forgotten too, forgotten as were all shattering things, the edge off them anybody's adventure.

The woman by the fire stirred, shivered a little. She must get back to bed.

Later, when the whole ward was settled into sleep, the firelight tossing darkness into corners, the door opened and a night-nurse pushed open the door. She wore a thick black cape against the chill of the stone corridors, and carried a storm lantern held high. Four figures came heavily into the room, bearing a stretcher. Silently they opened the bed next to Mrs. Stimpson and slid their burden into it. After a careful survey they went out again, four shadows following them to the door. There was no sound from the bed.

Once outside the matron put her arm round the doctor's shoulders. 'You did all you could, my dear. You were wonderful,' she said. 'It was not your fault. Not in the least. The girl—' she let her hand fall. 'Hopeless, disgraceful.'

'It's the first baby I've lost,' said the doctor. 'It's never happened before. To lose a life—' she shook her head.

'*You* didn't lose it,' said the matron sharply. 'I can't understand it. Such a dreadful thing to do – we must ask her – so wicked – wicked.'

'No, she must sleep now,' said the doctor. 'Must give her time.' Time. She was dazed with the strain and shock. Her mind was empty and yet terribly clear. I couldn't have saved the child. She saw to that. Too late . . .

The matron opened her sitting-room door. 'A cup of tea,' she said, 'before you go to bed.'

They sat down before the fire and the matron made tea. The doctor carefully built up the dying fire. The exactitude soothed her hands, she felt steadied. She could bring her mind round to face the thought that had been tugging at her all day, ever since the bitter knowledge of what the girl had done was clear to her. Theresa had known what she was going to do – perhaps she had discussed it over the phone, with the doctor in the room. But that was too horrible. Perhaps it was the letter. Or, worst of all, she may have done it knowing what a shattering effect it would have on her. She said in defence against the evil she felt beating at the walls of her house, 'Every child we bring into the world is some sort of victory. We must always be against the destroyers.'

The matron poured milk into the cups and tested the tea. Her face, smooth as a nun's, looked towards the other woman, with her young blonde head and the blue ribbon threading the hair. How young she looks, she thought. Yet I suppose she's right. I suppose that's what a hospital is for. And yet was it? To her a hospital entailed lists of necessities, changing faces, great quietness and clean smells. When I was young, she thought. But years pass and peaks become plains; the war against disease and germs becomes a routine thing. You win and you lose and miracles sometimes happen. I am old, she thought. I fight in my own way.

She shook her head.

'The risk,' she said in awe. 'What a risk to take, and how

wicked! Yes, wicked after all these months' – for an instant she knew grief at the thought of the flawless kicking child, a sound boy. Life in the shell – frail fingers and curled toes. To cut this life off, which was the world's life, belonged to the world – with – what, a hairpin? Wicked, wicked. Denying God a life. She shook this thought away, cast away too, the little cold curled body in the white wrappings. It would have to be buried.

'Your tea, my dear,' she said. 'I'll have to take you in hand, I can see. Can't have our doctor cracking up.'

In her own room later, the doctor remembered this phrase. Our doctor. It set the tempo of her dreams. Theresa at the end of a narrow corridor, a naked child held high, always eluding her. Theresa laughing, big-bellied; calling in the soundless medium of a dream-shout: Doctor! Our doctor! And near dawn, a procession of women passing, herself in a cage, and each woman having a key to fasten the many locks. Our doctor, said their devoted faces. Dear doctor.

All the next day Theresa slept. She had a pale, burnt-out look to her, and her mouth lay defenceless and innocent. What sort of woman is she? thought the doctor, what sort of life has she? Is she really married? What will she do? The doctor stood over her, thinking, probing. But the sleeping face was closed to her.

As she left the ward, she saw the dark look in Nurse Griffith's eyes and on impulse took her aside and said what was in her own mind, said it as much in warning to herself. 'We are here to get people well, nurse. Their lives outside are not our concern; we are not judges. I don't want the other women to hear about this. She lost her baby, that is all. And she is to be treated exactly as they are.' Looking into the tightened face she knew the ways an unpopular patient could be treated. A rough shouldering whilst making the

68

bed or changing dressings, delay with the bedpan, pillows set uncomfortably. A dozen small unkindnesses. 'Very well, doctor,' said the nurse stiffly.

It helped the doctor to give these instructions. It gave her ascendancy over that other world, sensed through a phone call, seen in a letter, but strangely missing from the relaxed face on the pillow. All that day she was at peace, she was taking no advantages, the two worlds lay quiescent.

The next morning she watched the girl wake up, turning on her back, the eyes suddenly wide and dark. Her arms were bent up from the elbows and the palms of her hands lay on the pillow either side of her face. 'Philip,' she said.

The doctor was moving forward to lay her hand on the girl's forehead, but the voice, so weak and certain, made her draw back sharply. Philip? Her husband? The action attract-ed the girl's gaze and in an instant she understood. 'Could I have something to drink?' she asked.

In the days that followed she gradually recovered. Silently she sat propped high and watched the other women as they knitted or talked or fed their children. At first they did these things almost furtively, feeling guilt in her quiet presence, but as the days passed they came to expect her silence and almost forgot her. If the peace of the room, with its six low oaken beds and warm mauve blankets flowed into her, she never showed it, although her face softened as her split body healed, and her eyes assumed an abiding sorrow, something indefinable which would never leave them.

One day, early on, at feeding time, the doctor was helping the woman in the next bed when Nurse Griffith dropped a glass and rubber instrument on to the girl's bed. 'You'll need this, Mrs. Jenkins,' she said as she passed on, 'I'll come back and show you how to use it.'

The girl and the doctor looked at it together. 'It's a breast pump,' said the doctor, her hand on the other woman's shoulder. 'You *must* relax your shoulders,' she said.

Theresa stared at it, then round at the others, busy with their children, each sunk into a cocoon of warm flowing milk.

'Let me show you,' said Nurse Griffith. 'Over here. So. Then pump gently here. It's quite easy.'

She went away after a minute and the girl watched the needle sprays of milk jetting into the glass bulb. Glancing across at the doctor she gave a short laugh. The doctor's fingers trembled. She knew what it meant: the final gesture. But from somewhere deep in her mind echoed the calm voice, the beloved voice: *don't choose medicine unless you believe in it.* . . . What did it say, what had he said, all those buried years ago? *People are lost, all of them. Lost in soul or body, mind or spirit, call it what you will. You can help them. You're a healer. I know it and you know. Help, heal . . .*

Help, who was to help whom? It was all lies, the voice from the past, your hand's cunning, lies to get you into a bright little, tight little hygienic cage, rubber-sprung – and still you helped nobody.

'Oh doctor,' said the woman beneath her hand. 'Oh doctor,' she said in pain.

The day Theresa Jenkins left Rowley Hall it was snowing again. Flakes hesitated in the still air, settling chill and furtive on windowsills, gravel and in the furrows of the ploughed field before the house. The doctor saw her as she came across from the stairs, holding a notice in her hand to pin to the board. Healed, departing, life in the ward behind her, the girl stood in the grey hall, thin and empty-armed. On impulse the doctor went up to her.

'Don't you want to see where your baby—?'

Theresa looked at her, moistening the lips she had red-
dened for the journey. 'No,' she said. 'Thank you for seeing
to all that.'

A car came up the drive, churning through the snow.
Theresa picked up her case and held out her hand.

'Good-bye,' she said, and the snow blew in as she opened
the door.

As the car slowly turned and brushed its way past the
overladen yews, the doctor ran on to the porch, leaning into
the snow and fighting an almost uncontrollable urge to run
after it. Suddenly she could not bear to see her go, knowing
nothing. It was as if the girl was driving into a void, travelling
always out from the place where the child lay, a cold body,
never to uncurl. As if with her, she took the whole meaning
of the doctor's life, her work. I can't stay here, she thought,
moving back to the board in the hall. She tore down an
old notice and crumpled it in one swift movement. Have to
get another job. Go out into the world. Do something. But
what? She looked at her hands; they had made her a doctor.
Healer's hands. But what was a doctor? An attendant upon
life only. Apart from the main stream: receiving and sending
forth, healing and bringing forth. But why? Where did they
all go, the healed in body? Looking at her hands, she thought
with panic: If I was asked to deliver a child now, what would
I do? What *do* you do? The printed page of one of her textbooks was before her. She saw clearly the form of the printed
page, the paragraphs, sub-headings. The diagrams, carefully
coloured. But the meaning was lost to her, the type meaningless. A nurse crossed the hall and disappeared into the
nursery, two babies tucked under her arms. She was smiling.
The doctor thought, I must have some reason for staying
here in the cold. Then she saw the notice she had to pin up.
'Permission must be obtained . . .' she smoothed it out, and

pinned it in a good light. When it was done another surge of irritation ran through her. Nurses and wards, patients and deliveries, was there no end to them? What of the free, the open life outside where you could be a woman, nothing more? Theresa Jenkins had no struggle there – her only problem was to be a woman, how to get through that way. A doctor had one path before her; everything must be seen in that one clear light, no muddleheads, no sidetracks, no envy. After all, in medicine you knew too much, perhaps that kept you apart. The earth was teeming, all you did was to direct the flow. We're all the same, she thought; bus-conductors, commissionaires, doctors. She laughed a little. But do they really trust us?

She shivered. She saw that the door was open again. How could that be?

She had not heard the charabanc churning up the drive, had missed the pull of brakes, and the women dropping heavy as honey bees to the white-felted ground. Sister Matthews had come through the hall and was gathering the women together, driving them in from the cold.

A touch, like a summons, fell on her arm.

'You're the doctor, aren't you?' said a small cockney voice. The doctor looked round, saw the customary fear, the pinched mouth, hair damp with melting snow. 'My friend, Mrs. Stimpson, told me about you. She said to tell you the baby's doing well, thanks to you. She said you'd take care of me. It's my first—' the woman paused. Woman? she was little more than a girl. 'A child's a precious thing,' she said shyly.

The doctor was staring at her. 'Yes,' she said, 'yes, I'm the doctor.' Although the world can turn up and around like the snowstorm in a glass ball, it will settle, and I am still the doctor: there is still humanity. She passed a hand over

72

her eyes, as if to wipe away a lifetime's doubt, a six-week torment.

'Don't you worry at all,' she said, 'I'll see you through.' And walking, along the hall with her, she knew she could.

ARTHUR CONAN DOYLE

SWEETHEARTS

IT IS HARD for the general practitioner who sits among his patients both morning and evening, and sees them in their homes between, to steal time for one little daily breath of cleanly air. To win it he must slip early from his bed and walk out between shuttered shops when it is chill but very clear, and all things are sharply outlined, as in a frost. It is an hour that has a charm of its own, when, but for a postman or a milkman, one has the pavement to oneself, and even the most common thing takes an ever-recurring freshness, as though causeway, and lamp, and signboard had all wakened to the new day. Then even an inland city may seem beautiful, and bear virtue in its smoke-tainted air.

But it was by the sea that I lived, in a town that was unlovely enough were it not for its glorious neighbour. And who cares for the town when one can sit on the bench at the headland, and look out over the huge blue bay, and the yellow scimitar that curves before it. I loved it when its great face was freckled with the fishing boats, and I loved it when the big ships went past, far out, a little hillock of white and no hull, with topsails curved like a bodice, so stately and demure. But most of all I loved it when no trace of man marred the majesty of Nature, and when the sun-bursts slanted down on it from between the drifting rain-clouds. Then I have seen the further edge draped in the gauze of the driving rain, with its thin grey shading under the slow clouds, while my headland was golden, and the sun gleamed upon the breakers and struck deep through the green waves beyond, showing up the purple patches where the beds of seaweed are lying. Such a morning as that, with the wind in his hair, and the spray on his lips, and the cry of the eddying gulls in his ear, may send a man back braced afresh to the reek of a sick-room, and the dead, drab weariness of practice.

It was on such another day that I first saw my old man. He came to my bench just as I was leaving it. My eye must have picked him out even in a crowded street, for he was a man of large frame and fine presence, with something of distinction in the set of his lip and the poise of his head. He limped up the winding path leaning heavily upon his stick, as though those great shoulders had become too much at last for the failing limbs that bore them. As he approached, my eyes caught Nature's danger signal, that faint bluish tinge in nose and lip which tells of a labouring heart.

'The brae is a little trying, sir,' said I. 'Speaking as a physician, I should say that you would do well to rest here before you go further.'

He inclined his head in a stately, old-world fashion, and seated himself upon the bench. Seeing that he had no wish to speak I was silent also, but I could not help watching him out of the corners of my eyes, for he was such a wonderful survival of the early half of the century, with his low-crowned, curly-brimmed hat, his black satin tie which fastened with a buckle at the back, and, above all, his large, fleshy, clean-shaven face shot with its mesh of wrinkles. Those eyes, ere they had grown dim, had looked out from the box-seat of mail coaches, and had seen the knots of navvies as they toiled on the brown embankments. Those lips had smiled over the first numbers of 'Pickwick,' and had gossiped of the promising young man who wrote them. The face itself was a seventy-year almanack, and every seam an entry upon it where public as well as private sorrow left its trace. That pucker on the forehead stood for the Mutiny, perhaps; that line of care for the Crimean winter, it may be; and that last little sheaf of wrinkles, as my fancy hoped, for the death of Gordon. And so, as I dreamed in my foolish way, the old gentleman with the shining stock was gone, and it was seventy years of a great nation's life that took shape before me on the headland in the morning.

But he soon brought me back to earth again. As he recovered his breath he took a letter out of his pocket, and, putting on a pair of horn-rimmed eye-glasses, he read it through very carefully. Without any design of playing the spy I could not help observing that it was in a woman's hand. When he had finished it he read it again, and then sat with the corners of his mouth drawn down and his eyes staring vacantly out over the bay, the most forlorn-looking old gentleman that ever I have seen. All that is kindly within me was set stirring by that wistful face, but I knew that he was in no humour for talk, and so, at last, with my breakfast and my patients calling me, I left him on the bench and started for home.

I never gave him another thought until the next morning, when, at the same hour, he turned up upon the headland, and shared the bench which I had been accustomed to look upon as my own. He bowed again before sitting down, but was no more inclined than formerly to enter into conversation. There had been a change in him during the last twenty-four hours, and all for the worse. The face seemed more heavy and more wrinkled, while that ominous venous tinge was more pronounced as he panted up the hill. The clean lines of his cheek and chin were marred by a day's growth of grey stubble, and his large, shapely head had lost something of the brave carriage which had struck me when first I glanced at him. He had a letter there, the same, or another, but still in a woman's hand, and over this he was moping and mumbling in his senile fashion, with his brow puckered, and the corners of his mouth drawn down like those of a fretting child. So I left him, with a vague wonder as to who he might be, and why a single spring day should have wrought such a change upon him.

So interested was I that next morning I was on the look out for him. Sure enough, at the same hour, I saw him coming up the hill; but very slowly, with a bent back and a heavy head. It was shocking to me to see the change in him as he approached.

'I am afraid that our air does not agree with you, sir,' I ventured to remark.

But it was as though he had no heart for talk. He tried, as I thought, to make some fitting reply, but it slurred off into a mumble and silence. How bent and weak and old he seemed – ten years older at the least than when first I had seen him! It went to my heart to see this fine old fellow wasting away before my eyes. There was the eternal letter which he unfolded with his shaking fingers. Who was this woman whose words moved him so? Some daughter, perhaps, or grand-daughter, who should have been the light of his home instead of— I smiled to find how bitter I was growing, and how swiftly I was weaving a romance round an unshaven old man and his correspondence. Yet all day he lingered in my mind, and I had fitful glimpses of those two trembling, blue-veined, knuckly hands with the paper rustling between them.

I had hardly hoped to see him again. Another day's decline must, I thought, hold him to his room, if not to his bed. Great, then, was my surprise when, as I approached my bench, I saw that he was already there. But as I came up to him I could scarce be sure that it was indeed the same man. There were the curly-brimmed hat, and the shining stock, and the horn glasses, but where were the stoop and the grey-stubbled, pitiable face? He was clean-shaven and firm lipped, with a bright eye and a head that poised itself upon his great shoulders like an eagle on a rock. His back was as straight and square as a grenadier's, and he switched at the pebbles with his stick in his exuberant vitality. In the button-hole of his well-brushed black coat there glinted a golden blossom, and the corner of a dainty red silk handkerchief lapped over from his breast-pocket. He might have been the eldest son of the weary creature who had sat there the morning before.

'Good morning, sir, good morning!' he cried with a merry waggle of his cane.

'Good morning!' I answered; 'how beautiful the bay is looking.'

'Yes, sir, but you should have seen it just before the sun rose.'

'What, have you been here since then?'

'I was here when there was scarce light to see the path.'

'You are a very early riser.'

'On occasion, sir; on occasion!' He cocked his eye at me as if to gauge whether I were worthy of his confidence. 'The fact is, sir, that my wife is coming back to me to-day.'

I suppose that my face showed that I did not quite see the force of the explanation. My eyes, too, may have given him assurance of sympathy, for he moved quite close to me and began speaking in a low, confidential voice, as if the matter were of such weight that even the seagulls must be kept out of our councils.

'Are you a married man, sir?'

'No, I am not.'

'Ah, then you cannot quite understand it. My wife and I have been married for nearly fifty years, and we have never been parted, never at all, until now.'

'Was it for long?' I asked.

'Yes, sir. This is the fourth day. She had to go to Scotland. A matter of duty, you understand, and the doctors would not let me go. Not that I would have allowed them to stop me, but she was on their side. Now, thank God! it is over, and she may be here at any moment.'

'Here!'

'Yes, here. This headland and bench were old friends of ours thirty years ago. The people with whom we stay are not, to tell the truth, very congenial, and we have little privacy among them. That is why we prefer to meet here. I could not be sure which train would bring her, but if she had come by the very earliest she would have found me waiting.'

'In that case—' said I, rising.

'No, sir, no,' he entreated, 'I beg that you will stay. It does not weary you, this domestic talk of mine?'

'On the contrary.'

'I have been so driven inwards during these few last days! Ah, what a nightmare it has been! Perhaps it may seem strange to you that an old fellow like me should feel like this.'

'It is charming.'

'No credit to me, sir! There's not a man on this planet but would feel the same if he had the good fortune to be married to such a woman. Perhaps, because you see me like this, and hear me speak of our long life together, you conceive that she is old, too.'

He laughed heartily, and his eyes twinkled at the humour of the idea.

'She's one of those women, you know, who have youth in

82

their hearts, and so it can never be very far from their faces. To me she's just as she was when she first took my hand in hers in '45. A wee little bit stouter, perhaps, but then, if she had a fault as a girl, it was that she was a shade too slender. She was above me in station, you know – I a clerk, and she the daughter of my employer. Oh! it was quite a romance, I give you my word, and I won her; and, somehow, I have never got over the freshness and the wonder of it. To think that that sweet, lovely girl has walked by my side all through life, and that I have been able—'

He stopped suddenly, and I glanced round at him in surprise. He was shaking all over, in every fibre of his great body. His hands were clawing at the woodwork, and his feet shuffling on the gravel. I saw what it was. He was trying to rise, but was so excited that he could not. I half extended my hand, but a higher courtesy constrained me to draw it back again and turn my face to the sea. An instant afterwards he was up and hurrying down the path.

A woman was coming towards us. She was quite close before he had seen her – thirty yards at the utmost. I know not if she had ever been as he described her, or whether it was but some ideal which he carried in his brain. The person upon whom I looked was tall, it is true, but she was thick and shapeless, with a ruddy, full-blown face, and a skirt grotesquely gathered up. There was a green ribbon in her hat, which jarred upon my eyes, and her blouse-like bodice was full and clumsy. And this was the lovely girl, the ever youthful! My heart sank as I thought how little such a woman might appreciate him, how unworthy she might be of his love.

She came up the path in her solid way, while he staggered along to meet her. Then, as they came together, looking discreetly out of the furthest corner of my eye, I saw that he put out both his hands, while she, shrinking from a public caress, took one of them in hers and shook it. As she did so I saw her face, and I was easy in my mind for my old man. God grant that when this hand is shaking, and when this back is bowed, a woman's eyes may look so into mine.

MIKHAIL BULGAKOV

THE EMBROIDERED
TOWEL

Translated by Michael Glenny

IF YOU HAVE never driven over country roads it is useless for me to tell you about it; you wouldn't understand anyway. But if you have, I would rather not remind you of it.

To cut a long story short, my driver and I spent exactly twenty-four hours covering the thirty-two miles which separate the district town of Grachyovka from Muryovo hospital. Indeed so nearly exactly twenty-four hours that it was uncanny: at 2 p.m. on 16 September 1916 we were at the last corn-chandler's store on the outskirts of the remarkable town of Grachyovka, and at five past two on 17 September of that same unforgettable year 1916, I was in the Muryovo hospital yard, standing on trampled, withered grass, flattened by the September rain. My legs were ossified with cold, so much so that as I stood there bemused, I mentally leafed through the textbook pages in an inane attempt to remember whether there was such a complaint as ossification of the muscles or whether it was an illness I had dreamed up while asleep the night before in the village of Grabilovka. What the devil was it in Latin? Every single muscle ached unbearably, like toothache. There is nothing I can say about my toes – they lay immobile in my boots, as rigid as wooden stumps. I confess that in a burst of cowardice I pronounced a whispered curse on the medical profession and on the application form I had handed in five years earlier to the rector of the university. All the time a fine rain was drizzling down as through a sieve. My coat had swelled like a sponge.

I vainly tried to grasp my suitcase with the fingers of my right hand, but in the end spat on the wet grass in disgust. My fingers were incapable of gripping anything. It was then, stuffed as I was with all sorts of knowledge from fascinating medical books, that I suddenly remembered the name of the illness – palsy. 'Paralysis', I said to myself in despair, God knows why.

'Your roads take some getting used to,' I muttered through stony, blue lips, staring resentfully at the driver, although the state of the road was hardly his fault.

'Ah, comrade doctor,' he answered, with lips equally stiff under their fair moustache, 'I've been driving fifteen years and I still can't get used to them.'

I shuddered and glanced round miserably at the peeling, white, two-storey hospital building, at the bare log walls of my assistant's house, and at my own future residence, a neat, two-storey house with mysterious windows blank as gravestones. I gave a long sigh. Suddenly instead of Latin words a faraway memory flashed through my head, a sweet phrase which a lusty tenor in blue stockings sang in my numbed and shaken head: *Salut, demeure chaste et pure . . .* Farewell, farewell, it will be a long time before I see you again, oh golden-red Bolshoi Theatre, Moscow, shop windows . . . ah, farewell.

'Next time, I'll wear a sheepskin coat,' I said to myself in angry desperation, tugging at the suitcase by its straps with my inflexible hands. 'I'll . . . though next time it'll be mid-October, I'll have to wear two sheepskin coats. I certainly shan't be going to Grachyovka for a month yet. Just think . . . I actually had to put up for the night en route! When we had only driven fifteen miles and it was as black as the tomb . . . it was night . . . we had to stop in Grabilovka, a school teacher put us up. This morning we set off at seven

88

in the morning, and here we are . . . God, it's been slower driving here than if we'd come on foot. One wheel got stuck in a ditch, the other swung up into the air, my case fell on to my feet with a crash, we slithered from side to side, lurching forward one moment, backward the next. And all the time a fine rain drizzling down and my bones turning to ice. Who'd believe you can freeze as easily in the middle of a grey, miserable September as in the depth of winter? Ah well, it seems you can. And as you die a slow death there's nothing to look at except the same endless monotony. On the right the bare, undulating fields and on the left a stunted copse, flanked by five or six grey, dilapidated shacks. Not a living soul in them, it seems, and not a sound to be heard.'

In the end the suitcase yielded. The driver lay on his stomach and shoved it down on top of me. I tried to catch it by the strap but my hand refused to perform and the beastly thing, crammed with books and all sorts of rubbish, flopped down on to the grass, crashing against my legs.

'Oh Lor . . .' the driver began fearfully, but I did not complain. My legs were no more sensitive than two sticks of wood.

'Hey, anybody at home? Hey!' the driver cried out and flapped his arms like a rooster flapping its wings. 'Hey, I've brought the doctor!'

At once faces appeared, pressed against the dark windows of the assistant's house. A door banged and I saw a man hobbling towards me in a ragged coat and worn old boots. He hurriedly and respectfully doffed his cap, ran up and stopped two paces short of me, then smiling somewhat bashfully he welcomed me in a hoarse voice:

'Good day, comrade doctor.'

'And who might you be?' I asked.

'I'm Yegorich,' he introduced himself, 'the watchman here. We've been expecting you.'

Without wasting a moment he grabbed the suitcase, swung it over his shoulder and carried it in. I limped after him, trying unsuccessfully to thrust my hand into my trouser pocket to get out my purse.

Man's basic needs are few. The first of them is fire. Back in Moscow, when I found out that I was to go to remote Muryovo, I had promised myself that I would behave in a dignified manner. My youthful appearance made life intolerable for me in those early days. I always made a point of introducing myself as 'Doctor So-and-So', and inevitably people raised their eyebrows and said:

'Really? I thought you were still a student.'

'No. I'm qualified,' I would answer sullenly, thinking: 'I must start wearing spectacles, that's what I must do.' But there was no point in this, as I had perfectly good vision, my eyes as yet unclouded by experience. Unable to wear glasses as a defence against those invariable, affectionately indulgent smiles, I tried to develop a special manner designed to induce respect. I tried to talk evenly and gravely, to repress impulsive movements as far as possible, to walk and not run as twenty-four-year-olds do who have just left university. Looking back, I now realise that the attempt did not come off at all.

At the moment in question I disobeyed my unwritten code of behaviour. I sat hunched up in front of the fire with my shoes off, not in the study but in the kitchen, like a fire-worshipper, fervently and passionately drawn to the birch logs blazing in the stove. On my left stood an upturned tub with my boots lying on top of it, next to them a plucked cockerel with a bloodstained neck, and its many-coloured feathers lying in a heap beside it. While still stiff with the cold, I had somehow managed to perform a whole set of vital actions. I had confirmed Yegorich's wife, the sharp-nosed Aksinya, in her position as my cook. As a result of this she had slaughtered the cockerel and I was to eat it. I had been introduced to everyone in turn. My *feldsher** was called Demyan Lukich, the midwives were Pelagea Ivanovna and Anna Nikolaevna. I had been shown round the hospital and was left in no doubt whatever that it was generously equipped. With equal certainty I was forced to admit (inwardly, of course) that I had no idea what very many of these shiny, unsullied instruments were for. Not only had I never held them in my hands, but to tell the truth I had never even seen them.

'Hm,' I mumbled significantly, 'must say you have an excellent set of instruments. Hm . . .'

'Oh sir,' Demyan Lukich remarked sweetly, 'this is all thanks to your predecessor Leopold Leopoldovich. You see, he used to operate from dawn till dusk.'

I was instantly covered with cold sweat and stared glumly at the gleaming cupboards.

We then went round the empty wards and I satisfied myself that they could easily hold forty patients.

'Leopold Leopoldovich sometimes had fifty in here,' Demyan Lukich said consolingly, and Anna Nikolaevna, a woman with a diadem of grey hair, chose to say:

'Doctor, you look so young, so very young . . . it's simply amazing. You look like a student.'

'Oh, hell,' I said to myself, 'really, you'd think they were doing it on purpose!'

Through clenched teeth I grunted:

'Hm . . . no, well, I . . . yes, rather young looking . . .'

* A partly-qualified medical assistant.

After that we went down to the pharmacy and a glance was enough to tell me that it was supplied with every conceivable medicine. Its two sombre rooms smelled strongly of herbs and its shelves were filled with an endless variety of preparations. There were even foreign patent medicines, which, need I add, I had never heard of.

'Leopold Leopoldovich ordered these,' Pelagea Ivanovna reported proudly.

'This Leopold was nothing short of a genius,' I thought and was filled with respect for the mysterious Leopold who had left the quiet little village of Muryovo behind him.

Besides fire, man also needs to find his bearings. I had long since eaten the cockerel, Yegorich had stuffed my mattress with straw and covered it with a sheet, and a light was burning in my study. Spellbound, I sat and stared at the legendary Leopold's third great achievement: the book-case was crammed with books. I counted roughly thirty volumes of surgery manuals in Russian and German. And the books on therapeutics! The beautiful leather-bound anatomical atlases!

Evening drew on and I started to find my bearings.

'It's not my fault,' I repeated to myself stubbornly and unhappily. 'I've got my degree and a first class one at that. Didn't I warn them back in town that I wanted to start off as a junior partner in a practice? But no, they just smiled and said, "You'll get your bearings." So now I've got to find my bearings. Suppose they bring me a hernia? Just tell me how I'll find my bearings with that? And more to the point, what will a hernia patient feel like when I get my hands on him? Will he find his bearings in the next world?' The thought made my blood run cold.

'What about peritonitis? Oh no! Or croup, that country children get? When is tracheotomy indicated? Even if it

doesn't need tracheotomy I shall be pretty much at sea . . .
What about . . . what about . . . deliveries! I forgot about
deliveries! Incorrect positions. What on earth will I do? What
a fool I was! I should have refused this job. I really should.
They should have found themselves another Leopold.'

Miserable, I paced up and down the twilit study. When
I came up to the lamp I caught sight of the reflection of
my pale face and of the light of the lamp in the window set
against the boundless darkness of the fields.

'I'm like Dmitry the Pretender – nothing but a sham,' I
thought stupidly and sat down at the table again.

I spent about two lonely hours of self-torment and only
stopped when my nerves could no longer bear the horrors
I had summoned up. Then I started to calm down and even
to work out a plan of action.

'Let's see now . . . they tell me admissions are almost nil
at the moment. They're braking flax in the villages, the roads
are impassable . . .'

'That's just when they will bring you a hernia,' thundered
a harsh voice in my mind, 'because a man with a cold won't
make the effort over impassable roads but rest assured they'll
bring you a hernia, my dear doctor.'

There was something in what the voice said. I shuddered.

'Be quiet,' I said to it. 'It won't necessarily be a hernia. Stop
being so neurotic. You can't back out once you've begun.'

'You said it!' the voice answered spitefully.

'All right then . . . I won't take a step without my reference
book . . . If I have to prescribe something I can think it
over while I wash my hands and the reference book will be
lying open on top of the patients' register. I shall make out
wholesome but simple prescriptions, say, sodium salicylate,
0.5 grammes in powder form three times a day.'

'You might as well prescribe baking soda! Why don't you

93

just prescribe soda?' the voice was blatantly making fun of me.

'What's soda got to do with it? I'll also prescribe an infusion of ipecacuanha, 180 c.c. Or 200 c.c. if you don't mind.'

And although no one was asking for ipecacuanha as I sat there alone by the lamp, I sheepishly turned the pages in the pharmacopoeia and checked ipecacuanha; meanwhile I automatically read in passing that there was a certain substance called 'Insipin' which is none other than 'ethereal sulphate of quinine-diglycolic acid'. Apparently it doesn't taste of quinine! What is it for? And how is it prescribed? What is it, a powder? To hell with it!

'That's all very well, but what are you going to do about a hernia?' The voice of Fear continued to pester me.

'I'll put them into a bath,' I defended myself in exasperation, 'and try to reduce it.'

'What if it's a strangulated one, old boy? Baths won't be much use then, will they! A strangulated hernia!' Fear chanted in a demoniac voice, 'You'll have to cut it out . . .!'

I gave in and all but burst into tears. I sent out a prayer to the darkness outside the window: please, anything but not a strangulated hernia.

Weariness then crooned:

'Go to bed, unhappy physician. Sleep on it. Calm down and stop being neurotic. Look how still the dark is outside the window, the fields are cold and sleeping, there is no hernia. You can think about it in the morning. You'll settle down . . . Sleep . . . drop that book of diagrams, you won't make head or tail of it anyway . . . hernial orifice . . .'

I don't remember him arriving. I only remember the bolt grating in the door, a shriek from Aksinya and a cart creaking out in the yard.

He was hatless, his sheepskin coat unbuttoned, his beard was dishevelled and there was a mad look in his eyes.

He crossed himself, fell on his knees and banged his forehead against the floor. This to me!

'I'm a lost man,' I thought wretchedly.

'Now, now – what's the matter?' I muttered and pulled at his grey sleeve.

His face twisted and he started mumbling a breathless and incoherent answer:

'Oh doctor, sir . . . sir . . . she's all I've got, she's all I've got, she's all I've got,' he burst out suddenly in a voice so young-sounding and powerful that the lampshade trembled. 'Oh, sir, oh . . .' He wrung his hands in misery and started knocking his forehead against the floorboards as if trying to smash them. 'Why? Why am I being punished? What have I done to deserve God's anger?'

'What is it? What's happened?' I cried out, feeling the blood draining from my face.

He jumped to his feet, rushed towards me and whispered:

'Anything you want, doctor, sir . . . I'll give you money, take as much money as you want. As much as you want. We'll pay you in food if you like. Only don't let her die. Don't let her die. Even if she's to be a cripple, I don't mind. I don't mind!' He shouted to the ceiling. 'I've got enough to feed her, I can manage.'

I could see Aksinya's pale face in the black rectangle of the door. I was overcome with anguish.

'Well, what is it? Speak!' I cried irritably.

He stopped. His eyes went blank and he whispered, as if telling me a secret:

'She fell into the brake.'

'Brake . . . brake? What's that?'

95

'Flax, they were braking flax, doctor,' Aksinya whispered in explanation, 'you know, brake, flax braking . . .'

'Here's a fine beginning. This is it. Oh why did I ever come?' I said to myself in horror.

'Who?'

'My daughter,' he answered in a whisper, and then shouted, 'Help me!' Once again he threw himself to the floor and his hair, cut like a mop in peasant fashion, fell into his eyes.

The pressure-lamp with its lopsided tin shade burned with hot beams of light. She lay on the operating table, on white, fresh-smelling oilcloth and when I saw her all thoughts of hernia vanished from my mind.

Her fair, almost reddish hair hung down from the table in a matted clump. She had a gigantic plait which reached to the floor.

Her calico skirt was torn and stained with blood in various shades from brown to oily scarlet. The light of the kerosene lamp was a lively yellow in comparison with her paper-white face, and her nose was beginning to sharpen. On her white face, motionless as a plaster cast, a truly rare beauty was fading away before my eyes. Seldom in life does one see such a face.

The operating theatre was completely silent for about ten seconds, but from behind the closed doors came the muffled sounds of someone shouting and banging his head over and over again.

'Gone out of his mind,' I thought. 'The nurses must be seeing to him. Why is she so beautiful? Though he does have good bone structure; the mother must have been a beautiful woman. He's a widower. . . .'

'Is he a widower?' I whispered automatically.

'Yes, he is,' Pelagea Ivanovna answered quietly.

Then Demyan Lukich, almost as if in anger, ripped the skirt from hem to waist, baring her instantly. I looked, and what I saw was even worse than I had expected. Strictly speaking there was no left leg. From the smashed knee down there were just bloody shreds, battered red flesh and splinters of white bone protruding in all directions. The right leg was fractured at the shin so that the tips of both bones had punctured the skin and her foot lay lifelessly on its side, as though disconnected.

'Yes . . .' the *feldsher* pronounced softly and that was all he said.

Thereupon I regained my wits and started feeling her pulse. Her cold wrist registered nothing. Only after a few seconds did I detect a barely perceptible, irregular ripple. It passed and was followed by a pause during which I had time to glance at her white lips and nostrils, which were turning blue. I already felt like saying 'It's all over', but fortunately controlled myself . . . there was another hint of a beat.

'The end of a mangled human being,' I said to myself. 'There's really nothing more to be done.'

But suddenly I said sternly, in a voice that I did not recognise:

'Camphor.'

Anna Nikolaevna bent over to my ear and whispered:

'What for, doctor? Don't torture her. What's the point of smashing her up any more? She'll die any minute now . . . you won't save her.'

I gave her an angry look and said:

'I asked for camphor . . .' in such a way that she flushed, marched resentfully to the little table and broke an ampoule. The *feldsher* obviously did not approve of the camphor either. Nonetheless he deftly and swiftly took hold of a syringe and the yellow oil went under the skin of her shoulder.

'Die. Die quickly,' I said to myself. 'Die. Otherwise what am I to do with you?'

'She'll die now,' whispered the *feldsher* as if guessing my thoughts. He glanced meaningfully at the sheet but apparently changed his mind. It seemed a pity to stain it with blood. But a few seconds later he had to cover her. She lay like a corpse, but did not die. Suddenly my head became quite clear, as if I were standing under the glass roof of the anatomy theatre in that faraway medical school.

'Camphor again,' I said hoarsely.

And once again the *feldsher* obediently injected the oil.

'Is she really not going to die?' I thought in despair. 'Will I really have to . . .'

Everything lit up in my mind and I suddenly became aware without any textbooks, without any advice or help (and with unshakeable conviction), that now, for the first time in my life I had to perform an amputation on a dying person. And that that person would die under the knife. She was bound to die under the knife; after all, there was no blood left in her body. It had all drained out through her shattered legs over six miles and there was not even a sign that she was conscious. She was silent. Oh, why didn't she die? What would her maddened father say to me?

'Prepare for an amputation,' I said to the assistant in a voice that was not my own.

The midwife gave me a fierce look but the *feldsher* showed a spark of sympathy in his eyes and began busying himself with the instruments. A primus-stove started to roar.

A quarter of an hour passed. I raised her cold eyelid and looked with superstitious fear at the expiring eye. It told me nothing. How could a semi-corpse stay alive? Drops of sweat ran uncontrollably down my forehead from under my white cap and Pelagea wiped away the salt sweat with gauze. What remained of the blood in the girl's veins was now diluted with caffeine. Ought it to have been injected or not? Anna Nikolaevna was gently massaging the swellings caused by the saline solution. And the girl lived on.

I picked up the knife, trying to imitate the man I had once in my life seen perform an amputation, at university. I entreated fate not to let her die at least in the next half hour. 'Let her die in the ward, when I've finished the operation . . .'

I had only common sense to rely on, and it was stimulated into action by the extraordinary situation. Like an experienced butcher, I made a neat circular incision in her thigh with the razor-sharp knife and the skin parted without exuding the smallest drop of blood. 'What will I do if the vessels start bleeding?' I thought, and without turning my head glanced at the row of forceps. I cut through a huge piece of female flesh together with one of the vessels – it looked like a little whitish pipe – but not a drop of blood emerged from it. I stopped it up with a pair of forceps and proceeded, clamping on forceps wherever I suspected the existence of a vessel. 'Arteria . . . arteria . . . what the devil is it called?' The operating theatre had begun to take on a thoroughly professional look. The forceps were hanging in clusters. My assistants drew them back with gauze, retracting the flesh, and I started sawing the round bone with a gleaming, fine-toothed saw. 'Why isn't she dying? It's astonishing . . . God, how people cling to life!'

The bone fell away. Demyan Lukich was left with what had been a girl's leg in his hands. Shreds of flesh and bone. This was all discarded and there remained on the table a young girl shortened, as it were, by a third, with a stump splayed out to one side. 'Just a little bit more . . . Please don't die,' I wished ardently, 'keep going till they take you to the ward, let me come out of this frightful episode with some credit.'

They tied the ligatures and then, knees knocking, I started sewing up the skin with widely-spaced stitches. Suddenly I stopped, brought to my senses by an inspired thought: I left a gap for drainage in which I inserted a gauze wick. My eyes were dimmed with sweat. I felt as if I were in a steam bath.

I heaved a sigh of relief. I looked wearily at the stump and at her waxen face and asked:

'Is she alive?'

'Yes, she's alive,' came the immediate and almost soundless echo as the *feldsher* and Anna Nikolaevna replied in unison.

'She'll last perhaps another minute or so,' the *feldsher* mouthed voicelessly into my ear. Then he hesitated and suggested tentatively:

'Perhaps you needn't touch the other leg, doctor. We could just bandage it, you know . . . otherwise she won't last till the ward . . . all right? Better if she doesn't die in the theatre.'

'Let's have the plaster,' I uttered hoarsely, urged on by some unknown force.

The floor was covered in white blobs of gypsum. We were all bathed in sweat. The body lay lifeless. Its right leg was encased in plaster and the shin showed through where in another inspired moment I had left a window to coincide with the fracture.

'She's alive,' the assistant breathed in surprise.

Then we started lifting her and an enormous cavity could be seen under the sheet – we had left a third of her body on the operating table.

Shadows flitted down the passage, nurses darted to and fro and I saw a dishevelled male figure shuffle past along the wall and let out a muffled howl. But he was led away. Silence fell.

In the operating room I washed off the blood which had stained my arms up to the elbow.

'I suppose you've done a lot of amputations, doctor?' Anna Nikolaevna asked suddenly. 'That was very good, no worse than Leopold.'

She invariably pronounced the name 'Leopold' as if she were talking about the dean of a medical school.

I glanced suspiciously at their faces and saw respect and astonishment in all of them, including Demyan Lukich and Pelagea Ivanovna.

'Hm, well, the fact is I've done only two . . .'

Why did I lie? I cannot understand it to this day.

The hospital was utterly silent.

'When she dies, be sure to send for me,' I told the *feldsher* in an undertone, and for some reason instead of just answering 'All right,' he said deferentially:

'Very good, sir.'

A few minutes later I was standing beside the green-shaded lamp in the study of the doctor's quarters. There was not a sound to be heard.

A pale face was reflected in the pitch-dark window.

'No, I don't look like Dmitry the Pretender, and, do you know, I seem to have aged, there's a furrow between my eyebrows . . . right now there'll be a knock . . . and they'll say, "She's dead".

'Yes, I'll go and have a last look, any minute now there'll be a knock . . .'

There was a knock at the door. It was two and a half months later. One of the first bright days of winter was shining through the window.

He came in; only then did I really look at him. Yes, he definitely had good features. Forty-five years old. Sparkling eyes.

Then a rustling sound. A young girl of enchanting beauty came bounding in on crutches; she had only one leg and was dressed in a very wide skirt with a red border at the hem.

She looked at me and her cheeks flushed pink.

'In Moscow . . . in Moscow,' I said and started writing down an address, 'they'll fix you up with a prosthesis – an artificial leg.'

'Kiss his hand,' the father suddenly commanded her.

I was so confused that I kissed her on the nose instead of the lips.

Then, hanging on her crutches, she undid a bundle and out fell a snow-white towel artlessly embroidered with a red cockerel. So that was what she'd been hiding under her pillow when I did my rounds in the ward! And indeed I remembered seeing some thread on her bedside table.

'I can't accept it,' I said sternly, and even shook my head. But she gave me such a look that I took it.

It hung in my bedroom in Muryovo and then went with me on my travels. In the end it grew threadbare, faded, wore out and disappeared just as memories fade and disappear.

ROBERT LOUIS STEVENSON

THE BODY-SNATCHER

EVERY NIGHT IN the year, four of us sat in the small parlour of the George at Debenham – the undertaker, and the landlord, and Fettes, and myself. Sometimes there would be more; but blow high, blow low, come rain or snow or frost, we four would be each planted in his own particular arm-chair. Fettes was an old drunken Scotchman, a man of education obviously, and a man of some property, since he lived in idleness. He had come to Debenham years ago, while still young, and by a mere continuance of living had grown to be an adopted townsman. His blue camlet cloak was a local antiquity, like the church-spire. His place in the parlour at the George, his absence from church, his old, crapulous, disreputable vices, were all things of course in Debenham. He had some vague Radical opinions and some fleeting infidelities, which he would now and again set forth and emphasise with tottering slaps upon the table. He drank rum – five glasses regularly every evening; and for the greater portion of his nightly visit to the George sat, with his glass in his right hand, in a state of melancholy alcoholic saturation. We called him the Doctor, for he was supposed to have some special knowledge of medicine, and had been known, upon a pinch, to set a fracture or reduce a dislocation; but beyond these slight particulars, we had no knowledge of his character and antecedents.

One dark winter night – it had struck nine some time before the landlord joined us – there was a sick man in the

George, a great neighbouring proprietor suddenly struck down with apoplexy on his way to Parliament; and the great man's still greater London doctor had been telegraphed to his bedside. It was the first time that such a thing had happened in Debenham, for the railway was but newly open, and we were all proportionately moved by the occurrence.

'He's come,' said the landlord, after he had filled and lighted his pipe.

'He?' said I. 'Who? – not the doctor?'

'Himself,' replied our host.

'What is his name?'

'Doctor Macfarlane,' said the landlord.

Fettes was far through his third tumbler, stupidly fuddled, now nodding over, now staring mazily around him; but at the last word he seemed to awaken, and repeated the name 'Macfarlane' twice, quietly enough the first time, but with sudden emotion at the second.

'Yes,' said the landlord, 'that's his name, Doctor Wolfe Macfarlane.'

Fettes became instantly sober; his eyes awoke, his voice became clear, loud, and steady, his language forcible and earnest. We were all startled by the transformation, as if a man had risen from the dead.

'I beg your pardon,' he said, 'I am afraid I have not been paying much attention to your talk. Who is this Wolfe Macfarlane?' And then, when he had heard the landlord out, 'It cannot be, it cannot be,' he added; 'and yet I would like well to see him face to face.'

'Do you know him, Doctor?' asked the undertaker, with a gasp.

'God forbid!' was the reply. 'And yet the name is a strange one; it were too much to fancy two. Tell me, landlord, is he old?'

'Well,' said the host, 'he's not a young man, to be sure, and his hair is white; but he looks younger than you.'

'He is older, though; years older. But,' with a slap upon the table, 'it's the rum you see in my face – rum and sin. This man, perhaps, may have an easy conscience and a good digestion. Conscience! Hear me speak. You would think I was some good, old, decent Christian, would you not? But no, not I; I never canted. Voltaire might have canted if he'd stood in my shoes; but the brains' – with a rattling fillip on his bald head – 'the brains were clear and active, and I saw and made no deductions.'

'If you know this doctor,' I ventured to remark, after a somewhat awful pause, 'I should gather that you do not share the landlord's good opinion.'

Fettes paid no regard to me.

'Yes,' he said, with sudden decision, 'I must see him face to face.'

There was another pause, and then a door was closed rather sharply on the first floor, and a step was heard upon the stair.

'That's the doctor,' cried the landlord. 'Look sharp, and you can catch him.'

It was but two steps from the small parlour to the door of the old George Inn; the wide oak staircase landed almost in the street; there was room for a Turkey rug and nothing more between the threshold and the last round of the descent; but this little space was every evening brilliantly lit up, not only by the light upon the stair and the great signal lamp below the sign, but by the warm radiance of the bar-room window. The George thus brightly advertised itself to passers-by in the cold street. Fettes walked steadily to the spot, and we, who were hanging behind, beheld the two men meet, as one of them had phrased it, face to face. Dr. Macfarlane was alert and vigorous. His white hair set off his pale and placid, although energetic, countenance. He was richly dressed in the finest of broadcloth and the whitest of linen, with a great gold watch-chain, and studs and spectacles of the same precious material. He wore a broad-folded tie, white and speckled with lilac, and he carried on his arm a comfortable driving-coat of fur. There was no doubt but he became his years, breathing, as he did, of wealth and consideration; and it was a surprising contrast to see our parlour sot – bald, dirty, pimpled, and robed in his old camlet cloak – confront him at the bottom of the stairs.

'Macfarlane!' he said somewhat loudly, more like a herald than a friend.

The great doctor pulled up short on the fourth step, as though the familiarity of the address surprised and somewhat shocked his dignity.

'Toddy Macfarlane!' repeated Fettes.

The London man almost staggered. He stared for the swiftest of seconds at the man before him, glanced behind him with a sort of scare, and then in a startled whisper, 'Fettes!' he said, 'you!'

'Ay', said the other, 'me! Did you think I was dead too? We are not so easy shut of our acquaintance.'

'Hush, hush!' exclaimed the doctor. 'Hush, hush! this meeting is so unexpected – I can see you are unmanned. I hardly knew you, I confess, at first; but I am overjoyed – overjoyed to have this opportunity. For the present it must be how-d'ye-do and good-bye in one, for my fly is waiting, and I must not fail the train; but you shall – let me see – yes – you shall give me your address, and you can count on early news of me. We must do something for you Fettes. I fear you are out at elbows; but we must see to that for auld lang syne, as once we sang at suppers.'

'Money!' cried Fettes; 'money from you! The money that I had from you is lying where I cast it in the rain.'

Dr. Macfarlane had talked himself into some measure of superiority and confidence, but the uncommon energy of this refusal cast him back into his first confusion.

A horrible, ugly look came and went across his almost venerable countenance. 'My dear fellow,' he said, 'be it as you please; my last thought is to offend you. I would intrude on none. I will leave you my address, however—'

'I do not wish it – I do not wish to know the roof that shelters you,' interrupted the other. 'I heard your name; I feared it might be you; I wished to know if, after all, there were a God; I know now that there is none. Begone!'

He still stood in the middle of the rug, between the stair and doorway; and the great London physician, in order to escape, would be forced to step to one side. It was plain that he hesitated before the thought of this humiliation. White as he was, there was a dangerous glitter in his spectacles; but while he still paused uncertain, he became aware that the driver of his fly was peering in from the street at this unusual scene and caught a glimpse at the same time of our little body from the parlour, huddled by the corner of the bar. The presence of so many witnesses decided him at once to flee. He crouched together, brushing on the wainscot, and made a dart like a serpent, striking for the door. But his tribulation was not entirely at an end, for even as he was passing Fettes clutched him by the arm and these words came in a whisper, and yet painfully distinct, 'Have you seen it again?'

The great rich London doctor cried out aloud with a sharp, throttling cry; he dashed his questioner across the open space, and, with his hands over his head, fled out of the door like a detected thief. Before it had occurred to one of us to make a movement the fly was already rattling toward the station. The scene was over like a dream, but the dream had left proofs and traces of its passage. Next day the servant found the fine gold spectacles broken on the threshold, and that very night we were all standing breathless by the bar-room window, and Fettes at our side, sober, pale, and resolute in look.

'God protect us, Mr. Fettes!' said the landlord, coming first into possession of his customary senses. 'What in the universe is all this? These are strange things you have been saying.'

Fettes turned toward us; he looked us each in succession in the face. 'See if you can hold your tongues,' said he. 'That man Macfarlane is not safe to cross; those that have done so already have repented it too late.'

And then, without so much as finishing his third glass, far less waiting for the other two, he bade us good-bye and went forth, under the lamp of the hotel, into the black night.

We three turned to our places in the parlour, with the big red fire and four clear candles; and as we recapitulated what had passed, the first chill of our surprise soon changed into a glow of curiosity. We sat late; it was the latest session I have known in the old George. Each man, before we parted, had his theory that he was bound to prove; and none of us had any nearer business in this world than to track out the past of our condemned companion, and surprise the secret that he shared with the great London doctor. It is no great boast, but I believe I was a better hand at worming out a story than either of my fellows at the George; and perhaps there is now no other man alive who could narrate to you the following foul and unnatural events.

In his young days Fettes studied medicine in the schools of Edinburgh. He had talent of a kind, the talent that picks up swiftly what it hears and readily retails it for its own.

He worked little at home; but he was civil, attentive, and intelligent in the presence of his masters. They soon picked him out as a lad who listened closely and remembered well; nay, strange as it seemed to me when I first heard it, he was in those days well favoured, and pleased by his exterior. There was, at that period, a certain extramural teacher of anatomy, whom I shall here designate by the letter K. His name was subsequently too well known. The man who bore it skulked through the streets of Edinburgh in disguise, while the mob that applauded at the execution of Burke called loudly for the blood of his employer. But Mr. K—— was then at the top of his vogue; he enjoyed a popularity due partly to his own talent and address, partly to the incapacity of his rival, the university professor. The students, at least, swore by his name, and Fettes believed himself, and was believed by others, to have laid the foundations of success when he acquired the favour of this meteorically famous man. Mr. K—— was a *bon vivant* as well as an accomplished teacher; he liked a sly illusion no less than a careful preparation. In both capacities Fettes enjoyed and deserved his notice, and by the second year of his attendance he held the half-regular position of second demonstrator, or sub-assistant in his class.

In this capacity the charge of the theatre and lecture-room devolved in particular upon his shoulders. He had to answer for the cleanliness of the premises and the conduct of the other students, and it was a part of his duty to supply, receive, and divide the various subjects. It was with a view to this last – at that time very delicate – affair that he was lodged by Mr. K—— in the same wynd, and at last in the same building, with the dissecting-rooms. Here, after a night of turbulent pleasures, his hand still tottering, his sight still misty and confused, he would be called out of bed in the black hours before the winter dawn by the unclean and desperate interlopers who supplied the table. He would open the door to these men, since infamous throughout the land. He would help them with their tragic burden, pay them their sordid price, and remain alone, when they were gone, with the unfriendly relics of humanity. From such a scene he would return to snatch another hour or two of slumber, to repair the abuses of the night, and refresh himself for the labours of the day.

Few lads could have been more insensible to the impressions of a life thus passed among the ensigns of mortality. His mind was closed against all general considerations. He was incapable of interest in the fate and fortunes of another, the slave of his own desires and low ambitions. Cold, light, and selfish in the last resort, he had that modicum of prudence, miscalled morality, which keeps a man from inconvenient drunkenness or punishable theft. He coveted, besides, a measure of consideration from his masters and his fellow-pupils, and he had no desire to fail conspicuously in the external parts of life. Thus he made it his pleasure to gain some distinction in his studies, and day after day rendered unimpeachable eye-service to his employer, Mr. K——. For his day of work he indemnified himself by nights of roaring, blackguardly enjoyment; and when that balance had been struck, the organ that he called his conscience declared itself content.

The supply of subjects was a continual trouble to him as well as to his master. In that large and busy class, the raw material of the anatomist kept perpetually running out; and the business thus rendered necessary was not only unpleasant in itself, but threatened dangerous consequences to all who were concerned. It was the policy of Mr. K—— to ask no questions in his dealings with the trade. 'They bring the body, and we pay the price,' he used to say, dwelling on the alliteration – '*quid pro quo.*' And, again, and somewhat profanely, 'Ask no questions,' he would tell his assistants, 'for conscience' sake.' There was no understanding that the subjects were provided by the crime of murder. Had that idea been broached to him in words, he would have recoiled in horror; but the lightness of his speech upon so grave a matter was, in itself, an offence against good manners, and a temptation to the men with whom he dealt. Fettes, for instance, had often remarked to himself upon the singular freshness of the bodies. He had been struck again and again by the hangdog, abominable looks of the ruffians who came to him before the dawn; and pulling things together clearly in his private thoughts, he perhaps attributed a meaning too immoral and too categorical to the unguarded counsels of his master. He understood his duty, in short, to have three branches: to take what was brought, to pay the price, and to avert the eye from any evidence of crime.

One November morning this policy of silence was put sharply to the test. He had been awake all night with a racking toothache – pacing his room like a caged beast or throwing himself in fury on his bed – and had fallen at last into that profound, uneasy slumber that so often follows on a night of pain, when he was awakened by the third or fourth angry repetition of the concerted signal. There was a thin, bright moonshine; it was bitter cold, windy, and frosty; the town had not yet awakened, but an indefinable stir already preluded the noise and business of the day. The ghouls had come later than usual, and they seemed more than usually eager to be gone. Fettes, sick with sleep, lighted them upstairs. He heard their grumbling Irish voices through a dream; and as they stripped the sack from their sad merchandise he leaned dozing, with his shoulder propped against the wall; he had to shake himself to find the men their money. As he did so his eyes lighted on the dead face. He started; he took two steps nearer, with the candle raised.

'God Almighty!' he cried. 'That is Jane Galbraith!'

The men answered nothing, but they shuffled nearer the door.

'I know her, I tell you,' he continued. 'She was alive and hearty yesterday. It's impossible she can be dead; it's impossible you should have got this body fairly.'

'Sure, sir, you're mistaken entirely,' said one of the men.

But the other looked Fettes darkly in the eyes, and demanded the money on the spot.

It was impossible to misconceive the threat or to exaggerate the danger. The lad's heart failed him. He stammered some excuses, counted out the sum, and saw his hateful visitors depart. No sooner were they gone than he hastened to confirm his doubts. By a dozen unquestionable marks he identified the girl he had jested with the day before. He saw, with horror, marks upon her body that might well betoken violence. A panic seized him, and he took refuge in his room. There he reflected at length over the discovery that he had made; considered soberly the bearing of Mr. K——'s instructions and the danger to himself of interference in so serious a business, and at last, in sore perplexity, determined to wait for the advice of his immediate superior, the class assistant.

This was a young doctor, Wolfe Macfarlane, a high favourite among all the reckless students, clever, dissipated, and unscrupulous to the last degree. He had travelled and studied abroad. His manners were agreeable and a little forward. He was an authority on the stage, skilful on the ice or the links with skate or golf-club; he dressed with nice audacity, and, to put the finishing touch upon his glory, he kept a gig and a strong trotting-horse. With Fettes he was on terms of intimacy; indeed, their relative positions called for some community of life; and when subjects were scarce the pair would drive far into the country in Macfarlane's gig, visit and desecrate some lonely graveyard, and return before dawn with their booty to the door of the dissecting-room.

On that particular morning Macfarlane arrived somewhat earlier than his wont. Fettes heard him, and met him on the stairs, told him his story, and showed him the cause of his alarm. Macfarlane examined the marks on her body.

'Yes,' he said, with a nod, 'it looks fishy.'

'Well, what should I do?' asked Fettes.

'Do?' repeated the other, 'Do you want to do anything? Least said soonest mended, I should say.'

'Someone else might recognise her,' objected Fettes. 'She was as well known as the Castle Rock.'

'We'll hope not,' said Macfarlane, 'and if anybody does – well, you didn't, don't you see, and there's an end. The fact is, this has been going on too long. Stir up the mud, and you'll get K—— into the most unholy trouble; you'll be in a shocking box yourself. So will I, if you come to that. I should like to know how any one of us would look, or what the devil we should have to say for ourselves, in any Christian witness-box. For me, you know there's one thing certain – that, practically speaking, all our subjects have been murdered.'

'Macfarlane!' cried Fettes.

'Come now!' sneered the other. 'As if you hadn't suspected it yourself!'

'Suspecting is one thing—'

'And proof another. Yes, I know; and I'm as sorry as you are this should have come here,' tapping the body with his cane. 'The next best thing for me is not to recognise it; and,' he added coolly, 'I don't. You may, if you please. I don't dictate, but I think a man of the world would do as I do; and I may add, I fancy that is what K—— would look for at our hands. The question is, Why did he choose us two for his assistants? And I answer, Because he didn't want old wives.'

This was the tone of all others to affect the mind of a lad like Fettes. He agreed to imitate Macfarlane. The body of the unfortunate girl was duly dissected, and no one remarked or appeared to recognise her.

One afternoon, when his day's work was over, Fettes dropped into a popular tavern and found Macfarlane sitting with a stranger. This was a small man, very pale and dark, with coal-black eyes. The cut of his features gave a promise of intellect and refinement which was but feebly realised in his manners, for he proved, upon a nearer acquaintance, coarse, vulgar, and stupid. He exercised, however, a very remarkable control over Macfarlane; issued orders like the Great Bashaw; became inflamed at the least discussion or delay, and commented rudely on the servility with which he was obeyed. This most offensive person took a fancy to Fettes on the spot, plied him with drinks, and honoured him with unusual confidences on his past career. If a tenth part of what he confessed were true, he was a very loathsome rogue; and the lad's vanity was tickled by the attention of so experienced a man.

'I'm a pretty bad fellow myself,' the stranger remarked, 'but Macfarlane is the boy – Toddy Macfarlane I call him. Toddy, order your friend another glass.' Or it might be, 'Toddy, you jump up and shut the door.' 'Toddy hates me,' he said again. 'Oh, yes, Toddy, you do!'

'Don't you call me that confounded name,' growled Macfarlane.

'Hear him! Did you ever see the lads play knife? He would like to do that all over my body,' remarked the stranger.

'We medicals have a better way than that,' said Fettes. 'When we dislike a dead friend of ours, we dissect him.'

Macfarlane looked up sharply, as though this jest were scarcely to his mind.

The afternoon passed. Gray, for that was the stranger's name, invited Fettes to join them at dinner, ordered a feast so sumptuous that the tavern was thrown into commotion, and when all was done commanded Macfarlane to settle the bill. It was late before they separated; the man Gray was incapably drunk. Macfarlane, sobered by his fury, chewed the cud of the money he had been forced to squander and the slights he had been obliged to swallow. Fettes, with various liquors singing in his head, returned home with devious footsteps and a mind entirely in abeyance. Next day Macfarlane was absent from the class, and Fettes smiled to himself as he imagined him still squiring the intolerable Gray from tavern to tavern. As soon as the hour of liberty had struck he posted from place to place in quest of his last night's companions. He could find them, however, nowhere; so returned, early to his rooms, went early to bed, and slept the sleep of the just.

At four in the morning he was awakened by the well-known signal. Descending to the door, he was filled with astonishment to find Macfarlane with his gig, and in the gig one of those long and ghastly packages with which he was so well acquainted.

'What?' he cried. 'Have you been out alone? How did you manage?'

But Macfarlane silenced him roughly, bidding him turn to business. When they had got the body upstairs and laid it on the table, Macfarlane made at first as if he were going away. Then he paused and seemed to hesitate; and then, 'You had better look at the face,' said he, in tones of some constraint. 'You had better,' he repeated, as Fettes only stared at him in wonder.

'But where, and how, and when did you come by it?' cried the other.

'Look at the face,' was the only answer.

Fettes was staggered; strange doubts assailed him. He looked from the young doctor to the body, and then back again. At last, with a start, he did as he was bidden. He had almost expected the sight that met his eyes, and yet the shock was cruel. To see, fixed in the rigidity of death and naked on that coarse layer of sackcloth, the man whom he had left well clad and full of meat and sin upon the threshold of a tavern, awoke, even in the thoughtless Fettes, some of the terrors of the conscience. It was a *cras tibi* which re-echoed in his soul, that two whom he had known should have come to lie upon these icy tables. Yet these were only secondary thoughts. His first concern regarded Wolfe. Unprepared for a challenge so momentous, he knew not how to look his comrade in the face. He durst not meet his eye, and he had neither words nor voice at his command.

It was Macfarlane himself who made the first advance. He came up quietly behind and laid his hand gently but firmly on the other's shoulder.

'Richardson,' said he, 'may have the head.'

Now Richardson was a student who had long been anxious for that portion of the human subject to dissect. There was no answer, and the murderer resumed: 'Talking of business, you must pay me; your accounts, you see, must tally.'

Fettes found a voice, the ghost of his own: 'Pay you!' he cried. 'Pay you for that?'

'Why, yes, of course you must. By all means and on every possible account, you must,' returned the other. 'I dare not give it for nothing, you dare not take it for nothing; it would compromise us both. This is another case like Jane Galbraith's. The more things are wrong the more we must act as if all were right. Where does old K—— keep his money?'

'There,' answered Fettes hoarsely, pointing to a cupboard in the corner.

'Give me the key, then,' said the other calmly, holding out his hand.

There was an instant's hesitation, and the die was cast. Macfarlane could not suppress a nervous twitch, the infinitesimal mark of an immense relief, as he felt the key between his fingers. He opened the cupboard, brought out pen and ink and a paper-book that stood in one compartment, and separated from the funds in a drawer a sum suitable to the occasion.

'Now, look here,' he said, 'there is the payment made – first proof of your good faith: first step to your security. You have now to clinch it by a second. Enter the payment in your book, and then you for your part may defy the devil.'

The next few seconds were for Fettes an agony of thought; but in balancing his terrors it was the most immediate that triumphed. Any future difficulty seemed almost welcome if he could avoid a present quarrel with Macfarlane. He set down the candle which he had been carrying all this time, and with a steady hand entered the date, the nature, and the amount of the transaction.

'And now,' said Macfarlane, 'it's only fair that you should pocket the lucre. I've had my share already. By-the-bye, when a man of the world falls into a bit of luck, has a few shillings extra in his pocket – I'm ashamed to speak of it, but there's a rule of conduct in the case. No treating, no purchase of expensive class-books, no squaring of old debts; borrow, don't lend.'

'Macfarlane,' began Fettes, still somewhat hoarsely, 'I have put my neck in a halter to oblige you.'

'To oblige me?' cried Wolfe. 'Oh, come! You did, as near as I can see the matter, what you downright had to do in self-defence. Suppose I got into trouble, where would you be? This second little matter flows clearly from the first. Mr. Gray is the continuation of Miss Galbraith. You can't begin and then stop. If you begin, you must keep on beginning; that's the truth. No rest for the wicked.'

A horrible sense of blackness and the treachery of fate seized hold upon the soul of the unhappy student.

'My God!' he cried, 'but what have I done? and when did I begin? To be made a class assistant – in the name of reason, where's the harm in that? Service wanted the position; Service might have got it. Would *he* have been where *I* am now!'

'My dear fellow,' said Macfarlane, 'what a boy you are! What harm *has* come to you? What harm *can* come to you if you hold your tongue? Why, man, do you know what this life is? There are two squads of us – the lions and the lambs. If you're a lamb, you'll come to lie upon these tables like Gray or Jane Galbraith; if you're a lion, you'll live and drive a horse like me, like K——, like all the world with any wit or courage. You're staggered at the first. But look at K——! My dear fellow, you're clever, you have pluck. I like you, and K—— likes you. You were born to lead the hunt; and I tell you, on my honour and my experience of life, three days from now you'll laugh at all these scarecrows like a High School boy at a farce.'

And with that Macfarlane took his departure and drove off up the wynd in his gig to get under cover before day-light. Fettes was thus left alone with his regrets. He saw the miserable peril in which he stood involved. He saw, with inexpressible dismay, that there was no limit to his weakness, and that, from concession to concession, he had fallen from the arbiter of Macfarlane's destiny to his paid and helpless accomplice. He would have given the world to have been a little braver at the time, but it did not occur to him that he might still be brave. The secret of Jane Galbraith and the cursed entry in the day-book closed his mouth.

Hours passed; the class began to arrive; the members of the unhappy Gray were dealt out to one and to another, and received without remark. Richardson was made happy with the head; and before the hour of freedom rang Fettes trembled with exultation to perceive how far they had already gone toward safety.

For two days he continued to watch, with increasing joy, the dreadful process of disguise.

On the third day Macfarlane made his appearance. He had been ill, he said; but he made up for lost time by the energy with which he directed the students. To Richardson in particular he extended the most valuable assistance and advice, and that student, encouraged by the praise of the demonstrator, burned high with ambitious hopes, and saw the medal already in his grasp.

Before the week was out Macfarlane's prophecy had been fulfilled. Fettes had outlived his terrors and had forgotten his baseness. He began to plume himself upon his courage, and had so arranged the story in his mind that he could look back on these events with an unhealthy pride. Of his accomplice he saw but little. They met, of course, in the business of the class; they received their orders together from Mr. K——. At times they had a word or two in private, and Macfarlane was from first to last particularly kind and jovial. But it was plain that he avoided any reference to their common secret; and even when Fettes whispered to him that he had cast in his lot with the lions and forsworn the lambs, he only signed to him smilingly to hold his peace.

At length an occasion arose which threw the pair once more into a closer union. Mr. K—— was again short of subjects; pupils were eager, and it was a part of this teacher's pretensions to be always well supplied. At the same time there came the news of a burial in the rustic graveyard of Glencorse. Time has little changed the place in question. It stood then, as now, upon a cross road, out of call of human habitations, and buried fathom deep in the foliage of six cedar trees. The cries of the sheep upon the neighbouring hills, the streamlets upon either hand, one loudly singing among pebbles, the other dripping furtively from pond to pond, the stir of the wind in mountainous old flowering chestnuts, and once in seven days the voice of the bell and the old tunes of the precentor, were the only sounds that disturbed the silence around the rural church. The Resurrection Man – to use a by-name of the period – was not to be deterred by any of the sanctities of customary piety. It was part of his trade to despise and desecrate the scrolls and trumpets of old tombs, the paths worn by the feet of worshippers and mourners, and the offerings and the inscriptions of bereaved affection. To rustic neighbourhoods, where love is more than commonly tenacious, and where some bonds of blood or fellowship unite the entire society of a parish, the body-snatcher, far from being repelled by natural respect, was attracted by the ease and safety of the task. To bodies that had been laid in earth, in joyful expectation of a far different awakening, there came that hasty, lamplit, terror-haunted resurrection of the spade and mattock. The coffin was forced, the cerements torn, and the melancholy relics, clad in sackcloth, after being rattled for hours on moonless byways, were at length exposed to uttermost indignities before a class of gaping boys.

Somewhat as two vultures may swoop upon a dying lamb, Fettes and Macfarlane were to be let loose upon a grave in that green and quiet resting-place. The wife of a farmer, a woman who had lived for sixty years, and been known for nothing but good butter and a godly conversation, was to be rooted from her grave at midnight and carried, dead and naked, to that far-away city that she had always honoured with her Sunday's best; the place beside her family was to be empty till the crack of doom; her innocent and almost venerable members to be exposed to that last curiosity of the anatomist.

Late one afternoon the pair set forth, well wrapped in cloaks and furnished with a formidable bottle. It rained without remission – a cold, dense, lashing rain. Now and again there blew a puff of wind, but these sheets of falling water kept it down. Bottle and all, it was a sad and silent drive as far as Penicuik, where they were to spend the evening. They stopped once, to hide their implements in a thick bush not far from the churchyard, and once again at the Fisher's Tryst, to have a toast before the kitchen fire and vary their nips of whisky with a glass of ale. When they reached their journey's end the gig was housed, the horse was fed and comforted, and the two young doctors in a private room sat down to the best dinner and the best wine the house afforded. The lights, the fire, the beating rain upon the window, the cold, incongruous work that lay before them, added zest to their enjoyment of the meal. With every glass their cordiality increased. Soon Macfarlane handed a little pile of gold to his companion.

'A compliment,' he said. 'Between friends these little d—d accommodations ought to fly like pipe-lights.'

Fettes pocketed the money, and applauded the sentiment to the echo. 'You are a philosopher,' he cried. 'I was an ass till I knew you. You and K—— between you, by the Lord Harry! but you'll make a man of me.'

'Of course we shall,' applauded Macfarlane. 'A man? I tell you, it required a man to back me up the other morning. There are some big, brawling, forty-year-old cowards who would have turned sick at the look of the d—d thing; but not you – you kept your head. I watched you.'

'Well, and why not?' Fettes thus vaunted himself. 'It was no affair of mine. There was nothing to gain on the one side but disturbance, and on the other I could count on your gratitude, don't you see?' And he slapped his pocket till the gold pieces rang.

Macfarlane somehow felt a certain touch of alarm at these unpleasant words. He may have regretted that he had taught his young companion so successfully, but he had no time to interfere, for the other noisily continued in this boastful strain: –

'The great thing is not to be afraid. Now, between you and me, I don't want to hang – that's practical; but for all cant, Macfarlane, I was born with a contempt. Hell, God, Devil, right, wrong, sin, crime, and all the old gallery of curiosities – they may frighten boys, but men of the world, like you and me, despise them. Here's to the memory of Gray!'

It was by this time growing somewhat late. The gig, according to order, was brought round to the door with both lamps brightly shining, and the young men had to pay their bill and take the road. They announced that they were bound for Peebles, and drove in that direction till they were clear of the last houses of the town; then, extinguishing the lamps, returned upon their course, and followed a by-road toward Glencorse. There was no sound but that of their own passage, and the incessant, strident pouring of the rain. It was pitch dark; here and there a white gate or a white stone in the wall guided them for a short space across the night; but for the most part it was at a foot pace, and almost groping, that they picked their way through that resonant blackness to their solemn and isolated destination. In the sunken woods that traverse the neighbourhood of the burying-ground the last glimmer failed them, and it became necessary to kindle a match and re-illumine one of the lanterns of the gig. Thus, under the dripping trees, and environed by huge and moving shadows, they reached the scene of their unhallowed labours.

They were both experienced in such affairs, and powerful with the spade; and they had scarce been twenty minutes at their task before they were rewarded by a dull rattle on the coffin lid. At the same moment, Macfarlane, having hurt his hand upon a stone, flung it carelessly above his head. The grave, in which they now stood almost to the shoulders, was close to the edge of the plateau of the graveyard; and the gig lamp had been propped, the better to illuminate their labours, against a tree, and on the immediate verge of the steep bank descending to the stream. Chance had taken a sure aim with the stone. Then came a clang of broken glass; night fell upon them; sounds alternately dull and ringing announced the bounding of the lantern down the bank, and its occasional collision with the trees. A stone or two, which it had dislodged in its descent, rattled behind it into the profundities of the glen; and then silence, like night, resumed its sway; and they might bend their hearing to its utmost pitch, but naught was to be heard except the rain, now marching to the wind, now steadily falling over miles of open country.

They were so nearly at an end of their abhorred task that they judged it wisest to complete it in the dark. The coffin was exhumed and broken open; the body inserted in the dripping sack and carried between them to the gig; one mounted to keep it in its place, and the other, taking the horse by the mouth, groped along by wall and bush until they reached the wider road by the Fisher's Tryst. Here was a faint, diffused radiancy, which they hailed like daylight; by that they pushed the horse to a good pace and began to rattle along merrily in the direction of the town.

They had both been wetted to the skin during their operations, and now, as the gig jumped among the deep ruts, the thing that stood propped between them fell now upon one and now upon the other. At every repetition of the horrid contact each instinctively repelled it with the greater haste; and the process, natural although it was, began to tell upon the nerves of the companions. Macfarlane made some ill-favoured jest about the farmer's wife, but it came hollowly from his lips, and was allowed to drop in silence. Still their unnatural burden bumped from side to side; and now the head would be laid, as if in confidence, upon their shoulders, and now the drenching sackcloth would flap icily about their faces. A creeping chill began to possess the soul of Fettes. He peered at the bundle, and it seemed somehow larger than at first. All over the country-side, and from every degree of distance, the farm dogs accompanied their passage with tragic ululations; and it grew and grew upon his mind that some unnatural miracle had been accomplished, that some nameless change had befallen the dead body, and that it was in fear of their unholy burden that the dogs were howling.

'For God's sake,' said he, making a great effort to arrive at speech, 'for God's sake, let's have a light!'

Seemingly Macfarlane was affected in the same direction; for, though he made no reply, he stopped the horse, passed the reins to his companion, got down, and proceeded to kindle the remaining lamp. They had by that time got no farther than the cross-road down to Auchenclinny. The rain still poured as though the deluge were returning, and it was no easy matter to make a light in such a world of wet and darkness. When at last the flickering blue flame had been transferred to the wick and began to expand and clarify, and shed a wide circle of misty brightness round the gig, it became possible for the two young men to see each other and the thing they had along with them. The rain had moulded the rough sacking to the outlines of the body underneath; the head was distinct from the trunk, the shoulders plainly modelled; something at once spectral and human riveted their eyes upon the ghastly comrade of their drive.

For some time Macfarlane stood motionless, holding up the lamp. A nameless dread was swathed, like a wet sheet, about the body, and tightened the white skin upon the face of Fettes; a fear that was meaningless, a horror of what could not be, kept mounting to his brain. Another beat of the watch, and he had spoken. But his comrade forestalled him.

'That is not a woman,' said Macfarlane, in a hushed voice.

'It was a woman when we put her in,' whispered Fettes.

'Hold that lamp,' said the other. 'I must see her face.'

And as Fettes took the lamp his companion untied the fastenings of the sack and drew down the cover from the head. The light fell very clear upon the dark, well-moulded features and smooth-shaven cheeks of a too familiar countenance, often beheld in dreams of both of these young men. A wild yell rang up into the night; each leaped from his own side into the roadway: the lamp fell, broke, and was extinguished; and the horse, terrified by this unusual commotion, bounded and went off toward Edinburgh at a gallop, bearing along with it, sole occupant of the gig, the body of the dead and long-dissected Gray.

J. G. BALLARD

MINUS ONE

'WHERE, MY GOD, *where* is he?'

Uttered in a tone of uncontrollable frustration as he paced up and down in front of the high-gabled window behind his desk, this *cri de coeur* of Dr Mellinger, Director of Green Hill Asylum, expressed the consternation of his entire staff at the mysterious disappearance of one of their patients. In the twelve hours that had elapsed since the escape, Dr Mellinger and his subordinates had progressed from surprise and annoyance to acute exasperation, and eventually to a mood of almost euphoric disbelief. To add insult to injury, not only had the patient, James Hinton, succeeded in becoming the first ever to escape from the asylum, but he had managed to do so without leaving any clues as to his route. Thus Dr Mellinger and his staff were tantalized by the possibility that Hinton had never escaped at all and was still safely within the confines of the asylum. At all events, everyone agreed that if Hinton *had* escaped, he had literally vanished into thin air.

However, one small consolation, Dr Mellinger reminded himself as he drummed his fingers on his desk, was that Hinton's disappearance had exposed the shortcomings of the asylum's security systems, and administered a salutary jolt to his heads of departments. As this hapless group, led by the Deputy Director, Dr Normand, filed into his office for the first of the morning's emergency conferences, Dr Mellinger cast a baleful glare at each in turn, but their sleepless faces remained mutely lowered to the carpeting, as if, despairing of finding Hinton anywhere else, they now sought his hiding place in its deep ruby pile.

At least, Dr Mellinger reflected, only one patient had disappeared, a negative sentiment which assumed greater meaning in view of the outcry that would be raised from the world outside when it was discovered that a patient – obviously a homicidal lunatic – had remained at large for over twelve hours before the police were notified.

This decision not to inform the civil authorities, an error of judgement whose culpability seemed to mount as the hours passed, alone prevented Dr Mellinger from finding an immediate scapegoat – a convenient one would have been little Dr Mendelsohn of the Pathology Department, an unimportant branch of the asylum – and sacrificing him on the altar of his own indiscretion. His natural caution, and reluctance to yield an inch of ground unless compelled, had prevented Dr Mellinger from raising the general alarm during the first hours after Hinton's disappearance, when some doubt still remained whether the latter had actually left the asylum. Although the failure to find Hinton might have been interpreted as a reasonable indication that he had successfully escaped, Dr Mellinger had characteristically refused to accept such faulty logic.

By now, over twelve hours later, his miscalculation had become apparent. As the thin smirk on Dr Normand's face revealed, and as his other subordinates would soon realize, his directorship of the asylum was now at stake. Unless they found Hinton within a few hours he would be placed in an untenable position before both the civil authorities and the trustees.

However, Dr Mellinger reminded himself, it was not without the exercise of considerable guile and resource that he had become Director of Green Hill in the first place.

'Where *is* he?'

Shifting his emphasis from the first of these interrogatories to the second, as if to illustrate that the fruitless search for Hinton's whereabouts had been superseded by an examination of his total existential role in the unhappy farce of which he was the author and principal star, Dr Mellinger turned upon his three breakfastless subordinates.

'Well, have you found him? Don't sit there dozing, gentlemen! You may have had a sleepless night, but I have still to wake from the nightmare.' With this humourless shaft, Dr Mellinger flashed a mordant eye into the rhododendron-lined drive, as if hoping to catch a sudden glimpse of the vanished patient. 'Dr Redpath, your report, please.'

'The search is still continuing, Director.' Dr Redpath, the registrar of the asylum, was nominally in charge of security. 'We have examined the entire grounds, dormitory blocks, garages and outbuildings – even the patients are taking part – but every trace of Hinton has vanished. Reluctantly, I am afraid there is no alternative but to inform the police.'

'Nonsense.' Dr Mellinger took his seat behind the desk, arms outspread and eyes roving the bare top for a minuscule replica of the vanished patient. 'Don't be disheartened by your inability to discover him, Doctor. Until the search is complete we would be wasting the police's time to ask for their help.'

'Of course, Director,' Dr Normand rejoined smoothly, 'but on the other hand, as we have now proved that the missing patient is not within the boundaries of Green Hill, we can conclude, ergo, that he is outside them. In such an event is it perhaps rather a case of *us* helping the police?'

'Not at all, my dear Normand,' Dr Mellinger replied pleasantly. As he mentally elaborated his answer, he realized that he had never trusted or liked his deputy; given the first opportunity he would replace him, most conveniently with Redpath, whose blunders in the 'Hinton affair', as it could be designated, would place him for ever squarely below the Director's thumb. 'If there were any evidence of the means by which Hinton made his escape – knotted sheets or footprints in the flower-beds – we could assume that he was no longer within these walls. But no such evidence has been found. For all we know – in fact, everything points inescapably to this conclusion – the patient is still within the confines of Green Hill, indeed by rights still within his cell. The bars on the window were not cut, and the only way out was through the door, the keys to which remained in the possession of Dr Booth' – he indicated the third member of the trio, a slim young man with a worried expression – 'throughout the period between the last contact with Hinton and the discovery of his disappearance. Dr Booth, as the physician actually responsible for Hinton, you are quite certain you were the last person to visit him?'

Dr Booth nodded reluctantly. His celebrity at having discovered Hinton's escape had long since turned sour. 'At seven o'clock, sir, during my evening round. But the last person to *see* Hinton was the duty nurse half an hour later. However, as no treatment had been prescribed – the patient had been admitted for observation – the door was not unlocked. Shortly after nine o'clock I decided to visit the patient—'

'Why?' Dr Mellinger placed the tips of his fingers together and constructed a cathedral spire and nave. 'This is one of the strangest aspects of the case, Doctor. Why should you have chosen, almost an hour and a half later, to leave your comfortable office on the ground floor and climb three flights of stairs merely to carry out a cursory inspection which could best be left to the duty staff? Your motives puzzle me, Doctor.'

'But, Director—!' Dr Booth was almost on his feet. 'Surely you don't suspect me of colluding in Hinton's escape? I assure you—'

'Doctor, please.' Dr Mellinger raised a smooth white hand. 'Nothing could be further from my mind. Perhaps I should have said: your *unconscious* motives.'

Again the unfortunate Booth protested: 'Director, there were no unconscious motives. I admit I can't remember precisely what prompted me to see Hinton, but it was some perfectly trivial reason. I hardly knew the patient.'

Dr Mellinger bent forwards across the desk. 'That is exactly what I meant, Doctor. To be precise, you did not know Hinton at all.' Dr Mellinger gazed at the distorted reflection of himself in the silver ink-stand. 'Tell me, Dr Booth, how would you describe Hinton's appearance?'

Booth hesitated. 'Well, he was of . . . medium height, if I remember, with . . . yes, brown hair and a pale complexion. His eyes were – I should have to refresh my memory from the file, Director.'

Dr Mellinger nodded. He turned to Redpath. 'Could you describe him, Doctor?'

'I'm afraid not, sir. I never saw the patient.' He gestured to the Deputy Director. 'I believe Dr Normand interviewed him on admission.'

With an effort Dr Normand cast into his memory. 'It was probably my assistant. If I remember, he was a man of average build with no distinguishing features. Neither short, nor tall. Stocky, one might say.' He pursed his lips. 'Yes. Or rather, no. I'm certain it was my assistant.'

'How interesting.' Dr Mellinger had visibly revived, the gleams of ironic humour which flashed from his eyes revealed some potent inner transformation. The burden of irritations and frustrations which had plagued him for the past day seemed to have been lifted. 'Does this mean, Dr Normand, that this entire institution has been mobilized in a search for a man whom no one here could recognize even if they found him? You surprise me, my dear Normand. I was under the impression that you were a man of cool and analytical intelligence, but in your search for Hinton you are obviously employing more arcane powers.'

'But, Director! I cannot be expected to memorize the face of every patient—'

'Enough, enough!' Dr Mellinger stood up with a flourish, and resumed his circuit of the carpet. 'This is all very disturbing. Obviously the whole relationship between Green Hill and its patients must be re-examined. Our patients are not faceless ciphers, gentlemen, but the possessors of unique and vital identities. If we regard them as nonentities and fail to invest them with any personal characteristics, is it surprising that they should seem to disappear? I suggest that we put aside the next few days and dedicate them to a careful re-appraisal. Let us scrutinize all those facile assumptions we make so readily.' Impelled by this vision, Dr Mellinger stepped into the light pouring through the window, as if to expose himself to this new revelation. 'Yes, this is the task that lies before us now; from its successful conclusion will emerge a new Green Hill, a Green Hill without shadows and conspiracies, where patients and physicians stand before each other in mutual trust and responsibility.'

A pregnant silence fell at the conclusion of this homily. At last Dr Redpath cleared his throat, reluctant to disturb Dr Mellinger's sublime communion with himself. 'And Hinton, sir?'

'Hinton? Ah, yes.' Dr Mellinger turned to face them, like

a bishop about to bless his congregation. 'Let us see Hinton as an illustration of this process of self-examination, a focus of our re-appraisal.'

'So the search should continue, sir?' Redpath pressed.

'Of course.' For a moment Dr Mellinger's attention wandered. 'Yes, we must find Hinton. He is here some-where; his essence pervades Green Hill, a vast metaphysical conundrum. Solve it, gentlemen, and you will have solved the mystery of his disappearance.'

For the next hour Dr Mellinger paced the carpet alone, now and then warming his hands at the low fire below the mantelpiece. Its few flames entwined in the chimney like the ideas playing around the periphery of his mind. At last, he felt, a means of breaking through the impasse had offered itself. He had always been certain that Hinton's miraculous disappearance represented more than a simple problem of breached security, and was a symbol of something grievously at fault with the very foundations of Green Hill.

Pursuing these thoughts, Dr Mellinger left his office and made his way down to the floor below which housed the administrative department. The offices were deserted; the entire staff of the building was taking part in the search. Occasionally the querulous cries of the patients demanding their breakfasts drifted across the warm, insulated air. For-tunately the walls were thick, and the rates charged by the asylum high enough to obviate the need for over-crowding.

Green Hill Asylum (motto, and principal attraction: 'There is a Green Hill Far, Far Away') was one of those insti-tutions which are patronized by the wealthier members of the community and in effect serve the role of private prisons. In such places are confined all those miscreant or unfortu-nate relatives whose presence would otherwise be a burden or embarrassment: the importunate widows of blacksheep sons, senile maiden aunts, elderly bachelor cousins paying the price for their romantic indiscretions – in short, all those abandoned casualties of the army of privilege. As far as the patrons of Green Hill were concerned, maximum security came first, treatment, if given at all, a bad second. Dr Mellinger's patients had disappeared conveniently from the world, and as long as they remained in this distant limbo those who paid the bills were satisfied. All this made Hinton's escape particularly dangerous.

Stepping through the open doorway of Normand's office, Dr Mellinger ran his eye cursorily around the room. On the desk, hastily opened, was a slim file containing a few documents and a photograph.

For a brief moment Dr Mellinger gazed abstractedly at the file. Then, after a discreet glance into the corridor, he slipped it under his arm and retraced his steps up the empty staircase.

Outside, muted by the dark groves of rhododendrons, the sounds of search and pursuit echoed across the grounds. Opening the file on his desk, Dr Mellinger stared at the photograph, which happened to be lying upside down. Without straightening it, he studied the amorphous features. The nose was straight, the forehead and cheeks symmetrical, the ears a little oversize, but in its inverted position the face lacked any cohesive identity.

Suddenly, as he started to read the file, Dr Mellinger was filled with a deep sense of resentment. The entire subject of Hinton and the man's precarious claims to reality over-whelmed him with a profound nausea. He refused to accept that this mindless cripple with his anonymous features could have been responsible for the confusion and anxiety of the previous day. Was it possible that these few pieces of paper constituted this meagre individual's full claim to reality?

Flinching slightly from the touch of the file to his fingers, Dr Mellinger carried it across to the fireplace. Averting his face, he listened with a deepening sense of relief as the flames flared briefly and subsided.

'My dear Booth! Do come in. It's good of you to spare the time.' With this greeting Dr Mellinger ushered him to a chair beside the fire and proffered his silver cigarette case. 'There's a certain small matter I wanted to discuss, and you are almost the only person who can help me.'

'Of course, Director,' Booth assured him. 'I am greatly honoured.'

Dr Mellinger seated himself behind his desk. 'It's a very curious case, one of the most unusual I have ever come across. It concerns a patient under your care, I believe.'

'May I ask for his name, sir?'

'Hinton,' Dr Mellinger said, with a sharp glance at Booth.

'Hinton, sir?'

'You show surprise,' Dr Mellinger continued before Booth could reply. 'I find that response particularly interesting.'

'The search is still being carried on,' Booth said uncertainly as Dr Mellinger paused to digest his remarks. 'I'm afraid we've found absolutely no trace of him. Dr Normand thinks we should inform—'

'Ah, yes, Dr Normand.' The Director revived suddenly. 'I have asked him to report to me with Hinton's file as soon as he is free. Dr Booth, does it occur to you that we may be chasing the wrong hare?'

'Sir—?'

'Is it in fact *Hinton* we are after? I wonder, perhaps, whether the search for Hinton is obscuring something larger

139

and more significant, the enigma, as I mentioned yesterday, which lies at the heart of Green Hill and to whose solution we must all now be dedicated.' Dr Mellinger savoured these reflections before continuing. 'Dr Booth, let us for a moment consider the role of Hinton, or to be more precise, the complex of overlapping and adjacent events that we identify loosely by the term "Hinton".'

'Complex, sir? You speak diagnostically?'

'No, Booth. I am now concerned with the phenomenology of Hinton, with his absolute metaphysical essence. To speak more plainly: has it occurred to you, Booth, how little we know of this elusive patient, how scanty the traces he has left of his own identity?'

'True, Director,' Booth agreed. 'I constantly reproach myself for not taking a closer interest in the patient.'

'Not at all, Doctor. I realize how busy you are. I intend to carry out a major reorganization of Green Hill, and I assure you that your tireless work here will not be forgotten. A senior administrative post would, I am sure, suit you excellently.' As Booth sat up, his interest in the conversation increasing several-fold, Dr Mellinger acknowledged his expression of thanks with a discreet nod. 'As I was saying, Doctor, you have so many patients, all wearing the same uniforms, housed in the same wards, and by and large prescribed the same treatment – is it surprising that they should lose their individual identities? If I may make a small confession,' he added with a roguish smile. 'I myself find that all the patients look alike. Why, if Dr Normand or yourself informed me that a new patient by the name of Smith or Brown had arrived, I would automatically furnish him with the standard uniform of identity at Green Hill – those same lustreless eyes and slack mouth, the same amorphous features.'

Unclasping his hands, Dr Mellinger leaned intently

across his desk. 'What I am suggesting, Doctor, is that this automatic mechanism may have operated in the case of the so-called Hinton, and that you may have invested an entirely non-existent individual with the fictions of a personality.'

Dr Booth nodded slowly. 'I see, sir. You suspect that Hinton – or what we have called Hinton up to now – was perhaps a confused memory of another patient?' He hesitated doubtfully, and then noticed that Dr Mellinger's eyes were fixed upon him with hypnotic intensity.

'Dr Booth, I ask you: what actual proof have we that Hinton ever existed?'

'Well, sir, there are the . . .' Booth searched about helplessly . . . 'the records in the administrative department. And the case notes.'

Dr Mellinger shook his head with a scornful flourish. 'My dear Booth, you are speaking of mere pieces of paper. These are not proof of a man's identity. A typewriter will invent anything you choose. The only conclusive proof is his physical existence in time and space or, failing that, a distinct memory of his tangible physical presence. Can you honestly say that either of these conditions is fulfilled?'

'No, sir. I suppose I can't. Though I did speak to a patient whom I assumed to be Hinton.'

'But was he?' The Director's voice was resonant and urgent. 'Search your mind, Booth; be honest with yourself. Was it perhaps another patient to whom you spoke? What doctor ever really looks at his patients? In all probability you merely saw Hinton's name on a list and assumed that he sat before you, an intact physical existence like your own.'

There was a knock upon the door. Dr Normand stepped into the office. 'Good afternoon, Director.'

'Ah, Normand. Do come in. Dr Booth and I have been having a most instructive conversation. I really believe we have found a solution to the mystery of Hinton's disappearance.'

Dr Normand nodded cautiously. 'I am most relieved, sir. I was beginning to wonder whether we should inform the civil authorities. It is now nearly forty-eight hours since . . .'

'My dear Normand, I am afraid you are rather out of touch. Our whole attitude to the Hinton case has changed radically. Dr Booth has been so helpful to me. We have been discussing the possibility that an administrative post might be found for him. You have the Hinton file?'

'Er, I regret not, sir,' Normand apologized, his eyes moving from Booth to the Director. 'I gather it's been temporarily displaced. I've instituted a thorough search and it will be brought to you as soon as possible.'

'Thank you, Normand, if you would.' Mellinger took Booth by the arm and led him to the door. 'Now, Doctor, I am most gratified by your perceptiveness. I want you to question your ward staff in the way I have questioned you. Strike through the mists of illusion and false assumption that swirl about their minds. Warn them of those illusions compounded on illusions which can assume the guise of reality. Remind them, too, that clear minds are required at Green Hill. I will be most surprised if any one of them can put her hand on her heart and swear that Hinton *really* existed.'

After Booth had made his exit, Dr Mellinger returned to his desk. For a moment he failed to notice his deputy.

'Ah, yes, Normand. I wonder where that file is? You didn't bring it?'

'No, sir. As I explained—'

'Well, never mind. But we mustn't become careless, Normand, too much is at stake. Do you realize that without that file we would know literally nothing whatever about Hinton? It would be most awkward.'

'I assure you, sir, the file—'

'Enough, Normand. Don't worry yourself.' Dr Mellinger turned a vulpine smile upon the restless Normand. 'I have the greatest respect for the efficiency of the administrative department under your leadership. I think it unlikely that they should have misplaced it. Tell me, Normand, are you sure that this file ever existed?'

'Certainly, sir,' Normand replied promptly. 'Of course, I have not actually seen it myself, but every patient at Green Hill has a complete personal file.'

'But Normand,' the Director pointed out gently, 'the patient in question is not *at* Green Hill. Whether or not this hypothetical file exists, Hinton does not.'

He stopped and waited as Normand looked up at him, his eyes narrowing.

A week later, Dr Mellinger held a final conference in his office. This was a notably more relaxed gathering; his subordinates lay back in the leather armchairs around the fire, while Dr Mellinger leaned against the desk, supervising the circulation of his best sherry.

'So, gentlemen,' he remarked in conclusion, 'we may look back on the past week as a period of unique self-discovery, a lesson for all of us to remember the true nature of our roles at Green Hill, our dedication to the task of separating reality from illusion. If our patients are haunted by chimeras, let us at least retain absolute clarity of mind, accepting the validity of any proposition only if all our senses corroborate it. Consider the example of the "Hinton affair". Here, by an accumulation of false assumptions, of illusions buttressing illusions, a vast edifice of fantasy was erected around the

143

wholly mythical identity of one patient. This imaginary figure, who by some means we have not discovered – most probably the error of a typist in the records department – was given the name "Hinton", was subsequently furnished with a complete personal identity, a private ward, attendant nurses and doctors. Such was the grip of this substitute world, this concatenation of errors, that when it crumbled and the lack of any substance behind the shadow was discovered, the remaining vacuum was automatically interpreted as the patient's escape.'

Dr Mellinger gestured eloquently, as Normand, Redpath and Booth nodded their agreement. He walked around his desk and took his seat. 'Perhaps, gentlemen, it is fortunate that I remain aloof from the day-to-day affairs of Green Hill. I take no credit upon myself, that I alone was sufficiently detached to consider the full implications of Hinton's disappearance and realize the only possible explanation – *that Hinton had never existed!*'

'A brilliant deduction,' Redpath murmured.

'Without doubt,' echoed Booth.

'A profound insight,' agreed Normand.

There was a sharp knock on the door. With a frown, Dr Mellinger ignored it and resumed his monologue.

'Thank you, gentlemen. Without your assistance that hypothesis, that Hinton was no more than an accumulation of administrative errors, could never have been confirmed.'

The knock on the door repeated itself. A staff sister appeared breathlessly. 'Excuse me, sir. I'm sorry to interrupt you, but—'

Dr Mellinger waved away her apologies. 'Never mind. What is it?'

'A visitor, Dr Mellinger.' She paused as the Director waited impatiently. 'Mrs Hinton, to see her husband.'

For a moment there was consternation. The three men around the fire sat upright, their drinks forgotten, while Dr Mellinger remained stock-still at his desk. A total silence filled the room, only broken by the light tapping of a woman's heels in the corridor outside.

But Dr Mellinger recovered quickly. Standing up, with a grim smile at his colleagues, he said: 'To see Mr Hinton? Impossible, Hinton never existed. The woman must be suffering from terrible delusions; she requires immediate treatment. Show her in.' He turned to his colleagues. 'Gentlemen, we must do everything we can to help her.'

Minus two.

JHUMPA LAHIRI

INTERPRETER OF
MALADIES

AT THE TEA stall Mr. and Mrs. Das bickered about who should take Tina to the toilet. Eventually Mrs. Das relented when Mr. Das pointed out that he had given the girl her bath the night before. In the rearview mirror Mr. Kapasi watched as Mrs. Das emerged slowly from his bulky white Ambassador, dragging her shaved, largely bare legs across the back seat. She did not hold the little girl's hand as they walked to the rest room.

They were on their way to see the Sun Temple at Konarak. It was a dry, bright Saturday, the mid-July heat tempered by a steady ocean breeze, ideal weather for sightseeing. Ordinarily Mr. Kapasi would not have stopped so soon along the way, but less than five minutes after he'd picked up the family that morning in front of Hotel Sandy Villa, the little girl had complained. The first thing Mr. Kapasi had noticed when he saw Mr. and Mrs. Das, standing with their children under the portico of the hotel, was that they were very young, perhaps not even thirty. In addition to Tina they had two boys, Ronny and Bobby, who appeared very close in age and had teeth covered in a network of flashing silver wires. The family looked Indian but dressed as foreigners did, the children in stiff, brightly colored clothing and caps with translucent visors. Mr. Kapasi was accustomed to foreign tourists; he was assigned to them regularly because he could speak English. Yesterday he had driven an elderly couple from Scotland, both with spotted faces and fluffy white hair so thin it exposed their sunburnt scalps. In comparison, the tanned, youthful faces of Mr. and Mrs. Das were all the more striking. When he'd introduced himself, Mr. Kapasi had pressed his palms together in greeting, but Mr. Das squeezed hands like an American so that Mr. Kapasi felt it in his elbow. Mrs. Das, for her part, had flexed one side of her mouth, smiling dutifully at Mr. Kapasi, without displaying any interest in him.

As they waited at the tea stall, Ronny, who looked like the older of the two boys, clambered suddenly out of the back seat, intrigued by a goat tied to a stake in the ground.

'Don't touch it,' Mr. Das said. He glanced up from his paperback tour book, which said 'INDIA' in yellow letters and looked as if it had been published abroad. His voice, somehow tentative and a little shrill, sounded as though it had not yet settled into maturity.

'I want to give it a piece of gum,' the boy called back as he trotted ahead.

Mr. Das stepped out of the car and stretched his legs by squatting briefly to the ground. A clean-shaven man, he looked exactly like a magnified version of Ronny. He had a sapphire blue visor, and was dressed in shorts, sneakers, and a T-shirt. The camera slung around his neck, with an impressive telephoto lens and numerous buttons and mark-ings, was the only complicated thing he wore. He frowned, watching as Ronny rushed toward the goat, but appeared to have no intention of intervening. 'Bobby, make sure that your brother doesn't do anything stupid.'

'I don't feel like it,' Bobby said, not moving. He was sitting in the front seat beside Mr. Kapasi, studying a picture of the elephant god taped to the glove compartment.

'No need to worry,' Mr. Kapasi said. 'They are quite tame.' Mr. Kapasi was forty-six years old, with receding hair that had gone completely silver, but his butterscotch complexion and his unlined brow, which he treated in spare moments to dabs of lotus-oil balm, made it easy to imagine what he must have looked like at an earlier age. He wore gray trousers and a matching jacket-style shirt, tapered at the waist, with short sleeves and a large pointed collar, made of a thin but durable synthetic material. He had specified both the cut and the fabric to his tailor – it was his preferred uniform for giving tours because it did not get crushed during his long hours behind the wheel. Through the windshield he watched as Ronny circled around the goat, touched it quickly on its side, then trotted back to the car.

'You left India as a child?' Mr. Kapasi asked when Mr. Das had settled once again into the passenger seat.

'Oh, Mina and I were both born in America,' Mr. Das announced with an air of sudden confidence. 'Born and raised. Our parents live here now. They retired. We visit them every couple years.' He turned to watch as the little girl ran toward the car, the wide purple bows of her sundress flopping on her narrow brown shoulders. She was holding to her chest a doll with yellow hair that looked as if it had been chopped, as a punitive measure, with a pair of dull scissors. 'This is Tina's first trip to India, isn't it, Tina?'

'I don't have to go to the bathroom anymore,' Tina announced.

'Where's Mina?' Mr. Das asked.

Mr. Kapasi found it strange that Mr. Das should refer to his wife by her first name when speaking to the little girl. Tina pointed to where Mrs. Das was purchasing something from one of the shirtless men who worked at the tea stall. Mr. Kapasi heard one of the shirtless men sing a phrase from a popular Hindi love song as Mrs. Das walked back to the car, but she did not appear to understand the words of the song, for she did not express irritation, or embarrassment, or react in any other way to the man's declarations.

He observed her. She wore a red-and-white-checkered skirt that stopped above her knees, slip-on shoes with a square wooden heel, and a close-fitting blouse styled like a man's undershirt. The blouse was decorated at chest-level with a calico appliqué in the shape of a strawberry. She was a short woman, with small hands like paws, her frosty pink fingernails painted to match her lips, and was slightly plump in her figure. Her hair, shorn only a little longer than her husband's, was parted far to one side. She was wearing large dark brown sunglasses with a pinkish tint to them, and carried a big straw bag, almost as big as her torso, shaped like a bowl, with a water bottle poking out of it. She walked slowly, carrying some puffed rice tossed with peanuts and chili peppers in a large packet made from newspapers. Mr. Kapasi turned to Mr. Das.

'Where in America do you live?'

'New Brunswick, New Jersey.'

'Next to New York?'

'Exactly. I teach middle school there.'

'What subject?'

'Science. In fact, every year I take my students on a trip to the Museum of Natural History in New York City. In a way we have a lot in common, you could say, you and I. How long have you been a tour guide, Mr. Kapasi?'

'Five years.'

Mrs. Das reached the car. 'How long's the trip?' she asked, shutting the door.

'About two and a half hours,' Mr. Kapasi replied.

At this Mrs. Das gave an impatient sigh, as if she had been traveling her whole life without pause. She fanned herself with a folded Bombay film magazine written in English.

'I thought that the Sun Temple is only eighteen miles north of Puri,' Mr. Das said, tapping on the tour book.

'The roads to Konarak are poor. Actually it is a distance of fifty-two miles,' Mr. Kapasi explained.

Mr. Das nodded, readjusting the camera strap where it had begun to chafe the back of his neck.

Before starting the ignition, Mr. Kapasi reached back to make sure the cranklike locks on the inside of each of the back doors were secured. As soon as the car began to move the little girl began to play with the lock on her side, clicking it with some effort forward and backward, but Mrs. Das said nothing to stop her. She sat a bit slouched at one end of the back seat, not offering her puffed rice to anyone. Ronny and Tina sat on either side of her, both snapping bright green gum.

'Look,' Bobby said as the car began to gather speed. He pointed with his finger to the tall trees that lined the road. 'Look.'

'Monkeys!' Ronny shrieked. 'Wow!'

They were seated in groups along the branches, with shining black faces, silver bodies, horizontal eyebrows, and crested heads. Their long gray tails dangled like a series of ropes among the leaves. A few scratched themselves with black leathery hands, or swung their feet, staring as the car passed.

'We call them the hanuman,' Mr. Kapasi said. 'They are quite common in the area.'

As soon as he spoke, one of the monkeys leaped into the middle of the road, causing Mr. Kapasi to brake suddenly. Another bounced onto the hood of the car, then sprang away. Mr. Kapasi beeped his horn. The children began to get excited, sucking in their breath and covering their faces partly with their hands. They had never seen monkeys

153

outside of a zoo, Mr. Das explained. He asked Mr. Kapasi to stop the car so that he could take a picture.

While Mr. Das adjusted his telephoto lens, Mrs. Das reached into her straw bag and pulled out a bottle of colorless nail polish, which she proceeded to stroke on the tip of her index finger.

The little girl stuck out a hand. 'Mine too. Mommy, do mine too.'

'Leave me alone,' Mrs. Das said, blowing on her nail and turning her body slightly. 'You're making me mess up.'

The little girl occupied herself by buttoning and unbuttoning a pinafore on the doll's plastic body.

'All set,' Mr. Das said, replacing the lens cap.

The car rattled considerably as it raced along the dusty road, causing them all to pop up from their seats every now and then, but Mrs. Das continued to polish her nails. Mr. Kapasi eased up on the accelerator, hoping to produce a smoother ride. When he reached for the gearshift the boy in front accommodated him by swinging his hairless knees out of the way. Mr. Kapasi noted that this boy was slightly paler than the other children. 'Daddy, why is the driver sitting on the wrong side in this car, too?' the boy asked.

'They all do that here, dummy,' Ronny said.

'Don't call your brother a dummy,' Mr. Das said. He turned to Mr. Kapasi. 'In America, you know . . . it confuses them.'

'Oh yes, I am well aware,' Mr. Kapasi said. As delicately as he could, he shifted gears again, accelerating as they approached a hill in the road. 'I see it on *Dallas*, the steering wheels are on the left-hand side.'

'What's *Dallas*?' Tina asked, banging her now naked doll on the seat behind Mr. Kapasi.

'It went off the air,' Mr. Das explained. 'It's a television show.'

They were all like siblings, Mr. Kapasi thought as they passed a row of date trees. Mr. and Mrs. Das behaved like an older brother and sister, not parents. It seemed that they were in charge of the children only for the day; it was hard to believe they were regularly responsible for anything other than themselves. Mr. Das tapped on his lens cap, and his tour book, dragging his thumbnail occasionally across the pages so that they made a scraping sound. Mrs. Das continued to polish her nails. She had still not removed her sunglasses. Every now and then Tina renewed her plea that she wanted her nails done, too, and so at one point Mrs. Das flicked a drop of polish on the little girl's finger before depositing the bottle back inside her straw bag.

'Isn't this an air-conditioned car?' she asked, still blowing on her hand. The window on Tina's side was broken and could not be rolled down.

'Quit complaining,' Mr. Das said. 'It isn't so hot.'

'I told you to get a car with air-conditioning,' Mrs. Das continued. 'Why do you do this, Raj, just to save a few stupid rupees. What are you saving us, fifty cents?'

Their accents sounded just like the ones Mr. Kapasi heard on American television programs, though not like the ones on *Dallas*.

'Doesn't it get tiresome, Mr. Kapasi, showing people the same thing every day?' Mr. Das asked, rolling down his own window all the way. 'Hey, do you mind stopping the car. I just want to get a shot of this guy.'

Mr. Kapasi pulled over to the side of the road as Mr. Das took a picture of a barefoot man, his head wrapped in a dirty turban, seated on top of a cart of grain sacks pulled by a pair of bullocks. Both the man and the bullocks were emaciated.

In the back seat Mrs. Das gazed out another window, at the sky, where nearly transparent clouds passed quickly in front of one another.

'I look forward to it, actually,' Mr. Kapasi said as they continued on their way. 'The Sun Temple is one of my favorite places. In that way it is a reward for me. I give tours on Fridays and Saturdays only. I have another job during the week.'

'Oh? Where?' Mr. Das asked.

'I work in a doctor's office.'

'You're a doctor?'

'I am not a doctor. I work with one. As an interpreter.'

'What does a doctor need an interpreter for?'

'He has a number of Gujarati patients. My father was Gujarati, but many people do not speak Gujarati in this area, including the doctor. And so the doctor asked me to work in his office, interpreting what the patients say.'

'Interesting. I've never heard of anything like that,' Mr. Das said.

Mr. Kapasi shrugged. 'It is a job like any other.'

'But so romantic,' Mrs. Das said dreamily, breaking her extended silence. She lifted her pinkish brown sunglasses and arranged them on top of her head like a tiara. For the first time, her eyes met Mr. Kapasi's in the rearview mirror: pale, a bit small, their gaze fixed but drowsy.

Mr. Das craned to look at her. 'What's so romantic about it?'

'I don't know. Something.' She shrugged, knitting her brows together for an instant. 'Would you like a piece of gum, Mr. Kapasi?' she asked brightly. She reached into her straw bag and handed him a small square wrapped in green-and-white-striped paper. As soon as Mr. Kapasi put the gum in his mouth a thick sweet liquid burst onto his tongue.

'Tell us more about your job, Mr. Kapasi,' Mrs. Das said.

'What would you like to know, madame?'

'I don't know,' again she shrugged, munching on some puffed rice and licking the mustard oil from the corners of her mouth. 'Tell us a typical situation.' She settled back in her seat, her head tilted in a patch of sun, and closed her eyes. 'I want to picture what happens.'

'Very well. The other day a man came in with a pain in his throat.'

'Did he smoke cigarettes?'

'No. It was very curious. He complained that he felt as if there were long pieces of straw stuck in his throat. When I told the doctor he was able to prescribe the proper medication.'

'That's so neat.'

'Yes,' Mr. Kapasi agreed after some hesitation.

'So these patients are totally dependent on you,' Mrs. Das said. She spoke slowly, as if she were thinking aloud. 'In a way, more dependent on you than the doctor.'

'How do you mean? How could it be?'

'Well, for example, you could tell the doctor that the pain felt like a burning, not straw. The patient would never know what you had told the doctor, and the doctor wouldn't know that you had told the wrong thing. It's a big responsibility.'

'Yes, a big responsibility you have there, Mr. Kapasi,' Mr. Das agreed.

Mr. Kapasi had never thought of his job in such complimentary terms. To him it was a thankless occupation. He found nothing noble in interpreting people's maladies, assiduously translating the symptoms of so many swollen bones, countless cramps of bellies and bowels, spots on people's palms that changed color, shape, or size. The doctor, nearly half his age, had an affinity for bell-bottom trousers and made humorless jokes about the Congress party. Together they worked in a stale little infirmary where Mr. Kapasi's smartly tailored clothes clung to him in the heat, in spite of the blackened blades of a ceiling fan churning over their heads.

The job was a sign of his failings. In his youth he'd been a devoted scholar of foreign languages, the owner of an impressive collection of dictionaries. He had dreamed of being an interpreter for diplomats and dignitaries, resolving conflicts between people and nations, settling disputes of which he alone could understand both sides. He was a self-educated man. In a series of notebooks, in the evenings before his parents settled his marriage, he had listed the common etymologies of words, and at one point in his life he was confident that he could converse, if given the opportunity, in English, French, Russian, Portuguese, and Italian, not to mention Hindi, Bengali, Oriya, and Gujarati. Now only a handful of European phrases remained in his memory, scattered words for things like saucers and chairs. English was the only non-Indian language he spoke fluently anymore. Mr. Kapasi knew it was not a remarkable talent. Sometimes he feared that his children knew better English than he did, just from watching television. Still, it came in handy for the tours.

He had taken the job as an interpreter after his first son, at the age of seven, contracted typhoid – that was how he had first made the acquaintance of the doctor. At the time Mr. Kapasi had been teaching English in a grammar school, and he bartered his skills as an interpreter to pay the increasingly exorbitant medical bills. In the end the boy had died one evening in his mother's arms, his limbs burning with fever, but then there was the funeral to pay for, and the other children who were born soon enough, and the newer, bigger house, and the good schools and tutors, and the fine shoes and the television, and the countless other ways he tried to console his wife and to keep her from crying in her sleep, and so when the doctor offered to pay him twice as much as he earned at the grammar school, he accepted. Mr. Kapasi knew that his wife had little regard for his career as an interpreter. He knew it reminded her of the son she'd lost, and that she resented the other lives he helped, in his own small way, to save. If ever she referred to his position, she used the phrase 'doctor's assistant,' as if the process of interpretation were equal to taking someone's temperature, or changing a bedpan. She never asked him about the patients who came to the doctor's office, or said that his job was a big responsibility.

For this reason it flattered Mr. Kapasi that Mrs. Das was so intrigued by his job. Unlike his wife, she had reminded him of its intellectual challenges. She had also used the word 'romantic.' She did not behave in a romantic way toward her husband, and yet she had used the word to describe him. He wondered if Mr. and Mrs. Das were a bad match, just as he and his wife were. Perhaps they, too, had little in common apart from three children and a decade of their lives. The signs he recognized from his own marriage were there – the bickering, the indifference, the protracted silences. Her sudden interest in him, an interest she did not express in either her husband or her children, was mildly intoxicating. When Mr. Kapasi thought once again about how she had said 'romantic,' the feeling of intoxication grew.

He began to check his reflection in the rearview mirror as he drove, feeling grateful that he had chosen the gray suit that morning and not the brown one, which tended to sag a little in the knees. From time to time he glanced through the mirror at Mrs. Das. In addition to glancing at her face he glanced at the strawberry between her breasts, and the golden brown hollow in her throat. He decided to tell Mrs. Das about another patient, and another: the young woman who had complained of a sensation of raindrops in her spine, the gentleman whose birthmark had begun to sprout hairs. Mrs. Das listened attentively, stroking her hair with a small plastic brush that resembled an oval bed of nails, asking more questions, for yet another example. The children were quiet, intent on spotting more monkeys in the trees, and Mr. Das was absorbed by his tour book, so it seemed like a private conversation between Mr. Kapasi and Mrs. Das. In this manner the next half hour passed, and when they stopped for lunch at a roadside restaurant that sold fritters and omelette sandwiches, usually something Mr. Kapasi looked forward to on his tours so that he could sit in peace and enjoy some hot tea, he was disappointed. As the Das family settled together under a magenta umbrella fringed with white and orange tassels, and placed their orders with one of the waiters who marched about in tricornered caps, Mr. Kapasi reluctantly headed toward a neighboring table.

'Mr. Kapasi, wait. There's room here,' Mrs. Das called out. She gathered Tina onto her lap, insisting that he accompany them. And so, together, they had bottled mango juice and sandwiches and plates of onions and potatoes deep-fried in graham-flour batter. After finishing two omelette sandwiches Mr. Das took more pictures of the group as they ate.

'How much longer?' he asked Mr. Kapasi as he paused to load a new roll of film in the camera.

'About half an hour more.'

By now the children had gotten up from the table to look at more monkeys perched in a nearby tree, so there was a considerable space between Mrs. Das and Mr. Kapasi. Mr.

Das placed the camera to his face and squeezed one eye shut, his tongue exposed at one corner of his mouth. 'This looks funny. Mina, you need to lean in closer to Mr. Kapasi.'

She did. He could smell a scent on her skin, like a mixture of whiskey and rosewater. He worried suddenly that she could smell his perspiration, which he knew had collected beneath the synthetic material of his shirt. He polished off his mango juice in one gulp and smoothed his silver hair with his hands. A bit of the juice dripped onto his chin. He wondered if Mrs. Das had noticed.

She had not. 'What's your address, Mr. Kapasi?' she inquired, fishing for something inside her straw bag.

'You would like my address?'

'So we can send you copies,' she said. 'Of the pictures.' She handed him a scrap of paper which she had hastily ripped from a page of her film magazine. The blank portion was limited, for the narrow strip was crowded by lines of text and a tiny picture of a hero and heroine embracing under a eucalyptus tree.

The paper curled as Mr. Kapasi wrote his address in clear, careful letters. She would write to him, asking about his days interpreting at the doctor's office, and he would respond eloquently, choosing only the most entertaining anecdotes, ones that would make her laugh out loud as she read them in her house in New Jersey. In time she would reveal the disappointment of her marriage, and he his. In this way their friendship would grow, and flourish. He would possess a picture of the two of them, eating fried onions under a magenta umbrella, which he would keep, he decided, safely tucked between the pages of his Russian grammar. As his mind raced, Mr. Kapasi experienced a mild and pleasant shock. It was similar to a feeling he used to experience long ago when, after months of translating with the aid of a dictionary, he would finally read a passage from a French novel, or an Italian sonnet, and understand the words, one after another, unencumbered by his own efforts. In those moments Mr. Kapasi used to believe that all was right with the world, that all struggles were rewarded, that all of life's mistakes made sense in the end. The promise that he would hear from Mrs. Das now filled him with the same belief.

When he finished writing his address Mr. Kapasi handed her the paper, but as soon as he did so he worried that he had either misspelled his name, or accidentally reversed the numbers of his postal code. He dreaded the possibility of a lost letter, the photograph never reaching him, hovering somewhere in Orissa, close but ultimately unattainable. He thought of asking for the slip of paper again, just to make sure he had written his address accurately, but Mrs. Das had already dropped it into the jumble of her bag.

They reached Konarak at two-thirty. The temple, made of sandstone, was a massive pyramid-like structure in the shape of a chariot. It was dedicated to the great master of life, the sun, which struck three sides of the edifice as it made its journey each day across the sky. Twenty-four giant wheels were carved on the north and south sides of the plinth. The whole thing was drawn by a team of seven horses, speeding as if through the heavens. As they approached, Mr. Kapasi explained that the temple had been built between A.D. 1243 and 1255, with the efforts of twelve hundred artisans, by the great ruler of the Ganga dynasty, King Narasimhadeva the First, to commemorate his victory against the Muslim army.

'It says the temple occupies about a hundred and seventy acres of land,' Mr. Das said, reading from his book.

'It's like a desert,' Ronny said, his eyes wandering across the sand that stretched on all sides beyond the temple.

'The Chandrabhaga River once flowed one mile north of here. It is dry now,' Mr. Kapasi said, turning off the engine.

They got out and walked toward the temple, posing first for pictures by the pair of lions that flanked the steps. Mr. Kapasi led them next to one of the wheels of the chariot, higher than any human being, nine feet in diameter.

' "The wheels are supposed to symbolize the wheel of life," ' Mr. Das read. ' "They depict the cycle of creation, preservation, and achievement of realization." Cool.' He turned the page of his book. ' "Each wheel is divided into eight thick and thin spokes, dividing the day into eight equal parts. The rims are carved with designs of birds and animals, whereas the medallions in the spokes are carved with women in luxurious poses, largely erotic in nature." '

What he referred to were the countless friezes of entwined naked bodies, making love in various positions, women clinging to the necks of men, their knees wrapped eternally around their lovers' thighs. In addition to these were assorted scenes from daily life, of hunting and trading, of deer being killed with bows and arrows and marching warriors holding swords in their hands.

It was no longer possible to enter the temple, for it had filled with rubble years ago, but they admired the exterior, as did all the tourists Mr. Kapasi brought there, slowly strolling along each of its sides. Mr. Das trailed behind, taking pictures. The children ran ahead, pointing to figures of naked people, intrigued in particular by the Nagamithunas, the half-human, half-serpentine couples who were said, Mr. Kapasi told them, to live in the deepest waters of the sea. Mr. Kapasi was pleased that they liked the temple, pleased especially that it appealed to Mrs. Das. She stopped every three or four paces, staring silently at the carved lovers, and the processions of elephants, and the topless female musicians beating on two-sided drums.

Though Mr. Kapasi had been to the temple countless times, it occurred to him, as he, too, gazed at the topless women, that he had never seen his own wife fully naked. Even when they had made love she kept the panels of her blouse hooked together, the string of her petticoat knotted around her waist. He had never admired the backs of his wife's legs the way he now admired those of Mrs. Das, walking as if for his benefit alone. He had, of course, seen plenty of bare limbs before, belonging to the American and European ladies who took his tours. But Mrs. Das was different. Unlike the other women, who had an interest only in the temple, and kept their noses buried in a guidebook, or their eyes behind the lens of a camera, Mrs. Das had taken an interest in him.

Mr. Kapasi was anxious to be alone with her, to continue their private conversation, yet he felt nervous to walk at her side. She was lost behind her sunglasses, ignoring her husband's requests that she pose for another picture, walking past her children as if they were strangers. Worried that he might disturb her, Mr. Kapasi walked ahead, to admire, as he always did, the three life-sized bronze avatars of Surya, the sun god, each emerging from its own niche on the temple facade to greet the sun at dawn, noon, and evening. They wore elaborate headdresses, their languid, elongated eyes closed, their bare chests draped with carved chains and amulets. Hibiscus petals, offerings from previous visitors, were strewn at their gray-green feet. The last statue, on the northern wall of the temple, was Mr. Kapasi's favorite. This Surya had a tired expression, weary after a hard day of work, sitting astride a horse with folded legs. Even his horse's eyes were drowsy. Around his body were smaller sculptures of women in pairs, their hips thrust to one side.

'Who's that?' Mrs. Das asked. He was startled to see that she was standing beside him.

'He is the Astachala-Surya,' Mr. Kapasi said. 'The setting sun.'

'So in a couple of hours the sun will set right here?' She slipped a foot out of one of her square-heeled shoes, rubbed her toes on the back of her other leg.

'That is correct.'

She raised her sunglasses for a moment, then put them back on again. 'Neat.'

Mr. Kapasi was not certain exactly what the word suggested, but he had a feeling it was a favorable response. He hoped that Mrs. Das had understood Surya's beauty, his power. Perhaps they would discuss it further in their letters. He would explain things to her, things about India, and she would explain things to him about America. In its own way this correspondence would fulfill his dream, of serving as an interpreter between nations. He looked at her straw bag, delighted that his address lay nestled among its contents. When he pictured her so many thousands of miles away he plummeted, so much so that he had an overwhelming urge to wrap his arms around her, to freeze with her, even for an instant, in an embrace witnessed by his favorite Surya. But Mrs. Das had already started walking.

'When do you return to America?' he asked, trying to sound placid.

'In ten days.'

He calculated: A week to settle in, a week to develop the pictures, a few days to compose her letter, two weeks to get to India by air. According to his schedule, allowing room for delays, he would hear from Mrs. Das in approximately six weeks' time.

* * *

The family was silent as Mr. Kapasi drove them back, a little past four-thirty, to Hotel Sandy Villa. The children had bought miniature granite versions of the chariot's wheels at a souvenir stand, and they turned them round in their hands. Mr. Das continued to read his book. Mrs. Das untangled Tina's hair with her brush and divided it into two little ponytails.

Mr. Kapasi was beginning to dread the thought of dropping them off. He was not prepared to begin his six-week wait to hear from Mrs. Das. As he stole glances at her in the rearview mirror, wrapping elastic bands around Tina's hair, he wondered how he might make the tour last a little longer. Ordinarily he sped back to Puri using a shortcut, eager to return home, scrub his feet and hands with sandalwood soap, and enjoy the evening newspaper and a cup of tea that his wife would serve him in silence. The thought of that silence, something to which he'd long been resigned, now oppressed him. It was then that he suggested visiting the hills at Udayagiri and Khandagiri, where a number of monastic dwellings were hewn out of the ground, facing one another across a defile. It was some miles away, but well worth seeing, Mr. Kapasi told them.

'Oh yeah, there's something mentioned about it in this book,' Mr. Das said. 'Built by a Jain king or something.'

'Shall we go then?' Mr. Kapasi asked. He paused at a turn in the road. 'It's to the left.'

Mr. Das turned to look at Mrs. Das. Both of them shrugged.

'Left, left,' the children chanted.

Mr. Kapasi turned the wheel, almost delirious with relief. He did not know what he would do or say to Mrs. Das once they arrived at the hills. Perhaps he would tell her what a

166

pleasing smile she had. Perhaps he would compliment her strawberry shirt, which he found irresistibly becoming. Perhaps, when Mr. Das was busy taking a picture, he would take her hand.

He did not have to worry. When they got to the hills, divided by a steep path thick with trees, Mrs. Das refused to get out of the car. All along the path, dozens of monkeys were seated on stones, as well as on the branches of the trees. Their hind legs were stretched out in front and raised to shoulder level, their arms resting on their knees.

'My legs are tired,' she said, sinking low in her seat. 'I'll stay here.'

'Why did you have to wear those stupid shoes?' Mr. Das said. 'You won't be in the pictures.'

'Pretend I'm there.'

'But we could use one of these pictures for our Christmas card this year. We didn't get one of all five of us at the Sun Temple. Mr. Kapasi could take it.'

'I'm not coming. Anyway, those monkeys give me the creeps.'

'But they're harmless,' Mr. Das said. He turned to Mr. Kapasi. 'Aren't they?'

'They are more hungry than dangerous,' Mr. Kapasi said. 'Do not provoke them with food, and they will not bother you.'

Mr. Das headed up the defile with the children, the boys at his side, the little girl on his shoulders. Mr. Kapasi watched as they crossed paths with a Japanese man and woman, the only other tourists there, who paused for a final photograph, then stepped into a nearby car and drove away. As the car disappeared out of view some of the monkeys called out, emitting soft whooping sounds, and then walked on their flat black hands and feet up the path. At one point a group of them formed a little ring around Mr. Das and the children. Tina screamed in delight. Ronny ran in circles around his father. Bobby bent down and picked up a fat stick on the ground. When he extended it, one of the monkeys approached him and snatched it, then briefly beat the ground.

'I'll join them,' Mr. Kapasi said, unlocking the door on his side. 'There is much to explain about the caves.'

'No. Stay a minute,' Mrs. Das said. She got out of the back seat and slipped in beside Mr. Kapasi. 'Raj has his dumb book anyway.' Together, through the windshield, Mrs. Das and Mr. Kapasi watched as Bobby and the monkey passed the stick back and forth between them.

'A brave little boy,' Mr. Kapasi commented.

'It's not so surprising,' Mrs. Das said.

'No?'

'He's not his.'

'I beg your pardon?'

'Raj's. He's not Raj's son.'

Mr. Kapasi felt a prickle on his skin. He reached into his shirt pocket for the small tin of lotus-oil balm he carried with him at all times, and applied it to three spots on his forehead. He knew that Mrs. Das was watching him, but he did not turn to face her. Instead he watched as the figures of Mr. Das and the children grew smaller, climbing up the steep path, pausing every now and then for a picture, surrounded by a growing number of monkeys.

'Are you surprised?' The way she put it made him choose his words with care.

'It's not the type of thing one assumes,' Mr. Kapasi replied slowly. He put the tin of lotus-oil balm back in his pocket.

'No, of course not. And no one knows, of course. No one

168

at all. I've kept it a secret for eight whole years.' She looked at Mr. Kapasi, tilting her chin as if to gain a fresh perspective. 'But now I've told you.'

Mr. Kapasi nodded. He felt suddenly parched, and his forehead was warm and slightly numb from the balm. He considered asking Mrs. Das for a sip of water, then decided against it.

'We met when we were very young,' she said. She reached into her straw bag in search of something, then pulled out a packet of puffed rice. 'Want some?'

'No, thank you.'

She put a fistful in her mouth, sank into the seat a little, and looked away from Mr. Kapasi, out the window on her side of the car. 'We married when we were still in college. We were in high school when he proposed. We went to the same college, of course. Back then we couldn't stand the thought of being separated, not for a day, not for a minute. Our parents were best friends who lived in the same town. My entire life I saw him every weekend, either at our house or theirs. We were sent upstairs to play together while our parents joked about our marriage. Imagine! They never caught us at anything, though in a way I think it was all more or less a setup. The things we did those Friday and Saturday nights, while our parents sat downstairs drinking tea . . . I could tell you stories, Mr. Kapasi.'

As a result of spending all her time in college with Raj, she continued, she did not make many close friends. There was no one to confide in about him at the end of a difficult day, or to share a passing thought or a worry. Her parents now lived on the other side of the world, but she had never been very close to them, anyway. After marrying so young she was overwhelmed by it all, having a child so quickly, and nursing, and warming up bottles of milk and testing their temperature against her wrist while Raj was at work, dressed in sweaters and corduroy pants, teaching his students about rocks and dinosaurs. Raj never looked cross or harried, or plump as she had become after the first baby.

Always tired, she declined invitations from her one or two college girlfriends, to have lunch or shop in Manhattan. Eventually the friends stopped calling her, so that she was left at home all day with the baby, surrounded by toys that made her trip when she walked or wince when she sat, always cross and tired. Only occasionally did they go out after Ronny was born, and even more rarely did they entertain. Raj didn't mind; he looked forward to coming home from teaching and watching television and bouncing Ronny on his knee. She had been outraged when Raj told her that a Punjabi friend, someone whom she had once met but did not remember, would be staying with them for a week for some job interviews in the New Brunswick area.

Bobby was conceived in the afternoon, on a sofa littered with rubber teething toys, after the friend learned that a London pharmaceutical company had hired him, while Ronny cried to be freed from his playpen. She made no protest when the friend touched the small of her back as she was about to make a pot of coffee, then pulled her against his crisp navy suit. He made love to her swiftly, in silence, with an expertise she had never known, without the meaningful expressions and smiles Raj always insisted on afterward. The next day Raj drove the friend to JFK. He was married now, to a Punjabi girl, and they lived in London still, and every year they exchanged Christmas cards with Raj and Mina, each couple tucking photos of their families into the envelopes. He did not know that he was Bobby's father. He never would.

'I beg your pardon, Mrs. Das, but why have you told me

this information?' Mr. Kapasi asked when she had finally finished speaking, and had turned to face him once again.

'For God's sake, stop calling me Mrs. Das. I'm twenty-eight. You probably have children my age.'

'Not quite.' It disturbed Mr. Kapasi to learn that she thought of him as a parent. The feeling he had had toward her, that had made him check his reflection in the rearview mirror as they drove, evaporated a little.

'I told you because of your talents.' She put the packet of puffed rice back into her bag without folding over the top.

'I don't understand,' Mr. Kapasi said.

'Don't you see? For eight years I haven't been able to express this to anybody, not to friends, certainly not to Raj. He doesn't even suspect it. He thinks I'm still in love with him. Well, don't you have anything to say?'

'About what?'

'About what I've just told you. About my secret, and about how terrible it makes me feel. I feel terrible looking at my children, and at Raj, always terrible. I have terrible urges, Mr. Kapasi, to throw things away. One day I had the urge to throw everything I own out the window, the television, the children, everything. Don't you think it's unhealthy?'

He was silent.

'Mr. Kapasi, don't you have anything to say? I thought that was your job.'

'My job is to give tours, Mrs. Das.'

'Not that. Your other job. As an interpreter.'

'But we do not face a language barrier. What need is there for an interpreter?'

'That's not what I mean. I would never have told you otherwise. Don't you realize what it means for me to tell you?'

'What does it mean?'

'It means that I'm tired of feeling so terrible all the time. Eight years, Mr. Kapasi, I've been in pain eight years. I was hoping you could help me feel better, say the right thing. Suggest some kind of remedy.'

He looked at her, in her red plaid skirt and strawberry T-shirt, a woman not yet thirty, who loved neither her husband nor her children, who had already fallen out of love with life. Her confession depressed him, depressed him all the more when he thought of Mr. Das at the top of the path, Tina clinging to his shoulders, taking pictures of ancient monastic cells cut into the hills to show his students in America, unsuspecting and unaware that one of his sons was not his own. Mr. Kapasi felt insulted that Mrs. Das should ask him to interpret her common, trivial little secret. She did not resemble the patients in the doctor's office, those who came glassy-eyed and desperate, unable to sleep or breathe or urinate with ease, unable, above all, to give words to their pains. Still, Mr. Kapasi believed it was his duty to assist Mrs. Das. Perhaps he ought to tell her to confess the truth to Mr. Das. He would explain that honesty was the best policy. Honesty, surely, would help her feel better, as she'd put it. Perhaps he would offer to preside over the discussion, as a mediator. He decided to begin with the most obvious question, to get to the heart of the matter, and so he asked, 'Is it really pain you feel, Mrs. Das, or is it guilt?'

She turned to him and glared, mustard oil thick on her frosty pink lips. She opened her mouth to say something, but as she glared at Mr. Kapasi some certain knowledge seemed to pass before her eyes, and she stopped. It crushed him; he knew at that moment that he was not even important enough to be properly insulted. She opened the car door and began walking up the path, wobbling a little on her square wooden heels, reaching into her straw bag to eat handfuls of puffed rice. It fell through her fingers, leaving a zigzagging trail, causing a monkey to leap down from a tree and devour the little white grains. In search of more, the monkey began to follow Mrs. Das. Others joined him, so that she was soon being followed by about half a dozen of them, their velvety tails dragging behind.

Mr. Kapasi stepped out of the car. He wanted to holler, to alert her in some way, but he worried that if she knew they were behind her, she would grow nervous. Perhaps she would lose her balance. Perhaps they would pull at her bag or her hair. He began to jog up the path, taking a fallen branch in his hand to scare away the monkeys. Mrs. Das continued walking, oblivious, trailing grains of puffed rice. Near the top of the incline, before a group of cells fronted by a row of squat stone pillars, Mr. Das was kneeling on the ground, focusing the lens of his camera. The children stood under the arcade, now hiding, now emerging from view.

'Wait for me,' Mrs. Das called out. 'I'm coming.'

Tina jumped up and down. 'Here comes Mommy!'

'Great,' Mr. Das said without looking up. 'Just in time. We'll get Mr. Kapasi to take a picture of the five of us.'

Mr. Kapasi quickened his pace, waving his branch so that the monkeys scampered away, distracted, in another direction.

'Where's Bobby?' Mrs. Das asked when she stopped.

Mr. Das looked up from the camera. 'I don't know. Ronny, where's Bobby?'

Ronny shrugged. 'I thought he was right here.'

'Where is he?' Mrs. Das repeated sharply. 'What's wrong with all of you?'

They began calling his name, wandering up and down the path a bit. Because they were calling, they did not initially

173

hear the boy's screams. When they found him, a little farther down the path under a tree, he was surrounded by a group of monkeys, over a dozen of them, pulling at his T-shirt with their long black fingers. The puffed rice Mrs. Das had spilled was scattered at his feet, raked over by the monkeys' hands. The boy was silent, his body frozen, swift tears running down his startled face. His bare legs were dusty and red with welts from where one of the monkeys struck him repeatedly with the stick he had given to it earlier.

'Daddy, the monkey's hurting Bobby,' Tina said.

Mr. Das wiped his palms on the front of his shorts. In his nervousness he accidentally pressed the shutter on his camera; the whirring noise of the advancing film excited the monkeys, and the one with the stick began to beat Bobby more intently. 'What are we supposed to do? What if they start attacking?'

'Mr. Kapasi,' Mrs. Das shrieked, noticing him standing to one side. 'Do something, for God's sake, do something!'

Mr. Kapasi took his branch and shooed them away, hissing at the ones that remained, stomping his feet to scare them. The animals retreated slowly, with a measured gait, obedient but unintimidated. Mr. Kapasi gathered Bobby in his arms and brought him back to where his parents and siblings were standing. As he carried him he was tempted to whisper a secret into the boy's ear. But Bobby was stunned, and shivering with fright, his legs bleeding slightly where the stick had broken the skin. When Mr. Kapasi delivered him to his parents, Mr. Das brushed some dirt off the boy's T-shirt and put the visor on him the right way. Mrs. Das reached into her straw bag to find a bandage which she taped over the cut on his knee. Ronny offered his brother a fresh piece of gum. 'He's fine. Just a little scared, right, Bobby?' Mr. Das said, patting the top of his head.

'God, let's get out of here,' Mrs. Das said. She folded her arms across the strawberry on her chest. 'This place gives me the creeps.'

'Yeah. Back to the hotel, definitely,' Mr. Das agreed.

'Poor Bobby,' Mrs. Das said. 'Come here a second. Let Mommy fix your hair.' Again she reached into her straw bag, this time for her hairbrush, and began to run it around the edges of the translucent visor. When she whipped out the hairbrush, the slip of paper with Mr. Kapasi's address on it fluttered away in the wind. No one but Mr. Kapasi noticed. He watched as it rose, carried higher and higher by the breeze, into the trees where the monkeys now sat, solemnly observing the scene below. Mr. Kapasi observed it too, knowing that this was the picture of the Das family he would preserve forever in his mind.

CONSULTATIONS

W. W. JACOBS

BACK TO BACK

MRS. SCUTTS, CONCEALED behind the curtain, gazed at the cab in uneasy amazement. The cabman clambered down from the box and, opening the door, stood by with his hands extended ready for any help that might be needed. A stranger was the first to alight, and, with his back towards Mrs. Scutts, seemed to be struggling with something in the cab. He placed a dangling hand about his neck and, staggering under the weight, reeled backwards supporting Mr. Scutts, whose other arm was round the neck of a third man. In a flash Mrs. Scutts was at the door.

'Oh, Bill!' she gasped. 'And by daylight, too!'

Mr. Scutts raised his head sharply and his lips parted; then his head sank again, and he became a dead weight in the grasp of his assistants.

'He's all right,' said one of them, turning to Mrs. Scutts.

A deep groan from Mr. Scutts confirmed the statement.

'What is it?' inquired his wife, anxiously.

'Just a little bit of a railway accident,' said one of the strangers. 'Train ran into some empty trucks. Nobody hurt – seriously,' he added, in response to a terrible and annoyed groan from Mr. Scutts.

With his feet dragging helplessly, Mr. Scutts was conveyed over his own doorstep and placed on the sofa.

'All the others went off home on their own legs,' said one of the strangers, reproachfully. 'He said he couldn't walk, and he wouldn't go to a hospital.'

'Wanted to die at home,' declared the sufferer. 'I ain't going to be cut about at no 'ospitals.'

The two strangers stood by watching him; then they looked at each other.

'I don't want – no – 'ospitals,' gasped Mr. Scutts. 'I'm going to have my own doctor.'

'Of course the company will pay the doctor's bill,' said one of the strangers to Mrs. Scutts; 'or they'll send their own doctor. I expect he'll be all right to-morrow.'

'I 'ope so,' said Mr. Scutts, 'but I don't think it. Thank you for bringing of me 'ome.'

He closed his eyes languidly, and kept them closed until the men had departed.

'Can't you walk, Bill?' inquired the tearful Mrs. Scutts.

Her husband shook his head. 'You go and fetch the doctor,' he said, slowly. 'That new one round the corner.'

'He looks such a boy,' objected Mrs. Scutts.

'You go and fetch 'im,' said Mr. Scutts, raising his voice. 'D'ye hear!'

'But—' began his wife.

'If I get up to you, my gal,' said the forgetful Mr. Scutts, 'you'll know it.'

'Why, I thought—' said his wife, in surprise.

Mr. Scutts raised himself on the sofa and shook his fist at her. Then, as a tribute to appearances, he sank back and groaned again. Mrs. Scutts, looking somewhat relieved, took her bonnet from a nail and departed.

The examination was long and tedious, but Mr. Scutts, beyond remarking that he felt chilly, made no complaint. He endeavoured, but in vain, to perform the tests suggested, and even did his best to stand, supported by his medical attendant. Self-preservation is the law of Nature, and when

Mr. Scutts's legs and back gave way he saw to it that the doctor was underneath.

'We'll have to get you up to bed,' said the latter, rising slowly and dusting himself.

Mr. Scutts, who was lying full length on the floor, acquiesced, and sent his wife for some neighbours. One of them was a professional furniture-remover, and, half-way up the narrow stairs, the unfortunate had to remind him that he was dealing with a British working man, and not a piano. Four pairs of hands deposited Mr. Scutts with mathematical precision in the centre of the bed and then proceeded to tuck him in, while Mrs. Scutts drew the sheet in a straight line under his chin.

'Don't *look* much the matter with 'im,' said one of the assistants.

'You can't tell with a face like that,' said the furniture-remover. 'It's wot you might call a 'appy face. Why, he was 'arf smiling as we carried 'im up the stairs.'

'You're a liar,' said Mr. Scutts, opening his eyes.

'All right, mate,' said the furniture-remover; 'all right. There's no call to get annoyed about it. Good old English pluck, I call it. Where d'you feel the pain?'

'All over,' said Mr. Scutts, briefly.

His neighbours regarded him with sympathetic eyes, and then, led by the furniture-remover, filed out of the room on tip-toe. The doctor, with a few parting instructions, also took his departure.

'If you're not better by the morning,' he said, pausing at the door, 'you must send for your club doctor.'

Mr. Scutts, in a feeble voice, thanked him, and lay with a twisted smile on his face listening to his wife's vivid narrative to the little crowd which had collected at the front door. She came back, followed by the next-door neighbour, Mr. James

183

Flynn, whose offers of assistance ranged from carrying Mr. Scutts out pick-a-back when he wanted to take the air, to filling his pipe for him and fetching his beer.

'But I dare say you'll be up and about in a couple o' days,' he concluded. 'You wouldn't look so well if you'd got anything serious the matter; rosy, fat cheeks and—'

'That'll do,' said the indignant invalid. 'It's my back that's hurt, not my face.'

'I know,' said Mr. Flynn, nodding sagely; 'but if it was hurt bad your face would be as white as that sheet – whiter.'

'The doctor said as he was to be kep' quiet,' remarked Mrs. Scutts, sharply.

'Right-o,' said Mr. Flynn. 'Ta-ta, old pal. Keep your pecker up, and if you want your back rubbed with turps, or anything of that sort, just knock on the wall.'

He went, before Mr. Scutts could think of a reply suitable for an invalid and, at the same time, bristling with virility. A sinful and foolish desire to leap out of bed and help Mr. Flynn downstairs made him more rubicund than ever.

He sent for the club doctor next morning, and, pending his arrival, partook of a basin of arrowroot and drank a little beef-tea. A bottle of castor-oil and an empty pill-box on the table by the bedside added a little local colour to the scene.

'Any pain?' inquired the doctor, after an examination in which bony and very cold fingers had played a prominent part.

'Not much pain,' said Mr. Scutts. 'Don't seem to have no strength in my back.'

'Ah!' said the doctor.

'I tried to get up this morning to go to my work,' said Mr. Scutts, 'but I can't stand – I couldn't get out of bed.'

'Fearfully upset, he was, pore dear,' testified Mrs. Scutts. 'He can't bear losing a day. I s'pose – I s'pose the railway company will 'ave to do something if it's serious, won't they, sir?'

'Nothing to do with me,' said the doctor. 'I'll put him on the club for a few days; I expect he will be all right soon. He's got a healthy colour – a very healthy colour.'

Mr. Scutts waited until he had left the house and then made a few remarks on the colour question that for impurity of English and strength of diction have probably never been surpassed.

A second visitor that day came after dinner – a tall man in a frock-coat, bearing in his hand a silk hat, which, after a careful survey of the room, he hung on a knob of the bed-post.

'Mr. Scutts?' he inquired, bowing.

'That's me,' said Mr. Scutts, in a feeble voice.

'I've called from the railway company,' said the stranger. 'We have seen now all those who left their names and addresses on Monday afternoon, and I am glad to say that nobody was really hurt. Nobody.'

Mr. Scutts, in a faint voice, said he was glad to hear it.

'Been a wonder if they had,' said the other, cheerfully. 'Why, even the paint wasn't knocked off the engine. The most serious damage appears to be two top-hats crushed and an umbrella broken.'

He leaned over the bed-rail and laughed joyously. Mr. Scutts, through half-closed eyes, gazed at him in silent reproach.

'I don't say that one or two people didn't receive a little bit of a shock to their nerves,' said the visitor, thoughtfully. 'One lady even stayed in bed next day. However, I made it all right with them. The company is very generous, and although of course there is no legal obligation, they made several of them a present of a few pounds so that they could go away for a little change, or anything of that sort, to quiet their nerves.'

Mr. Scutts, who had been listening with closed eyes, opened them languidly and said, 'Oh.'

'I gave one gentleman twen-ty pounds!' said the visitor, jingling some coins in his trouser-pocket. 'I never saw a man so pleased and grateful in my life. When he signed the receipt for it – I always get them to sign a receipt, so that the company can see that I haven't kept the money for myself – he nearly wept with joy.'

'I should think he would,' said Mr. Scutts, slowly – 'if he wasn't hurt.'

'You're the last on my list,' said the other, hastily. He produced a slip of paper from his pocket-book and placed it on the small table, with a fountain pen. Then, with a smile that was both tender and playful, he plunged his hand in his pocket and poured a stream of gold on the table.

'What do you say to thir-ty pounds?' he said, in a hushed voice. 'Thir-ty golden goblins?'

'What for?' inquired Mr. Scutts, with a notable lack of interest.

'For – well, to go away for a day or two,' said the visitor. 'I find you in bed; it may be a cold or a bilious attack; or perhaps you had a little upset of the nerves when the trains kissed each other.'

'I'm in bed – because – I can't walk – or stand,' said Mr. Scutts, speaking very distinctly. 'I'm on my club, and if as 'ow I get well in a day or two, there's no reason why the company should give me any money. I'm pore, but I'm honest.'

'Take my advice as a friend,' said the other; 'take the money while you can get it.'

He nodded significantly at Mr. Scutts and closed one eye. Mr. Scutts closed both of his.

'I 'ad my back hurt in the collision,' he said, after a long pause. 'I 'ad to be helped 'ome. So far it seems to get worse, but I 'ope for the best.'

'Dear me,' said the visitor; 'how sad! I suppose it has been coming on for a long time. Most of these back cases do. At least all the doctors say so.'

'It was done in the collision,' said Mr. Scutts, mildly but firmly. 'I was as right as rain before then.'

The visitor shook his head and smiled. 'Ah! you would have great difficulty in proving that,' he said, softly; 'in fact, speaking as man to man, I don't mind telling you it would be impossible. I'm afraid I'm exceeding my duty, but, as you're the last on my list, suppose – suppose we say forty pounds. Forty! A small fortune.'

He added some more gold to the pile on the table, and gently tapped Mr. Scutts's arm with the end of the pen.

'Good afternoon,' said the invalid.

The visitor, justly concerned at his lack of intelligence, took a seat on the edge of the bed and spoke to him as a friend and a brother, but in vain. Mr. Scutts reminded him at last that it was medicine-time, after which, pain and weakness permitting, he was going to try to get a little sleep.

'Forty pounds!' he said to his wife, after the official had departed. 'Why didn't 'e offer me a bag 'o sweets?'

'It's a lot o' money,' said Mrs. Scutts, wistfully.

'So's a thousand,' said her husband. 'I ain't going to 'ave my back broke for nothing, I can tell you. Now, you keep that mouth o' yours shut, and if I get it, you shall 'ave a new pair o' boots.'

'A thousand!' exclaimed the startled Mrs. Scutts. 'Have you took leave of your senses, or what?'

'I read a case in the paper where a man got it,' said Mr.

Scutts. 'He 'ad his back 'urt too, pore chap. How would you like to lay on your back all your life for a thousand pounds?'

'Will you 'ave to lay abed all your life?' inquired his wife, staring.

'Wait till I get the money,' said Mr. Scutts; 'then I might be able to tell you better.'

He gazed wistfully at the window. It was late October, but the sun shone and the air was clear. The sound of traffic and cheerful voices ascended from the little street. To Mr. Scutts it all seemed to be a part of a distant past.

'If that chap comes round to-morrow and offers me five hundred,' he said, slowly, 'I don't know as I won't take it. I'm sick of this mouldy bed.'

He waited expectantly next day, but nothing happened, and after a week of bed he began to realize that the job might be a long one. The monotony, to a man of his active habits, became almost intolerable, and the narrated adventures of Mr. James Flynn, his only caller, filled him with an uncontrollable longing to be up and doing.

The fine weather went, and Mr. Scutts, in his tumbled bed, lay watching the rain beating softly on the window-panes. Then one morning he awoke to the darkness of a London fog.

'It gets worse and worse,' said Mrs. Scutts, as she returned home in the afternoon with a relish for his tea. 'Can't see your 'and before your face.'

Mr. Scutts looked thoughtful. He ate his tea in silence, and after he had finished lit his pipe and sat up in bed smoking.

'Penny for your thoughts,' said his wife.

'I'm going out,' said Mr. Scutts, in a voice that defied opposition. 'I'm going to 'ave a walk, and when I'm far enough away I'm going to 'ave one or two drinks. I believe this fog is sent a-purpose to save my life.'

Mrs. Scutts remonstrated, but in vain, and at half-past six the invalid, with his cap over his eyes and a large scarf tied round the lower part of his face, listened for a moment at his front door and then disappeared in the fog.

Left to herself, Mrs. Scutts returned to the bedroom and, poking the tiny fire into a blaze, sat and pondered over the wilfulness of men.

She was awakened from a doze by a knocking at the street-door. It was just eight o'clock, and, inwardly congratulating her husband on his return to common sense and home, she went down and opened it. Two tall men in silk hats entered the room.

'Mrs. Scutts?' said one of them.

Mrs. Scutts, in a dazed fashion, nodded.

'We have come to see your husband,' said the intruder. 'I am a doctor.'

The panic-stricken Mrs. Scutts tried in vain to think.

'He – he's asleep,' she said, at last.

'Doesn't matter,' said the doctor.

'Not a bit,' said his companion.

'You – you can't see him,' protested Mrs. Scutts. 'He ain't to be seen.'

'He'd be sorry to miss me,' said the doctor, eyeing her keenly as she stood on guard by the inner door. 'I suppose he's at home?'

'Of course,' said Mrs. Scutts, stammering and flushing. 'Why, the pore man can't stir from his bed.'

'Well, I'll just peep in at the door, then,' said the doctor. 'I won't wake him. You can't object to that. If you do—'

Mrs. Scutts's head began to swim. 'I'll go up and see whether he's awake,' she said.

She closed the door on them and stood with her hand to her throat, thinking. Then, instead of going upstairs, she

189

passed into the yard and, stepping over the fence, opened Mr. Flynn's back door.

'Halloa!' said that gentleman, who was standing in the scullery removing mud from his boots. 'What's up?'

In a frenzied gabble Mrs. Scutts told him. 'You must be 'im,' she said, clutching him by the coat and dragging him towards the door. 'They've never seen 'im, and they won't know the difference.'

'But—' exclaimed the astonished James.

'Quick!' she said, sharply. 'Go into the back room and undress, then nip into his room and get into bed. And mind, be fast asleep all the time.'

Still holding the bewildered Mr. Flynn by the coat, she led him into the house and waved him upstairs, and stood below listening until a slight creaking of the bed announced that he had obeyed orders. Then she entered the parlour.

'He's fast asleep,' she said, softly; 'and mind, I won't 'ave him disturbed. It's the first real sleep he's 'ad for nearly a week. If you promise not to wake 'im you may just have a peep.'

'We won't disturb him,' said the doctor, and, followed by his companion, noiselessly ascended the stairs and peeped into the room. Mr. Flynn was fast asleep, and not a muscle moved as the two men approached the bed on tip-toe and stood looking at him. The doctor turned after a minute and led the way out of the room.

'We'll call again,' he said, softly.

'Yes, sir,' said Mrs. Scutts. 'When?'

The doctor and his companion exchanged glances. 'I'm very busy just at present,' he said, slowly. 'We'll look in some time and take our chance of catching him awake.'

Mrs. Scutts bowed them out, and in some perplexity returned to Mr. Flynn. 'I don't like the look of 'em,' she said, shaking her head. 'You'd better stay in bed till Bill comes 'ome in case they come back.'

'Right-o,' said the obliging Mr. Flynn. 'Just step in and tell my landlady I'm 'aving a chat with Bill.'

He lit his pipe and sat up in bed smoking until a knock at the front door at half-past eleven sent him off to sleep again. Mrs. Scutts, who was sitting downstairs, opened it and admitted her husband.

'All serene?' he inquired. 'What are you looking like that for? What's up?'

He sat quivering with alarm and rage as she told him, and then, mounting the stairs with a heavy tread, stood gazing in helpless fury at the slumbering form of Mr. James Flynn.

'Get out o' my bed,' he said at last, in a choking voice.

'What, Bill!' said Mr. Flynn, opening his eyes.

'Get out o' my bed,' repeated the other. 'You've made a nice mess of it between you. It's a fine thing if a man can't go out for 'arf a pint without coming home and finding all the riff-raff of the neighbourhood in 'is bed.'

''Ow's the pore back, Bill?' inquired Mr. Flynn, with tenderness.

Mr. Scutts gurgled at him. 'Outside!' he said as soon as he could get his breath.

'Bill,' said the voice of Mrs. Scutts, outside the door.

'Halloa,' growled her husband.

'He mustn't go,' said Mrs. Scutts. 'Those gentlemen are coming again, and they think he is you.'

'WHAT!' roared the infuriated Mr. Scutts.

'Don't you see? It's me what's got the pore back now, Bill,' said Mr. Flynn. 'You can't pass yourself off as me, Bill; you ain't good-looking enough.'

Mr. Scutts, past speech, raised his clenched fists to the ceiling.

'He'll 'ave to stay in your bed,' continued the voice of Mrs. Scutts. 'He's got a good 'art, and I know he'll do it; won't you, Jim?

Mr. Flynn pondered. 'Tell my landlady in the morning that I've took your back room,' he said. 'What a fortunit thing it is I'm out o' work. What are you walking up and down like that for, Bill? Back coming on agin?'

'Then o' course,' pursued the voice of Mrs. Scutts, in meditative accents, 'there's the club doctor and the other gentleman that knows Bill. They might come at any moment. There's got to be two Bills in bed, so that if one party comes one Bill can nip into the back room, and if the other Bill – party, I mean – comes, the other Bill – you know what I mean!'

Mr. Scutts swore himself faint.

'That's 'ow it is, mate,' said Mr. Flynn. 'It's no good standing there saying your little piece of poetry to yourself. Take off your clo'es and get to bed like a little man. Now! now! Naughty! Naughty!'

'P'r'aps I oughtn't to 'ave let 'em up, Bill,' said his wife; 'but I was afraid they'd smell a rat if I didn't. Besides, I was took by surprise.'

'You get off to bed,' said Mr. Scutts. 'Get off to bed while you're safe.'

'And get a good night's rest,' added the thoughtful Mr. Flynn. 'If Bill's back is took bad in the night I'll look after it.'

Mr. Scutts turned a threatening face on him. 'For two pins—' he began.

'For two pins I'll go back 'ome and stay there,' said Mr. Flynn.

He put one muscular leg out of bed, and then, at the earnest request of Mr. Scutts, put it back again. In a few simple, manly words the latter apologized, by putting all the blame on Mrs. Scutts, and, removing his clothes, got into bed.

Wrapped in bedclothes, they passed the following day listening for knocks at the door and playing cards. By evening both men were weary, and Mr. Scutts made a few pointed remarks concerning dodging doctors and deceitful visitors to which Mr. Flynn listened in silent approval.

'They mightn't come for a week,' he said, dismally. 'It's all right for you, but where do I come in? Halves?'

Mr. Scutts had a rush of blood to the head.

'You leave it to me, mate,' he said, controlling himself by an effort. 'If I get ten quid, say, you shall have 'arf.'

'And suppose you get more?' demanded the other.

'We'll see,' said Mr. Scutts, vaguely.

Mr. Flynn returned to the charge next day, but got no satisfaction. Mr. Scutts preferred to talk instead of the free board and lodging his friend was getting. On the subject of such pay for such work he was almost eloquent.

'I'll bide my time,' said Mr. Flynn, darkly. 'Treat me fair and I'll treat you fair.'

His imprisonment came to an end on the fourth day. There was a knock at the door, and the sound of men's voices, followed by the hurried appearance of Mrs. Scutts.

'It's *Jim's* lot,' she said, in a hurried whisper. 'I've just come up to get the room ready.'

Mr. Scutts took his friend by the hand, and after warmly urging him not to forget the expert instructions he had received concerning his back, slipped into the back room, and, a prey to forebodings, awaited the result.

'Well, he looks better,' said the doctor, regarding Mr. Flynn.

'Much better,' said his companion.

Mrs. Scutts shook her head. 'His pore back don't seem no

better, sir,' she said in a low voice. 'Can't you do something for it?'

'Let me have a look at it,' said the doctor. 'Undo your shirt.'

Mr. Flynn, with slow fingers, fumbled with the button at his neck and looked hard at Mrs. Scutts.

'She can't bear to see me suffer,' he said, in a feeble voice, as she left the room.

He bore the examination with the fortitude of an early Christian martyr. In response to inquiries he said he felt as though the mainspring of his back had gone.

'How long since you walked?' inquired the doctor.

'Not since the accident,' said Mr. Flynn, firmly.

'Try now,' said the doctor.

Mr. Flynn smiled at him reproachfully.

'You can't walk because you think you can't,' said the doctor; 'that is all. You'll have to be encouraged the same way that a child is. I should like to cure you, and I think I can.'

He took a small canvas bag from the other man and opened it. 'Forty pounds,' he said. 'Would you like to count it?'

Mr. Flynn's eyes shone.

'It is all yours,' said the doctor, 'if you can walk across the room and take it from that gentleman's hand.'

'Honour bright?' asked Mr. Flynn, in tremulous tones, as the other man held up the bag and gave him an encouraging smile.

'Honour bright,' said the doctor.

With a spring that nearly broke the bed, Mr. Flynn quitted it and snatched the bag, and at the same moment Mrs. Scutts, impelled by a maddened arm, burst into the room.

'Your back!' she moaned. 'It'll kill you. Get back to bed.'

'I'm cured, lovey,' said Mr. Flynn, simply.

'His back is as strong as ever,' said the doctor, giving it a thump.

Mr. Flynn, who had taken his clothes from a chair and was hastily dressing himself, assented.

'But if you'll wait 'arf a tick I'll walk as far as the corner with you,' he said, quickly. 'I'd like to make sure it's all right.'

He paused at the foot of the stairs and, glancing up at the pallid and murderous face of Mr. Scutts, which protruded from the back bedroom, smiled at him rapturously. Then, with a lordly air, he tossed him five pieces of gold.

GUY DE MAUPASSANT

A COUP D'ÉTAT

PARIS HAD JUST learnt of the disaster of Sedan. The Republic was proclaimed. All France was panting at the outset of a delirium that lasted until after the Commune. Everybody was playing soldiers from one end of the country to the other.

Hatters became colonels, assuming the duties of generals; revolvers and daggers were displayed on large rotund paunches, enveloped in red sashes; common citizens became temporary warriors, commanding battalions of noisy volunteers, and swearing like troopers to emphasise their importance.

The mere fact of bearing arms and handling guns excited people who hitherto had only handled weighing-scales, and made them formidable to the first comer, without reason. They even executed a few innocent people to prove that they knew how to kill; and, in roaming through country places as yet innocent of Prussians, they shot stray dogs, cows chewing the cud in peace, or sick horses put out to pasture. Every man believed himself called upon to play a great rôle in military affairs. The cafés of the smallest villages, full of tradesmen in uniform, resembled barracks or field-hospitals.

Now, the town of Canneville did not yet know the news of the army and the Capital, but a violent agitation had been disturbing it for a month, and the rival parties had confronted each other. The Mayor, Vicomte de Varnetot, a small, thin man, already old, a Legitimist who had rallied recently to the Empire, spurred by ambition, had seen rising up against him a powerful adversary in Doctor Massarel, a stout, full-blooded man, head of the Republican party in the district, venerable chief of the Masonic Lodge in the county town, president of the Society of Agriculture, chairman of the Fire Department banquet, and organiser of the rural militia which was to save the country.

In two weeks he had induced sixty-three married men and fathers of families to volunteer in defence of their country, prudent farmers and merchants of the town, and he drilled them every morning on the square in front of the Town Hall.

Whenever the mayor happened to appear at the Local Government building, Commander Massarel, covered with pistols, sword in hand, passing proudly up and down in front of his troops, would make them shout, 'Long live our country!' And this, they noticed, disturbed the little Vicomte, who no doubt heard in it menace and defiance, and perhaps some odious recollection of the great Revolution.

On the morning of the Fifth of September the doctor, in uniform, his revolver on the table, was giving a consultation to an old peasant couple of whom the husband had suffered with varicose veins for seven years, but had waited until his wife had the same complaint before coming to see the doctor, when the postman arrived with the newspaper.

Doctor Massarel opened it, grew pale, straightened himself abruptly and, raising his arms to heaven in a gesture of exaltation, cried out with all his might, in the face of the amazed rustics:

'Long live the Republic! Long live the Republic! Long live the Republic!'

Then he dropped into his arm-chair weak with emotion.

When the peasant explained again that this sickness had begun with a feeling as if ants were running up and down in his legs, the doctor exclaimed: 'Leave me in peace. I have no time to waste on such nonsense. The Republic is proclaimed! The Emperor is a prisoner! France is saved! Long live the Republic!' And, running to the door, he bellowed: 'Céleste! Quick! Céleste!'

The frightened maid hastened in. He stuttered, so rapidly did he try to speak: 'My boots, my sword – my cartridge box – and – the Spanish dagger, which is on my night table. Hurry now!'

The obstinate peasant, taking advantage of the moment's silence, began again: 'They became like knots that hurt me when I walked.'

The exasperated doctor shouted: 'Shut up, for Heaven's sake! If you had washed your feet oftener, it would not have happened.' Then, seizing him by the neck, he hissed in his face: 'Can't you understand that we are living in a Republic, idiot?'

But a sense of his profession calmed him suddenly, and he let the astonished old couple out of the house, repeating:

'Come back to-morrow, come back to-morrow, my friends; I have no time to-day.'

While equipping himself from head to foot, he gave another series of urgent orders to the maid:

'Run to Lieutenant Picart's and to Sub-lieutenant Pommel's and tell them that I want them here immediately. Send Torchebeuf to me, too, with his drum. Quick, now! Quick!' And when Céleste was gone, he collected his thoughts and prepared to overcome the difficulties of the situation.

The three men arrived together. They were in their working clothes. The Commander, who had expected to see them in uniform, gave a start of surprise.

'Good Lord! You know nothing, then? The Emperor has

been taken prisoner. A Republic is proclaimed. We must take action. My position is delicate, I might almost say perilous.'

He reflected for some minutes in the presence of his astonished subordinates and then continued:

'We must act without hesitation. Minutes now are worth hours in times like these. Everything depends upon promptness of decision. You, Picart, go and find the priest and order him to ring the bell to bring the people together, so that I can inform them. You, Torchebeuf, beat the call in every part of the district, as far as the hamlets of Gerisaie and Salmare, to assemble the militia in arms, in the square. You, Pommel, put on your uniform at once, that is, the jacket and cap. We, together, are going to take possession of the Town Hall and summon M. de Varnetot to transfer his authority to me. Do you understand?'

'Yes.'

'Act, then, and promptly. I will accompany you to your house, Pommel, since we are to work together.'

Five minutes later, the Commandant and his subaltern, armed to the teeth, appeared in the square, just at the moment when the little Vicomte de Varnetot, wearing hunting gaiters, and with his rifle on his shoulder, came along by another street, walking rapidly and followed by three gamekeepers in green jackets, each carrying a knife at his side and a gun over his shoulder.

While the doctor stopped in amazement, the four men entered the Town Hall and the door closed behind them.

'We have been forestalled,' murmured the doctor. 'Now we shall have to wait for reinforcements; nothing can be done for the time being.'

Lieutenant Picart reappeared: 'The priest refuses to obey,' said he; 'he has even shut himself up in the church with the beadle and the usher.'

On the other side of the square, opposite the white, closed front of the Town Hall, the church, silent and sombre, showed its great oak door with the wrought-iron trimmings.

Then, as the puzzled inhabitants put their heads out of the windows, or came out upon their thresholds, the rolling of a drum was heard, and Torchebeuf suddenly appeared, beating with fury the three quick strokes of the call to arms. He crossed the square with disciplined step, and then disappeared along the road leading to the country.

The Commandant drew his sword, advanced alone about half-way between the two buildings where the enemy was barricaded and, waving his weapon above his head, roared at the top of his lungs: 'Long live the Republic! Death to traitors!' Then he fell back where his officers were. The butcher, the baker, and the apothecary, feeling a little uncertain, put up their shutters and closed their shops. The grocery alone remained open.

Meanwhile the men of the militia were gradually arriving, variously clothed, but all wearing caps with red braid, the cap constituting the whole uniform of the corps. They were armed with their old, rusty guns, guns that had hung over chimney-pieces in kitchens for thirty years, and looked quite like a detachment of foresters.

When there were about thirty around him, the Commandant explained in a few words the state of affairs. Then, turning toward his general staff, he said: 'Now, we must act.'

While the inhabitants collected, looked on, and discussed the matter, the doctor quickly formed his plan of campaign:

'Lieutenant Picart, you advance to the windows of the Town Hall and order M. de Varnetot to surrender it to me, in the name of the Republic.'

But the Lieutenant was a master-mason and refused.

'You are very clever, aren't you? Trying to make a target

of me! Those fellows in there are good shots, you know. No, thanks! Execute your commissions yourself!'

The Commandant turned red: 'I order you to go in the name of discipline,' said he.

The Lieutenant rebelled:

'I am not going to have my features spoiled without knowing the reason why.'

The notables of the village, in a group near by, began to laugh. One of them called out: 'You are right, Picart, it is not the proper time.' The doctor, under his breath, muttered 'Cowards!' And, placing his sword and his revolver in the hands of a soldier, he advanced with measured step, his eyes fixed on the windows, as if he expected to see the muzzle of a gun pointed at him.

When he was within a few steps of the building the doors at the two ends, affording an entrance to two schools, opened, and a flood of little creatures, boys on one side, girls on the other, poured out and began playing in the open space, chattering around the doctor like a flock of birds. He could hardly make himself heard.

As soon as they were all out, the two doors closed. The greater part of the little monkeys finally scattered, and then the Commandant called out in a loud voice:

'Monsieur de Varnetot!' A window in the first storey opened and M. de Varnetot appeared.

The Commandant began: 'Monsieur, you are aware of the great events which have changed the system of Government. The party you represent no longer exists. The side I repre-sent now comes into power. Under these sad but decisive circumstances, I come to summon you, in the name of the new Republic, to place in my hands the authority vested in you by the out-going power.'

M. de Varnetot replied: 'Doctor Massarel, I am Mayor of

Canneville, so placed by the proper authorities, and Mayor of Canneville I shall remain until the title is revoked and replaced by an order from my superiors. As Mayor, I am at home in the Town Hall and, there I shall stay. Furthermore, just try to put me out.' And he closed the window.

The Commandant returned to his troops. But, before explaining anything, measuring Lieutenant Picart from head to foot, he said:

'You are a fine fellow, you are – a goose, the disgrace of the army. I degrade you.'

The Lieutenant replied: 'I don't care a damn.' And he went over to the group of grumbling citizens.

Then the doctor hesitated. What should he do? Make an assault? Would his men obey him? And then, was he in the right? Then he had a bright idea. He ran to the telegraph office opposite the Town Hall, on the other side of the square, and sent three dispatches: 'To the Members of the Republican Government, at Paris'; 'To the New Republican Prefect of the Seine-Inférieure, at Rouen'; 'To the New Republican Sub-prefect of Dieppe.'

He explained the situation fully; told of the danger which the district incurred by remaining in the hands of the monarchist mayor, offered his loyal services, asked for orders and signed his name, followed by all his titles. Then he returned to his army corps and, drawing ten francs out of his pocket, said:

'Now, my men, go and eat and drink a little something. Only leave here a detachment of ten men, so that no one leaves the town hall.'

Ex-Lieutenant Picart, chatting with the watchmaker, overheard this. With a sneer he remarked: 'Pardon me, but if they go out, you will have a chance to go in. Otherwise, I can't see how you are to get in there!'

The doctor made no reply, but went off to lunch. In the afternoon, he placed guards all about town, as if it were threatened by a surprise. Many times he passed before the doors of the Town Hall and of the church, without noticing anything suspicious; one might have believed the two buildings were empty.

The butcher, the baker, and the apothecary reopened their shops. There was a lot of talking in the houses. If the Emperor had been taken prisoner, there must be a traitor somewhere. They did not know exactly which Republic had been restored.

Night came on. Toward nine o'clock, the doctor returned quietly and alone to the entrance to the Town Hall, persuaded that his adversary had retired. And, as he was trying to force an entrance with a few blows of a pickaxe, the loud voice of a sentry demanded suddenly: 'Who goes there?' Monsieur Massarel beat a retreat at top speed.

Another day dawned without any change in the situation. The militia in arms occupied the square. The inhabitants stood around them, awaiting the solution. People from neighbouring villages came to look on. Finally, the doctor, realising that his reputation was at stake, resolved to settle the thing in one way or another. He had just decided that it must be something energetic, when the door of the telegraph office opened and the little servant of the postmistress appeared, holding in her hand two papers.

First she went to the Commandant and gave him one of the dispatches; then, crossing the deserted centre of the square, intimidated by so many eyes fixed upon her, with lowered head and running steps, she rapped gently at the door of the barricaded house, as if unaware that a party of men in arms was concealed there.

The door opened slightly; the hand of a man received the

message, and the girl returned, blushing and ready to weep, from being stared at by the whole country-side.

In vibrating tones the doctor shouted: 'Silence, please.' And, when the populace became quiet, he continued proudly:

'Here is a communication which I have received from the Government.' And raising the telegram, he read:

'Old Mayor recalled. Please attend to urgent matters. Instructions will follow.

'For the Sub-prefect,
'SAPIN, Councillor.'

He had triumphed. His heart was beating with joy. His hands were shaking. But Picart, his old subaltern, cried out to him from a neighbouring group: 'That's all right; but if the others in there won't get out, that piece of paper will not do you much good.' M. Massarel turned pale. Supposing the others would not get out? He would now have to take the offensive. It was not only his right, but his duty. And he looked anxiously at the Town Hall, hoping that he might see the door open and his adversary retreat. But the door remained closed. What was to be done? The crowd was increasing, surrounding the militia. People were laughing.

One thought, especially, tortured the doctor. If he should make an assault, he must march at the head of his men; and as, once he were killed, there would be no opposition, it would be at him, and at him alone that M. de Varnetot and the three gamekeepers would aim. And their aim was good, very good! Picart had reminded him of that.

But an idea occurred to him, and turning to Pommel, he said: 'Go, quickly, and ask the chemist to lend me a napkin and a pole.'

The Lieutenant hurried off. The doctor was going to make a political banner, a white one, that would, perhaps, rejoice the Legitimist heart of the old mayor.

Pommel returned with the piece of linen required, and a broom handle. With some pieces of string, they improvised a flag, which Massarel seized in both hands. Again, he advanced towards the Town Hall, bearing the standard before him. When in front of the door, he called out: 'Monsieur de Varnetot!'

The door opened suddenly, and M. de Varnetot and his three gamekeepers appeared on the threshold. The doctor recoiled, instinctively. Then, he saluted his enemy courteously, and announced, almost strangled by emotion: 'I have come, sir, to communicate to you the instructions I have just received.'

That gentleman, without any salutation whatever, replied: 'I am going to withdraw, sir, but you must understand that it is not because of fear, or in obedience to an odious Government that has usurped power.' And, biting off each word, he declared: 'I do not wish to have the appearance of serving the Republic for a single day. That is all.'

Massarel, amazed, made no reply; and M. de Varnetot, walking off at a rapid pace, disappeared around the corner, followed closely by his escort. Then the doctor, mad with pride, returned to the crowd. When he was near enough to be heard, he cried: 'Hurrah! Hurrah! The Republic triumphs all along the line!'

But no emotion was manifested. The doctor tried again: 'The people are free! You are free and independent! Do you understand? Be proud of it!'

The listless villagers looked at him with eyes unlit by glory. In his turn, he looked at them, indignant at their indifference, seeking for some word that could make a grand impression, electrify this placid country and make good his mission. The inspiration came, and turning to Pommel, he said: 'Lieutenant, go and get the bust of the Ex-Emperor, which is in the Municipal Council Hall, and bring it to me with a chair.'

And soon the man reappeared, carrying on his right shoulder, Napoleon III in plaster, and holding in his left hand a straw-bottomed chair.

Massarel met him, took the chair, placed it on the ground, put the white image upon it, fell back a few steps and called out, in sonorous voice:

'Tyrant! Tyrant! At last you have fallen! Fallen in the dust and in the mire. An expiring country groaned beneath your foot. Avenging fate has struck you down. Defeat and shame cling to you. You fall conquered, a prisoner to the Prussians, and upon the ruins of the crumbling Empire the young and radiant Republic arises, picking up your broken sword.'

He awaited applause. But not a shout was raised, not a hand clapped. The bewildered peasants remained silent. And the bust, with its pointed moustaches extending beyond the cheeks on each side, the bust, as motionless and well groomed as a hairdresser's sign, seemed to be looking at M. Massarel with a plaster smile, an ineffaceable and mocking smile.

They remained thus face to face, Napoleon on the chair, the doctor in front of him about three steps away. Suddenly the Commandant grew angry. What was to be done? What was there that would move these people, and bring about a definite victory of opinion? His hand happened to rest on his hip and to come in contact there with the butt-end of his revolver, under his red sash. No inspiration, no further word would come. So he drew his pistol, advanced two steps, and, taking aim, fired at the late monarch. The ball entered the forehead, leaving a little, black hole, like a spot, nothing more. It made no effect. Then he fired a second shot, which made a second hole; then, a third; and then, without stopping, he emptied his revolver. The brow of Napoleon disappeared in white powder, but the eyes, the nose, and the fine points of the moustaches remained intact. Then, the exasperated doctor overturned the chair with a blow of his fist and, resting a foot on the remainder of the bust in an attitude of triumph, he turned to the flabbergasted public and shouted: 'So let all tyrants perish!'

Still no enthusiasm was manifest, and as the spectators seemed to be in a kind of stupor from astonishment, the Commandant called to the militiamen: 'You may now go to your homes.' And he went toward his own house with great strides, as if he were pursued.

His maid, when he appeared, told him that some patients had been waiting in his office for three hours. He hastened in. There were the two varicose-vein patients, who had returned at daybreak, obstinate and patient.

The old man immediately began his explanation: 'This began by a feeling like ants running up and down my legs.'

GRAHAM GREENE

DOCTOR CROMBIE

AN UNFORTUNATE CIRCUMSTANCE in my life has just recalled to mind a certain Doctor Crombie and the conversations I used to hold with him when I was young. He was the school doctor until the eccentricity of his ideas became generally known. After he had ceased to attend the school the rest of his practice was soon reduced to a few old people, almost as eccentric as himself – there were, I remember, Colonel Parker, a British Israelite, Miss Warrender who kept twenty-five cats, and a man called Horace Turner who invented a system for turning the National Debt into a National Credit.

Doctor Crombie lived all alone half a mile from the school in a red-brick villa in King's Road. Luckily he possessed a small private income, for at the end his work had come to be entirely paperwork – long articles for the *Lancet* and the *British Medical Journal* which were never published. It was long before the days of television; otherwise a corner might have been found for him in some magazine programme, and his views would have reached a larger public than the random gossips of Bankstead – with who knows what result? – for he spoke with sincerity, and when I was young he certainly to me carried a measure of conviction.

Our school, which had begun as a grammar school during the reign of Henry VIII, had, by the twentieth century, just edged its way into the *Public Schools Year Book*. There were many day-boys, of whom I was one, for Bankstead was only an hour from London by train, and in the days of the old London Midland and Scottish Railways there were frequent and rapid services for commuters. In a boarding-school where the boys are isolated for months at a time like prisoners on Dartmoor, Doctor Crombie's views would have become known more slowly. By the time a boy went home for the holidays he would have forgotten any curious details, and the parents, dotted about England in equal isolation, would have been unable to get together and check up on any unusual stories. It was different at Bankstead, where parents lived a community life and attended sing-songs, but even here Doctor Crombie's views had a long innings.

The headmaster was a progressively minded man, and, when the boys emerged, at the age of thirteen, from the junior school, he arranged, with the consent of the parents, that Doctor Crombie should address them in small groups on the problems of personal hygiene and the dangers which lay ahead. I have only faint memories of the occasion, of the boys who sniggered, of the boys who blushed, of the boys who stared at the ground as though they had dropped something, but I remember vividly the explicit and plain-speaking Doctor Crombie, with his melancholy moustache, which remained blond from nicotine long after his head was grey, and his gold-rimmed spectacles – gold rims, like a pipe, always give me the impression of a rectitude I can never achieve. I understood very little of what he was saying, but I do remember later that I asked my parents what he meant by 'playing with oneself'. Being an only child I was accustomed to play with myself. For example, in the case of my model railway, I was in turn driver, signalman and station-master, and I felt no need of an assistant.

My mother said she had forgotten to speak to the cook and left us alone.

'Doctor Crombie,' I told my father, 'says that it causes cancer.'

'Cancer!' my father exclaimed. 'Are you sure he didn't say insanity?' (It was a great period for insanity: loss of vitality leading to nervous debility and nervous debility becoming melancholia and eventually melancholia becoming madness. For some reasons these effects were said to come before marriage and not after.)

'He said cancer. An incurable disease, he said.'

'Odd!' my father remarked. He reassured me about playing trains, and Doctor Crombie's theory went out of my head for some years. I don't think my father can have mentioned it to anyone else except possibly my mother and that only as a joke. Cancer was as good a scare during puberty as madness – the standard of dishonesty among parents is a high one. They had themselves long ceased to believe in the threat of madness, but they used it as a convenience, and only after some years did they reach the conclusion that Doctor Crombie was a strictly honest man.

I had just left school by that time and I had not yet gone up to the university; Doctor Crombie's head was quite white by then, though his moustache stayed blond. We had become close friends, for we both liked observing trains, and sometimes on a summer's day we took a picnic-lunch and sat on the green mound of Bankstead Castle from which we could watch the line and see below it the canal with the bright-painted barges drawn by slow horses in the direction of Birmingham. We drank ginger-beer out of stone bottles and ate ham sandwiches while Doctor Crombie studied *Bradshaw.* When I want an image for innocence I think of those afternoons.

But the peace of the afternoon I am remembering now was disturbed. An immense goods-train of coal-waggons went by us – I counted sixty-three, which approached our record, but when I asked for his confirmation, Doctor Crombie had inexplicably forgotten to count.

'Is something the matter?' I asked.

'The school has asked me to resign,' he said, and he took off the gold-rimmed glasses and wiped them.

'Good heavens! Why?'

'The secrets of the consulting-room, my dear boy, are one-sided,' he said. 'The patient, though not the doctor, is at liberty to tell everything.'

A week later I learnt a little of what had happened. The story had spread rapidly from parent to parent, for this was not something which concerned small boys – this concerned all of them. Perhaps there was even an element of fear in the talk – fear that Doctor Crombie might be right. Incredible thought!

A boy whom I knew, a little younger than myself, called Fred Wright, who was still in the sixth form, had visited Doctor Crombie because of certain pains in the testicles. He had had his first woman in a street off Leicester Square on a half-day excursion – there were half-day excursions in those happy days of rival railway-companies – and he had taken his courage in his hands and visited Doctor Crombie. He was afraid that he had caught what was then known as a social disease. Doctor Crombie had reassured him – he was suffering from acidity, that was all, and he should be careful not to eat tomatoes, but Doctor Crombie went on, rashly and unnecessarily, to warn him, as he had warned all of us at thirteen . . .

Fred Wright had no reason to feel ashamed. Acidity can happen to anyone, and he didn't hesitate to tell his parents of the further advice which Doctor Crombie had given him. When I returned home that afternoon and questioned my parents, I found the story had already reached them as it had reached the school authorities. Parent after parent had checked with one another, and afterwards child after child was interrogated. Cancer as the result of masturbation was one thing – you had to discourage it somehow – but what right had Doctor Crombie to say that cancer was the result of prolonged sexual relations, even in a proper marriage recognized by Church and State? (It was unfortunate that Fred Wright's very virile father, unknown to his son, had already fallen a victim to the dread disease.)

I was even a little shaken myself. I had great affection for Doctor Crombie and great confidence in him. (I had never played trains all by myself after thirteen with the same pleasure as before his hygienic talk.) And the worst of it was that now I had fallen in love, hopelessly in love, with a girl in Castle Street with what we called then bobbed hair; she resembled in an innocent and provincial way two famous society sisters whose photographs appeared nearly every week in the *Daily Mail*. (The years seem to be returning on their tracks, and I see now everywhere the same face, the same hair, as I saw then, but alas, with little or no emotion.)

The next time I went out with Doctor Crombie to watch the trains I tackled him – shyly; there were still words I didn't like to use with my elders. 'Did you really tell Fred Wright that – marriage – is a cause of cancer?'

'Not marriage in itself, my boy. Any form of sexual congress.'

'Congress?' It was the first time I had heard the word used in that way. I thought of the Congress of Vienna.

'Making love,' Doctor Crombie said gruffly. 'I thought I had explained all that to you at the age of thirteen.'

'I just thought you were talking about playing trains alone,' I said.

'What do you mean, playing trains?' he asked with bewilderment as a fast passenger-train went by, in and out of Bankstead station, leaving a great ball of steam at either end of No. 2 platform. 'The 3.45 from Newcastle,' he said. 'I make it a minute and a quarter slow.'

'Three-quarters of a minute,' I said. We had no means of checking our watches. It was before the days of radio.

'I am ahead of the time,' Doctor Crombie said, 'and I expect to suffer inconvenience. The strange thing is that people here have only just noticed. I have been speaking to you boys on the subject of cancer for years.'

'Nobody realized that you meant marriage,' I said.

'One begins with first things first. You were, none of you, in those symposiums which I held, of an age to marry.'

'But maiden ladies,' I objected, 'they die of cancer too.'

'The definition of maiden in common use,' Doctor Crombie replied, looking at his watch as a goods-train went by towards Bletchley, 'is an unbroken hymen. A lady may have had prolonged sexual relations with herself or another without injuring the maidenhead.'

I became curious. A new world was opening to me.

'You mean girls play with themselves too?'

'Of course.'

'But the young don't often die of cancer, do they?'

'They can lay the foundations with their excesses. It was from that I wished to save you all.'

'And the saints,' I said, 'did none of them die of cancer?'

'I know very little about saints. I would hazard a guess that the percentage of such deaths in their case was a small one, but I have never taught that sexual congress is the sole cause of cancer: only that it is the most frequent.'

'But all married people don't die that way?'

'My boy, you would be surprised how seldom many

married people make love. A burst of enthusiasm and then a long retreat. The danger is necessarily less in those cases.'

'The more you love the greater the danger?'

'I'm afraid that is a truth which applies to more than the danger of cancer.'

I was too much in love myself to be easily convinced, but his answers came, I had to admit, quickly and readily. When I made some remark about statistics he quickly closed that avenue of hope. 'If they demand statistics,' Doctor Crombie said, 'statistics they shall have. They have suspected many causes in the past and based their suspicion on dubious and debatable statistics. White flour for example. It would not surprise me if one day they did not come to suspect even this little innocent comfort of mine' (he waved his cigarette in the direction of the Grand Junction Canal), 'but can they deny that statistically my solution outweighs all others? Almost one hundred per cent of those who die of cancer have practised sex.'

It was a statement impossible to deny, and for a little it silenced me. 'Aren't you afraid yourself?' I asked him at last.

'You know that I live alone. I am one of the few who have never been greatly tempted in that direction.'

'If all of us followed your advice,' I said gloomily, 'the world would cease to exist.'

'You mean the human race. The inter-pollination of flowers seems to have no ill side-effects.'

'And men were created only to die out.'

'I am no believer in the God of Genesis, young man. I think that the natural processes of evolution see to it that an animal becomes extinct when it makes a wrong accidental deviation. Man will perhaps follow the dinosaurs.' He looked at his watch. 'Now here is something wholly abnormal. The time is close on 4.10 and the four o'clock from Bletchley has not even been signalled. Yes, you may check the time, but this delay cannot be accounted for by a difference in watches.'

I have quite forgotten why the four o'clock was so delayed, and I had even forgotten Doctor Crombie and our conversation until this afternoon. Doctor Crombie survived his ruined practice for a few years and then died quietly one winter night of pneumonia following flu. I married four times, so little had I heeded Doctor Crombie's advice, and I only remembered his theory today when my specialist broke to me with rather exaggerated prudence and gravity the fact that I am suffering from cancer of the lungs. My sexual desires, now that I am past sixty, are beginning to diminish, and I am quite content to follow the dinosaurs into obscurity. Of course the doctors attribute the disease to my heavy indulgence in cigarettes, but it amuses me all the same to believe with Doctor Crombie that it has been caused by excesses of a more agreeable nature.

ANNA KAVAN

AIRING A GRIEVANCE

YESTERDAY I WENT to see my official advisor. I have visited him fairly often during the last three months in spite of the inconvenience and expense of these interviews. When one's affairs are in such a desperate state as mine, one is simply obliged to make use of any possible help; and this man D has been my last hope. He has been the only source of advice and assistance available to me, the only person with whom I could discuss my affairs: in fact, the only person to whom I could speak openly about the intolerable situation in which I have been placed. With everybody else I have had to be reserved and suspicious, remembering the motto, 'Silence is a friend that never betrays anyone'. For how can I tell whether the person to whom I am talking is not an enemy, or perhaps connected with my accusers or with those who will ultimately decide my fate?

Even with D I have always been on my guard. From the start there have been days when something seemed to warn me that he was not altogether to be trusted: yet on other occasions he filled me with confidence; and what was to become of me if I were deprived even of his support – unsatisfactory as it might be? No, I really couldn't face the future entirely alone, and so, for my own sake, I *must* not distrust him.

I went to him confidently enough in the first place. His name was known to me as that of a man, still young, but already very near the top of his profession. I considered myself lucky to have been placed in his charge, notwithstanding the long journey which separated me from him: in those early days I did not anticipate having to visit him frequently. At the beginning, I was favourably impressed by his solid town house, and by the room in which he received me with its wine-coloured velvet curtains, its comfortable arm-chairs, its valuable looking pieces of tapestry.

About the man himself I was not so certain. I have always believed that people of similar physical characteristics fall into corresponding mental groups, and he belonged to a type which I have constantly found unsympathetic. All the same, there could be no doubt as to his ability, he was excellently qualified to take charge of my case, and as I was only to meet him occasionally – and then in a professional and not in a social capacity – the fact of our being basically antipathetic to one another seemed of little significance. The main thing was that he should devote sufficient time to my affairs, that he should study my interests seriously; and this, to begin with, he seemed quite prepared to do.

It was only later, as things went from bad to worse, and I was obliged to consult him at shorter and shorter intervals, that I started to feel dubious about his goodwill towards me.

At our early meetings he always treated me with extreme consideration, even with deference, listening with the closest attention to everything I had to say, and in general impressing me with the grave importance of my case. Irrational as it may sound, it was this very attitude of his – originally so gratifying – which aroused my first vague suspicions. If he were really looking after my interests as thoroughly as he asserted, why was it necessary for him to behave in this almost propitiatory way which suggested either that he was trying to distract my attention from some possible negligence on his part, or that matters were not progressing as favourably as he affirmed? Yet, as I have previously mentioned, he had a knack of inspiring confidence, and with a few encouraging, convincing phrases he could dispel all my tenuous doubts and fears.

But presently another cause for suspicion pricked my uneasy mind. Ever since my introduction to D I had been aware of something dimly familiar about his face with the very black brows accentuating deep-set eyes into which I never looked long enough or directly enough to determine their colour but which I assumed to be dark brown. From time to time my thoughts idly pursued the half-remembered image which I could never quite manage to bring into full consciousness. Without ever really giving much attention to the subject, I think I finally decided that D must remind me of some portrait seen long before in a gallery, most probably somewhere abroad; for his countenance was decidedly foreign, and contained the curious balance of latent sensuality and dominant intellectualism seen to the best advantage in some of the work of El Greco. Then one day, just as I was leaving his house, the complete memory which had eluded me for so long, suddenly came to me with an impact sharp as a collision with a fellow pedestrian. It was no ancient portrait that D's face recalled to my mind, but a press photograph, and one that I had seen comparatively recently, one that was contained in an illustrated periodical which was probably still lying about somewhere in my living-room.

As soon as I got home I started to search through the papers which, in my preoccupied state of mind, I had allowed to accumulate in an untidy pile. It was not long before I found what I was looking for. The face of the young assassin, gazing darkly at me from the page, was, in all essentials, the same black-browed face that had confronted me a short time previously in the curtained seclusion of his handsome room.

Why did this accidental likeness make such an impression on me, I wonder? It is possible for a man to resemble a certain murderer in his outward appearance without possessing himself any violent tendencies; or if, as is more likely, he does possess them, without lacking sufficient restraint to hold them in check. One has only to think of D's responsible position, to look at his controlled, serene, intelligent face, to realize the fantastic nature of the comparison. The whole sequence of ideas is utterly grotesque, utterly illogical. And yet there it is; I can't banish it from my mind.

One must remember, too, that the man in the photograph was no common assassin, but a fanatic, a man of extraordinarily strong convictions, who killed not for personal gain, but for a principle, for what he considered to be the right. Is this an argument against D or in his favour? Sometimes I think one way, sometimes the other: I am quite unable to decide.

As a result of these prejudices – and of course there were others which would take too long to write down here – I decided to put my case in the hands of a different advisor. This was a serious step, not to be taken lightly, and I expended a great deal of time considering the subject before I finally sent off my application. Even after I had posted the letter I could not feel at all sure that I had done the right thing. Certainly, I had heard of people who changed their advisors, not once but several times, and of some who seemed to spend their whole time running from one to another: but I had always rather despised them for their instability, and the general feeling in the public mind was that the cases of these individuals would terminate badly. Still, on the whole, I felt that the exceptional circumstances warranted the change where I was concerned. In wording my letter of application I was particularly careful to avoid any statement that could possibly be taken as detrimental to D, merely stressing the point of how expensive and awkward it was for me to be continually undertaking the long journey to his house, and asking for my case to be transferred to someone in the university town near my home.

For several days I waited anxiously for an answer, only to receive at the end of that time a bundle of complicated forms to be filled up in duplicate. These I completed, sent off, and then waited again. How much of my life lately has consisted of this helpless, soul-destroying suspense! The waiting goes on and on, day after day, week after week, and yet one never gets used to it. Well, at last the reply came back on the usual stiff, pale blue paper, the very sight of which I have learned to dread. My request was refused. No explanation was given as to why a favour which had been granted to hundreds of people should be denied to me. But of course one can't expect explanations from these officials; their conduct is always completely autocratic and incalculable. All they condescended to add to the categorical negative was the statement that I was at liberty to dispense altogether with the services of an advisor should I prefer to do so.

I was so cast down after the receipt of this arbitrary communication that for two whole weeks I remained at home, absolutely inactive. I had not even the heart to go out of doors, but stayed in my room, saying that I was ill and seeing no one except the servant who brought my meals. Indeed, the plea of illness was no untruth, for I felt utterly wretched in body as well as in mind, exhausted, listless and depressed as if after a severe fever.

Alone in my room, I pondered endlessly over the situation. Why, in heaven's name, had the authorities refused my application when I knew for a fact that other people were allowed to change their advisors at will? Did the refusal mean that there was some special aspect of my case which differentiated it from the others? If this were so, it must surely indicate that a more serious view was taken of mine than of the rest, as I was to be denied ordinary privileges. If only I knew – if only I could find out something definite! With extreme care I drafted another letter and sent it off to the official address, politely, I'm afraid even servilely, beseeching an answer to my questions. What a fool I was to humiliate myself so uselessly, most likely for the benefit of a roomful of junior clerks who doubtless had a good laugh over my laboriously-thought-out composition before tossing it into the waste-paper basket! Naturally, no reply was forthcoming.

I waited a few days longer in a state of alternate agitation and despair that became hourly more unbearable. At last – yesterday – I reached a point where I could no longer endure so much tension. There was only one person in the whole world to whom I could unburden my mind, only one person who might conceivably be able to relieve my suspense, and that was D who was still, when all was said, my official advisor.

On the spur of the moment I decided to go and see him again. I was in a condition in which to take action of some sort had become an urgent necessity. I put on my things and went out to catch the train.

The sun was shining, and I was astonished to see that during the period I had remained indoors, too preoccupied with my troubles even to look out of the window, the season seemed to have passed from winter to spring. When last I had looked objectively at the hills I had seen a Breughel-like landscape of snow and sepia trees, but now the snow had vanished except for a narrow whiteness bordering the northern edge of the highest point of the wood. From the windows of the train I saw hares playing among the fine, emerald green lines of the winter wheat: the newly-ploughed earth in the valleys looked rich as velvet. I opened the carriage window and felt the soft rush of air which, not far away, carried the plover in their strange, reeling love dance. When the train slowed down between high banks I saw the glossy yellow cups of celandines in the grass.

Even in the city there was a feeling of gladness, of renewed life. People walked briskly towards appointments or dawdled before the shop windows with contented faces. Some whistled or sang quietly to themselves under cover of the traffic's noise, some swung their arms, some thrust their hands deep in their pockets, others had already discarded their overcoats. Flowers were being sold at the street corners. Although the sunlight could not reach to the bottom of the deep streets the house-tops were brightly gilded, and many eyes were raised automatically to the burnished roofs and the soft, promising sky.

I, too, was influenced by the beneficent atmosphere of the day. As I walked along, I determined to put the whole matter of the letter and its answer frankly before D, to conceal nothing from him, but to ask him what he thought lay behind this new official move. After all, I had not done anything that should offend him; my request for a change of advisor was perfectly justifiable on practical grounds. Nor had I any real reason for distrusting him. On the contrary, it was now more than ever essential that I should have implicit faith in him, since he alone was empowered to advance my cause. Surely, if only for the sake of his own high reputation, he would do everything possible to help me.

I reached his house and stood waiting for the door to be opened. A beggar was standing close to the area railings holding a tray of matches in front of him, a thin, youngish man of middle-class appearance, carefully shaved, and wearing a very old, neat, dark blue suit. Of course, the whole town is full of destitute people, one sees them everywhere, but I couldn't help wishing that I had not caught sight, just at this moment, of this particular man who looked as though he might be a schoolmaster fallen on evil days. We were so close together that I expected him to beg from me; but instead of that he stood without even glancing in my direction, without even troubling to display his matches to the passers-by, an expression of complete apathy on his face that in an instant began to dissipate for me all the optimistic influence of the day.

As I went inside the door, some part of my attention remained fixed on the respectable looking beggar, with whom I seemed in some way to connect myself. The thought crossed my mind that perhaps one day I, no longer able to work, my small fortune absorbed in advisor's fees, my friends irreparably alienated, might be placed in the same situation as he.

The manservant informed me that D had been called out on urgent business but that he would be back before long. I was shown into a room and asked to wait. Alone here, all my depression, briefly banished by the sun, began to return. After the spring-like air outside, the room felt close and oppressive, but a sort of gloomy inertia prevented me from opening one of the thickly draped windows. An enormous grandfather clock in the corner didactically ticked the minutes away. Listening to that insistent ticking, a sense of abysmal futility gradually overwhelmed me. The fact of D's absence, that he should choose to-day of all days to keep me waiting in this dismal room, created the worst possible impression on my overwrought nerves. A feeling of despair, as if every effort I might make would inevitably be in vain, took possession of me. I sat lethargically on a straight-backed, uncomfortable chair with a leather seat, gazing indifferently at the clock, the hands of which had now completed a half circle since my arrival. I thought of going away, but lacked even the energy to move. An apathy, similar to that displayed by the beggar outside, had come over me. I felt convinced that already, before I had even spoken to D, the visit had been a failure.

Suddenly the servant returned to say that D was at my disposal. But now I no longer wanted to see him, it was only with the greatest difficulty that I forced myself to stand up and follow the man into the room where my advisor sat at his desk. I don't know why the sight of him sitting in his accustomed pose should have suggested to me the idea that he had not really been called out at all, but had been sitting there the whole time, keeping me waiting for some ulterior motive of his own; perhaps to produce in me just such a sensation of despair as I now experienced.

We shook hands, I sat down and began to speak, driving my sluggish tongue to frame words that seemed useless even before they were uttered. Was it my fancy that D listened less attentively than on previous occasions, fidgeting with his fountain pen or with the papers in front of him? It was not long before something in his attitude convinced me that he was thoroughly acquainted with the whole story of my letter of application and its sequel. No doubt the authorities had referred the matter to him – with what bias, with what implication? And now my indifferent mood changed to one of suspicion and alarm as I tried to guess what this intercommunication portended.

I heard myself advancing the old argument of inconvenience, explaining in hesitant tones that in order to spend less than an hour with him I must be nearly six hours on the double journey. And then I heard him answer that I should no longer have cause to complain of this tedious travelling, as he was just about to start on a holiday of indefinite length and would undertake no further work until his return.

If I felt despairing before you can imagine how this information affected me. Somehow I took leave of him, somehow found my way through the streets, somehow reached the train which carried me across the now sunless landscape.

How hard it is to sit at home with nothing to do but wait. To wait – the most difficult thing in the whole world. To wait – with no living soul in whom to confide one's doubts, one's fears, one's relentless hopes. To wait – not knowing whether D's words are to be construed into an official edict depriving me of all assistance, or whether he intends to take up my case again in the distant future, or whether the case is already concluded. To wait – only to wait – without even the final merciful deprivation of hope.

Sometimes I think that some secret court must have tried and condemned me, unheard, to this heavy sentence.

W. SOMERSET MAUGHAM

LORD MOUNTDRAGO

DR. AUDLIN LOOKED at the clock on his desk. It was twenty minutes to six. He was surprised that his patient was late, for Lord Mountdrago prided himself on his punctuality; he had a sententious way of expressing himself which gave the air of an epigram to a commonplace remark, and he was in the habit of saying that punctuality is a compliment you pay to the intelligent and a rebuke you administer to the stupid. Lord Mountdrago's appointment was for five-thirty.

There was in Dr. Audlin's appearance nothing to attract attention. He was tall and spare, with narrow shoulders and something of a stoop; his hair was grey and thin; his long, sallow face deeply lined. He was not more than fifty, but he looked older. His eyes, pale-blue and rather large, were weary. When you had been with him for a while you noticed that they moved very little; they remained fixed on your face, but so empty of expression were they that it was no discomfort. They seldom lit up. They gave no clue to his thoughts nor changed with the words he spoke. If you were of an observant turn it might have struck you that he blinked much less often than most of us. His hands were on the large side, with long, tapering fingers; they were soft, but firm, cool but not clammy. You could never have said what Dr. Audlin wore unless you had made a point of looking. His clothes were dark. His tie was black. His dress made his sallow lined face paler, and his pale eyes more wan. He gave you the impression of a very sick man.

Dr. Audlin was a psycho-analyst. He had adopted the profession by accident and practised it with misgiving. When the war broke out he had not been long qualified and was getting experience at various hospitals; he offered his services to the authorities, and after a time was sent out to France. It was then that he discovered his singular gift. He could allay certain pains by the touch of his cool, firm hands, and by talking to them often induce sleep in men who were suffering from sleeplessness. He spoke slowly. His voice had no particular colour, and its tone did not alter with the words he uttered, but it was musical, soft and lulling. He told the men that they must rest, that they mustn't worry, that they must sleep; and rest stole into their jaded bones, tranquillity pushed their anxieties away, like a man finding a place for himself on a crowded bench, and slumber fell on their tired eyelids like the light rain of spring upon the fresh-turned earth. Dr. Audlin found that by speaking to men with that low, monotonous voice of his, by looking at them with his pale, quiet eyes, by stroking their weary foreheads with his long firm hands, he could soothe their perturbations, resolve the conflicts that distracted them and banish the phobias that made their lives a torment. Sometimes he effected cures that seemed miraculous. He restored speech to a man who, after being buried under the earth by a bursting shell, had been struck dumb, and he gave back the use of his limbs to another who had been paralysed after a crash in a plane. He could not understand his powers; he was of a sceptical turn, and though they say that in circumstances of this kind the first thing is to believe in yourself, he never quite succeeded in doing that; and it was only the outcome of his activities, patent to the most incredulous observer, that obliged him to admit that he had some faculty, coming from he knew not where, obscure and uncertain, that enabled him to do things for which he could offer no explanation. When the war was over he went to Vienna and studied there, and afterwards to Zurich; and then settled down in London to practise the art he had so strangely acquired. He had been practising now for fifteen years, and had attained, in the speciality he followed, a distinguished reputation. People told one another of the amazing things he had done, and though his fees were high, he had as many patients as he had time to see. Dr. Audlin knew that he had achieved some very extraordinary results; he had saved men from suicide, others from the lunatic asylum, he had assuaged griefs that embittered useful lives, he had turned unhappy marriages into happy ones, he had eradicated abnormal instincts and thus delivered not a few from a hateful bondage, he had given health to the sick in spirit; he had done all this, and yet at the back of his mind remained the suspicion that he was little more than a quack.

It went against his grain to exercise a power that he could not understand, and it offended his honesty to trade on the faith of the people he treated when he had no faith in himself. He was rich enough now to live without working, and the work exhausted him; a dozen times he had been on the point of giving up practice. He knew all that Freud and Jung and the rest of them had written. He was not satisfied; he had an intimate conviction that all their theory was hocus-pocus, and yet there the results were, incomprehensible, but manifest. And what had he not seen of human nature during the fifteen years that patients had been coming to his dingy back room in Wimpole Street? The revelations that had been poured into his ears, sometimes only too willingly, sometimes with shame, with reservations, with anger, had long ceased to surprise him. Nothing could shock him any longer. He knew by now that men were liars, he knew how extravagant was their vanity; he knew far worse than that about them; but he knew that it was not for him to judge or to condemn. But year by year as these terrible confidences were imparted to him his face grew a little greyer, its lines a little more marked and his pale eyes more weary. He seldom laughed, but now and again when for relaxation he read a novel he smiled. Did their authors really think the men and women they wrote of were like that? If they only knew how much more complicated they were, how much more unexpected, what irreconcilable elements coexisted within their souls and what dark and sinister contentions afflicted them!

It was a quarter to six. Of all the strange cases he had been called upon to deal with Dr. Audlin could remember none stranger than that of Lord Mountdrago. For one thing the personality of his patient made it singular. Lord Mountdrago was an able and a distinguished man. Appointed Secretary for Foreign Affairs when still under forty, now after three years in office he had seen his policy prevail. It was generally acknowledged that he was the ablest politician in the Conservative Party, and only the fact that his father was a peer, on whose death he would no longer be able to sit in the House of Commons, made it impossible for him to aim at the premiership. But if in these democratic times it is out of the question for a Prime Minister of England to be in the House of Lords, there was nothing to prevent Lord Mountdrago from continuing to be Secretary for Foreign Affairs in successive Conservative administrations and so for long directing the foreign policy of his country.

Lord Mountdrago had many good qualities. He had intelligence and industry. He was widely travelled, and spoke several languages fluently. From early youth he had specialized in foreign affairs, and had conscientiously made himself acquainted with the political and economic circumstances of other countries. He had courage, insight and determination. He was a good speaker, both on the platform and in the House, clear, precise and often witty. He was a brilliant debater and his gift of repartee was celebrated. He had a fine presence: he was a tall, handsome man, rather bald and somewhat too stout, but this gave him solidity and an air of maturity that were of service to him. As a young man he had been something of an athlete and had rowed in the Oxford boat, and he was known to be one of the best shots in England. At twenty-four he had married a girl of eighteen whose father was a duke and her mother a great American heiress, so that she had both position and wealth, and by her he had had two sons. For several years they had lived privately apart, but in public united, so that appearances were saved, and no other attachment on either side had given the gossips occasion to whisper. Lord Mountdrago indeed was too ambitious, too hard-working, and it must be added too patriotic, to be tempted by any pleasures that might interfere with his career. He had, in short, a great deal to make him a popular and successful figure. He had unfortunately great defects.

He was a fearful snob. You would not have been surprised at this if his father had been the first holder of the title. That the son of an ennobled lawyer, a manufacturer or a distiller, should attach an inordinate importance to his rank is understandable. The earldom held by Lord Mountdrago's father was created by Charles II, and the barony held by the first Earl dated from the Wars of the Roses. For three hundred years the successive holders of the title had allied themselves with the noblest families of England. But Lord Mountdrago was as conscious of his birth as a *nouveau riche* is conscious of his money. He never missed an opportunity of impressing it upon others. He had beautiful manners when he chose to display them, but this he did only with people whom he regarded as his equals. He was coldly insolent to those whom he looked upon as his social inferiors. He was rude to his servants and insulting to his secretaries. The subordinate officials in the government offices to which he had been successively attached feared and hated him. His arrogance was horrible. He knew that he was a great deal cleverer than most of the persons he had to do with, and never hesitated to apprise them of the fact. He had no patience with the infirmities of human nature. He felt himself born to command and was irritated with people who expected him to listen to their arguments or wished to hear the reasons for his decisions. He was immeasurably selfish. He looked upon any service that was rendered him as a right due to his rank and intelligence and therefore deserving of no gratitude. It never entered his head that he was called upon to do anything for others. He had many enemies: he despised them. He knew no one who merited his assistance, his sympathy or his compassion. He had no friends. He was distrusted by his chiefs, because they doubted his loyalty; he was unpopular with his party, because he was overbearing and discourteous; and yet his merit was so great, his patriotism so evident, his intelligence so solid and his management of affairs so brilliant, that they had to put up with him. And what made it possible to do this was that on occasion he could be enchanting: when he was with persons whom he considered his equals, or whom he wished to captivate, in the company of foreign dignitaries or women of distinction, he could be gay, witty and debonair; his manners then reminded you that in his veins ran the same blood as had run in the veins of Lord Chesterfield; he could tell a story with point, he could be natural, sensible and even profound. You were surprised at the extent of his knowledge and the sensitiveness of his taste. You thought him the best company in the world; you forgot that he had insulted you the day before and was quite capable of cutting you dead the next.

Lord Mountdrago almost failed to become Dr. Audlin's patient. A secretary rang up the doctor and told him that his lordship, wishing to consult him, would be glad if he would come to his house at ten o'clock on the following morning. Dr. Audlin answered that he was unable to go to Lord Mountdrago's house, but would be pleased to give him an appointment at his consulting-room at five o'clock on the next day but one. The secretary took the message and presently rang back to say that Lord Mountdrago insisted on seeing Dr. Audlin in his own house and the doctor could fix his own fee. Dr. Audlin replied that he only saw patients in his consulting-room and expressed his regret that unless Lord Mountdrago was prepared to come to him he could not give him his attention. In a quarter of an hour a brief message was delivered to him that his lordship would come not next day but one, but next day, at five.

When Lord Mountdrago was then shown in he did not come forward, but stood at the door and insolently looked the doctor up and down. Dr. Audlin perceived that he was in a rage; he gazed at him, silently, with still eyes. He saw a big heavy man, with greying hair, receding on the forehead so that it gave nobility to his brow, a puffy face with bold regular features and an expression of haughtiness. He had somewhat the look of one of the Bourbon sovereigns of the eighteenth century.

'It seems that it is as difficult to see you as a Prime Minister, Dr. Audlin. I'm an extremely busy man.'

'Won't you sit down?' said the doctor.

His face showed no sign that Lord Mountdrago's speech in any way affected him. Dr. Audlin sat in his chair at the desk. Lord Mountdrago still stood and his frown darkened.

'I think I should tell you that I am His Majesty's Secretary for Foreign Affairs,' he said acidly.

'Won't you sit down?' the doctor repeated.

Lord Mountdrago made a gesture, which might have suggested that he was about to turn on his heel and stalk out of the room; but if that was his intention he apparently thought better of it. He seated himself. Dr. Audlin opened a large book and took up his pen. He wrote without looking at his patient.

'How old are you?'

'Forty-two.'

'Are you married?'

'Yes.'

'How long have you been married?'

'Eighteen years.'

'Have you any children?'

'I have two sons.'

Dr. Audlin noted down the facts as Lord Mountdrago abruptly answered his questions. Then he leaned back in his chair and looked at him. He did not speak; he just looked, gravely, with pale eyes that did not move.

'Why have you come to see me?' he asked at length.

'I've heard about you. Lady Canute is a patient of yours, I understand. She tells me you've done her a certain amount of good.'

Dr. Audlin did not reply. His eyes remained fixed on the other's face, but they were so empty of expression that you might have thought he did not even see him.

'I can't do miracles,' he said at length. Not a smile, but the shadow of a smile flickered in his eyes. 'The Royal College of Physicians would not approve of it if I did.'

Lord Mountdrago gave a brief chuckle. It seemed to lessen his hostility. He spoke more amiably.

'You have a very remarkable reputation. People seem to believe in you.'

'Why have you come to me?' repeated Dr. Audlin.

Now it was Lord Mountdrago's turn to be silent. It looked as though he found it hard to answer. Dr. Audlin waited. At last Lord Mountdrago seemed to make an effort. He spoke.

'I'm in perfect health. Just as a matter of routine I had myself examined by my own doctor the other day, Sir Augustus Fitzherbert, I daresay you've heard of him, and he tells me I have the physique of a man of thirty. I work hard, but I'm never tired, and I enjoy my work. I smoke very little and I'm an extremely moderate drinker. I take a sufficiency of exercise and I lead a regular life. I am a perfectly sound, normal, healthy man. I quite expect you to think it very silly and childish of me to consult you.'

Dr. Audlin saw that he must help him.

'I don't know if I can do anything to help you. I'll try. You're distressed?'

Lord Mountdrago frowned.

'The work that I'm engaged in is important. The decisions I am called upon to make can easily affect the welfare of the country and even the peace of the world. It is essential that my judgement should be balanced and my brain clear. I look upon it as my duty to eliminate any cause of worry that may interfere with my usefulness.'

Dr. Audlin had never taken his eyes off him. He saw a great deal. He saw behind his patient's pompous manner and arrogant pride an anxiety that he could not dispel.

'I asked you to be good enough to come here because I know by experience that it's easier for someone to speak openly in the dingy surroundings of a doctor's consulting-room than in his accustomed environment.'

'They're certainly dingy,' said Lord Mountdrago acidly. He paused. It was evident that this man who had so much self-assurance, so quick and decided a mind that he was never at a loss, at this moment was embarrassed. He smiled in order to show the doctor that he was at his ease, but his eyes betrayed his disquiet. When he spoke again it was with unnatural heartiness.

'The whole thing's so trivial that I can hardly bring myself to bother you with it. I'm afraid you'll just tell me not to be a fool and waste your valuable time.'

'Even things that seem very trivial may have their importance. They can be a symptom of a deep-seated derangement. And my time is entirely at your disposal.'

Dr. Audlin's voice was low and grave. The monotone in which he spoke was strangely soothing. Lord Mountdrago at length made up his mind to be frank.

'The fact is I've been having some very tiresome dreams lately. I know it's silly to pay any attention to them, but – well, the honest truth is that I'm afraid, they've got on my nerves.'

'Can you describe any of them to me?'

Lord Mountdrago smiled, but the smile that tried to be careless was only rueful.

'They're so idiotic, I can hardly bring myself to narrate them.'

'Never mind.'

'Well, the first I had was about a month ago. I dreamt that I was at a party at Connemara House. It was an official party. The King and Queen were to be there and of course decorations were worn. I was wearing my ribbon and my star. I went into a sort of cloakroom they have to take off my coat.

There was a little man there called Owen Griffiths, who's a Welsh Member of Parliament, and to tell you the truth, I was surprised to see him. He's very common, and I said to myself: "Really, Lydia Connemara is going too far, whom will she ask next?" I thought he looked at me rather curiously, but I didn't take any notice of him; in fact I cut the little bounder and walked upstairs. I suppose you've never been there?'

'Never.'

'No, it's not the sort of house you'd ever be likely to go to. It's a rather vulgar house, but it's got a very fine marble staircase, and the Connemaras were at the top receiving their guests. Lady Connemara gave me a look of surprise when I shook hands with her, and began to giggle; I didn't pay much attention, she's a very silly, ill-bred woman and her manners are no better than those of her ancestress whom King Charles II made a duchess. I must say the reception rooms at Connemara House are stately. I walked through, nodding to a number of people and shaking hands; then I saw the German Ambassador talking with one of the Austrian Archdukes. I particularly wanted to have a word with him, so I went up and held out my hand. The moment the Archduke saw me he burst into a roar of laughter. I was deeply affronted. I looked him up and down sternly, but he only laughed the more. I was about to speak to him rather sharply, when there was a sudden hush and I realized that the King and Queen had come. Turning my back on the Archduke, I stepped forward, and then, quite suddenly, I noticed that I hadn't got any trousers on. I was in short silk drawers, and I wore scarlet sock-suspenders. No wonder Lady Connemara had giggled; no wonder the Archduke had laughed! I can't tell you what that moment was. An agony of shame. I awoke in a cold sweat. Oh, you don't know the relief I felt to find it was only a dream.'

'It's the kind of dream that's not so very uncommon,' said Dr. Audlin.

'I daresay not. But an odd thing happened next day. I was in the lobby of the House of Commons, when that fellow Griffiths walked slowly past me. He deliberately looked down at my legs and then he looked me full in the face and I was almost certain he winked. A ridiculous thought came to me. He'd been there the night before and seen me make that ghastly exhibition of myself and was enjoying the joke. But of course I knew that was impossible because it was only a dream. I gave him an icy glare and he walked on. But he was grinning his head off.'

Lord Mountdrago took his handkerchief out of his pocket and wiped the palms of his hands. He was making no attempt now to conceal his perturbation. Dr. Audlin never took his eyes off him.

'Tell me another dream.'

'It was the night after, and it was even more absurd than the first one. I dreamt that I was in the House. There was a debate on foreign affairs which not only the country, but the world, had been looking forward to with the gravest concern. The government had decided on a change in their policy which vitally affected the future of the Empire. The occasion was historic. Of course the House was crowded. All the ambassadors were there. The galleries were packed. It fell to me to make the important speech of the evening. I had prepared it carefully. A man like me has enemies, there are a lot of people who resent my having achieved the position I have at an age when even the cleverest men are content with situations of relative obscurity, and I was determined that my speech should not only be worthy of the occasion, but should silence my detractors. It excited me to think that the whole world was hanging on my lips. I rose to my feet.

If you've ever been in the House you'll know how members chat to one another during a debate, rustle papers and turn over reports. The silence was the silence of the grave when I began to speak. Suddenly I caught sight of that odious little bounder on one of the benches opposite, Griffiths the Welsh member; he put out his tongue at me. I don't know if you've ever heard a vulgar music-hall song called *A Bicycle Made for Two*. It was very popular a great many years ago. To show Griffiths how completely I despised him I began to sing it. I sang the first verse right through. There was a moment's surprise, and when I finished they cried "Hear, hear," on the opposite benches. I put up my hand to silence them and sang the second verse. The House listened to me in stony silence and I felt the song wasn't going down very well. I was vexed, for I have a good baritone voice, and I was determined that they should do me justice. When I started the third verse the members began to laugh; in an instant the laughter spread; the ambassadors, the strangers in the Distinguished Strangers' Gallery, the ladies in the Ladies' Gallery, the reporters, they shook, they bellowed, they held their sides, they rolled in their seats; everyone was overcome with laughter except the ministers on the Front Bench immediately behind me. In that incredible, in that unprecedented uproar, they sat petrified. I gave them a glance, and suddenly the enormity of what I had done fell upon me. I had made myself the laughing-stock of the whole world. With misery I realized that I should have to resign. I woke and knew it was only a dream.'

Lord Mountdrago's grand manner had deserted him as he narrated this, and now having finished he was pale and trembling. But with an effort he pulled himself together. He forced a laugh to his shaking lips.

'The whole thing was so fantastic that I couldn't help being amused. I didn't give it another thought, and when I went into the House on the following afternoon I was feeling in very good form. The debate was dull, but I had to be there, and I read some documents that required my attention. For some reason I chanced to look up and I saw that Griffiths was speaking. He has an unpleasant Welsh accent and an unprepossessing appearance. I couldn't imagine that he had anything to say that it was worth my while to listen to, and I was about to return to my papers when he quoted two lines from *A Bicycle Made for Two*. I couldn't help glancing at him and I saw that his eyes were fixed on me with a grin of bitter mockery. I faintly shrugged my shoulders. It was comic that a scrubby little Welsh member should look at me like that. It was an odd coincidence that he should quote two lines from that disastrous song that I'd sung all through in my dream. I began to read my papers again, but I don't mind telling you that I found it difficult to concentrate on them. I was a little puzzled. Owen Griffiths had been in my first dream, the one at Connemara House, and I'd received a very definite impression afterwards that he knew the sorry figure I'd cut. Was it a mere coincidence that he had just quoted those two lines? I asked myself if it was possible that he was dreaming the same dreams as I was. But of course the idea was preposterous and I determined not to give it a second thought.'

There was a silence. Dr. Audlin looked at Lord Mountdrago and Lord Mountdrago looked at Dr. Audlin.

'Other people's dreams are very boring. My wife used to dream occasionally and insist on telling me her dreams next day with circumstantial detail. I found it maddening.'

Dr. Audlin faintly smiled.

'You're not boring me.'

'I'll tell you one more dream I had a few days later.

I dreamt that I went into a public-house at Limehouse. I've never been to Limehouse in my life and I don't think I've ever been in a public-house since I was at Oxford, and yet I saw the street and the place I went into as exactly as if I were at home there. I went into a room, I don't know whether they call it the saloon bar or the private bar; there was a fireplace and a large leather armchair on one side of it, and on the other a small sofa; a bar ran the whole length of the room and over it you could see into the public bar. Near the door was a round marble-topped table and two armchairs beside it. It was a Saturday night and the place was packed. It was brightly lit, but the smoke was so thick that it made my eyes smart. I was dressed like a rough, with a cap on my head and a handkerchief round my neck. It seemed to me that most of the people there were drunk. I thought it rather amusing. There was a gramophone going, or the radio, I don't know which, and in front of the fireplace two women were doing a grotesque dance. There was a little crowd round them, laughing, cheering and singing. I went up to have a look and some man said to me: "'Ave a drink, Bill?" There were glasses on the table full of a dark liquid which I understand is called brown ale. He gave me a glass and not wishing to be conspicuous I drank it. One of the women who were dancing broke away from the other and took hold of the glass. "'Ere, what's the idea?" she said. "That's my beer you're putting away." "Oh, I'm so sorry," I said, "this gentleman offered it me and I very naturally thought it was his to offer." "All right, mate," she said, "I don't mind. You come an' 'ave a dance with me." Before I could protest she'd caught hold of me and we were dancing together. And then I found myself sitting in the armchair with the woman on my lap and we were sharing a glass of beer. I should tell you that sex has never played any great part in my life. I married young because in my position it was desirable that I should marry, but also in order to settle once for all the question of sex. I had the two sons I had made up my mind to have, and then I put the whole matter on one side. I've always been too busy to give much thought to that kind of thing, and living so much in the public eye as I do it would have been madness to do anything that might give rise to scandal. The greatest asset a politician can have is a blameless record as far as women are concerned. I have no patience with the men who smash up their careers for women. I only despise them. The woman I had on my knees was drunk; she wasn't pretty and she wasn't young: in fact, she was just a blowsy old prostitute. She filled me with disgust, and yet when she put her mouth to mine and kissed me, though her breath stank of beer and her teeth were decayed, though I loathed myself, I wanted her – I wanted her with all my soul. Suddenly I heard a voice. "That's right, old boy, have a good time." I looked up and there was Owen Griffiths. I tried to spring out of the chair, but that horrible woman wouldn't let me. "Don't you pay no attention to 'im," she said, "'e's only one of them nosy-parkers." "You go to it," he said. "I know Moll. She'll give you your money's worth all right." You know, I wasn't so much annoyed at his seeing me in that absurd situation as angry that he should address me as "old boy." I pushed the woman aside and stood up and faced him. "I don't know you and I don't want to know you," I said. "I know you all right," he said. "And my advice to you, Molly, is, see that you get your money, he'll bilk you if he can." There was a bottle of beer standing on the table close by. Without a word I seized it by the neck and hit him over the head with it as hard as I could. I made such a violent gesture that it woke me up.'

'A dream of that sort is not incomprehensible,' said Dr.

Audlin. 'It is the revenge nature takes on persons of un-impeachable character.'

'The story's idiotic. I haven't told it you for its own sake. I've told it you for what happened next day. I wanted to look up something in a hurry and I went into the library of the House. I got the book and began reading. I hadn't noticed when I sat down that Griffiths was sitting in a chair close by me. Another of the Labour Members came in and went up to him. "Hullo, Owen," he said to him, "you're looking pretty dicky to-day." "I've got an awful headache," he answered. "I feel as if I'd been cracked over the head with a bottle."'

Now Lord Mountdrago's face was grey with anguish.

'I knew then that the idea I'd had and dismissed as preposterous was true. I knew that Griffiths was dreaming my dreams and that he remembered them as well as I did.'

'It may also have been a coincidence.'

'When he spoke he didn't speak to his friend, he deliberately spoke to me. He looked at me with sullen resentment.'

'Can you offer any suggestion why this same man should come into your dreams?'

'None.'

Dr. Audlin's eyes had not left his patient's face and he saw that he lied. He had a pencil in his hand and he drew a straggling line or two on his blotting-paper. It often took a long time to get people to tell the truth, and yet they knew that unless they told it he could do nothing for them.

'The dream you've just described to me took place just over three weeks ago. Have you had any since?'

'Every night.'

'And does this man Griffiths come into them all?'

'Yes.'

The doctor drew more lines on his blotting-paper. He

wanted the silence, the drabness, the dull light of that little room to have its effect on Lord Mountdrago's sensibility. Lord Mountdrago threw himself back in his chair and turned his head away so that he should not see the other's grave eyes.

'Dr. Audlin, you must do something for me. I'm at the end of my tether. I shall go mad if this goes on. I'm afraid to go to sleep. Two or three nights I haven't. I've sat up reading and when I felt drowsy put on my coat and walked till I was exhausted. But I must have sleep. With all the work I have to do I must be at concert pitch; I must be in complete control of all my faculties. I need rest; sleep brings me none. I no sooner fall asleep than my dreams begin, and he's always there, that vulgar little cad, grinning at me, mocking me, despising me. It's a monstrous persecution. I tell you, doctor, I'm not the man of my dreams; it's not fair to judge me by them. Ask anyone you like. I'm an honest, upright, decent man. No one can say anything against my moral character either private or public. My whole ambition is to serve my country and maintain its greatness. I have money, I have rank, I'm not exposed to many of the temptations of lesser men, so that it's no credit to me to be incorruptible; but this I can claim, that no honour, no personal advantage, no thought of self would induce me to swerve by a hair's-breadth from my duty. I've sacrificed everything to become the man I am. Greatness is my aim. Greatness is within my reach and I'm losing my nerve. I'm not that mean, despicable, cowardly, lewd creature that horrible little man sees. I've told you three of my dreams; they're nothing; that man has seen me do things that are so beastly, so horrible, so shameful, that even if my life depended on it I wouldn't tell them. And he remembers them. I can hardly meet the derision and disgust I see in his eyes and I even hesitate to speak because I know

252

my words can seem to him nothing but utter humbug. He's seen me do things that no man with any self-respect would do, things for which men are driven out of the society of their fellows and sentenced to long terms of imprisonment; he's heard the foulness of my speech; he's seen me not only ridiculous, but revolting. He despises me and he no longer pretends to conceal it. I tell you that if you can't do something to help me I shall either kill myself or kill him.'

'I wouldn't kill him if I were you,' said Dr. Audlin, coolly, in that soothing voice of his. 'In this country the consequences of killing a fellow-creature are awkward.'

'I shouldn't be hanged for it, if that's what you mean. Who would know that I'd killed him? That dream of mine has shown me how. I told you, the day after I'd hit him over the head with a beer-bottle he had such a headache that he couldn't see straight. He said so himself. That shows that he can feel with his waking body what happens to his body asleep. It's not with a bottle I shall hit him next time. One night, when I'm dreaming, I shall find myself with a knife in my hand or a revolver in my pocket, I must because I want to so intensely, and then I shall seize my opportunity. I'll stick him like a pig; I'll shoot him like a dog. In the heart. And then I shall be free of this fiendish persecution.'

Some people might have thought that Lord Mountdrago was mad; after all the years during which Dr. Audlin had been treating the diseased souls of men he knew how thin a line divides those whom we call sane from those whom we call insane. He knew how often in men who to all appearance were healthy and normal, who were seemingly devoid of imagination, and who fulfilled the duties of common life with credit to themselves and with benefit to their fellows, when you gained their confidence, when you tore away the mask they wore to the world, you found not only hideous abnormality, but kinks so strange, mental extravagances so fantastic, that in that respect you could only call them lunatic. If you put them in an asylum not all the asylums in the world would be large enough. Anyhow, a man was not certifiable because he had strange dreams and they had shattered his nerve. The case was singular, but it was only an exaggeration of others that had come under Dr. Audlin's observation; he was doubtful, however, whether the methods of treatment that he had so often found efficacious would here avail.

'Have you consulted any other member of my profession?' he asked.

'Only Sir Augustus. I merely told him that I suffered from nightmares. He said I was overworked and recommended me to go for a cruise. That's absurd. I can't leave the Foreign Office just now when the international situation needs constant attention. I'm indispensable, and I know it. On my conduct at the present juncture my whole future depends. He gave me sedatives. They had no effect. He gave me tonics. They were worse than useless. He's an old fool.'

'Can you give any reason why it should be this particular man who persists in coming into your dreams?'

'You asked me that question before. I answered it.'

That was true. But Dr. Audlin had not been satisfied with the answer.

'Just now you talked of persecution. Why should Owen Griffiths want to persecute you?'

'I don't know.'

Lord Mountdrago's eyes shifted a little. Dr. Audlin was sure that he was not speaking the truth.

'Have you ever done him an injury?'

'Never.'

Lord Mountdrago made no movement, but Dr. Audlin had a queer feeling that he shrank into his skin. He saw before him a large, proud man who gave the impression that the questions put to him were an insolence, and yet for all that, behind that façade, was something shifting and startled that made you think of a frightened animal in a trap. Dr. Audlin leaned forward and by the power of his eyes forced Lord Mountdrago to meet them.

'Are you quite sure?'

'Quite sure. You don't seem to understand that our ways lead along different paths. I don't wish to harp on it, but I must remind you that I am a Minister of the Crown and Griffiths is an obscure Member of the Labour Party. Naturally there's no social connection between us; he's a man of very humble origin, he's not the sort of person I should be likely to meet at any of the houses I go to; and politically our respective stations are so far separated that we could not possibly have anything in common.'

'I can do nothing for you unless you tell me the complete truth.'

Lord Mountdrago raised his eyebrows. His voice was rasping.

'I'm not accustomed to having my word doubted, Dr. Audlin. If you're going to do that I think to take up any more of your time can only be a waste of mine. If you will kindly let my secretary know what your fee is he will see that a cheque is sent to you.'

For all the expression that was to be seen on Dr. Audlin's face you might have thought that he simply had not heard what Lord Mountdrago said. He continued to look steadily into his eyes and his voice was grave and low.

'Have you done anything to this man that *he* might look upon as an injury?'

Lord Mountdrago hesitated. He looked away, and then, as though there were in Dr. Audlin's eyes a compelling force that he could not resist, looked back. He answered sulkily:

'Only if he was a dirty, second-rate little cad.'

'But that is exactly what you've described him to be.'

Lord Mountdrago sighed. He was beaten. Dr. Audlin knew that the sigh meant he was going at last to say what he had till then held back. Now he had no longer to insist. He dropped his eyes and began again drawing vague geometrical figures on his blotting-paper. The silence lasted two or three minutes.

'I'm anxious to tell you everything that can be of any use to you. If I didn't mention this before, it's only because it was so unimportant that I didn't see how it could possibly have anything to do with the case. Griffiths won a seat at the last election and he began to make a nuisance of himself almost at once. His father's a miner, and he worked in a mine himself when he was a boy; he's been a schoolmaster in the board schools and a journalist. He's that half-baked, conceited intellectual, with inadequate knowledge, ill-considered ideas and impractical plans, that compulsory education has brought forth from the working-classes. He's a scrawny, grey-faced man, who looks half-starved, and he's always very slovenly in appearance; heaven knows members nowadays don't bother much about their dress, but his clothes are an outrage to the dignity of the House. They're ostentatiously shabby, his collar's never clean and his tie's never tied properly; he looks as if he hadn't had a bath for a month and his hands are filthy. The Labour Party have two or three fellows on the Front Bench who've got a certain ability, but the rest of them don't amount to much. In the kingdom of the blind the one-eyed man is king: because Griffiths is glib and has a lot of superficial information on a number of subjects, the Whips on his side began to put him up to speak whenever there was a chance. It appeared that he fancied himself on foreign affairs, and he was continually asking me silly, tiresome questions. I don't mind telling you that I made a point of snubbing him as soundly as I thought he deserved. From the beginning I hated the way he talked, his whining voice and his vulgar accent; he had nervous mannerisms that intensely irritated me. He talked rather shyly, hesitatingly, as though it were torture to him to speak and yet he was forced to by some inner passion, and often he used to say some very disconcerting things. I'll admit that now and again he had a sort of tub-thumping eloquence. It had a certain influence over the ill-regulated minds of the members of his party. They were impressed by his earnestness and they weren't, as I was, nauseated by his sentimentality. A certain sentimentality is the common coin of political debate. Nations are governed by self-interest, but they prefer to believe that their aims are altruistic, and the politician is justified if with fair words and fine phrases he can persuade the electorate that the hard bargain he is driving for his country's advantage tends to the good of humanity. The mistake people like Griffiths make is to take these fair words and fine phrases at their face value. He's a crank, and a noxious crank. He calls himself an idealist. He has at his tongue's end all the tedious blather that the intelligentsia have been boring us with for years. Non-resistance. The brotherhood of man. You know the hopeless rubbish. The worst of it was that it impressed not only his own party, it even shook some of the sillier, more sloppy-minded members of ours. I heard rumours that Griffiths was likely to get office when a Labour Government came in; I even heard it suggested that he might get the Foreign Office. The notion was grotesque but not impossible. One day I had occasion to wind up a debate on foreign affairs which Griffiths had opened. He'd spoken for an hour. I thought it a very good opportunity to cook his goose, and by God, sir, I cooked it. I tore his speech to pieces. I pointed out the faultiness of his reasoning and emphasized the deficiency of his knowledge. In the House of Commons the most devastating weapon is ridicule: I mocked him; I bantered him; I was in good form that day and the House rocked with laughter. Their laughter excited me and I excelled myself. The Opposition sat glum and silent, but even some of them couldn't help laughing once or twice; it's not intolerable, you know, to see a colleague, perhaps a rival, made a fool of. And if ever a man was made a fool of I made a fool of Griffiths. He shrank down in his seat, I saw his face go white, and presently he buried it in his hands. When I sat down I'd killed him. I'd destroyed his prestige for ever; he had no more chance of getting office when a Labour Government came in than the policeman at the door. I heard afterwards that his father, the old miner, and his mother had come up from Wales, with various supporters of his in the constit-uency, to watch the triumph they expected him to have. They had seen only his utter humiliation. He'd won the constituency by the narrowest margin. An incident like that might very easily lose him his seat. But that was no business of mine.'

'Should I be putting it too strongly if I said you had ruined his career?' asked Dr. Audlin.

'I don't suppose you would.'

'That is a very serious injury you've done him.'

'He brought it on himself.'

'Have you never felt any qualms about it?'

'I think perhaps if I'd known that his father and mother were there I might have let him down a little more gently.'

There was nothing further for Dr. Audlin to say, and he set about treating his patient in such a manner as he thought might avail. He sought by suggestion to make him forget his dreams when he awoke; he sought to make him sleep so deeply that he would not dream. He found Lord Mountdrago's resistance impossible to break down. At the end of an hour he dismissed him. Since then he had seen Lord Mountdrago half a dozen times. He had done him no good. The frightful dreams continued every night to harass the unfortunate man, and it was clear that his general condition was growing rapidly worse. He was worn out. His irritability was uncontrollable. Lord Mountdrago was angry because he received no benefit from his treatment, and yet continued it, not only because it seemed his only hope, but because it was a relief to him to have someone with whom he could talk openly. Dr. Audlin came to the conclusion at last that there was only one way in which Lord Mountdrago could achieve deliverance, but he knew him well enough to be assured that of his own free will he would never, never take it. If Lord Mountdrago was to be saved from the breakdown that was threatening he must be induced to take a step that must be abhorrent to his pride of birth and his self-complacency. Dr. Audlin was convinced that to delay was impossible. He was treating his patient by suggestion, and after several visits found him more susceptible to it. At length he managed to get him into a condition of somnolence. With his low, soft, monotonous voice he soothed his tortured nerves. He repeated the same words over and over again. Lord Mountdrago lay quite still, his eyes closed; his breathing was regular, and his limbs were relaxed. Then Dr. Audlin in the same quiet tone spoke the words he had prepared.

'You will go to Owen Griffiths and say that you are sorry that you caused him that great injury. You will say that you will do whatever lies in your power to undo the harm that you have done him.'

The words acted on Lord Mountdrago like the blow of a whip across his face. He shook himself out of his hypnotic state and sprang to his feet. His eyes blazed with passion and he poured forth upon Dr. Audlin a stream of angry vituperation such as even he had never heard. He swore at him. He cursed him. He used language of such obscenity that Dr. Audlin, who had heard every sort of foul word, sometimes from the lips of chaste and distinguished women, was surprised that he knew it.

'Apologize to that filthy little Welshman? I'd rather kill myself.'

'I believe it to be the only way in which you can regain your balance.'

Dr. Audlin had not often seen a man presumably sane in such a condition of uncontrollable fury. He grew red in the face and his eyes bulged out of his head. He did really foam at the mouth. Dr. Audlin watched him coolly, waiting for the storm to wear itself out, and presently he saw that Lord Mountdrago, weakened by the strain to which he had been subjected for so many weeks, was exhausted.

'Sit down,' he said then, sharply.

Lord Mountdrago crumpled up into a chair.

'Christ, I feel all in. I must rest a minute and then I'll go.'

For five minutes perhaps they sat in complete silence. Lord Mountdrago was a gross, blustering bully, but he was also a gentleman. When he broke the silence he had recovered his self-control.

'I'm afraid I've been very rude to you. I'm ashamed of the things I've said to you and I can only say you'd be justified if you refused to have anything more to do with me. I hope you won't do that. I feel that my visits to you do help me. I think you're my only chance.'

'You mustn't give another thought to what you said. It was of no consequence.'

'But there's one thing you mustn't ask me to do, and that is to make excuses to Griffiths.'

'I've thought a great deal about your case. I don't pretend to understand it, but I believe that your only chance of release is to do what I proposed. I have a notion that we're none of us one self, but many, and one of the selves in you has risen up against the injury you did Griffiths and has taken on the form of Griffiths in your mind and is punishing you for what you cruelly did. If I were a priest I should tell you that it is your conscience that has adopted the shape and lineaments of this man to scourge you to repentance and persuade you to reparation.'

'My conscience is clear. It's not my fault if I smashed the man's career. I crushed him like a slug in my garden. I regret nothing.'

It was on these words that Lord Mountdrago had left him. Reading through his notes, while he waited, Dr. Audlin considered how best he could bring his patient to the state of mind that, now that his usual methods of treatment had failed, he thought alone could help him. He glanced at his clock. It was six. It was strange that Lord Mountdrago did not come. He knew he had intended to because a secretary had rung up that morning to say that he would be with him at the usual hour. He must have been detained by pressing work. This notion gave Dr. Audlin something else to think of: Lord Mountdrago was quite unfit to work and in no condition to deal with important matters of state. Dr. Audlin wondered whether it behoved him to get in touch with someone in authority, the Prime Minister or the Permanent Under Secretary for Foreign Affairs, and impart to him his conviction that Lord Mountdrago's mind was so unbalanced that it was dangerous to leave affairs of moment in his hands. It was a ticklish thing to do. He might cause needless trouble and get roundly snubbed for his pains. He shrugged his shoulders.

'After all,' he reflected, 'the politicians have made such a mess of the world during the last five-and-twenty years, I don't suppose it makes much odds if they're mad or sane.'

He rang the bell.

'If Lord Mountdrago comes now will you tell him that I have another appointment at six-fifteen and so I'm afraid I can't see him.'

'Very good, sir.'

'Has the evening paper come yet?'

'I'll go and see.'

In a moment the servant brought it in. A huge headline ran across the front page: Tragic Death of Foreign Minister.

'My God!' cried Dr. Audlin.

For once he was wrenched out of his wonted calm. He was shocked, horribly shocked, and yet he was not altogether surprised. The possibility that Lord Mountdrago might commit suicide had occurred to him several times, for that it was suicide he could not doubt. The paper said that Lord Mountdrago had been waiting in a tube station, standing on the edge of the platform, and as the train came in was seen to fall on the rail. It was supposed that he had had a sudden attack of faintness. The paper went on to say that Lord Mountdrago had been suffering for some weeks from the effects of overwork, but had felt it impossible to absent himself while the foreign situation demanded his unremitting attention. Lord Mountdrago was another victim of the strain that modern politics placed upon those who played the more important parts in it. There was a neat little piece about the talents and industry, the patriotism and vision, of the deceased statesman, followed by various surmises upon the Prime Minister's choice of his successor. Dr. Audlin read all this. He had not liked Lord Mountdrago. The chief emotion that his death caused in him was dissatisfaction with himself because he had been able to do nothing for him.

Perhaps he had done wrong in not getting into touch with Lord Mountdrago's doctor. He was discouraged, as always when failure frustrated his conscientious efforts, and repulsion seized him for the theory and practice of this empiric doctrine by which he earned his living. He was dealing with dark and mysterious forces that it was perhaps beyond the powers of the human mind to understand. He was like a man blindfold trying to feel his way to he knew not whither. Listlessly he turned the pages of the paper. Suddenly he gave a great start, and an exclamation once more was forced from his lips. His eyes had fallen on a small paragraph near the bottom of a column. Sudden Death of an M.P., he read. Mr. Owen Griffiths, member for so-and-so, had been taken ill in Fleet Street that afternoon and when he was brought to Charing Cross Hospital life was found to be extinct. It was supposed that death was due to natural causes, but an inquest would be held. Dr. Audlin could hardly believe his eyes. Was it possible that the night before Lord Mountdrago had at last in his dream found himself possessed of the weapon, knife or gun, that he had wanted, and had killed his tormentor, and had that ghostly murder, in the same way as the blow with the bottle had given him a racking headache on the following day, taken effect a certain number of hours later on the waking man? Or was it, more mysterious and more frightful, that when Lord Mountdrago sought relief in death, the enemy he had so cruelly wronged, unappeased, escaping from his own mortality, had pursued him to some other sphere there to torment him still? It was strange. The sensible thing was to look upon it merely as an odd coincidence. Dr. Audlin rang the bell.

'Tell Mrs. Milton that I'm sorry I can't see her this evening. I'm not well.'

It was true; he shivered as though of an ague. With some kind of spiritual sense he seemed to envisage a bleak, a horrible void. The dark night of the soul engulfed him, and he felt a strange, primeval terror of he knew not what.

JULIAN MACLAREN-ROSS

I HAD TO GO SICK

I HADN'T BEEN in the army long at the time. About a week, not more. We were marching round the square one afternoon and I couldn't keep in step. The corporal kept calling out 'Left, left,' but it didn't do any good. In the end the corporal told me to fall out. The platoon sergeant came rushing up and said, 'What the hell's wrong with you, man? Why can't you hold the step?'

I didn't know, I couldn't tell him. There was an officer on the square, and the sergeant-major, and they were both watching us.

'Got anything wrong with your leg?' the sergeant said.

'Your left leg?'

'I've got a scar on it Sergeant,' I told him.

'Dekko,' the sergeant said.

So I rolled up my trouser leg and showed him the scar on my knee. The sergeant looked at it and shook his head. 'That don't look too good, lad,' he said. 'How'd you come to get it?'

'I was knocked down by a bike. Years ago.'

By this time the sergeant-major had come up and he looked at the scar too. 'What's your category, lad?' he asked me. 'A1?'

'Yes sir.'

'Well you go sick tomorrow morning and let the MO have a look at that leg. Meantime sit in that shed over there till it's time to fall out.'

There was a Bren Gun lesson going on in the shed when I got there. My arrival interrupted it. 'Who the hell are you?' the NCO taking the lesson asked me. 'What d'you want?'

'I've been sent over here to sit down Corporal.'

'To sit down?'

'Sergeant-major sent me.'

'Oh well if he sent you that's all right. But don't go opening your trap, see? Keep mum and don't say nothing.'

'Very good Corporal.'

'Not so much of it,' the corporal said.

The lesson went on. I listened but couldn't understand what it was all about. I'd never seen a Bren Gun before. And then the corporal's pronunciation didn't help matters. I sat there in the shed until everyone else had fallen out. Then the sergeant-major came over to me.

'Fall out,' he said. 'What're you waiting for. Parade's over for the day, you're dismissed. And don't forget – you go sick tomorrow morning,' he shouted after me.

'How do I go sick?' I asked the other fellows, back in the barrack-room.

They didn't know, none of them had ever been sick. 'Ask the Sarnt,' they said.

But I couldn't find the sergeant, or the corporal either. They'd gone off to a dance in the town. So I went down to the cookhouse and there was an old sweat sitting on a bucket outside, peeling spuds. You could see he was an old sweat because he was in shirt sleeves and his arms were tattooed all over. So I asked him how to go sick and he said 'Ah, swinging the lead, eh? MO'll mark you down in red ink, likely.'

'What happens if he does that?'

'CB for a cert. Scrubbing, or mebbe a spot of spud bashing. You won't get less than seven days, anyhow.'

'What, seven days CB for going sick?'

'Sure, if you're swinging the lead. Stands to reason. There ain't nothing wrong with you now is there? AI, aintcher?'

'Yes.'

'There you are then. You'll get seven all right,' said the sweat. 'What d'you expect. All you lads are alike. Bleeding lead swingers the lot of you.'

He spat on the ground and went on peeling spuds. I could see he wasn't going to say any more so I walked on. Further along I stopped by another old sweat. This second sweat was even older and more tattooed than the first one. And he hadn't any teeth.

'Excuse me,' I said. 'Can you tell me how to go sick?'

'Go sick?' said this second, toothless sweat. 'You don't want to do that.'

'Why not?' I said.

'Well look at me. Went sick I did with a pain in the guts, and what's the MO do? Silly bleeder sent me down the Dental Centre and had them take all me teeth out. I ask you, do it make sense? Course it don't. You got the guts-ache and they pull out all your teeth. Bleeding silly. And they ain't given me no new teeth neither and here I been waiting six munce. No,' said the sweat, 'you don't want to go sick. Take my tip, lad: keep away from that there MO long as you can.'

'But I've got to go sick. I've been ordered to.'

'Who by?'

'Sergeant-major.'

'What's wrong with you?'

'My leg, so they say.'

'Your leg? Then mebbe they'll take your teeth out too. Ain't no knowing what they'll do once they start on you. I'm bleeding browned-off with the bleeding sick I am.'

'Well how do I go about it?'

* * *

On the door of the orderly sergeant's bunk it said KNOCK AND WAIT. I did both and a voice shouted 'Come in, come in. Don't need to bash the bleeding door down.'

There was a corporal sitting at a table covered with a blanket writing laboriously on a sheet of paper.

'Yes?' he said, looking up. 'What d'you want?'

'I was looking for the Orderly Sergeant,' I said.

'I'm the Orderly Sergeant,' said the corporal. 'State your business and be quick about it. I ain't got all night.'

'I want to go sick Sergeant. I mean Corporal.'

'Don't you go making no smart cracks here,' said the corporal. 'And stand properly to attention when you speak to an NCO.'

'Sorry Corporal.'

'Ain't no such word in the British army,' the corporal told me. 'Now what's your name? Age? Service? Religion? Medical Category? Okay, you parade outside here 8.30 tomorrow morning. On the dot.'

I went to go out, but the corporal called me back. 'Here, half a mo. How d'you spell Picquet? One K or two?'

'No Ks at all Corporal,' I told him.

'Listen didn't I tell you not to be funny? I'll stick you on a chitty so help me if you ain't careful. How d'you mean, no Ks? How can you spell Picquet without no Ks?'

I explained. The corporal looked suspicious. 'Sure? You ain't trying to be funny?'

'No Corporal. P-i-c-q-u-e-t.'

'Okay.' He wrote it down. 'Need a bleeding dictionary to write this bastard out,' he muttered, and then looking up: 'All right, what're you waiting for. Scram. Gillo! And don't forget: 0830 tomorrow. Bring your small kit in case.'

I didn't like to ask him in case of what. I got out quick

before he gave me scrubbing or spud-bashing or tried to take my teeth out maybe.

I didn't sleep too well that night, I can tell you. Next morning at 0830 there I was outside the orderly sergeant's bunk with my small kit: I'd found out from our sergeant what that was. There were quite a lot of other fellows there as well. It's funny how they pass you A1 into the army and then find out you're nothing of the sort. One of these fellows had flat feet, another weak lungs, and a third reckoned he was ruptured.

After a while the corporal came out. 'All right,' he said. 'Get fell in the sick.'

We fell in and were marched down to the MI Room.

'Keep in step, you!' the corporal shouted at me. 'Christ, can't you keep step?'

Down at the MI Room it said on the walls NO SMOK-ING, NO SPITTING, and we sat around waiting for our names to be called out. At last mine was called and I went in. The MO looked up. 'Yes, what's wrong with you?'

I looked round. There were two fellows standing behind me waiting their turn. A third was putting on his trousers in a corner. More crowded in the doorway behind. I felt silly with all these fellows listening in. I didn't know what to say.

'Come on, out with it,' said the MO. 'Or perhaps it's something you'd rather say in private?'

'Well sir, I would prefer it.'

'Right. Come back at five tonight.'

I went out again.

'What'd you get?' the orderly sergeant asked me.

'He said to come back at five Corporal.'

'What's wrong? Got the clap?'

'No Corporal.'

'Crabs, maybe?'

'No, not crabs.'

'Well what the hell you want to see him in private for, then? Only blokes with VD see him in private as a rule. Unless they've crabs.'

At five I reported back to the MI Room.

'Right,' said the medical corporal. 'This way. Cap off. Don't salute.'

The MO said, 'Ah yes. Sit down and tell me about it.'

I did. He seemed a bit disappointed that I hadn't VD but in the end he examined my leg.

'Does it hurt? No? What about if you kneel on it? H'm, yes, there's something wrong there. You'd better see the specialist. Report here tomorrow at ten.'

The specialist was at a hospital some miles away from the camp. He said 'Try and straighten the leg. What, you can't? All right. Put your trousers on and wait outside.'

Pretty soon an orderly came out with a chitty. 'You're to have treatment twice a week,' he told me. 'Electrical massage. This way.'

I followed him down a lot of corridors and finally out into the grounds and up some steps into a hut with MASSAGE on a board outside it. There I lay down on a table and a nurse strapped some sort of pad on my thigh. After that they gave me a series of shocks from an electric battery. It lasted about half an hour.

'Feeling better?' the nurse asked me when it was over.

'No,' I said.

I could hardly walk.

'That'll wear off by and by,' said the nurse.

I drove in by an ambulance to the MI Room.

'Had your treatment?'

'Yes sir.'

272

The MO started to write something on a piece of paper. I was a bit nervous in case he used the red ink. But he didn't after all. He used blue ink instead. 'Give this to your orderly sergeant,' he said.

On the piece of paper it said 'Att. C.'

'Attend C!' said the orderly sergeant. 'Cor you got it cushy ain't you?'

'What's it mean Corporal?' I asked.

'Attend C? Excused all duties. Bleeding march coming off tomorrow and all.'

Two days later I went to the hospital again. After a week or two of treatment I'd developed quite a limp. The fellows all said I was swinging the lead. I limped about the camp doing nothing, in the intervals of having more electric shock. Then, after about three weeks, the MO sent for me again.

'Is your leg any better now?'

'No sir,' I said.

'Treatment not doing you any good?'

'No sir.'

'H'm. Well I'd better put you down for a medical board in that case.'

So I didn't even go to the hospital any more. I used to lie on my bed all day long reading a book. But I got tired of that because I only had one book and I wasn't allowed out owing to being on sick. There weren't any other books in the camp. Meanwhile the fellows were marching and drilling and firing on the range, and the man in the next bed to me suddenly developed a stripe. This shook me, so I thought I'd go and see the sergeant-major.

I was a bit nervous when I got to his office. The sergeant-major had an alarming appearance. He looked almost exactly like an ape. Only he'd less hair on him, of course. But he was quite a decent fellow really.

When I came in he was telling two clerks and an ATS girl how he'd nailed a native's hand to his desk during his active service in India. He broke off this recital when he saw me standing there. 'Yes, lad, what d'you want?'

I explained that I was waiting for a medical board and meantime had nothing to do, as I was excused parades.

'But d'you WANT something to do?' the sergeant-major asked. He seemed stupefied.

'Yes sir,' I said. 'I didn't join the army to do nothing all day.'

The two clerks looked up when I said that, and the ATS stared at me with her mouth open. The sergeant-major breathed heavily through his nose. Then he said, 'Can you use a typewriter, lad?'

'Yes sir,' I said.

'Ah!' He jumped up from his table. 'Then sit you down here and show us how to use this ruddy thing. It's only just been sent us, see, and none of us know how to make the bleeder go.'

It was a very old typewriter, an Oliver. I'd used one before, so I didn't find it too difficult. Soon I was typing out long lists of names and other stuff full of initials and abbreviations that I didn't know the meaning of. Sometimes I couldn't read the handwriting, especially if one of the officers had written it, but the ATS used to translate for me.

Then one day the company commander walked in.

'Who's this man?' he said, pointing at me with his stick.

'Sick man, sir,' the sergeant-major said. 'Waiting a medical board.'

'Well he can't wait for it here. We're not allowed any more clerks. You've enough clerks already,' and he walked out again, after hitting my table a whack with his stick.

'All right, fall out,' the sergeant-major said to me. 'Back to your bunk.'

'Now we've no one to work the typewriter,' he said. 'Have to do it all by hand. Hell.'

Next day the orderly sergeant told me to go sick again. I'd got used to it by now. The other fellows called me the MO's right marker.

This time it was a new MO: the other one had been posted elsewhere.

'Well what's wrong with you?' he said.

I explained my case all over again.

'Let's see your leg.' He looked at it for a moment and then said, 'Well there's nothing wrong with that, is there?'

'Isn't there, sir?'

'No.' He poked at the scar, seized hold of my leg, bent it, straightened it a few times and then looked puzzled. 'H'm. There is something wrong after all. You'd better have a medical board.'

'I'm down for one already, sir.'

'What? Well why the devil didn't you say so then? Wasting my time. All right. You can go now.'

In the morning the orderly sergeant came into our hut. 'Get your small kit together,' he said, 'and be down the MI Room in ten minutes. You're for a medical board. It came through just now.'

At the hospital I sat for some time in a waiting room and nobody came near me. It was another hospital, not the one I used to go to for treatment. Then at last an officer came in. I stood up. He was a colonel.

'Carry on, carry on,' he said, and smiled very kindly. 'What's your trouble eh?'

'I'm waiting for a medical board, sir.'

'A medical board? What for?'

'I have trouble with my knee, sir.'

'Oh? What happens? Does it swell up?'

'No sir.'

'What, no swelling? H'm. Well come with me, we'll soon have you fixed up.' I followed this kindly colonel to the reception desk. 'Take this man along to Ward 9,' he told an orderly.

So I went along to Ward 9 and all the beds in it were empty except for one man sitting up in bed doing a jigsaw puzzle.

'Watcher, mate,' this man said. 'What you got? Ulcers, maybe?'

'Ulcers? No,' I said.

Then a nurse came in. 'Ah, you're the new patient. This way to the bathroom. Here are the pyjamas you change into afterwards.'

'Pyjamas?' I said.

'Yes,' said the nurse. 'And directly you've bathed and got your pyjamas on you hop into this bed here,' and she pointed to one next to the man with ulcers.

'But I don't want to go to bed,' I said. 'I'm not a bed patient. There's nothing wrong with me.'

'Then why are you here?'

'Nothing wrong with me like that, I mean. I'm waiting for a medical board.'

'Oh. Wait here a moment, please.' She fetched the orderly.

The orderly said, 'SMO's orders he was to be brought here. Said it hisself. The SMO Ward 9, he said.'

'But this ward is for gastric cases,' the nurse said. 'This man isn't a gastric case.'

'I don't know nothing about that,' the orderly told her.

The nurse said, 'There's some mistake. I'll see about it while you have your bath.'

So I had a bath and when I came out she gave me some clothes and a shirt and a red tie to put on and said I needn't go to bed.

'You'll have to stay here until we get this straightened out,' she said. 'Would you like anything to eat?'

'I would, thank you Nurse.'

'Well there's only milk pudding. This ward's for gastrics you see.'

'You won't get very fat on that, mate,' the man with ulcers said.

He was right. I ate two lots of milk pudding but still felt hungry afterwards. Then later on the MO came round. A lieutenant, he was. Quite young. He looked at my leg and said, 'This man's a surgical case, Nurse. What's he doing in here?'

'SMO's orders, doctor.'

'Oh. Well he'll have to stay here then.'

'How long will it be before I get this medical board, sir?' I said.

'Medical board? Might be months. Meantime you stay here. Yes, you can have chicken. Give him some chicken, Nurse.'

So he went away and I ate the chicken.

'Wish I was you, mate,' said the man with ulcers.

It wasn't so bad being in the hospital except that you only got eight-and-six on pay day. Every morning I used to go down to the massage department. 'Electrical massage's no good for your trouble,' said the MO. 'We'll try ordinary massage.' So I had ordinary massage and then sat on a table with a weight tied to my leg swinging it to-and-fro.

'Now I know what swinging the lead means,' I said.

I used to have to lie down for two hours a day to recover from the treatment. I was limping quite heavily by the time the MO put his head in one morning and said 'You're for a Board today. Twelve o'clock down in my office.'

I waited outside the office nervously. I thought they might order me to have my teeth out. But they didn't. I was called in and there were three medical officers, one a lieutenant-colonel, who asked me a lot of questions and examined my leg, and then I went back to the ward.

'How'd you get on, mate?' asked the ulcers-man. 'What'd they do?'

'I don't know,' I said. 'They didn't tell me.'

But that evening the MO came in and said, 'You've been graded B2.'

'What does that mean, sir?'

'Garrison duties at home and abroad.'

'Can I go back to the camp then, sir?'

'Not till the papers come through.'

A few days later he sent for me. In his office. 'Something's gone wrong,' he said. 'We've slipped up. It seems you should have seen the surgical specialist before having the Board. But you didn't, so these papers aren't valid. You'll have to have another Board now.'

'What'll that be, sir?'

'I don't know. Don't ask me.'

So that afternoon I saw the surgical specialist. He was a major, although he seemed quite young. He was very nice and cheerful and laughed a lot.

'Lie down on the table,' he said. 'That's right. Relax. Now bend the knee. Now straighten it. Hold it. Hold it. Try to hold it steady. Ha ha! You can't, can you? Ha ha! Of course you can't. You've got no tendon in it, that's why. The tendon. It's bust. How long ago did you say the accident . . .? Sixteen years? Good lord, nothing we can do about it now. You'll have to be awfully careful, though. No running, no jumping.

If you were to jump down into a trench your leg'd snap like a twig. Can't understand how they ever passed you A1. Ha ha! Well I'll make my report on you right away. Oughtn't to be in the infantry with a leg like that at all.'

I went back to Ward 9. It was supper time. Junket.

'Can't keep it down,' said the man with ulcers, and he proved this by bringing it up again.

Well then the MO went on leave.

'Now you stay here,' he told me, 'until the next Board comes off. Don't suppose it'll be till I'm back from my seven days. Meantime you stay put.'

'Yes sir,' I said.

But in the morning a new MO came round. He was a captain. With him was the Matron. 'Stand by your beds!' he called out as he came in.

The ward had filled up in the last week or two, but most of the patients were in bed, so they couldn't obey. The five of us who were up came belatedly to attention.

'Bad discipline in this ward Matron,' the captain said. 'Very slack. Who's the senior NCO here?'

There was only one NCO among the lot of us: a lance-corporal. He was up, as it happened, so he came in for an awful chewing-off.

'You've got to keep better order than this, Corporal,' said the captain. 'See that the men pay proper respect to an Officer when he enters the ward. If I've any further cause for complaint I shall hold you responsible. Also the beds aren't properly in line. I'm not satisfied with this ward, not satisfied at all. I hope to see some improvement when I come round tomorrow. Otherwise . . .'

He walked on round the beds examining the patients in turn. The ward was electrified. He ordered most of the bed patients to get up and those who were up to go to bed.

Except the lance-corporal, who had to keep order, and me. As for the man with ulcers, he was ordered out of the ward altogether. I was last on the list, standing by the end bed, when he came up.

'This man is fit to return to his unit Matron,' he said when he'd looked at me.

'But he's awaiting a medical board Doctor,' the matron said.

'Well he can wait for it at his unit. We're not running a home for soldiers awaiting medical boards. I never heard of such a thing.'

'Lieutenant Jackson said . . .'

'Never mind what he said. I'm in charge here now, and I've just given an order. This man will return to his unit forthwith.'

Then he walked out and the matron went too. Two nurses came in and helped the man with ulcers into a wheel-chair. 'So long, mates,' he said, then they wheeled him away. I don't know what became of him: he just disappeared. After that we straightened the beds and got them all in line.

'Keep order,' said the lance-corporal. 'Why the hell should I keep order. I'm not an NCO no more, they'll revert me soon's I get back. I'm Y listed, see? A bloody private, so why should I bother? Bleeding sauce.'

I wondered when they were going to chuck me out. Forthwith, he'd said, and forthwith turned out to be the next day.

I left about two o'clock. In a lorry. It dropped me at the station and I'd two hours to wait for a train. At last I got back to the camp and it looked all changed somehow, with no one about. Everything seemed shut up. I reported to the sergeant's bunk. Sitting in it was a corporal I'd never seen before.

'Who're you?' he said. 'What d'you want?'

I told him.

'No one told us you was coming,' said this new corporal, scratching his head. 'All the others have cleared off. Jerry been bombing the camp, see? We've been evacuated. Last draft leaves tomorrow.'

'Am I on it?'

'You'll be on it all right.'

'Well where do I sleep? And what about my kit.'

'That'll be in the stores, I suppose. Buggered if I know. I'm from another company, I don't know nothing about you. Wait here, I'll see the storeman.'

But the storeman was out, and the stores were locked up. The corporal came back scratching his head.

'Buggered if I know when he'll be back. Gone on the piss I shouldn't wonder. You better find a place to kip down. Here's a coupla blankets, if that's any use to you.'

Eventually I found a barrack room that wasn't locked: all the other huts were closed up. There were two other blokes in this room, both out of hospital. 'Where're we going to, mate?' they asked me.

'Damned if I know.'

'Nobody bloody well does know, that's the rub.'

At last, after a lot of conjecture, we dossed down for the night. It was autumn by now and turning cold and my two blankets didn't keep me very warm. I slept in all my clothes. Jerry came over during the night but didn't drop any bombs, or if he did we didn't hear them.

Then in the morning the corporal appeared. 'I've found some of your kit left.' Most of it had been pinched. My overcoat was gone and another one, much too small, left in its place.

'I don't know nothing about it,' said the storeman.

'You better get some breakfast,' the corporal said. 'I'll sort this lot out for you.'

Breakfast was a bacon sandwich, all the cookhouse fires had been let out.

'Bloody lark this is, ain't it?' said the cooks.

'You're telling us,' we said.

Then we paraded on the square, about forty of us. Don't know where all the others came from. Other companies I suppose. A lieutenant was in charge of us.

'Where's your equipment?' he asked me.

'I've never been issued with it, sir,' I said.

'Never been issued with equipment!'

'No sir. I was excused parades. And then I've just got out of hospital. I have the papers here, sir, that they gave me.'

'Oh all right. I'll take charge of them.' He took the long envelope from me. Then a sergeant turned up and shouted, 'Shun! By the left, quick – MARCH!'

We started off.

'Keep in step, there!' the sergeant shouted at me. 'Can't you keep in step? What the hell's the matter with yer!'

'I'm excused marching, Sergeant,' I said. 'I've just come from hospital.'

'Oh. All right lad. Fall out. Wait here.' He went up to the officer and saluted. ''Scuse me, sir, there's a man here excused marching, sir.'

'What's that? Excused marching? Well he'll have to bloody well march. This isn't a convalescent home.'

'It's five miles to the station, sir.'

'Oh well, damn it, what d'you want done? Shove him on a truck or something. Can't march, indeed. He'd march soon enough if Jerry was after him.'

So the sergeant told a truck to stop and helped me to board it. It was full of kits and very uncomfortable, I nearly fell off twice. I felt a mass of bruises when we got to the station, and my leg had begun to ache. I sat down on a trolley and waited for the train to come in. It didn't come in for an hour, and the men who'd marched up meantime stood around and argued about where we were going. Some said Egypt, but others said no because we weren't in tropical kit. So then they said Scotland and *then* Egypt. I personally didn't care where we were going. I was fed-up with the whole business, and my leg ached badly: I'd hit my bad knee getting down from the truck.

Then the train came in and it turned out to be full of recruits from another regiment going to wherever we were going, a new camp somewhere or other, and so we'd nowhere to sit. We stood for a long time in the corridor and then I tried sitting on my kit but that wasn't a success because fellows kept falling over me and one of them kicked my bad leg. I was pretty browned-off by this time, so I got up and was going to sock him, but another chap got in front of me and said, 'You can't hit a sick man.'

'Who's a sick man?' I said. 'I'm a sick man.'

'So am I,' said the man I wanted to sock. 'I'm sick too. Hell I got a hernia so bad they daren't operate. I'm waiting my ticket.'

'Sorry, mate,' I said, 'I didn't know.'

'That's okay,' he said so we shook hands and he gave me some chocolate out of his haversack: we'd got bloody hungry by now.

'What about some grub?' everyone was saying. 'Where's the grub?'

By and by it came round in tins. A sergeant brought it.

'What's this?' we said.

'Beans. Take one.'

'Where's the meat?'

'You've had it,' said the sergeant. Everyone cursed. Then an officer came round, a captain. 'Any complaints?'

'What about some more food, sir,' we said.

'There isn't any. I've had none myself,' he said. 'Mistake somewhere.'

'You're telling us,' we said, but not to him.

It was dark when we got to this other town and the search-lights were up overhead. We formed up outside the station. Our sergeant appeared and recognized me. 'I'll see to you in a minute,' he said. But he couldn't, because all the transport had already gone. So I had to march after all. It was three miles, and after all that standing about I felt done in when we got to the new camp. We had a hot meal and I'd have slept like the dead if Jerry hadn't dropped a bomb somewhere near the barracks and woken me up.

'Bugger it,' I said. 'Now we'll have to go to the trenches.'

But they didn't blow the alarm after all, so we went off to sleep again.

In the morning I was down for sick, but the MO at this camp proved to be a much tougher proposition than any I'd yet encountered.

He said, 'What d'you mean, you've had a medical board? How can you have had a medical board? Where're your papers?'

'I gave them to the officer in charge of the draft, sir,' I said.

'Well I haven't got them. What was the officer's name?'

'I don't know, sir.'

'You don't know. My God you give your papers to an officer and you don't even know his name.' The MO held his head in his hands. 'God deliver me,' he said, 'from such idiocy.'

'I don't think I'm especially idiotic, sir,' I said.

'Your opinion of yourself is entirely irrelevant,' said the MO. 'And you must remember who you're talking to.'

'Yes sir,' I said.

'Silence!' said the medical corporal, who'd come up at this.

The MO said, 'Now what's all this nonsense about a medical board? What happened? Were you re-graded?'

'Yes sir. B2.'

'Let's see your pay-book. Corporal, get his AB64 Part I.'

I produced my pay-book.

'Not in it, sir,' said the corporal. 'A1 it says here.'

'I know,' I said, 'but . . .'

'Silence!' said the corporal. 'Speak only when you're spoken to.'

The MO had his head in his hands again. 'All this shouting,' he said. 'If that man gives any more trouble you'll have to charge him, corporal.'

'Yes sir,' said the corporal.

'Now listen,' the MO said to me, speaking very quietly. 'You say you've had a medical board. You say you've been re-graded. Well you haven't. It's not in your pay-book. Therefore you've not been re-graded at all. You're lucky not to be charged with stating a falsehood, understand? Now don't come here again with any more nonsensical stories or you'll find yourself in trouble. Corporal, march this man out.'

'But sir . . .,' I said.

'Come on, you!' the corporal said. So I went. Two days later we started training, and the new sergeant found out I couldn't march and sent me sick again. It was another MO this time and he had my papers, they'd turned up again, and he said I've got to have another medical board.

That was a month ago, and I'm still waiting. I've not done much training so far, and I've had to pay for all the kit I had pinched at the other camp, and all I hope is this: that when they give me the Board, I don't have to go sick any more afterwards. I don't care if they grade me Z2 or keep me A1, so long as I don't have to go sick. I've had enough of it. I'm fed-up.

LORRIE MOORE

PEOPLE LIKE THAT
ARE THE ONLY PEOPLE
HERE: CANONICAL
BABBLING IN PEED ONK

A BEGINNING, an end: there seems to be neither. The whole thing is like a cloud that just lands and everywhere inside it is full of rain. A start: the Mother finds a blood clot in the Baby's diaper. What is the story? Who put this here? It is big and bright, with a broken khaki-colored vein in it. Over the weekend, the Baby had looked listless and spacey, clayey and grim. But today he looks fine – so what is this thing, startling against the white diaper, like a tiny mouse heart packed in snow? Perhaps it belongs to someone else. Perhaps it is something menstrual, something belonging to the Mother or to the Babysitter, something the Baby has found in a wastebasket and for his own demented baby reasons stowed away here. (Babies: they're crazy! What can you do?) In her mind, the Mother takes this away from his body and attaches it to someone else's. There. Doesn't that make more sense?

Still, she phones the clinic at the children's hospital. 'Blood in the diaper,' she says, and, sounding alarmed and perplexed, the woman on the other end says, 'Come in now.'

Such pleasingly instant service! Just say 'blood.' Just say 'diaper.' Look what you get!

In the examination room, pediatrician, nurse, head resident – all seem less alarmed and perplexed than simply perplexed. At first, stupidly, the Mother is calmed by this. But soon, besides peering and saying 'Hmmmm,' the pediatrician, nurse, and head resident are all drawing their mouths in, bluish and tight – morning glories sensing noon. They fold their arms across their white-coated chests, unfold them again and jot things down. They order an ultrasound. Bladder and kidneys. 'Here's the card. Go downstairs; turn left.'

In Radiology, the Baby stands anxiously on the table, naked against the Mother as she holds him still against her legs and waist, the Radiologist's cold scanning disc moving about the Baby's back. The Baby whimpers, looks up at the Mother. *Let's get out of here*, his eyes beg. *Pick me up!* The Radiologist stops, freezes one of the many swirls of oceanic gray, and clicks repeatedly, a single moment within the long, cavern-ous weather map that is the Baby's insides.

'Are you finding something?' asks the Mother. Last year, her uncle Larry had had a kidney removed for something that turned out to be benign. These imaging machines! They are like dogs, or metal detectors: they find everything, but don't know what they've found. That's where the surgeons come in. They're like the owners of the dogs. 'Give me that,' they say to the dog. 'What the heck is that?'

'The surgeon will speak to you,' says the Radiologist.

'Are you finding something?'

'The surgeon will speak to you,' the Radiologist says again. 'There seems to be something there, but the surgeon will talk to you about it.'

'My uncle once had something on his kidney,' says the Mother. 'So they removed the kidney and it turned out the something was benign.'

The Radiologist smiles a broad, ominous smile. 'That's always the way it is,' he says. 'You don't know exactly what it is until it's in the bucket.'

' "In the bucket," ' the Mother repeats.

The Radiologist's grin grows scarily wider – is that even possible? 'That's doctor talk,' he says.

'It's very appealing,' says the Mother. 'It's a very appealing way to talk.' Swirls of bile and blood, mustard and maroon in a pail, the colors of an African flag or some exuberant salad bar: *in the bucket* – she imagines it all.

'The Surgeon will see you soon,' he says again. He tousles the Baby's ringletty hair. 'Cute kid,' he says.

'Let's see now,' says the Surgeon in one of his examining rooms. He has stepped in, then stepped out, then come back in again. He has crisp, frowning features, sharp bones, and a tennis-in-Bermuda tan. He crosses his blue-cottoned legs. He is wearing clogs.

The Mother knows her own face is a big white dumpling of worry. She is still wearing her long, dark parka, holding the Baby, who has pulled the hood up over her head because he always thinks it's funny to do that. Though on certain windy mornings she would like to think she could look vaguely romantic like this, like some French Lieutenant's Woman of the Prairie, in all of her saner moments she knows she doesn't. Ever. She knows she looks ridiculous – like one of those animals made out of twisted party balloons. She lowers the hood and slips one arm out of the sleeve. The Baby wants to get up and play with the light switch. He fidgets, fusses, and points.

'He's big on lights these days,' explains the Mother.

'That's okay,' says the Surgeon, nodding toward the light switch. 'Let him play with it.' The Mother goes and stands by it, and the Baby begins turning the lights off and on, off and on.

'What we have here is a Wilms' tumor,' says the Surgeon,

suddenly plunged into darkness. He says 'tumor' as if it were the most normal thing in the world.

'Wilms'?' repeats the Mother. The room is quickly on fire again with light, then wiped dark again. Among the three of them here, there is a long silence, as if it were suddenly the middle of the night. 'Is that apostrophe *s* or *s* apostrophe?' the Mother says finally. She is a writer and a teacher. Spelling can be important – perhaps even at a time like this, though she has never before been at a time like this, so there are barbarisms she could easily commit and not know.

The lights come on: the world is doused and exposed.

'*S* apostrophe,' says the Surgeon. 'I think.' The lights go back out, but the Surgeon continues speaking in the dark. 'A malignant tumor on the left kidney.'

Wait a minute. Hold on here. The Baby is only a baby, fed on organic applesauce and soy milk – a little prince! – and he was standing so close to her during the ultrasound. How could he have this terrible thing? It must have been *her* kidney. A fifties kidney. A DDT kidney. The Mother clears her throat. 'Is it possible it was my kidney on the scan? I mean, I've never heard of a baby with a tumor, and, frankly, I was standing very close.' She would make the blood hers, the tumor hers; it would all be some treacherous, farcical mistake.

'No, that's not possible,' says the Surgeon. The light goes back on.

'It's not?' says the Mother. Wait until it's *in the bucket*, she thinks. Don't be so sure. *Do we have to wait until it's in the bucket to find out a mistake has been made?*

'We will start with a radical nephrectomy,' says the Surgeon, instantly thrown into darkness again. His voice comes from nowhere and everywhere at once. 'And then we'll begin with chemotherapy after that. These tumors usually respond very well to chemo.'

'I've never heard of a baby having chemo,' the Mother says. *Baby* and *Chemo*, she thinks: they should never even appear in the same sentence together, let alone the same life. In her other life, her life before this day, she had been a believer in alternative medicine. Chemotherapy? Unthinkable. Now, suddenly, alternative medicine seems the wacko maiden aunt to the Nice Big Daddy of Conventional Treatment. How quickly the old girl faints and gives way, leaves one just standing there. Chemo? Of course: chemo! Why by all means: chemo. Absolutely! Chemo!

The Baby flicks the switch back on, and the walls reappear, big wedges of light checkered with small framed watercolors of the local lake. The Mother has begun to cry: all of life has led her here, to this moment. After this, there is no more life. There is something else, something stumbling and unlivable, something mechanical, something for robots, but not life. Life has been taken and broken, quickly, like a stick. The room goes dark again, so that the Mother can cry more freely. How can a baby's body be stolen so fast? How much can one heaven-sent and unsuspecting child endure? Why has he not been spared this inconceivable fate?

Perhaps, she thinks, she is being punished: too many baby-sitters too early on. ('Come to Mommy! Come to Mommy-Baby-sitter!' she used to say. But it was a joke!) Her life, perhaps, bore too openly the marks and wigs of deepest drag. Her unmotherly thoughts had all been noted: the panicky hope that his nap would last longer than it did; her occasional desire to kiss him passionately on the mouth (to make out with her baby!); her ongoing complaints about the very vocabulary of motherhood, how it degraded the speaker ('Is this a poopie onesie! Yes, it's a very poopie onesie!'). She had, moreover, on three occasions used the formula bottles as flower vases. She twice let the Baby's ears get fudgy with wax. A few afternoons last month, at snacktime, she placed a bowl of Cheerios on the floor for him to eat, like a dog. She let him play with the Dust-buster. Just once, before he was born, she said, 'Healthy? I just want the kid to be rich.' A joke, for God's sake! After he was born she announced that her life had become a daily sequence of mind-wrecking chores, the same ones over and over again, like a novel by Mrs. Camus. Another joke! These jokes will kill you! She had told too often, and with too much enjoyment, the story of how the Baby had said 'Hi' to his high chair, waved at the lake waves, shouted 'Goody-goody-goody' in what seemed to be a Russian accent, pointed at his eyes and said 'Ice.' And all that nonsensical baby talk: wasn't it a stitch? 'Canonical babbling,' the language experts called it. He recounted whole stories in it – totally made up, she could tell. He embroidered; he fished; he exaggerated. What a card! To friends, she spoke of his eating habits (carrots yes, tuna no). She mentioned, too much, his sidesplitting giggle. Did she have to be so boring? Did she have no consideration for others, for the intellectual demands and courtesies of human society? Would she not even attempt to be more interesting? It was a crime against the human mind not even to try.

Now her baby, for all these reasons – lack of motherly gratitude, motherly judgment, motherly proportion – will be taken away.

The room is fluorescently ablaze again. The Mother digs around in her parka pocket and comes up with a Kleenex. It is old and thin, like a mashed flower saved from a dance; she dabs it at her eyes and nose.

'The Baby won't suffer as much as you,' says the Surgeon. And who can contradict? Not the Baby, who in his Slavic

Betty Boop voice can say only *mama*, *dada*, *cheese*, *ice*, *bye-bye*, *outside*, *boogie-boogie*, *goody-goody*, *eddy-eddy*, and *car*. (Who is Eddy? They have no idea.) This will not suffice to express his mortal suffering. Who can say what babies do with their agony and shock? Not they themselves. (Baby talk: isn't it a stitch?) They put it all no place anyone can really see. They are like a different race, a different species: they seem not to experience pain the way *we* do. Yeah, that's it: their nervous systems are not as fully formed, and *they just don't experience pain the way we do*. A tune to keep one humming through the war. 'You'll get through it,' the Surgeon says.

'How?' asks the Mother. 'How does one get through it?'

'You just put your head down and go,' says the Surgeon. He picks up his file folder. He is a skilled manual laborer. The tricky emotional stuff is not to his liking. The babies. The babies! What can be said to console the parents about the babies? 'I'll go phone the oncologist on duty to let him know,' he says, and leaves the room.

'Come here, sweetie,' the Mother says to the Baby, who has toddled off toward a gum wrapper on the floor. 'We've got to put your jacket on.' She picks him up and he reaches for the light switch again. Light, dark. Peekaboo: where's baby? Where did baby go?

At home, she leaves a message – 'Urgent! Call me!' – for the Husband on his voice mail. Then she takes the Baby upstairs for his nap, rocks him in the rocker. The Baby waves good-bye to his little bears, then looks toward the window and says, 'Bye-bye, outside.' He has, lately, the habit of waving good-bye to everything, and now it seems as if he senses an imminent departure, and it breaks her heart to hear him. *Bye-bye!* She sings low and monotonously, like a small appliance, which is how he likes it. He is drowsy, dozy, drifting off. He has grown so much in the last year, he hardly fits in her lap anymore; his limbs dangle off like a pietà. His head rolls slightly inside the crook of her arm. She can feel him falling backward into sleep, his mouth round and open like the sweetest of poppies. All the lullabies in the world, all the melodies threaded through with maternal melancholy now become for her – abandoned as a mother can be by working men and napping babies – the songs of hard, hard grief. Sitting there, bowed and bobbing, the Mother feels the entirety of her love as worry and heartbreak. A quick and irrevocable alchemy: there is no longer one unworried scrap left for happiness. 'If you go,' she keens low into his soapy neck, into the ranunculus coil of his ear, 'we are going with you. We are nothing without you. Without you, we are a heap of rocks. We are gravel and mold. Without you, we are two stumps, with nothing any longer in our hearts. Wherever this takes you, we are following. We will be there. Don't be scared. We are going, too. That is that.'

'Take Notes,' says the Husband, after coming straight home from work, midafternoon, hearing the news, and saying all the words out loud – *surgery, metastasis, dialysis, transplant* – then collapsing in a chair in tears. 'Take notes. We are going to need the money.'

'Good God,' cries the Mother. Everything inside her suddenly begins to cower and shrink, a thinning of bones. Perhaps this is a soldier's readiness, but it has the whiff of death and defeat. It feels like a heart attack, a failure of will and courage, a power failure: a failure of everything. Her face, when she glimpses it in a mirror, is cold and bloated with shock, her eyes scarlet and shrunk. She has already started to wear sunglasses indoors, like a celebrity widow. From where will her own strength come? From some philosophy? From some frigid little philosophy? She is neither stalwart nor realistic and has trouble with basic concepts, such as the one that says events move in one direction only and do not jump up, turn around, and take themselves back.

The Husband begins too many of his sentences with 'What if.' He is trying to piece everything together like a train wreck. He is trying to get the train to town.

'We'll just take all the steps, move through all the stages. We'll go where we have to go. We'll hunt; we'll find; we'll pay what we have to pay. What if we can't pay?'

'Sounds like shopping.'

'I cannot believe this is happening to our little boy,' he says, and starts to sob again. 'Why didn't it happen to one of us? It's so unfair. Just last week, my doctor declared me in perfect health: the prostate of a twenty-year-old, the heart of a ten-year-old, the brain of an insect – or whatever it was he said. What a nightmare this is.'

What words can be uttered? You turn just slightly and there it is: the death of your child. It is part symbol, part devil, and in your blind spot all along, until, if you are unlucky, it is completely upon you. Then it is a fierce little country abducting you; it holds you squarely inside itself like a cellar room – the best boundaries of you are the boundaries of it. Are there windows? Sometimes aren't there windows?

The Mother is not a shopper. She hates to shop, is generally bad at it, though she does like a good sale. She cannot stroll meaningfully through anger, denial, grief, and acceptance. She goes straight to bargaining and stays there. How much? she calls out to the ceiling, to some makeshift construction of holiness she has desperately, though not uncreatively, assembled in her mind and prayed to; a doubter, never

297

before given to prayer, she must now reap what she has not sown; she must assemble from scratch an entire altar of worship and begging. She tries for noble abstractions, nothing too anthropomorphic, just some Higher Morality, though if this particular Highness looks something like the manager at Marshall Field's, sucking a Frango mint, so be it. Amen. Just tell me what you want, requests the Mother. And how do you want it? More charitable acts? A billion starting now. Charitable thoughts? Harder, but of course! Of course! I'll do the cooking, honey; I'll pay the rent. Just tell me. *Excuse me?* Well, if not to you, to whom do I speak? Hello? To whom do I have to speak around here? A higher-up? A superior? Wait? I can wait. I've got all day. I've got the whole damn day.

The Husband now lies next to her in bed, sighing. 'Poor little guy could survive all this, only to be killed in a car crash at the age of sixteen,' he says.

The wife, bargaining, considers this. 'We'll take the car crash,' she says.

'What?'

'Let's Make a Deal! Sixteen Is a Full Life! We'll take the car crash. We'll take the car crash, in front of which Carol Merrill is now standing.'

Now the Manager of Marshall Field's reappears. 'To take the surprises out is to take the life out of life,' he says.

The phone rings. The Husband gets up and leaves the room.

'But I don't want these surprises,' says the Mother. 'Here! You take these surprises!'

'To know the narrative in advance is to turn yourself into a machine,' the Manager continues. 'What makes humans human is precisely that they do not know the future. That is why they do the fateful and amusing things they do: who

298

can say how anything will turn out? Therein lies the only hope for redemption, discovery, and – let's be frank – fun, fun, fun! There might be things people will get away with. And not just motel towels. There might be great illicit loves, enduring joy, faith-shaking accidents with farm machinery. But you have to not know in order to see what stories your life's efforts bring you. The mystery is all.'

The Mother, though shy, has grown confrontational. 'Is this the kind of bogus, random crap they teach at merchandising school? We would like fewer surprises, fewer efforts and mysteries, thank you. K through eight; can we just get K through eight?' It now seems like the luckiest, most beautiful, most musical phrase she's ever heard: K through eight. The very lilt. The very thought.

The Manager continues, trying things out. 'I mean, the whole conception of "the story," of cause and effect, the whole idea that people have a clue as to how the world works is just a piece of laughable metaphysical colonialism perpetrated upon the wild country of time.'

Did they own a gun? The Mother begins looking through drawers.

The Husband comes back into the room and observes her. 'Ha! The Great Havoc that is the Puzzle of all Life!' he says of the Marshall Field's management policy. He has just gotten off a conference call with the insurance company and the hospital. The surgery will be Friday. 'It's all just some dirty capitalist's idea of a philosophy.'

'Maybe it's just a fact of narrative and you really can't politicize it,' says the Mother. It is now only the two of them.

'Whose side are you on?'

'I'm on the Baby's side.'

'Are you taking notes for this?'

'No.'

'You're not?'

'No. I can't. Not this! I write fiction. This isn't fiction.'

'Then write nonfiction. Do a piece of journalism. Get two dollars a word.'

'Then it has to be true and full of information. I'm not trained. I'm not that skilled. Plus, I have a convenient personal principle about artists not abandoning art. One should never turn one's back on a vivid imagination. Even the whole memoir thing annoys me.'

'Well, make things up, but pretend they're real.'

'I'm not that insured.'

'You're making me nervous.'

'Sweetie, darling, I'm not that good. I can't *do this*. I can do – what can I do? I can do quasi-amusing phone dialogue. I can do succinct descriptions of weather. I can do screwball outings with the family pet. Sometimes I can do those. Honey, I only do what I can. I do *the careful ironies of day-dream*. I do *the marshy ideas upon which intimate life is built*. But this? Our baby with cancer? I'm sorry. My stop was two stations back. This is irony at its most gaudy and careless. This is a Hieronymus Bosch of facts and figures and blood and graphs. This is a nightmare of narrative slop. This cannot be designed. This cannot even be noted in preparation for a design—'

'We're going to need the money.'

'To say nothing of the moral boundaries of pecuniary recompense in a situation such as this—'

'What if the other kidney goes? What if he needs a trans- plant? Where are the moral boundaries there? What are we going to do, have bake sales?'

'We can sell the house. I hate this house. It makes me crazy.'

'And we'll live – where again?'

'The Ronald McDonald place. I hear it's nice. It's the least McDonald's can do.'

'You have a keen sense of justice.'

'I try. What can I say?' She pauses. 'Is all this really happening? I keep thinking that soon it will be over – the life expectancy of a cloud is supposed to be only twelve hours – and then I realize something has occurred that can never ever be over.'

The Husband buries his face in his hands: 'Our poor baby. How did this happen to him?' He looks over and stares at the bookcase that serves as the nightstand. 'And do you think even one of these baby books is any help?' He picks up the Leach, the Spock, the *What to Expect*. 'Where in the pages or index of any of these does it say "chemotherapy" or "Hickman catheter" or "renal sarcoma"? Where does it say "carcinogenesis"? You know what these books are obsessed with? *Holding a fucking spoon*.' He begins hurling the books off the night table and against the far wall.

'Hey,' says the Mother, trying to soothe. 'Hey, hey, hey.' But compared to his stormy roar, her words are those of a backup singer – a Shondell, a Pip – a doo-wop ditty. Books, and now more books, continue to fly.

Take Notes.

Is *fainthearted* one word or two? Student prose has wrecked her spelling.

It's one word. Two words – *Faint Hearted* – what would that be? The name of a drag queen.

Take Notes. In the end, you suffer alone. But at the beginning you suffer with a whole lot of others. When your child has cancer, you are instantly whisked away to another planet: one of bald-headed little boys. Pediatric Oncology.

Peed Onk. You wash your hands for thirty seconds in anti-bacterial soap before you are allowed to enter through the swinging doors. You put paper slippers on your shoes. You keep your voice down. A whole place has been designed and decorated for your nightmare. Here is where your nightmare will occur. We've got a room all ready for you. We have cots. We have refrigerators. 'The children are almost entirely boys,' says one of the nurses. 'No one knows why. It's been documented, but a lot of people out there still don't realize it.' The little boys are all from sweet-sounding places – Janesville and Appleton – little heartland towns with giant landfills, agricultural runoff, paper factories, Joe McCarthy's grave (Alone, a site of great toxicity, thinks the Mother. The soil should be tested).

All the bald little boys look like brothers. They wheel their IVs up and down the single corridor of Peed Onk. Some of the lively ones, feeling good for a day, ride the lower bars of the IV while their large, cheerful mothers whiz them along the halls. *Wheee!*

The Mother does not feel large and cheerful. In her mind, she is scathing, acid-tongued, wraith-thin, and chain-smoking out on a fire escape somewhere. Beneath her lie the gentle undulations of the Midwest, with all its aspirations to be – to be what? To be Long Island. How it has succeeded! Strip mall upon strip mall. Lurid water, poisoned potatoes. The Mother drags deeply, blowing clouds of smoke out over the disfigured cornfields. When a baby gets cancer, it seems stupid ever to have given up smoking. When a baby gets cancer, you think, Whom are we kidding? Let's all light up. When a baby gets cancer, you think, Who came up with *this* idea? What celestial abandon gave rise to *this*? Pour me a drink, so I can refuse to toast.

The Mother does not know how to be one of these other mothers, with their blond hair and sweatpants and sneakers and determined pleasantness. She does not think that she can be anything similar. She does not feel remotely like them. She knows, for instance, too many people in Greenwich Village. She mail-orders oysters and tiramisu from a shop in SoHo. She is close friends with four actual homosexuals. Her husband is asking her to Take Notes.

Where do these women get their sweatpants? She will find out.

She will start, perhaps, with the costume and work from there.

She will live according to the bromides. Take one day at a time. Take a positive attitude. *Take a hike!* She wishes that there were more interesting things that were useful and true, but it seems now that it's only the boring things that are useful and true. *One day at a time.* And *at least we have our health.* How ordinary. How obvious. One day at a time. You need a brain for that?

While the Surgeon is fine-boned, regal, and laconic – they have correctly guessed his game to be doubles – there is a bit of the mad, overcaffeinated scientist to the Oncologist. He speaks quickly. He knows a lot of studies and numbers. He can do the math. Good! Someone should be able to do the math! 'It's a fast but wimpy tumor,' he explains. 'It typically metastasizes to the lung.' He rattles off some numbers, time frames, risk statistics. Fast but wimpy: the Mother tries to imagine this combination of traits, tries to think and think, and can only come up with Claudia Osk from the fourth grade, who blushed and almost wept when called on in class, but in gym could outrun everyone in the quarter-mile fire-door-to-fence dash. The Mother thinks now of this

303

tumor as Claudia Osk. They are going to get Claudia Osk, make her sorry. All right! Claudia Osk must die. Though it has never been mentioned before, it now seems clear that Claudia Osk should have died long ago. Who was she anyway? So conceited: not letting anyone beat her in a race. Well, hey, hey, hey: don't look now, Claudia!

The Husband nudges her. 'Are you listening?'

'The chances of this happening even just to one kidney are one in fifteen thousand. Now given all these other factors, the chances on the second kidney are about one in eight.'

'One in eight,' says the Husband. 'Not bad. As long as it's not one in fifteen thousand.'

The Mother studies the trees and fish along the ceiling's edge in the Save the Planet wallpaper border. Save the Planet. Yes! But the windows in this very building don't open and diesel fumes are leaking into the ventilating system, near which, outside, a delivery truck is parked. The air is nauseous and stale.

'Really,' the Oncologist is saying, 'of all the cancers he could get, this is probably the best.'

'We win,' says the Mother.

'*Best*, I know, hardly seems the right word. Look, you two probably need to get some rest. We'll see how the surgery and histology go. Then we'll start with chemo the week following. A little light chemo: vincristine and—'

'Vincristine?' interrupts the Mother. 'Wine of Christ?'

'The names are strange, I know. The other one we use is actinomycin-D. Sometimes called "dactinomycin." People move the *D* around to the front.'

'They move the *D* around to the front,' repeats the Mother.

'Yup!' the Oncologist says. 'I don't know why – they just do!'

'Christ didn't survive his wine,' says the Husband.

'But of course he did,' says the Oncologist, and nods toward the Baby, who has now found a cupboard full of hospital linens and bandages and is yanking them all out onto the floor. 'I'll see you guys tomorrow, after the surgery.' And with that, the Oncologist leaves.

'Or, rather, Christ *was* his wine,' mumbles the Husband. Everything he knows about the New Testament, he has gleaned from the sound track of *Godspell*. 'His blood was the wine. What a great beverage idea.'

'A little light chemo. Don't you like that one?' says the Mother. '*Eine kleine* dactinomycin. I'd like to see Mozart write that one up for a big wad o' cash.'

'Come here, honey,' the Husband says to the Baby, who has now pulled off both his shoes.

'It's bad enough when they refer to medical science as "an inexact science,"' says the Mother. 'But when they start referring to it as "an art," I get extremely nervous.'

'Yeah. If we wanted art, Doc, we'd go to an art museum.' The Husband picks up the Baby. 'You're an artist,' he says to the Mother, with the taint of accusation in his voice. 'They probably think you find creativity reassuring.'

The Mother sighs. 'I just find it inevitable. Let's go get something to eat.' And so they take the elevator to the cafeteria, where there is a high chair, and where, not noticing, they all eat a lot of apples with the price tags still on them.

Because his surgery is not until tomorrow, the Baby likes the hospital. He likes the long corridors, down which he can run. He likes everything on wheels. The flower carts in the lobby! ('Please keep your boy away from the flowers,' says the vendor. 'We'll buy the whole display,' snaps the Mother, adding, 'Actual children in a children's hospital – unbelievable, isn't it?') The Baby likes the other little boys. Places to

305

go! People to see! Rooms to wander into! There is Intensive Care. There is the Trauma Unit. The Baby smiles and waves. What a little Cancer Personality! Bandaged citizens smile and wave back. In Peed Onk, there are the bald little boys to play with. Joey, Eric, Tim, Mort, and Tod (Mort! Tod!). There is the four-year-old, Ned, holding his little deflated rubber ball, the one with the intriguing curling hose. The Baby wants to play with it. 'It's mine. Leave it alone,' says Ned. 'Tell the Baby to leave it alone.'

'Baby, you've got to share,' says the Mother from a chair some feet away.

Suddenly, from down near the Tiny Tim Lounge, comes Ned's mother, large and blond and sweatpanted. 'Stop that! Stop it!' she cries out, dashing toward the Baby and Ned and pushing the Baby away. 'Don't touch that!' she barks at the Baby, who is only a Baby and bursts into tears because he has never been yelled at like this before.

Ned's mom glares at everyone. 'This is drawing fluid from Neddy's liver!' She pats at the rubber thing and starts to cry a little.

'Oh my God,' says the Mother. She comforts the Baby, who is also crying. She and Ned, the only dry-eyed people, look at each other. 'I'm so sorry,' she says to Ned and then to his mother. 'I'm so stupid. I thought they were squabbling over a toy.'

'It does look like a toy,' agrees Ned. He smiles. He is an angel. All the little boys are angels. Total, sweet, bald little angels, and now God is trying to get them back for himself. Who are they, mere mortal women, in the face of this, this powerful and overwhelming and inscrutable thing, God's will? They are the mothers, that's who. You can't have him! they shout every day. You dirty old man! *Get out of here! Hands off!*

'I'm so sorry,' says the Mother again. 'I didn't know.'

Ned's mother smiles vaguely. 'Of course you didn't know,' she says, and walks back to the Tiny Tim Lounge.

The Tiny Tim Lounge is a little sitting area at the end of the Peed Onk corridor. There are two small sofas, a table, a rocking chair, a television and a VCR. There are various videos: *Speed*, *Dune*, and *Star Wars*. On one of the lounge walls there is a gold plaque with the singer Tiny Tim's name on it: his son was treated once at this hospital and so, five years ago, he donated money for this lounge. It is a cramped little lounge, which, one suspects, would be larger if Tiny Tim's son had actually lived. Instead, he died here, at this hospital and now there is this tiny room which is part gratitude, part generosity, part *fuck-you*.

Sifting through the videocassettes, the Mother wonders what science fiction could begin to compete with the science fiction of cancer itself – a tumor with its differentiated muscle and bone cells, a clump of wild nothing and its mad, ambitious desire to be something: something inside you, instead of you, another organism, but with a monster's architecture, a demon's sabotage and chaos. Think of leukemia, a tumor diabolically taking liquid form, better to swim about incognito in the blood. George Lucas, direct that!

Sitting with the other parents in the Tiny Tim Lounge, the night before the surgery, having put the Baby to bed in his high steel crib two rooms down, the Mother begins to hear the stories: leukemia in kindergarten, sarcomas in Little League, neuroblastomas discovered at summer camp. 'Eric slid into third base, but then the scrape didn't heal.' The parents pat one another's forearms and speak of other children's hospitals as if they were resorts. 'You were at St. Jude's last winter? So were we. What did you think of it? We loved the staff.' Jobs have been quit, marriages hacked up, bank accounts ravaged; the parents have seemingly endured the unendurable. They speak not of the *possibility* of comas brought on by the chemo, but of the *number* of them. 'He was in his first coma last July,' says Ned's mother. 'It was a scary time, but we pulled through.'

Pulling through is what people do around here. There is a kind of bravery in their lives that isn't bravery at all. It is automatic, unflinching, a mix of man and machine, consuming and unquestionable obligation meeting illness move for move in a giant even-steven game of chess – an unending round of something that looks like shadowboxing, though between love and death, which is the shadow? 'Everyone admires us for our courage,' says one man. 'They have no idea what they're talking about.'

I could get out of here, thinks the Mother. I could just get on a bus and go, never come back. Change my name. A kind of witness relocation thing.

'Courage requires options,' the man adds.

The Baby might be better off.

'There are options,' says a woman with a thick suede headband. 'You could give up. You could fall apart.'

'No, you can't. Nobody does. I've never seen it,' says the man. 'Well, not *really* fall apart.' Then the lounge falls quiet. Over the VCR someone has taped the fortune from a fortune cookie. 'Optimism,' it says, 'is what allows a teakettle to sing though up to its neck in hot water.' Underneath, someone else has taped a clipping from a summer horoscope. 'Cancer rules!' it says. Who would tape this up? Somebody's twelve-year-old brother. One of the fathers – Joey's father – gets up and tears them both off, makes a small wad in his fist.

There is some rustling of magazine pages.

The Mother clears her throat. 'Tiny Tim forgot the wet bar,' she says.

Ned, who is still up, comes out of his room and down the corridor, whose lights dim at nine. Standing next to her chair, he says to the Mother, 'Where are you from? What is wrong with your baby?'

In the tiny room that is theirs, she sleeps fitfully in her sweat-pants, occasionally leaping up to check on the Baby. This is what the sweatpants are for: leaping. In case of fire. In case of anything. In case the difference between day and night starts to dissolve, and there is no difference at all, so why pretend? In the cot beside her, the Husband, who has taken a sleeping pill, is snoring loudly, his arms folded about his head in a kind of origami. How could either of them have stayed back at the house, with its empty high chair and empty crib? Occasionally the Baby wakes and cries out, and she bolts up, goes to him, rubs his back, rearranges the linens. The clock on the metal dresser shows that it is five after three. Then twenty to five. And then it is really morning, the beginning of this day, nephrectomy day. Will she be glad when it's over, or barely alive, or both? Each day this week has arrived huge, empty, and unknown, like a spaceship, and this one especially is lit a bright gray.

'He'll need to put this on,' says John, one of the nurses, bright and early, handing the Mother a thin greenish gar-ment with roses and teddy bears printed on it. A wave of nausea hits her; this smock, she thinks, will soon be splat-tered with – with what?

The Baby is awake but drowsy. She lifts off his pajamas. 'Don't forget, *bubeleh*,' she whispers, undressing and dressing him. 'We will be with you every moment, every step. When you think you are asleep and floating off far

309

away from everybody, Mommy will still be there.' If she hasn't fled on a bus. 'Mommy will take care of you. And Daddy, too.' She hopes the Baby does not detect her own fear and uncertainty, which she must hide from him, like a limp. He is hungry, not having been allowed to eat, and he is no longer amused by this new place, but worried about its hardships. Oh, my baby, she thinks. And the room starts to swim a little. The Husband comes in to take over. 'Take a break,' he says to her. 'I'll walk him around for five minutes.'

She leaves but doesn't know where to go. In the hallway, she is approached by a kind of social worker, a customer-relations person, who had given them a video to watch about the anesthesia: how the parent accompanies the child into the operating room, and how gently, nicely the drugs are administered.

'Did you watch the video?'

'Yes,' says the Mother.

'Wasn't it helpful?'

'I don't know,' says the Mother.

'Do you have any questions?' asks the video woman. 'Do you have any questions?' asked of someone who has recently landed in this fearful, alien place seems to the Mother an absurd and amazing little courtesy. The very specificity of a question would give a lie to the overwhelming strangeness of everything around her.

'Not right now,' says the Mother. 'Right now, I think I'm just going to go to the bathroom.'

When she returns to the Baby's room, everyone is there: the surgeon, the anesthesiologist, all the nurses, the social worker. In their blue caps and scrubs, they look like a clutch of forget-me-nots, and forget them, who could? The Baby, in his little teddy-bear smock, seems cold and scared. He

310

reaches out and the Mother lifts him from the Husband's arms, rubs his back to warm him.

'Well, it's time!' says the Surgeon, forcing a smile.

'Shall we go?' says the Anesthesiologist.

What follows is a blur of obedience and bright lights. They take an elevator down to a big concrete room, the anteroom, the greenroom, the backstage of the operating room. Lining the walls are long shelves full of blue surgical outfits. 'Children often become afraid of the color blue,' says one of the nurses. But of course. Of course! 'Now, which one of you would like to come into the operating room for the anesthesia?'

'I will,' says the Mother.

'Are you sure?' asks the Husband.

'Yup.' She kisses the Baby's hair. 'Mr. Curlyhead,' people keep calling him here, and it seems both rude and nice. Women look admiringly at his long lashes and exclaim, 'Always the boys! Always the boys!'

Two surgical nurses put a blue smock and a blue cotton cap on the Mother. The Baby finds this funny and keeps pulling at the cap. 'This way,' says another nurse, and the Mother follows. 'Just put the Baby down on the table.'

In the video, the mother holds the baby and fumes are gently waved under the baby's nose until he falls asleep. Now, out of view of camera or social worker, the Anesthesiologist is anxious to get this under way and not let too much gas leak out into the room generally. The occupational hazard of this, his chosen profession, is gas exposure and nerve damage, and it has started to worry him. No doubt he frets about it to his wife every night. Now he turns the gas on and quickly clamps the plastic mouthpiece over the baby's cheeks and lips.

The Baby is startled. The Mother is startled. The Baby

starts to scream and redden behind the plastic, but he cannot be heard. He thrashes. 'Tell him it's okay,' says the nurse to the Mother.

Okay? 'It's okay,' repeats the Mother, holding his hand, but she knows he can tell it's not okay, because he can see not only that she is still wearing that stupid paper cap but that her words are mechanical and swallowed, and she is biting her lips to keep them from trembling. Panicked, he attempts to sit. He cannot breathe; his arms reach up. *Bye-bye, outside.* And then, quite quickly, his eyes shut; he untenses and has fallen not *into* sleep but aside to sleep, an odd, kidnapping kind of sleep, his terror now hidden someplace deep inside him.

'How did it go?' asks the social worker, waiting in the concrete outer room. The Mother is hysterical. A nurse has ushered her out.

'It wasn't at all like the filmstrip!' she cries. 'It wasn't like the filmstrip at all!'

'The filmstrip? You mean the video?' asks the social worker.

'It wasn't like that at all! It was brutal and unforgivable.'

'Why that's terrible,' she says, her role now no longer misinformational but janitorial, and she touches the Mother's arm, though the Mother shakes it off and goes to find the Husband.

She finds him in the large mulberry Surgery Lounge, where he has been taken and where there is free hot chocolate in small Styrofoam cups. Red cellophane garlands festoon the doorways. She has totally forgotten it is as close to Christmas as this. A pianist in the corner is playing 'Carol of the Bells,' and it sounds not only unfestive but scary, like the theme from *The Exorcist*.

There is a giant clock on the far wall. It is a kind of

porthole into the operating room, a way of assessing the Baby's ordeal: forty-five minutes for the Hickman implant; two and a half hours for the nephrectomy. And then, after that, three months of chemotherapy. The magazine on her lap stays open at a ruby-hued perfume ad.

'Still not taking notes,' says the Husband.

'Nope.'

'You know, in a way, this is the kind of thing you've *always* written about.'

'You are really something, you know that? This is life. This isn't a "kind of thing."'

'But this is the kind of thing that fiction is: it's the unlivable life, the strange room tacked onto the house, the extra moon that is circling the earth unbeknownst to science.'

'I told you that.'

'I'm quoting you.'

She looks at her watch, thinking of the Baby. 'How long has it been?'

'Not long. Too long. In the end, maybe those're the same things.'

'What do you suppose is happening to him right this second?'

Infection? Slipping knives? 'I don't know. But you know what? I've gotta go. I've gotta just walk a bit.' The Husband gets up, walks around the lounge, then comes back and sits down.

The synapses between the minutes are unswimmable. An hour is thick as fudge. The Mother feels depleted; she is a string of empty tin cans attached by wire, something a goat would sniff and chew, something now and then enlivened by a jolt of electricity.

She hears their names being called over the intercom. 'Yes? Yes?' She stands up quickly. Her words have flown

313

out before her, an exhalation of birds. The piano music has stopped. The pianist is gone. She and the Husband approach the main desk, where a man looks up at them and smiles. Before him is a xeroxed list of patients' names. 'That's our little boy right there,' says the Mother, seeing the Baby's name on the list and pointing at it. 'Is there some word? Is everything okay?'

'Yes,' says the man. 'Your boy is doing fine. They've just finished with the catheter, and they are moving on to the kidney.'

'But it's been two hours already! Oh my God, did something go wrong? What happened? What went wrong?'

'Did something go wrong?' The Husband tugs at his collar.

'Not really. It just took longer than they expected. I'm told everything is fine. They wanted you to know.'

'Thank you,' says the Husband. They turn and walk back toward where they were sitting.

'I'm not going to make it.' The Mother sighs, sinking into a fake leather chair shaped somewhat like a baseball mitt. 'But before I go, I'm taking half this hospital out with me.'

'Do you want some coffee?' asks the Husband.

'I don't know,' says the Mother. 'No, I guess not. No. Do you?'

'Nah, I don't, either, I guess,' he says.

'Would you like part of an orange?'

'Oh, maybe, I guess, if you're having one.' She takes an orange from her purse and just sits there peeling its difficult skin, the flesh rupturing beneath her fingers, the juice trickling down her hands, stinging the hangnails. She and the Husband chew and swallow, discreetly spit the seeds into Kleenex, and read from photocopies of the latest medical research, which they begged from the intern. They read, and underline, and sigh and close their eyes, and after some time, the surgery is over. A nurse from Peed Onk comes down to tell them.

'Your little boy's in recovery right now. He's doing well. You can see him in about fifteen minutes.'

How can it be described? How can any of it be described? The trip and the story of the trip are always two different things. The narrator is the one who has stayed home, but then, afterward, presses her mouth upon the traveler's mouth, in order to make the mouth work, to make the mouth say, say, say. One cannot go to a place and speak of it; one cannot both see and say, not really. One can go, and upon returning make a lot of hand motions and indications with the arms. The mouth itself, working at the speed of light, at the eye's instructions, is necessarily struck still; so fast, so much to report, it hangs open and dumb as a gutted bell. All that unsayable life! That's where the narrator comes in. The narrator comes with her kisses and mimicry and tidying up. The narrator comes and makes a slow, fake song of the mouth's eager devastation.

It is a horror and a miracle to see him. He is lying in his crib in his room, tubed up, splayed like a boy on a cross, his arms stiffened into cardboard 'no-no's' so that he cannot yank out the tubes. There is the bladder catheter, the nasal-gastric tube, and the Hickman, which, beneath the skin, is plugged into his jugular, then popped out his chest wall and capped with a long plastic cap. There is a large bandage taped over his abdomen. Groggy, on a morphine drip, still he is able to look at her when, maneuvering through all the vinyl wiring, she leans to hold him, and when she does, he begins to cry, but cry silently, without motion or noise. She has never seen a baby cry without motion or noise. It is the

315

crying of an old person: silent, beyond opinion, shattered. In someone so tiny, it is frightening and unnatural. She wants to pick up the Baby and run – out of there, out of there. She wants to whip out a gun: *No-no's, eh? This whole thing is what I call a no-no.* Don't you touch him! she wants to shout at the surgeons and the needle nurses. Not anymore! No more! No more! She would crawl up and lie beside him in the crib if she could. But instead, because of all his intricate wiring, she must lean and cuddle, sing to him, songs of peril and flight: 'We gotta get out of this place, if it's the last thing we ever do. We gotta get out of this place . . . there's a better life for me and you.'

Very 1967. She was eleven then and impressionable.

The Baby looks at her, pleadingly, his arms splayed out in surrender. To where? Where is there to go? Take me! Take me!

That night, postop night, the Mother and Husband lie afloat in the cot together. A fluorescent lamp near the crib is kept on in the dark. The Baby breathes evenly but thinly in his drugged sleep. The morphine in its first flooding doses apparently makes him feel as if he were falling backward – or so the Mother has been told – and it causes the Baby to jerk, to catch himself over and over, as if he were being dropped from a tree. 'Is this right? Isn't there something that should be done?' The nurses come in hourly, different ones – the night shifts seem strangely short and frequent. If the Baby stirs or frets, the nurses give him more morphine through the Hickman catheter, then leave to tend to other patients. The Mother rises to check on him in the low light. There is gurgling from the clear plastic suction tube coming out of his mouth. Brownish clumps have collected in the tube. What is going on? The Mother rings for the nurse. Is it Renée or Sarah or Darcy? She's forgotten.

'What, what is it?' murmurs the Husband, waking up.

'Something is wrong,' says the Mother. 'It looks like blood in his N-G tube.'

'What?' The Husband gets out of bed. He, too, is wearing sweatpants.

The nurse – Valerie – pushes open the heavy door to the room and enters quietly. 'Everything okay?'

'There's something wrong here. The tube is sucking blood out of his stomach. It looks like it may have perforated his stomach and that now he's bleeding internally. Look!'

Valerie is a saint, but her voice is the standard hospital saint voice: an infuriating, pharmaceutical calm. It says, Everything is normal here. Death is normal. Pain is normal. Nothing is abnormal. So there is nothing to get excited about. 'Well now, let's see.' She holds up the plastic tube and tries to see inside it. 'Hmmm,' she says. 'I'll call the attending physician.'

Because this is a research and teaching hospital, all the regular doctors are at home sleeping in their Mission-style beds. Tonight, as is apparently the case every weekend night, the attending physician is a medical student. He looks fifteen. The authority he attempts to convey, he cannot remotely inhabit. He is not even in the same building with it. He shakes everyone's hands, then strokes his chin, a gesture no doubt gleaned from some piece of dinner theater his parents took him to once. As if there were an actual beard on that chin! As if beard growth on that chin were even possible! *Our Town*! *Kiss Me Kate*! *Barefoot in the Park*! He is attempting to convince, if not to impress.

'We're in trouble,' the Mother whispers to the Husband. She is tired, tired of young people grubbing for grades. 'We've got Dr. "Kiss Me Kate," here.'

The Husband looks at her blankly, a mix of disorientation and divorce.

The medical student holds the tubing in his hands. 'I don't really see anything,' he says.

He flunks! 'You don't?' The Mother shoves her way in, holds the clear tubing in both hands. 'That,' she says. 'Right here and here.' Just this past semester, she said to one of her own students, 'If you don't see how this essay is better than that one, then I want you just to go out into the hallway and stand there until you do.' Is it important to keep one's voice down? The Baby stays asleep. He is drugged and dreaming, far away.

'Hmmm,' says the medical student. 'Perhaps there's a little irritation in the stomach.'

'A little irritation?' The Mother grows furious. 'This is blood. These are clumps and clots. This stupid thing is sucking the life right out of him!' Life! She is starting to cry.

They turn off the suction and bring in antacids, which they feed into the Baby through the tube. Then they turn the suction on again. This time on low.

'What was it on before?' asks the Husband.

'High,' says Valerie. 'Doctor's orders, though I don't know why. I don't know why these doctors do a lot of the things they do.'

'Maybe they're . . . not all that bright?' suggests the Mother. She is feeling relief and rage simultaneously: there is a feeling of prayer and litigation in the air. Yet essentially, she is grateful. Isn't she? She thinks she is. And still, and still: look at all the things you have to do to protect a child, a hospital merely an intensification of life's cruel obstacle course.

* * *

The Surgeon comes to visit on Saturday morning. He steps in and nods at the Baby, who is awake but glazed from the morphine, his eyes two dark unseeing grapes. 'The boy looks fine,' the Surgeon announces. He peeks under the Baby's bandage. 'The stitches look good,' he says. The Baby's abdomen is stitched all the way across like a baseball. 'And the other kidney, when we looked at it yesterday face-to-face, looked fine. We'll try to wean him off the morphine a little, and see how he's doing on Monday.' He clears his throat. 'And now,' he says, looking about the room at the nurses and medical students, 'I would like to speak with the Mother, alone.'

The Mother's heart gives a jolt. 'Me?'

'Yes,' he says, motioning, then turning.

She gets up and steps out into the empty hallway with him, closing the door behind her. What can this be about? She hears the Baby fretting a little in his crib. Her brain fills with pain and alarm. Her voice comes out as a hoarse whisper. 'Is there something—'

'There is a particular thing I need from you,' says the Surgeon, turning and standing there very seriously.

'Yes?' Her heart is pounding. She does not feel resilient enough for any more bad news.

'I need to ask a favor.'

'Certainly,' she says, attempting very hard to summon the strength and courage for this occasion, whatever it is; her throat has tightened to a fist.

From inside his white coat, the surgeon removes a thin paperback book and thrusts it toward her. 'Will you sign my copy of your novel?'

The Mother looks down and sees that it is indeed a copy of a novel she has written, one about teenaged girls.

She looks up. A big, spirited grin is cutting across his face.

'I read this last summer,' he says, 'and I still remember parts of it! Those girls got into such trouble!'

Of all the surreal moments of the last few days, this, she thinks, might be the most so.

'Okay,' she says, and the Surgeon merrily hands her a pen.

'You can just write To Dr.— Oh, I don't need to tell you what to write.'

The Mother sits down on a bench and shakes ink into the pen. A sigh of relief washes over and out of her. Oh, the pleasure of a sigh of relief, like the finest moments of love; has anyone properly sung the praises of sighs of relief? She opens the book to the title page. She breathes deeply. What is he doing reading novels about teenaged girls, anyway? And why didn't he buy the hardcover? She inscribes something grateful and true, then hands the book back to him.

'Is he going to be okay?'

'The boy? The boy is going to be fine,' he says, then taps her stiffly on the shoulder. 'Now you take care. It's Saturday. Drink a little wine.'

Over the weekend, while the Baby sleeps, the Mother and Husband sit together in the Tiny Tim Lounge. The Husband is restless and makes cafeteria and sundry runs, running errands for everyone. In his absence, the other parents regale her further with their sagas. Pediatric cancer and chemo stories: the children's amputations, blood poisoning, teeth flaking like shale, the learning delays and disabilities caused by chemo frying the young, budding brain. But strangely optimistic codas are tacked on – endings as stiff and loopy as carpenter's lace, crisp and empty as lettuce, reticulate as a net – ah, words. 'After all that business with the tutor, he's better now, and fitted with new incisors by my wife's cousin's husband, who did dental school in two and a half years, if you can believe that. We hope for the best. We take things as they come. Life is hard.'

'Life's a big problem,' agrees the Mother. Part of her welcomes and invites all their tales. In the few long days since this nightmare began, part of her has become addicted to disaster and war stories. She wants only to hear about the sadness and emergencies of others. They are the only situations that can join hands with her own; everything else bounces off her shiny shield of resentment and unsympathy. Nothing else can even stay in her brain. From this, no doubt, the philistine world is made, or should one say recruited? Together, the parents huddle all day in the Tiny Tim Lounge – no need to watch *Oprah*. They leave Oprah in the dust. Oprah has nothing on them. They chat matter-of-factly, then fall silent and watch *Dune* or *Star Wars*, in which there are bright and shiny robots, whom the Mother now sees not as robots at all but as human beings who have had terrible things happen to them.

Some of their friends visit with stuffed animals and soft greetings of 'Looking good' for the dozing baby, though the room is way past the stuffed-animal limit. The Mother arranges, once more, a plateful of Mint Milano cookies and cups of take-out coffee for guests. All her nutso pals stop by – the two on Prozac, the one obsessed with the word *penis* in the word *happiness*, the one who recently had her hair foiled green. 'Your friends put the *de* in *fin de siècle*,' says the Husband. Overheard, or recorded, all marital conversation sounds as if someone must be joking, though usually no one is.

She loves her friends, especially loves them for coming, since there are times they all fight and don't speak for weeks.

Is this friendship? For now and here, it must do and is, and is, she swears it is. For one, they never offer impromptu spiritual lectures about death, how it is part of life, its natural ebb and flow, how we all must accept that, or other such utterances that make her want to scratch out some eyes. Like true friends, they take no hardy or elegant stance loosely choreographed from some broad perspective. They get right in there and mutter 'Jesus Christ!' and shake their heads. Plus, they are the only people who not only will laugh at her stupid jokes but offer up stupid ones of their own. *What do you get when you cross Tiny Tim with a pit bull?* A child's illness is a strain on the mind. They know how to laugh in a fluty, desperate way – unlike the people who are more her husband's friends and who seem just to deepen their sorrow-ful gazes, nodding their heads with Sympathy. How exiling and estranging are everybody's Sympathetic Expressions! When anyone laughs, she thinks, Okay! Hooray: a buddy. In disaster as in show business.

Nurses come and go; their chirpy voices both startle and soothe. Some of the other Peed Onk parents stick their heads in to see how the Baby is and offer encouragement.

Green Hair scratches her head. 'Everyone's so friendly here. Is there someone in this place who isn't doing all this airy, scripted optimism – or are people like that the only people here?'

'It's Modern Middle Medicine meets the Modern Middle Family,' says the Husband. 'In the Modern Middle West.'

Someone has brought in take-out lo mein, and they all eat it out in the hall by the elevators.

Parents are allowed use of the Courtesy Line.

'You've got to have a second child,' says a different friend on the phone, a friend from out of town. 'An heir and a spare. That's what we did. We had another child to ensure we wouldn't off ourselves if we lost our first.'

'Really?'

'I'm serious.'

'A formal suicide? Wouldn't you just drink yourself into a lifelong stupor and let it go at that?'

'Nope. I knew how I would do it even. For a while, until our second came along, I had it all planned.'

'What did you plan?'

'I can't go into too much detail, because – Hi, honey! – the kids are here now in the room. But I'll spell out the general idea: R-O-P-E.'

Sunday evening, she goes and sinks down on the sofa in the Tiny Tim Lounge next to Frank, Joey's father. He is a short, stocky man with the currentless, flatlined look behind the eyes that all the parents eventually get here. He has shaved his head bald in solidarity with his son. His little boy has been battling cancer for five years. It is now in the liver, and the rumor around the corridor is that Joey has three weeks to live. She knows that Joey's mother, Heather, left Frank years ago, two years into the cancer, and has remarried and had another child, a girl named Brittany. The Mother sees Heather here sometimes with her new life – the cute little girl and the new, young, full-haired husband who will never be so maniacally and debilitatingly obsessed with Joey's illness the way Frank, her first husband, was. Heather comes to visit Joey, to say hello and now good-bye, but she is not Joey's main man. Frank is.

Frank is full of stories – about the doctors, about the food, about the nurses, about Joey. Joey, affectless from his meds, sometimes leaves his room and comes out to watch TV in his bathrobe. He is jaundiced and bald, and though he is nine, he looks no older than six. Frank has devoted the last four and a half years to saving Joey's life. When the cancer was first diagnosed, the doctors gave Joey a 20 percent chance of living six more months. Now here it is, almost five years later, and Joey's still here. It is all due to Frank, who, early on, quit his job as vice president of a consulting firm in order to commit himself totally to his son. He is proud of everything he's given up and done, but he is tired. Part of him now really believes things are coming to a close, that this is the end. He says this without tears. There are no more tears.

'You have probably been through more than anyone else on this corridor,' says the Mother.

'I could tell you stories,' he says. There is a sour odor between them, and she realizes that neither of them has bathed for days.

'Tell me one. Tell me the worst one.' She knows he hates his ex-wife and hates her new husband even more.

'The worst? They're all the worst. Here's one: one morning, I went out for breakfast with my buddy – it was the only time I'd left Joey alone ever; left him for two hours is all – and when I came back, his N-G tube was full of blood. They had the suction on too high, and it was sucking the guts right out of him.'

'Oh my God. That just happened to us,' said the Mother.

'It did?'

'Friday night.'

'You're kidding. They let that happen again? I gave them such a chewing-out about that!'

'I guess our luck is not so good. We get your very worst story on the second night we're here.'

'It's not a bad place, though.'

'It's not?'

'Naw. I've seen worse. I've taken Joey everywhere.'

'He seems very strong.' Truth is, at this point, Joey seems like a zombie and frightens her.

'Joey's a fucking genius. A biological genius. They'd given him six months, remember.'

The Mother nods.

'Six months is not very long,' says Frank. 'Six months is nothing. He was four and a half years old.'

All the words are like blows. She feels flooded with affection and mourning for this man. She looks away, out the window, out past the hospital parking lot, up toward the black marbled sky and the electric eyelash of the moon. 'And now he's nine,' she says. 'You're his hero.'

'And he's mine,' says Frank, though the fatigue in his voice seems to overwhelm him. 'He'll be that forever. Excuse me,' he says, 'I've got to go check. His breathing hasn't been good. Excuse me.'

'Good news and bad,' says the Oncologist on Monday. He has knocked, entered the room, and now stands there. Their cots are unmade. One wastebasket is overflowing with coffee cups. 'We've got the pathologist's report. The bad news is that the kidney they removed had certain lesions, called "rests," which are associated with a higher risk for disease in the other kidney. The good news is that the tumor is stage one, regular cell structure, and under five hundred grams, which qualifies you for a national experiment in which chemotherapy isn't done but your boy is monitored with ultrasound instead. It's not all that risky, given that the patient's watched closely, but here is the literature on it. There are forms to sign, if you decide to do that. Read all this and we can discuss it further. You have to decide within four days.'

Lesions? Rests? They dry up and scatter like M&M's on the floor. All she hears is the part about no chemo. Another sigh of relief rises up in her and spills out. In a life where there is only the bearable and the unbearable, a sigh of relief is an ecstasy.

'No chemo?' says the Husband. 'Do you recommend that?'

The Oncologist shrugs. What casual gestures these doctors are permitted! 'I know chemo. I like chemo,' says the Oncologist. 'But this is for you to decide. It depends how you feel.'

The Husband leans forward. 'But don't you think that now that we have the upper hand with this thing, we should keep going? Shouldn't we stomp on it, beat it, smash it to death with the chemo?'

The Mother swats him angrily and hard. 'Honey, you're delirious!' She whispers, but it comes out as a hiss. 'This is our lucky break!' Then she adds gently, 'We don't want the Baby to have chemo.'

The Husband turns back to the Oncologist. 'What do *you* think?'

'It could be,' he says, shrugging. 'It could be that this is your lucky break. But you won't know for sure for five years.'

The Husband turns back to the Mother. 'Okay,' he says. 'Okay.'

The Baby grows happier and strong. He begins to move and sit and eat. Wednesday morning, they are allowed to leave, and leave without chemo. The Oncologist looks a little nervous. 'Are you nervous about this?' asks the Mother.

'Of course I'm nervous.' But he shrugs and doesn't look that nervous. 'See you in six weeks for the ultrasound,' he says, waves and then leaves, looking at his big black shoes as he does.

The Baby smiles, even toddles around a little, the sun

bursting through the clouds, an angel chorus crescendoing. Nurses arrive. The Hickman is taken out of the Baby's neck and chest; antibiotic lotion is dispensed. The Mother packs up their bags. The Baby sucks on a bottle of juice and does not cry.

'No chemo?' says one of the nurses. 'Not even a *little* chemo?'

'We're doing watch and wait,' says the Mother.

The other parents look envious but concerned. They have never seen any child get out of there with his hair and white blood cells intact.

'Will you be okay?' asks Ned's mother.

'The worry's going to kill us,' says the Husband.

'But if all we have to do is worry,' chides the Mother, 'every day for a hundred years, it'll be easy. It'll be nothing. I'll take all the worry in the world, if it wards off the thing itself.'

'That's right,' says Ned's mother. 'Compared to everything else, compared to all the actual events, the worry is nothing.'

The Husband shakes his head. 'I'm such an amateur,' he moans.

'You're both doing admirably,' says the other mother. 'Your baby's lucky, and I wish you all the best.'

The Husband shakes her hand warmly. 'Thank you,' he says. 'You've been wonderful.'

Another mother, the mother of Eric, comes up to them. 'It's all very hard,' she says, her head cocked to one side. 'But there's a lot of collateral beauty along the way.'

Collateral beauty? Who is entitled to such a thing? A child is ill. No one is entitled to any collateral beauty!

'Thank you,' says the Husband.

Joey's father, Frank, comes up and embraces them both.

327

'It's a journey,' he says. He chucks the Baby on the chin. 'Good luck, little man.'

'Yes, thank you so much,' says the Mother. 'We hope things go well with Joey.' She knows that Joey had a hard, terrible night.

Frank shrugs and steps back. 'Gotta go,' he says. 'Good-bye!'

'Bye,' she says, and then he is gone. She bites the inside of her lip, a bit tearily, then bends down to pick up the diaper bag, which is now stuffed with little animals; helium balloons are tied to its zipper. Shouldering the thing, the Mother feels she has just won a prize. All the parents have now vanished down the hall in the opposite direction. The Husband moves close. With one arm, he takes the Baby from her; with the other, he rubs her back. He can see she is starting to get weepy.

'Aren't these people nice? Don't you feel better hearing about their lives?' he asks.

Why does he do this, form clubs all the time; why does even this society of suffering soothe him? When it comes to death and dying, perhaps someone in this family ought to be more of a snob.

'All these nice people with their brave stories,' he continues as they make their way toward the elevator bank, waving good-bye to the nursing staff as they go, even the Baby waving shyly. *Bye-bye! Bye-bye!* 'Don't you feel consoled, knowing we're all in the same boat, that we're all in this together?'

But who on earth would want to be in this boat? the Mother thinks. This boat is a nightmare boat. Look where it goes: to a silver-and-white room, where, just before your eyesight and hearing and your ability to touch or be touched disappear entirely, you must watch your child die.

Rope! Bring on the rope.

'Let's make our own way,' says the Mother, 'and not in this boat.'

Woman Overboard! She takes the Baby back from the Husband, cups the Baby's cheek in her hand, kisses his brow and then, quickly, his flowery mouth. The Baby's heart – she can hear it – drums with life. 'For as long as I live,' says the Mother, pressing the elevator button – up or down, everyone in the end has to leave this way – 'I never want to see any of these people again.'

There are the notes.

Now where is the money?

DEALING WITH ILLNESS

RUDYARD KIPLING

'SWEPT AND GARNISHED'

WHEN THE FIRST waves of feverish cold stole over Frau Ebermann she very wisely telephoned for the doctor and went to bed. He diagnosed the attack as mild influenza, prescribed the appropriate remedies, and left her to the care of her one servant in her comfortable Berlin flat. Frau Ebermann, beneath the thick coverlet, curled up with what patience she could until the aspirin should begin to act, and Anna should come back from the chemist with the forma-mint, the ammoniated quinine, the eucalyptus, and the little tin steam-inhaler. Meantime, every bone in her body ached; her head throbbed; her hot, dry hands would not stay the same size for a minute together; and her body, tucked into the smallest possible compass, shrank from the chill of the well-warmed sheets.

Of a sudden she noticed that an imitation-lace cover which should have lain mathematically square with the imitation-marble top of the radiator behind the green plush sofa had slipped away so that one corner hung over the bronze-painted steam pipes. She recalled that she must have rested her poor head against the radiator-top while she was taking off her boots. She tried to get up and set the thing straight, but the radiator at once receded toward the horizon, which, unlike true horizons, slanted diagonally, exactly parallel with the dropped lace edge of the cover. Frau Ebermann groaned through sticky lips and lay still.

'Certainly, I have a temperature,' she said. 'Certainly,

I have a grave temperature. I should have been warned by that chill after dinner.'

She resolved to shut her hot-lidded eyes, but opened them in a little while to torture herself with the knowledge of that ungeometrical thing against the far wall. Then she saw a child – an untidy, thin-faced little girl of about ten, who must have strayed in from the adjoining flat. This proved – Frau Ebermann groaned again at the way the world falls to bits when one is sick – proved that Anna had forgotten to shut the outer door of the flat when she went to the chemist. Frau Ebermann had had children of her own, but they were all grown up now, and she had never been a child-lover in any sense. Yet the intruder might be made to serve her scheme of things.

'Make – put,' she muttered thickly, 'that white thing straight on the top of that yellow thing.'

The child paid no attention, but moved about the room, investigating everything that came in her way – the yellow cut-glass handles of the chest of drawers, the stamped bronze hook to hold back the heavy puce curtains, and the mauve enamel, New Art finger-plates on the door. Frau Ebermann watched indignantly.

'Aie! That is bad and rude. Go away!' she cried, though it hurt her to raise her voice. 'Go away by the road you came!' The child passed behind the bed-foot, where she could not see her. 'Shut the door as you go. I will speak to Anna, but – first, put that white thing straight.'

She closed her eyes in misery of body and soul. The outer door clicked, and Anna entered, very penitent that she had stayed so long at the chemist's. But it had been difficult to find the proper type of inhaler, and—

'Where did the child go?' moaned Frau Ebermann – 'the child that was here?'

'There was no child,' said startled Anna. 'How should any child come in when I shut the door behind me after I go out? All the keys of the flats are different.'

'No, no! You forgot this time. But my back is aching, and up my legs also. Besides, who knows what it may have fingered and upset? Look and see.'

'Nothing is fingered, nothing is upset,' Anna replied, as she took the inhaler from its paper box.

'Yes, there is. Now I remember all about it. Put – put that white thing, with the open edge – the lace, I mean – quite straight on that—' she pointed. Anna, accustomed to her ways, understood and went to it.

'Now, is it quite straight?' Frau Ebermann demanded.

'Perfectly,' said Anna. 'In fact, in the very centre of the radiator.' Anna measured the equal margins with her knuckle, as she had been told to do when she first took service.

'And my tortoise-shell hair-brushes?' Frau Ebermann could not command her dressing-table from where she lay.

'Perfectly straight, side by side in the big tray, and the comb laid across them. Your watch also in the coralline watch-holder. Everything' – she moved round the room to make sure – 'everything is as you have it when you are well.' Frau Ebermann sighed with relief. It seemed to her that the room and her head had suddenly grown cooler.

'Good!' said she. 'Now warm my nightgown in the kitchen, so it will be ready when I have perspired. And the towels also. Make the inhaler steam, and put in the eucalyptus; that is good for the larynx. Then sit you in the kitchen, and come when I ring. But, first, my hot-water bottle.'

It was brought and scientifically tucked in.

'What news?' said Frau Ebermann drowsily. She had not been out that day.

337

'Another victory,' said Anna. 'Many more prisoners and guns.'

Frau Ebermann purred, one might almost say grunted, contentedly.

'That is good, too,' she said; and Anna, after lighting the inhaler lamp, went out.

Frau Ebermann reflected that in an hour or so the aspirin would begin to work, and all would be well. To-morrow – no, the day after – she would take up life with something to talk over with her friends at coffee. It was rare – every one knew it – that she should be overcome by any ailment. Yet in all her distresses she had not allowed the minutest deviation from daily routine and ritual. She would tell her friends – she ran over their names one by one – exactly what measures she had taken against the lace cover on the radiator-top and in regard to her two tortoise-shell hair-brushes and the comb at right angles. How she had set everything in order – everything in order. She roved further afield as she wriggled her toes luxuriously on the hot-water bottle. If it pleased our dear God to take her to Himself, and she was not so young as she had been – there was that plate of the four lower ones in the blue tooth-glass, for instance – He should find all her belongings fit to meet His eye. 'Swept and garnished' were the words that shaped themselves in her intent brain. 'Swept and garnished for—'

No, it was certainly not for the dear Lord that she had swept; she would have her room swept out to-morrow or the day after, and garnished. Her hands began to swell again into huge pillows of nothingness. Then they shrank, and so did her head, to minute dots. It occurred to her that she was waiting for some event, some tremendously important event, to come to pass. She lay with shut eyes for a long time till her head and hands should return to their proper size.

338

She opened her eyes with a jerk.

'How stupid of me,' she said aloud, 'to set the room in order for a parcel of dirty little children!'

They were there – five of them, two little boys and three girls – headed by the anxious-eyed ten-year-old whom she had seen before. They must have entered by the outer door, which Anna had neglected to shut behind her when she returned with the inhaler. She counted them backward and forward as one counts scales – one, two, three, four, five.

They took no notice of her, but hung about, first on one foot then on the other, like strayed chickens, the smaller ones holding by the larger. They had the air of utterly wearied passengers in a railway waiting-room, and their clothes were disgracefully dirty.

'Go away!' cried Frau Ebermann at last, after she had struggled, it seemed to her, for years to shape the words.

'You called?' said Anna at the living-room door.

'No,' said her mistress. 'Did you shut the flat door when you came in?'

'Assuredly,' said Anna. 'Besides, it is made to catch of itself.'

'Then go away,' said she, very little above a whisper. If Anna pretended not to see the children, she would speak to Anna later on.

'And now,' she said, turning toward them as soon as the door closed. The smallest of the crowd smiled at her, and shook his head before he buried it in his sister's skirts.

'Why – don't – you – go – away?' she whispered earnestly.

Again they took no notice, but, guided by the elder girl, set themselves to climb, boots and all, on to the green plush sofa in front of the radiator. The little boys had to be pushed, as they could not compass the stretch unaided. They settled themselves in a row, with small gasps of relief, and pawed the plush approvingly.

'I ask you – I ask you why do you not go away – why do you not go away?' Frau Ebermann found herself repeating the question twenty times. It seemed to her that everything in the world hung on the answer. 'You know you should not come into houses and rooms unless you are invited. Not houses and bedrooms, you know.'

'No,' a solemn little six-year-old repeated, 'not houses nor bedrooms, nor dining-rooms, nor churches, nor all those places. Shouldn't come in. It's rude.'

'Yes, he said so,' the younger girl put in proudly. 'He said it. He told them only pigs would do that.' The line nodded and dimpled one to another with little explosive giggles, such as children use when they tell deeds of great daring against their elders.

'If you know it is wrong, that makes it much worse,' said Frau Ebermann.

'Oh yes; much worse,' they assented cheerfully, till the smallest boy changed his smile to a baby wail of weariness.

'When will they come for us?' he asked, and the girl at the head of the row hauled him bodily into her square little capable lap.

'He's tired,' she explained. 'He is only four. He only had his first breeches this Spring.' They came almost under his armpits, and were held up by broad linen braces, which, his sorrow diverted for the moment, he patted proudly.

'Yes, beautiful, dear,' said both girls.

'Go away!' said Frau Ebermann. 'Go home to your father and mother!'

Their faces grew grave at once.

'H'sh! We *can't*,' whispered the eldest. 'There isn't anything left.'

'All gone,' a boy echoed, and he puffed through pursed lips. 'Like *that*, uncle told me. Both cows too.'

'And my own three ducks,' the boy on the girl's lap said sleepily.

'So, you see, we came here.' The elder girl leaned forward a little, caressing the child she rocked.

'I – I don't understand,' said Frau Ebermann. 'Are you lost, then? You must tell our police.'

'Oh no; we are only waiting.'

'But what are you waiting *for*?'

'We are waiting for our people to come for us. They told us to come here and wait for them. So we are waiting till they come,' the eldest girl replied.

'Yes. We are waiting till our people come for us,' said all the others in chorus.

'But,' said Frau Ebermann very patiently – 'but now tell me, for I tell you that I am not in the least angry, where do you come from? Where do you come from?'

The five gave the names of two villages of which she had read in the papers.

'That is silly,' said Frau Ebermann. 'The people fired on us, and they were punished. Those places are wiped out, stamped flat.'

'Yes, yes, wiped out, stamped flat. That is why and – I have lost the ribbon off my pigtail,' said the younger girl. She looked behind her over the sofa-back.

'It is not here,' said the elder. 'It was lost before. Don't you remember?'

'Now, if you are lost, you must go and tell our police. They will take care of you and give you food,' said Frau Ebermann. 'Anna will show you the way there.'

'No,' – this was the six-year-old with the smile, – 'we must wait here till our people come for us. Mustn't we, sister?'

'Of course. We wait here till our people come for us. All the world knows that,' said the eldest girl.

'Yes.' The boy in her lap had waked again. 'Little children, too – as little as Henri, and *he* doesn't wear trousers yet. As little as all that.'

'I don't understand,' said Frau Ebermann, shivering. In spite of the heat of the room and the damp breath of the steam-inhaler, the aspirin was not doing its duty.

The girl raised her blue eyes and looked at the woman for an instant.

'You see,' she said, emphasising her statements with her fingers, '*they* told *us* to wait *here* till *our* people came for us. So we came. We wait till our people come for us.'

'That is silly again,' said Frau Ebermann. 'It is no good for you to wait here. Do you know what this place is? You have been to school? It is Berlin, the capital of Germany.'

'Yes, yes,' they all cried; 'Berlin, capital of Germany. We know that. That is why we came.'

'So, you see, it is no good,' she said triumphantly, 'because your people can never come for you here.'

'They told us to come here and wait till our people came for us.' They delivered this as if it were a lesson in school. Then they sat still, their hands orderly folded on their laps, smiling as sweetly as ever.

'Go away! Go away!' Frau Ebermann shrieked.

'You called?' said Anna, entering.

'No. Go away! Go away!'

'Very good, old cat,' said the maid under her breath. 'Next time you *may* call,' and she returned to her friend in the kitchen.

'I ask you – ask you, *please* to go away,' Frau Ebermann pleaded. 'Go to my Anna through that door, and she will

342

give you cakes and sweeties. It is not kind of you to come into my room and behave so badly.'

'Where else shall we go now?' the elder girl demanded, turning to her little company. They fell into discussion. One preferred the broad street with trees, another the railway station; but when she suggested an Emperor's palace, they agreed with her.

'We will go then,' she said, and added half apologetically to Frau Ebermann, 'You see, they are so little they like to meet all the others.'

'What others?' said Frau Ebermann.

'The others – hundreds and hundreds and thousands and thousands of the others.'

'That is a lie. There cannot be a hundred even, much less a thousand,' cried Frau Ebermann.

'So?' said the girl politely.

'Yes. *I* tell you; and I have very good information. I know how it happened. You should have been more careful. You should not have run out to see the horses and guns passing. That is how it is done when our troops pass through. My son has written me so.'

They had clambered down from the sofa, and gathered round the bed with eager, interested eyes.

'Horses and guns going by – how fine!' some one whispered.

'Yes, yes; believe me, *that* is how the accidents to the children happen. You must know yourself that it is true. One runs out to look—'

'But I never saw any at all,' a boy cried sorrowfully. 'Only one noise I heard. That was when Aunt Emmeline's house fell down.'

'But listen to me. *I* am telling you! One runs out to look, because one is little and cannot see well. So one peeps

343

between the man's legs, and then – you know how close those big horses and guns turn the corners – then one's foot slips and one gets run over. That's how it happens. Several times it had happened, but not many times; certainly not a hundred, perhaps not twenty. So, you see, you *must* be all. Tell me now that you are all that there are, and Anna shall give you the cakes.'

'Thousands,' a boy repeated monotonously. 'Then we all come here to wait till our people come for us.'

'But now we will go away from here. The poor lady is tired,' said the elder girl, plucking his sleeve.

'Oh, you hurt, you hurt!' he cried, and burst into tears.

'What is that for?' said Frau Ebermann. 'To cry in a room where a poor lady is sick is very inconsiderate.'

'Oh, but look, lady!' said the elder girl.

Frau Ebermann looked and saw.

'*Au revoir*, lady.' They made their little smiling bows and curtseys undisturbed by her loud cries. '*Au revoir*, lady. We will wait till our people come for us.'

When Anna at last ran in, she found her mistress on her knees, busily cleaning the floor with the lace cover from the radiator, because, she explained, it was all spotted with the blood of five children – she was perfectly certain there could not be more than five in the whole world – who had gone away for the moment, but were now waiting round the corner, and Anna was to find them and give them cakes to stop the bleeding, while her mistress swept and garnished that Our dear Lord when He came might find everything as it should be.

O. HENRY

LET ME FEEL YOUR PULSE

SO I WENT to a doctor.

'How long has it been since you took any alcohol into your system?' he asked.

Turning my head sideways, I answered, 'Oh, quite a while.'

He was a young doctor, somewhere between twenty and forty. He wore heliotrope socks, but he looked like Napoleon. I liked him immensely.

'Now,' said he, 'I am going to show you the effect of alcohol upon your circulation.' I think it was 'circulation' he said; though it may have been 'advertising.'

He bared my left arm to the elbow, brought out a bottle of whisky, and gave me a drink. He began to look more like Napoleon. I began to like him better.

Then he put a tight compress on my upper arm, stopped my pulse with the fingers, and squeezed a rubber bulb connected with an apparatus on a stand that looked like a thermometer. The mercury jumped up and down without seeming to stop anywhere; but the doctor said it registered two hundred and thirty-seven or one hundred and sixty-five or some such number.

'Now,' said he, 'you see what alcohol does to the blood-pressure.'

'It's marvellous,' said I, 'but do you think it a sufficient test? Have one on me, and let's try the other arm.' But, no!

Then he grasped my hand. I thought I was doomed and

347

he was saying good-bye. But all he wanted to do was to jab a needle into the end of a finger and compare the red drop with a lot of fifty-cent. poker chips that he had fastened to a card.

'It's the haemoglobin test,' he explained. 'The colour of your blood is wrong.'

'Well,' said I, 'I know it should be blue; but this is a country of mix-ups. Some of my ancestors were cavaliers; but they got thick with some people on Nantucket Island, so—'

'I mean,' said the doctor, 'that the shade of red is too light.'

'Oh,' said I, 'it's a case of matching instead of matches.'

The doctor then pounded me severely in the region of the chest. When he did that I don't know whether he reminded me most of Napoleon or Battling or Lord Nelson. Then he looked grave and mentioned a string of grievances that the flesh is heir to – most ending in 'itis.' I immediately paid him fifteen dollars on account.

'Is or are it or some or any of them necessarily fatal?' I asked. I thought my connection with the matter justified my manifesting a certain amount of interest.

'All of them,' he answered cheerfully. 'But their progress may be arrested. With care and proper continuous treatment you may live to be eighty-five or ninety.'

I began to think of the doctor's bill. 'Eighty-five would be sufficient, I am sure,' was my comment. I paid him ten dollars more on account.

'The first thing to do,' he said, with renewed animation, 'is to find a sanatorium where you will get a complete rest for awhile, and allow your nerves to get into a better condition. I myself will go with you and select a suitable one.'

So he took me to a mad-house in the Catskills. It was on a bare mountain frequented only by infrequent frequenters.

You could see nothing but stones and boulders, some patches of snow, and scattered pine trees. The young physician in charge was most agreeable. He gave me a stimulant without applying a compress to the arm. It was luncheon time, and we were invited to partake. There were about twenty inmates at little tables in the dining-room. The young physician in charge came to our table and said: 'It is a custom with our guests not to regard themselves as patients, but merely as tired ladies and gentlemen taking a rest. Whatever slight maladies they may have are never alluded to in conversation.'

My doctor called loudly to a waitress to bring some phosphoglycerate of lime hash, dog-bread, bromo-seltzer pancakes, and nux vomica tea for my repast. Then a sound arose like a sudden wind storm among pine trees. It was produced by every guest in the room whispering loudly, 'Neurasthenia!' – except one man with a nose, whom I distinctly heard say, 'Chronic alcoholism.' I hope to meet him again. The physician in charge turned and walked away.

An hour or so after luncheon he conducted us to the workshop – say fifty yards from the house. Thither the guests had been conducted by the physician in charge's understudy and sponge-holder – a man with feet and a blue sweater. He was so tall that I was not sure he had a face; but the Armour Packing Company would have been delighted with his hands.

'Here,' said the physician in charge, 'our guests find relaxation from past mental worries by devoting themselves to physical labour – reaction, in reality.'

There were turning-lathes, carpenter's outfits, clay-modelling tools, spinning-wheels, weaving-frames, tread-mills, bass drums, enlarged crayon-portrait apparatuses, blacksmith forges, and everything seemingly, that could interest the paying lunatic guests of a first-rate sanatorium.

'The lady making mud-pies in the corner,' whispered the physician in charge, 'is no other than – Lula Lulington, the authoress of the novel entitled *Why Love Loves*. What she is doing now is simply to rest her mind after performing that piece of work.'

I had seen the book. 'Why doesn't she do it by writing another one instead?' I asked.

As you see, I wasn't as far gone as they thought I was.

'The gentleman pouring water through the funnel,' continued the physician in charge, 'is a Wall Street broker broken down from overwork.'

I buttoned my coat.

Others, he pointed out, were architects playing with Noah's arks, ministers reading Darwin's *Theory of Evolution*, lawyers sawing wood, tired-out society ladies talking Ibsen to the blue-sweatered sponge-holder, a neurotic millionaire lying asleep on the floor, and a prominent artist drawing a little red wagon around the room.

'You look pretty strong,' said the physician in charge to me. 'I think the best mental relaxation for you would be throwing small boulders over the mountain-side and then bringing them up again.'

I was a hundred yards away before my doctor over-took me.

'What's the matter?' he asked.

'The matter is,' said I, 'that there are no aeroplanes handy. So I am going to merrily and hastily jog the foot-pathway to yon station and catch the first unlimited-soft-coal express back to town.'

'Well,' said the doctor, 'perhaps you are right. This seems hardly the place suitable for you. But what you need is rest – absolute rest and exercise.'

That night I went to an hotel in the city, and said to the clerk: 'What I need is absolute rest and exercise. Can you give me a room with one of those tall folding-beds in it, and a relay of bell-boys to work it up and down while I rest?'

The clerk rubbed a speck off one of his finger-nails and glanced sideways at a tall man in a white hat sitting in the lobby. That man came over and asked me politely if I had seen the shrubbery at the west entrance. I had not, so he showed it to me and then looked me over.

'I thought you had 'em,' he said, not unkindly, 'but I guess you're all right. You'd better go see a doctor, old man.'

A week afterward my doctor tested my blood-pressure again without the preliminary stimulant. He looked to me a little less like Napoleon. And his socks were of a shade of tan that did not appeal to me.

'What you need,' he decided, 'is sea air and companionship.'

'Would a mermaid—' I began; but he slipped on his professional manner.

'I myself,' he said, 'will take you to the Hotel Bonair off the coast of Long Island and see that you get in good shape. It is a quiet, comfortable resort where you will soon recuperate.'

The Hotel Bonair proved to be a nine-hundred-room fashionable hostelry on an island off the main shore. Everybody who did not dress for dinner was shoved into a side dining-room and given only a terrapin and champagne table d'hôte. The bay was a great stamping-ground for wealthy yachtsmen. The *Corsair* anchored there the day we arrived. I saw Mr. Morgan standing on deck eating a cheese sandwich and gazing longingly at the hotel. Still, it was a very inexpensive place. Nobody could afford to pay their prices. When you went away you simply left your baggage, stole a skiff, and beat it for the mainland in the night.

When I had been there one day I got a pad of mono-grammed telegraph blanks at the clerk's desk and began to wire to all my friends for get-away money. My doctor and I played one game of croquet on the golf links and went to sleep on the lawn.

When we got back to town a thought seemed to occur to him suddenly. 'By the way,' he asked, 'how do you feel?'

'Relieved of very much,' I replied.

Now a consulting physician is different. He isn't exactly sure whether he is to be paid or not, and this uncertainty ensures you either the most careful or the most careless attention. My doctor took me to see a consulting physician. He made a poor guess and gave me careful attention. I liked him immensely. He put me through some co-ordination exercises.

'Have you a pain in the back of your head?' he asked. I told him I had not.

'Shut your eyes,' he ordered, 'put your feet close together, and jump backwards as far as you can.'

I was always a good backward jumper with my eyes shut, so I obeyed. My head struck the edge of the bathroom door, which had been left open and was only three feet away. The doctor was very sorry. He had overlooked the fact that the door was open. He closed it.

'Now touch your nose with your right forefinger,' he said.

'Where is it?' I asked.

'On your face,' said he.

'I mean my right forefinger,' I explained.

'Oh, excuse me,' said he. He reopened the bathroom door, and I took my finger out of the crack of it. After I had performed the marvellous digito-nasal feat I said:

'I do not wish to deceive you as to symptoms, doctor; I really have something like a pain in the back of my head.'

352

He ignored the symptom and examined my heart carefully with a latest-popular-air-penny-in-the-slot ear-trumpet. I felt like a ballad.

'Now,' he said, 'gallop like a horse for about five minutes around the room.'

I gave the best imitation I could of a disqualified Percheron being led out of Madison Square Garden. Then, without dropping in a penny, he listened to my chest again.

'No glanders in our family, Doc,' I said.

The consulting physician held up his forefinger within three inches of my nose. 'Look at my finger,' he commanded.

'Did you ever try Pears'—' I began; but he went on with his test rapidly.

'Now look across the bay. At my finger. Across the bay. At my finger. Across the bay. Across the bay. At my finger. Across the bay.' This for about three minutes.

He explained that this was a test of the action of the brain. It seemed easy to me. I never once mistook his finger for the bay. I'll bet that if he had used the phrases: 'Gaze, as it were, unpreoccupied, outward – or rather laterally – in the direction of the horizon, underlaid, so to speak, with the adjacent fluid inlet,' and 'Now, returning – or rather, in a manner, withdrawing your attention, bestow it upon my upraised digit' – I'll bet, I say, that Harry James himself could have passed the examination.

After asking me if I had ever had a grand uncle with curvature of the spine or a cousin with swelled ankles, the two doctors retired to the bathroom and sat on the edge of the bath tub for their consultation. I ate an apple, and gazed first at my finger and then across the bay.

The doctors came out looking grave. More: they looked tombstones and Tennessee-papers-please-copy. They wrote out a diet list to which I was to be restricted. It had everything that I had ever heard of to eat on it, except snails. And I never eat a snail unless it overtakes me and bites me first.

'You must follow this diet strictly,' said the doctors.

'I'd follow it a mile if I could get one-tenth of what's on it,' I answered.

'Of next importance,' they went on, 'is outdoor air and exercise. And here is a prescription that will be of great benefit to you.'

Then all of us took something. They took their hats, and I took my departure.

I went to a druggist and showed him the prescription.

'It will be $2.87 for an ounce bottle,' he said.

'Will you give me a piece of your wrapping cord?' said I.

I made a hole in the prescription, ran the cord through it, tied it around my neck, and tucked it inside. All of us have a little superstition, and mine runs to a confidence in amulets.

Of course there was nothing the matter with me, but I was very ill. I couldn't work, sleep, eat, or bowl. The only way I could get any sympathy was to go without shaving for four days. Even then somebody would say: 'Old man, you look as hardy as a pine-knot. Been up for a jaunt in the Maine woods, eh?'

Then, suddenly, I remembered that I must have outdoor air and exercise. So I went down South to John's. John is an approximate relative by verdict of a preacher standing with a little book in his hands in a bower of chrysanthemums while a hundred thousand people looked on. John has a country house seven miles from Pineville. It is at an altitude and on the Blue Ridge Mountains in a state too dignified to be dragged into this controversy. John is mica, which is more valuable and clearer than gold.

354

He met me at Pineville, and we took the trolley car to his home. It is a big neighbourless cottage on a hill surrounded by a hundred mountains. We got off at his little private station, where John's family and Amaryllis met and greeted us. Amaryllis looked at me a trifle anxiously.

A rabbit came bounding across the hill between us and the house. I threw down my suit-case and pursued it hot-foot. After I had run twenty yards and seen it disappear, I sat down on the grass and wept disconsolately.

'I can't catch a rabbit any more,' I sobbed. 'I'm of no further use in the world. I may as well be dead.'

'Oh, what is it – what is it, Brother John?' I heard Amaryllis say.

'Nerves a little unstrung,' said John in his calm way. 'Don't worry. Get up, you rabbit-chaser, and come on to the house before the biscuits get cold.' It was about twilight, and the mountains came up nobly to Miss Murfree's descriptions of them.

Soon after dinner I announced that I believed I could sleep for a year or two, including legal holidays. So I was shown to a room as big and cool as a flower garden, where there was a bed as broad as a lawn. Soon afterward the remainder of the household retired, and then there fell upon the land a silence.

I had not heard a silence before in years. It was absolute. I raised myself on my elbow and listened to it. Sleep! I thought that if I only could hear a star twinkle or a blade of grass sharpen itself I could compose myself to rest. I thought once that I heard a sound like the sail of a catboat flapping as it veered about in a breeze, but I decided that it was probably only a tack in the carpet. Still I listened.

Suddenly some belated little bird alighted upon the window-sill, and, in what he no doubt considered sleepy tones, enunciated the noise generally translated as 'cheep!'

I leaped into the air.

'Hey! what's the matter down there?' called John from his room above mine.

'Oh, nothing,' I answered, 'except that I accidentally bumped my head against the ceiling.'

The next morning I went out on the porch and looked at the mountains. There were forty-seven of them in sight. I shuddered, went into the big hall sitting-room of the house, selected *Pancoast's Family Practice of Medicine* from a bookcase, and began to read. John came in, took the book away from me, and led me outside. He has a farm of three hundred acres furnished with the usual complement of barns, mules, peasantry, and harrows with three front teeth broken off. I had seen such things in my childhood, and my heart began to sink.

Then John spoke of alfalfa, and I brightened at once. 'Oh, yes,' said I, 'wasn't she in the chorus of – let's see—'

'Green, you know,' said John, 'and tender, and you plough it under after the first season.'

'I know,' said I, 'and the grass grows over her.'

'Right,' said John. 'You know something about farming, after all.'

'I know something of some farmers,' said I, 'and a sure scythe will mow them down some day.'

On the way back to the house a beautiful and inexplicable creature walked across our path. I stopped irresistibly fascinated, gazing at it. John waited patiently, smoking his cigarette. He is a modern farmer. After ten minutes he said: 'Are you going to stand there looking at that chicken all day? Breakfast is nearly ready.'

'A chicken?' said I.

'A White Orpington hen, if you want to particularize.'

'A White Orpington hen?' I repeated, with intense inter-est. The fowl walked slowly away with graceful dignity, and I followed like a child after the Pied Piper. Five minutes more were allowed me by John, and then he took me by the sleeve and conducted me to breakfast.

After I had been there a week I began to grow alarmed. I was sleeping and eating well and actually beginning to enjoy life. For a man in my desperate condition that would never do. So I sneaked down to the trolley-station, took the car for Pineville, and went to see one of the best physicians in town. By this time I knew exactly what to do when I needed medical treatment. I hung my hat on the back of a chair, and said rapidly:

'Doctor, I have cirrhosis of the heart, indurated arteries, neurasthenia, neuritis, acute indigestion, and convalescence. I am going to live on a strict diet. I shall also take a tepid bath at night and a cold one in the morning. I shall endeavour to be cheerful, and fix my mind on pleasant subjects. In the way of drugs I intend to take a phosphorus pill three times a day, preferably after meals, and a tonic composed of the tinctures of gentian, cinchona, calisaya, and cardamom compound. Into each tablespoonful of this I shall mix tincture of nux vomica, beginning with one drop and increasing it a drop each day until the maximum dose is reached. I shall drop this with a medicine-dropper, which can be procured at a trifling cost at any pharmacy. Good morning.'

I took my hat and walked out. After I had closed the door I remembered something that I had forgotten to say. I opened it again. The doctor had not moved from where he had been sitting, but he gave a slightly nervous start when he saw me again.

'I forgot to mention,' said I, 'that I shall also take absolute rest and exercise.'

After this consultation I felt much better. The re-establishing in my mind of the fact that I was hopelessly ill gave me so much satisfaction that I almost became gloomy again. There is nothing more alarming to a neurasthenic than to feel himself growing well and cheerful.

John looked after me carefully. After I had evinced so much interest in his White Orpington chicken he tried his best to divert my mind, and was particular to lock his hen house of nights. Gradually the tonic mountain air, the wholesome food, and the daily walks among the hills so alleviated my malady that I became utterly wretched and despondent. I heard of a country doctor who lived in the mountains near-by. I went to see him and told him the whole story. He was a grey-bearded man with clear, blue, wrinkled eyes, in a home-made suit of grey jeans.

In order to save time I diagnosed my case, touched my nose with my right forefinger, struck myself below the knee to make my foot kick, sounded my chest, stuck out my tongue, and asked him the price of cemetery lots in Pineville.

He lit his pipe and looked at me for about three minutes. 'Brother,' he said, after awhile, 'you are in a mighty bad way. There's a chance for you to pull through, but it's a mighty slim one.'

'What can it be?' I asked eagerly. 'I have taken arsenic and gold, phosphorus, exercise, nux vomica, hydrotherapeutic baths, rest, excitement, codein, and aromatic spirits of ammonia. Is there anything left in the pharmacopoeia?'

'Somewhere in these mountains,' said the doctor, 'there's a plant growing – a flowering plant that'll cure you, and it's about the only thing that will. It's of a kind that's as old as the world; but of late it's powerful scarce and hard to find. You and I will have to hunt it up. I'm not engaged in active practice now; I'm getting along in years; but I'll take your

358

case. You'll have to come every day in the afternoon and help me hunt for this plant till we find it. The city doctors may know a lot about new scientific things, but they don't know much about the cures that Nature carries around in her saddlebags.'

So every day the old doctor and I hunted the cure-all plant among the mountains and valleys of the Blue Ridge. Together we toiled up steep heights so slippery with fallen autumn leaves that we had to catch every sapling and branch within our reach to save us from falling. We waded through forges and chasms, breast-deep with laurel and ferns; we followed the banks of mountain streams for miles; we wound our way like Indians through brakes of pine – road-side, hill-side, river-side, mountain-side we explored in our search for the miraculous plant.

As the old doctor said, it must have grown scarce and hard to find. But we followed our quest. Day by day we plumbed the valleys, scaled the heights, and tramped the plateaux in search of the miraculous plant. Mountain bred, he never seemed to tire. I often reached home too fatigued to do anything except fall into bed and sleep until morning. This we kept up for a month.

One evening after I had returned from a six-mile tramp with the old doctor, Amaryllis and I took a little walk under the trees near the road. We looked at the mountains drawing their royal-purple robes around them for their night's repose.

'I'm glad you're well again,' she said. 'When you first came you frightened me. I thought you were really ill.'

'Well again!' I almost shrieked. 'Do you know that I have only one chance in a thousand to live?'

Amaryllis looked at me in surprise. 'Why,' said she, 'you are as strong as one of the plough-mules, you sleep ten or twelve hours every night, and you are eating us out of house and home. What more do you want?'

'I tell you,' said I, 'that unless we find the magic – that is, the plant we are looking for – in time, nothing can save me. The doctor tells me so.'

'What doctor?'

'Doctor Tatum – the old doctor who lives halfway up Black Oak Mountain. Do you know him?'

'I have known him since I was able to talk. And is that where you go every day – is it he who takes you on these long walks and climbs that have brought back your health and strength? God bless the old doctor.'

Just then the old doctor himself drove slowly down the road in his rickety old buggy. I waved my hand at him and shouted that I would be on hand the next day at the usual time. He stopped his horse and called to Amaryllis to come to him. They talked for five minutes while I waited. Then the old doctor drove on.

When we got to the house Amaryllis lugged out an encyclopaedia and sought a word in it. 'The doctor said,' she told me, 'that you needn't call any more as a patient, but he'd be glad to see you any time as a friend. And then he told me to look up my name in the encyclopaedia and tell you what it means. It seems to be the name of a genus of flowering plants, and also the name of a country girl in Theocritus and Virgil. What do you suppose the doctor meant by that?'

'I know what he meant,' said I. 'I know now.'

A word to a brother who may have come under the spell of the unquiet Lady Neurasthenia.

The formula was true. Even though gropingly at times, the physicians of the walled cities had put their fingers upon the specific medicament.

And so for the exercise one is referred to good Doctor Tatum on Black Oak Mountain – take the road to your right at the Methodist meeting-house in the pine-grove.

Absolute rest and exercise.

What rest more remedial than to sit with Amaryllis in the shade, and, with a sixth sense, read the wordless Theocritan idyll of the gold-bannered blue mountains marching orderly into the dormitories of the night?

WILLIAM CARLOS WILLIAMS

THE PAID NURSE

WHEN I CAME in, approaching eleven o'clock Sunday evening, there had been a phone call for me. I don't know what it is, Mrs. Corcoran called up, said Floss, about an accident of some sort that happened to George. You know, Andy's friend. What kind of an accident? An explosion, I don't know, something like that, I couldn't make it out. He wants to come up and see you. She'll call back in a minute or two.

As I sat down to finish the morning paper the phone rang again as usual. His girl friend had heard about it and was taking him up to her doctor in Norwood. Swell.

But next day he came to see me anyhow. What in hell's happened to you, George? I said when I saw him. His right arm was bandaged to the shoulder, the crook of his left elbow looked like overdone bacon, his lips were blistered, his nose was shiny with grease and swollen out of shape and his right ear was red and thickened.

They want me to go back to work, he said. They told me if I didn't go back I wouldn't get paid. I want to see you.

What happened?

I work for the General Bearings Company, in Jersey City. You know what that means. They're a hard-boiled outfit. I'm not kidding myself about that, but they can't make me work the way I feel. Do you think I have to work with my arms like this? I want your opinion. That fellow in Norwood said it wasn't anything but I couldn't sleep last night. I was in agony. He gave me two capsules and told me to take one. I took one around three o'clock and that just made me feel worse. I tried to go back this morning but I couldn't do it.

Wait a minute, wait a minute. You haven't told me what happened yet.

Well, they had me cleaning some metal discs. It wasn't my regular job. So I asked the boss, What is this stuff? Benzol, he said. It is inflammable? I said. Not very, he said. We use it here all the time. I didn't believe him right then because I could smell it, it had a kind of smell like gasoline or cleaning fluid of some kind.

What I had to do was to pick those pieces out of a pail of the stuff on this side of me, my left side, and turn and place them in the oven to dry them. Two hundred degrees temperature in there. Then I'd turn and pick up another lot and so on into the dryer and back again. I had on long rubber gauntlets up almost to my elbow.

Well, I hadn't hardly started when, blup! it happened. I didn't know what it was at first. You know you don't realize those things right away – until I smelt burnt hair and cloth and saw my gloves blazing. The front of my shirt was burning too – lucky it wasn't soaked with the stuff. I jumped back into the aisle and put my hands back of me and shook the gloves off on the floor. The pail was blazing too.

Everybody came on the run and rushed me into the emergency room. Everybody was excited, but as soon as they saw that I could see and wasn't going to pass out on them they went back to their jobs and left me there with the nurse to fix me up.

Then I began to feel it. The flames from the shirt must have come up into my face because inside my nostrils was burnt and you can see what it did to my eyebrows and eyelashes. She called the doctor but he didn't come any nearer

than six feet from me. That's not very bad, he said. So the
nurse put a little dressing, of tannic acid, I think she said it
was, on my right arm which got the worst of it. I was just
turning away from the oven when it happened, lucky for me,
so I got it mostly on my right side.

What do I do now? I asked her. Go home? I was feeling
rotten.

No, of course not, she told me. That's not bad. Go on
back to work.

What! I said.

Yes, she said. And come back tomorrow morning. If
you don't you won't get paid. And, by the way, she said,
don't go to any other doctor. You come back here tomorrow
morning and go to work as usual. Do you think that was
right?

The bastards. Go ahead. Wasn't there someone you could
appeal to there? Don't you belong to a union?

No, said George. There's nothing like that there. Only the
teamsters and the pressmen have unions, they've had them
long enough so that the company can't interfere.

All right. Go ahead.

So I went back to the job. They gave me something else
to do but the pain got so bad I couldn't stand it so I told the
boss I had to quit. All right, he said, go on home but be back
here tomorrow morning. That would be today.

You went back this morning?

I couldn't sleep all night. Look at my arm.

All right. Let's look at it. The worst was the right elbow
and forearm, almost to the shoulder in fact. It was cooked
to about the color of ham rind with several areas where the
Norwood doctor had opened several large blisters the night
before. The arm was, besides that, swollen to a size at least a
third greater than its normal volume and had begun to turn

367

a deep, purplish red just above the wrist. The ear and nose were not too bad but in all the boy looked sick.

So you went back this morning?

Yes.

Did they dress it?

No, just looked at it and ordered me on the floor. They gave me a job dragging forty-pound cases from the stack to the elevator. I couldn't use my right arm so I tried to do it with my left but I couldn't keep it up. I told 'em I was going home.

Well?

The nurse gave me hell. She called me a baby and told me it wasn't anything. The men work with worse things than that the matter with them every day, she said.

That don't make any difference to me, I told her, I'm going home.

All right, she said, but if you don't show up here tomorrow for work you don't get any pay. That's why I'm here, he continued. I can't work. What do you say?

Well, I said, I'll call up the Senator, which I did at once. And was told, of course, that the man didn't have to go to work if I said he wasn't able to do so. They can be reported to the Commission, if necessary. Or better perhaps, I can write them a letter first. You tell him not to go to work.

You're not to go to work, I told the boy. O.K., that settles it. Want to see me tomorrow? Yeah. And quit those damned capsules he gave you, I told him. No damned good. Here, here's something much simpler that won't at least leave you walking on your ear till noon the next day. Thanks. See you tomorrow.

Then it began to happen. Late in the afternoon the nurse called him up to remind him to report for duty next morning. I told her I'd been to you, he said, and that you wanted the compensation papers. She won't listen to it. She says they're sending the company car for me tomorrow morning to take me in to see their doctor. Do I go?

Not on your life.

But the next day I was making rounds in the hospital at about ten A.M. when the office reached me on one of the floors. Hold the wire. It was George. The car is here and they want me to go back with them. What do I do?

Wait a minute, I said. What's their phone number? And what's that nurse's name? I'll talk to them. You wait till I call you back. So I got the nurse and talked to her. I hear you had an explosion down at your plant, I told her. What do you mean? she said. What are you trying to do, cover it up, I asked her, so the insurance company won't find out about it? We don't do that sort of thing in this company. What are you doing now? I asked her again. She blurted and bubbled till I lost my temper and let her have it. What is that, what is that? she kept saying. You know what I'm talking about, I told her. Our doctors take care of our own cases, she told me. You mean they stand off six feet from a man and tell him he's all right when the skin is half-burned off of him and the insides of his nostrils are all scorched? That isn't true, she said. He had no right to go to an outside doctor. What! I said, when he's in agony in the middle of the night from the pains of his burns, he has no right to get advice and relief? Is that what you mean? He has the privilege of calling our own doctor if he needs one, she says. In the middle of the night? I asked her. I tell you what you do, I said, you send me the compensation papers to sign. You heard me, I said, and make it snappy if you know what's good for you. We want our own doctor to see him, she insisted. All right, I said, your own doctor can see him but he's not to go to work. Get that through your head, I said. And that's what I told him.

369

He went back to their doctor in the company car.

It was funny. We were at supper that evening when he came to the house door. I didn't have any office hours that night. Floss asked him to come in and join us but he had eaten. He had a strange look on his face, half-amused and half-bewildered.

I don't know, he said. I couldn't believe it. You ought to see the way I was treated. I was all ready to be bawled out but, oh no! The nurse was all smiles. Come right in, George. Do you feel all right, George? You don't look very well. Don't you want to lie down here on the couch? I thought she was kidding me. But she meant it. What a difference! That isn't the way they treated me the first time. Then she says, It's so hot in here I'll turn on the fan so as to cool you a little. And here, here's a nice glass of orange juice. No kiddin'. What a difference!

Floss and I burst out laughing in spite of ourselves. Oh, everything's lovely now, he said. But you're not working? No, I don't have to work. They sent me back home in the company car and they're calling for me tomorrow morning. The only thing is they brought in the man who got me the job. That made me feel like two cents. You shouldn't have acted like that, George, he told me. We'll take care of you. We always take care of our men.

I can take it, sir, I told him. But I simply couldn't go back to work after the burning I got. You didn't have to go back to work, he said. Yes, I did, I said. They had me dragging forty-pound cases around the floor. . . .

Really? he said.

He didn't know that, did he? I interposed. I'm glad you spoke up. And they want you to go back tomorrow?

All right, but don't work till I tell you. But he did. After all, jobs aren't so easy to get nowadays even with a hard-boiled firm like that. I won't get any compensation either, they told me, not even for a scar.

Is that so?

And they said they're not going to pay you, either.

We'll see what the Senator says about that.

He came back two days later to tell me the rest of it. I get it now, he said. It seems after you've been there a year they insure you, but before that you don't get any protection. After a year one of the fellows was telling me – why, they had a man there that just sprained his ankle a little. It wasn't much. But they kept him out on full pay for five months, what do you know about that? They wouldn't let him work when he wanted to.

Good night!

Geez, it was funny today, he went on. They were dressing my arm and a big piece of skin had all worked loose and they were peeling it off. It hurt me a little, oh, you know, not much but I showed I could feel it, I guess. My God! the nurse had me lie down on the couch before I knew what she was doing. And do you know, that was around one-thirty. I didn't know what happened to me. When I woke up it was four o'clock. I'd been sleeping all that time! They had a blanket over me and everything.

Good!

How much do I owe you? Because I want to pay you. No use trying to get it from them. If I make any trouble they'll blackball me all over the country they tell me.

JOSEPH CONRAD

AMY FOSTER

KENNEDY IS A country doctor, and lives in Colebrook, on the shores of Eastbay. The high ground rising abruptly behind the red roofs of the little town crowds the quaint High Street against the wall which defends it from the sea. Beyond the sea-wall there curves for miles in a vast and regular sweep the barren beach of shingle, with the village of Brenzett standing out darkly across the water, a spire in a clump of trees; and still further out the perpendicular column of a lighthouse, looking in the distance no bigger than a lead-pencil, marks the vanishing-point of the land. The country at the back of Brenzett is low and flat; but the bay is fairly well sheltered from the seas, and occasionally a big ship, windbound or through stress of weather, makes use of the anchoring ground a mile and a half due north from you as you stand at the back door of the 'Ship Inn' in Brenzett. A dilapidated windmill near by, lifting its shattered arms from a mound no loftier than a rubbish-heap, and a Martello tower squatting at the water's edge half a mile to the south of the Coastguard cottages, are familiar to the skippers of small craft. These are the official sea-marks for the patch of trustworthy bottom represented on the Admiralty charts by an irregular oval of dots enclosing several figures six, with a tiny anchor engraved among them, and the legend 'mud and shells' over all.

The brow of the upland overtops the square tower of the Colebrook Church. The slope is green and looped by a white road. Ascending along this road, you open a valley broad and shallow, a wide green trough of pastures and hedges merging inland into a vista of purple tints and flowing lines closing the view.

In this valley down to Brenzett and Colebrook and up to Darnford, the market town fourteen miles away, lies the practice of my friend Kennedy. He had begun life as surgeon in the Navy, and afterwards had been the companion of a famous traveller, in the days when there were continents with unexplored interiors. His papers on the fauna and flora made him known to scientific societies. And now he had come to a country practice – from choice. The penetrating power of his mind, acting like a corrosive fluid, had destroyed his ambition, I fancy. His intelligence is of a scientific order, of an investigating habit, and of that unappeasable curiosity which believes that there is a particle of a general truth in every mystery.

A good many years ago now, on my return from abroad, he invited me to stay with him. I came readily enough, and as he could not neglect his patients to keep me company, he took me on his rounds – thirty miles or so of an afternoon, sometimes. I waited for him on the roads; the horse reached after the leafy twigs, and, sitting high in the dogcart, I could hear Kennedy's laugh through the half-open door of some cottage. He had a big, hearty laugh that would have fitted a man twice his size, a brisk manner, a bronzed face, and a pair of gray, profoundly attentive eyes. He had the talent of making people talk to him freely, and an inexhaustible patience in listening to their tales.

One day, as we trotted out of a large village into a shady bit of road, I saw on our left hand a low, black cottage, with diamond panes in the windows, a creeper on the end wall, a roof of shingle, and some roses climbing on the rickety trellis-work of the tiny porch. Kennedy pulled up to a walk. A woman, in full sunlight, was throwing a dripping blanket over a line stretched between two old apple-trees. And as the bobtailed, long-necked chestnut, trying to get his head, jerked the left hand, covered by a thick dogskin glove, the doctor raised his voice over the hedge: 'How's your child, Amy?'

I had the time to see her dull face, red, not with a mantling blush, but as if her flat cheeks had been vigorously slapped, and to take in the squat figure, the scanty, dusty brown hair drawn into a tight knot at the back of the head. She looked quite young. With a distinct catch in her breath, her voice sounded low and timid.

'He's well, thank you.'

We trotted again. 'A young patient of yours,' I said; and the doctor, flicking the chestnut absently, muttered, 'Her husband used to be.'

'She seems a dull creature,' I remarked, listlessly.

'Precisely,' said Kennedy. 'She is very passive. It's enough to look at the red hands hanging at the end of those short arms, at those slow, prominent brown eyes, to know the inertness of her mind – an inertness that one would think made it everlastingly safe from all the surprises of imagination. And yet which of us is safe? At any rate, such as you see her, she had enough imagination to fall in love. She's the daughter of one Isaac Foster, who from a small farmer has sunk into a shepherd; the beginning of his misfortunes dating from his runaway marriage with the cook of his widowed father – a well-to-do, apoplectic grazier, who passionately struck his name off his will, and had been heard to utter threats against his life. But this old affair, scandalous enough to serve as a motive for a Greek tragedy, arose from the similarity of their characters. There are other tragedies, less scandalous and of

377

a subtler poignancy, arising from irreconcilable differences and from that fear of the Incomprehensible that hangs over all our heads – over all our heads. . . .'

The tired chestnut dropped into a walk; and the rim of the sun, all red in a speckless sky, touched familiarly the smooth top of a ploughed rise near the road as I had seen it times innumerable touch the distant horizon of the sea. The uniform brownness of the harrowed field glowed with a rose tinge, as though the powdered clods had sweated out in minute pearls of blood the toil of uncounted ploughmen. From the edge of a copse a waggon with two horses was rolling gently along the ridge. Raised above our heads upon the sky-line, it loomed up against the red sun, triumphantly big, enormous, like a chariot of giants drawn by two slow-stepping steeds of legendary proportions. And the clumsy figure of the man plodding at the head of the leading horse projected itself on the background of the Infinite with a heroic uncouthness. The end of his carter's whip quivered high up in the blue. Kennedy discoursed.

'She's the eldest of a large family. At the age of fifteen they put her out to service at the New Barns Farm. I attended Mrs. Smith, the tenant's wife, and saw that girl there for the first time. Mrs. Smith, a genteel person with a sharp nose, made her put on a black dress every afternoon. I don't know what induced me to notice her at all. There are faces that call your attention by a curious want of definiteness in their whole aspect, as, walking in a mist, you peer attentively at a vague shape which, after all, may be nothing more curious or strange than a signpost. The only peculiarity I perceived in her was a slight hesitation in her utterance, a sort of pre-liminary stammer which passes away with the first word. When sharply spoken to, she was apt to lose her head at once; but her heart was of the kindest. She had never been heard to express a dislike for a single human being, and she was tender to every living creature. She was devoted to Mrs. Smith, to Mr. Smith, to their dogs, cats, canaries; and as to Mrs. Smith's gray parrot, its peculiarities exercised upon her a positive fascination. Nevertheless, when that outlandish bird, attacked by the cat, shrieked for help in human accents, she ran out into the yard stopping her ears, and did not prevent the crime. For Mrs. Smith this was another evidence of her stupidity; on the other hand, her want of charm, in view of Smith's well-known frivolousness, was a great recommendation. Her short-sighted eyes would swim with pity for a poor mouse in a trap, and she had been seen once by some boys on her knees in the wet grass helping a toad in difficulties. If it's true, as some German fellow has said, that without phosphorus there is no thought, it is still more true that there is no kindness of heart without a certain amount of imagination. She had some. She had even more than is necessary to understand suffering and to be moved by pity. She fell in love under circumstances that leave no room for doubt in the matter; for you need imagination to form a notion of beauty at all, and still more to discover your ideal in an unfamiliar shape.

'How this aptitude came to her, what it did feed upon, is an inscrutable mystery. She was born in the village, and had never been further away from it than Colebrook or perhaps Darnford. She lived for four years with the Smiths. New Barns is an isolated farm-house a mile away from the road, and she was content to look day after day at the same fields, hollows, rises; at the trees and the hedgerows; at the faces of the four men about the farm, always the same – day after day, month after month, year after year. She never showed a desire for conversation, and, as it seemed to me, she did not know how to smile. Sometimes of a fine Sunday afternoon she would put on her best dress, a pair of stout boots, a large gray hat trimmed with a black feather (I've seen her in that finery), seize an absurdly slender parasol, climb over two stiles, tramp over three fields and along two hundred yards of road – never further. There stood Foster's cottage. She would help her mother to give their tea to the younger children, wash up the crockery, kiss the little ones, and go back to the farm. That was all. All the rest, all the change, all the relaxation. She never seemed to wish for anything more. And then she fell in love. She fell in love silently, obstinately – perhaps helplessly. It came slowly, but when it came it worked like a powerful spell; it was love as the Ancients understood it: an irresistible and fateful impulse – a possession! Yes, it was in her to become haunted and possessed by a face, by a presence, fatally, as though she had been a pagan worshipper of form under a joyous sky – and to be awakened at last from that mysterious forgetfulness of self, from that enchantment, from that transport, by a fear resembling the unaccountable terror of a brute. . . .'

With the sun hanging low on its western limit, the expanse of the grass-lands framed in the counter-scarps of the rising ground took on a gorgeous and sombre aspect. A sense of penetrating sadness, like that inspired by a grave strain of music, disengaged itself from the silence of the fields. The men we met walked past, slow, unsmiling, with downcast eyes, as if the melancholy of an over-burdened earth had weighted their feet, bowed their shoulders, borne down their glances.

'Yes,' said the doctor to my remark, 'one would think the earth is under a curse, since of all her children these that cling to her the closest are uncouth in body and as leaden of gait as if their very hearts were loaded with chains. But here on this same road you might have seen amongst these heavy men a being lithe, supple and long-limbed, straight like a pine, with something striving upwards in his appearance as though the heart within him had been buoyant. Perhaps it was only the force of the contrast, but when he was passing one of these villagers here, the soles of his feet did not seem to me to touch the dust of the road. He vaulted over the stiles, paced these slopes with a long elastic stride that made him noticeable at a great distance, and had lustrous black eyes. He was so different from the mankind around that, with his freedom of movement, his soft – a little startled, glance, his olive complexion and graceful bearing, his humanity suggested to me the nature of a woodland creature. He came from there.'

The doctor pointed with his whip, and from the summit of the descent seen over the rolling tops of the trees in a park by the side of the road, appeared the level sea far below us, like the floor of an immense edifice inlaid with bands of dark ripple, with still trails of glitter, ending in a belt of glassy water at the foot of the sky. The light blurr of smoke, from an invisible steamer, faded on the great clearness of the horizon like the mist of a breath on a mirror; and, inshore, the white sails of a coaster, with the appearance of disentangling themselves slowly from under the branches, floated clear of the foliage of the trees.

'Shipwrecked in the bay?' I said.

'Yes; he was a castaway. A poor emigrant from Central Europe bound to America and washed ashore here in a storm. And for him, who knew nothing of the earth, England was an undiscovered country. It was some time before he learned its name; and for all I know he might have expected to find wild beasts or wild men here, when, crawling in the dark over the sea-wall, he rolled down the other side into a dyke, where it was another miracle he didn't get drowned. But he struggled instinctively like an animal under a net, and this blind struggle threw him out into a field. He must have been, indeed, of a tougher fibre than he looked to withstand without expiring such buffetings, the violence of his exertions, and so much fear. Later on, in his broken English that resembled curiously the speech of a young child, he told me himself that he put his trust in God, believing he was no longer in this world. And truly – he would add – how was he to know? He fought his way against the rain and the gale on all fours, and crawled at last among some sheep huddled close under the lee of a hedge. They ran off in all directions, bleating in the darkness, and he welcomed the first familiar sound he heard on these shores. It must have been two in the morning then. And this is all we know of the manner of his landing, though he did not arrive unattended by any means. Only his grisly company did not begin to come ashore till much later in the day. . . .'

The doctor gathered the reins, clicked his tongue; we trotted down the hill. Then turning, almost directly, a sharp corner into High Street, we rattled over the stones and were home.

Late in the evening Kennedy, breaking a spell of moodiness that had come over him, returned to the story. Smoking his pipe, he paced the long room from end to end. A reading-lamp concentrated all its light upon the papers on his desk; and, sitting by the open window, I saw, after the windless, scorching day, the frigid splendour of a hazy sea lying motionless under the moon. Not a whisper, not a splash, not a stir of the shingle, not a footstep, not a sigh came up from the earth below – never a sign of life but the scent of climbing jasmine: and Kennedy's voice, speaking behind me, passed through the wide casement, to vanish outside in a chill and sumptuous stillness.

'. . . The relations of shipwrecks in the olden time tell us of much suffering. Often the castaways were only saved from drowning to die miserably from starvation on a barren coast; others suffered violent death or else slavery, passing through years of precarious existence with people to whom their strangeness was an object of suspicion, dislike or fear. We read about these things, and they are very pitiful. It is indeed hard upon a man to find himself a lost stranger, helpless, incomprehensible, and of a mysterious origin, in some obscure corner of the earth. Yet amongst all the adventurers shipwrecked in all the wild parts of the world, there is not one, it seems to me, that ever had to suffer a fate so simply tragic as the man I am speaking of, the most innocent of adventurers cast out, by the sea in the bight of this bay, almost within sight from this very window.

'He did not know the name of his ship. Indeed, in the course of time we discovered he did not even know that ships had names – "like Christian people"; and when, one day, from the top of Talfourd Hill, he beheld the sea lying open to his view, his eyes roamed afar, lost in an air of wild surprise, as though he had never seen such a sight before. And probably he had not. As far as I could make out, he had been hustled together with many others on board an emigrant ship at the mouth of the Elbe, too bewildered to take note of his surroundings, too weary to see anything, too anxious to care. They were driven below into the 'tween-deck and battened down from the very start. It was a low timber dwelling – he would say – with wooden beams overhead, like the houses in his country, but you went into it down a ladder. It was very large, very cold, damp and sombre, with places in the manner of wooden boxes where people had to sleep one above another, and it kept on rocking all ways at once all the time. He crept into one of these boxes and lay down there in the clothes in which he had left his home many days before, keeping his bundle and his stick by his side. People groaned, children cried, water dripped, the lights went out, the walls of the place creaked, and everything was being shaken so that in one's little box one dared not lift one's head. He had lost touch with his only companion (a young man from the same valley, he said), and all the time a great noise of wind went on outside and heavy blows fell – boom! boom! An awful sickness overcame him, even to the point of making him neglect his prayers. Besides, one could not tell whether it was morning or evening. It seemed always to be night in that place.

'Before that he had been travelling a long, long time on the iron track. He looked out of the window, which had a wonderfully clear glass in it, and the trees, the houses, the fields, and the long roads seemed to fly round and round about him till his head swam. He gave me to understand that he had on his passage beheld uncounted multitudes of people – whole nations – all dressed in such clothes as the rich wear. Once he was made to get out of the carriage, and slept through a night on a bench in a house of bricks with his bundle under his head; and once for many hours he had to sit on a floor of flat stones, dozing, with his knees up and with his bundle between his feet. There was a roof over him, which seemed made of glass, and was so high that the tallest mountain-pine he had ever seen would have had room to grow under it. Steam-machines rolled in at one end and out at the other. People swarmed more than you can see on a feast-day round the miraculous Holy Image in the yard of the Carmelite Convent down in the plains where, before he left his home, he drove his mother in a wooden cart: – a pious old woman who wanted to offer prayers and make a vow for his safety. He could not give me an idea of how large and lofty and full of noise and smoke and gloom, and clang of iron, the place was, but someone had told him it was called Berlin. Then they rang a bell, and another steam-machine came in, and again he was taken on and on through a land that wearied his eyes by its flatness without a single bit of a hill to be seen anywhere. One more night he spent shut up in a building like a good stable with a litter of straw on the floor, guarding his bundle amongst a lot of men, of whom not one could understand a single word he said. In the morning they were all led down to the stony shores of an extremely broad muddy river, flowing not between hills but between houses that seemed immense. There was a steam-machine that went on the water, and they all stood upon it packed tight, only now there were with them many women and children who made much noise. A cold rain fell, the wind blew in his face; he was wet through, and his teeth chattered. He and the young man from the same valley took each other by the hand.

'They thought they were being taken to America straight away, but suddenly the steam-machine bumped against the side of a thing like a great house on the water. The walls were smooth and black, and there uprose, growing from the roof as it were, bare trees in the shape of crosses, extremely high. That's how it appeared to him then, for he had never seen a ship before. This was the ship that was going to swim all the way to America. Voices shouted, everything swayed; there was a ladder dipping up and down. He went up on his hands and knees in mortal fear of falling into the water below, which made a great splashing. He got separated from his companion, and when he descended into the bottom of that ship his heart seemed to melt suddenly within him.

'It was then also, as he told me, that he lost contact for good and all with one of those three men who the summer before had been going about through all the little towns in the foothills of his country. They would arrive on market-days driving in a peasant's cart, and would set up an office in an inn or some other Jew's house. There were three of them, of whom one with a long beard looked venerable; and they had red cloth collars round their necks and gold lace on their sleeves like Government officials. They sat proudly behind a long table; and in the next room, so that the common people shouldn't hear, they kept a cunning telegraph machine, through which they could talk to the Emperor of America. The fathers hung about the door, but the young men of the mountains would crowd up to the table asking many questions, for there was work to be got all the year round at three dollars a day in America, and no military service to do.

'But the American Kaiser would not take everybody. Oh, no! He himself had a great difficulty in getting accepted, and the venerable man in uniform had to go out of the room several times to work the telegraph on his behalf. The American Kaiser engaged him at last at three dollars, he being young and strong. However, many able young men backed out, afraid of the great distance; besides, those only who had some money could be taken. There were some who sold their huts and their land because it cost a lot of money to get to America; but then, once there, you had three dollars a day, and if you were clever you could find places where true gold could be picked up on the ground. His father's house was getting over full. Two of his brothers were married and had children. He promised to send money home from America by post twice a year. His father sold an old cow, a pair of piebald mountain ponies of his own raising, and a cleared plot of fair pasture land on the sunny slope of a pine-clad pass to a Jew innkeeper, in order to pay the people of the ship that took men to America to get rich in a short time.

'He must have been a real adventurer at heart, for how many of the greatest enterprises in the conquest of the earth had for their beginning just such a bargaining away of the paternal cow for the mirage or true gold far away! I have been telling you more or less in my own words what I learned fragmentarily in the course of two or three years, during which I seldom missed an opportunity of a friendly chat with him. He told me this story of his adventure with many flashes of white teeth and lively glances of black eyes, at first in a sort of anxious baby-talk, then, as he acquired the language, with great fluency, but always with that singing, soft, and at the same time vibrating intonation that instilled a strangely penetrating power into the sound of the most familiar English words, as if they had been the words of an unearthly language. And he always would come to an end, with many emphatic shakes of his head, upon that awful sensation of his heart melting within him directly he set foot on board that ship. Afterwards there seemed to come for him a period of blank ignorance, at any rate as to facts. No doubt he must have been abominably seasick and abominably unhappy – this soft and passionate adventurer, taken thus out of his knowledge, and feeling bitterly as he lay in his emigrant bunk his utter loneliness; for his was a highly sensitive nature. The next thing we know of him for certain is that he had been hiding in Hammond's pig-pound by the side of the road to Norton, six miles, as the crow flies, from the sea. Of these experiences he was unwilling to speak: they seemed to have seared into his soul a sombre sort of wonder and indignation. Through the rumours of the country-side, which lasted for a good many days after his arrival, we know that the fishermen of West Colebrook had been disturbed and startled by heavy knocks against the walls of weather-board cottages, and by a voice crying piercingly strange words in the night. Several of them turned out even, but, no doubt, he had fled in sudden alarm at their rough angry tones hailing each other in the darkness. A sort of frenzy must have helped him up the steep Norton hill. It was he, no doubt, who early the following morning had been seen lying (in a swoon, I should say) on the roadside grass by the Brenzett carrier, who actually got down to have a nearer look, but drew back, intimidated by the perfect immobility, and by something queer in the aspect of that tramp, sleeping so still under the showers. As the day advanced, some children came dashing into school at Norton in such a fright that the schoolmistress went out and spoke indignantly to a "horrid-looking man" on the road. He edged away, hanging his head, for a few steps, and then suddenly ran off with extraordinary fleetness. The driver of Mr. Bradley's milk-cart made no secret of it that he had lashed with his whip at a hairy sort of gipsy fellow who, jumping up at a turn of the road by the Vents, made a snatch at the pony's bridle. And he caught him a good one, too, right over the face, he said, that made him drop down in the mud a jolly sight quicker than he had jumped up; but it was a good half a mile before he could stop the pony. Maybe that in his desperate endeavours to get help, and in his need to get in touch with someone, the poor devil had tried to stop the cart. Also three boys confessed afterwards to throwing stones at a funny tramp, knocking about all wet and muddy, and, it seemed, very drunk, in the narrow deep lane by the limekilns. All this was the talk of three villages for days; but we have Mrs. Finn's (the wife of Smith's waggoner) unimpeachable testimony that she saw him get over the low wall of Hammond's pig-pound and lurch straight at her, babbling aloud in a voice that was enough to make one die of fright. Having the baby with her in a perambulator, Mrs. Finn called out to him to go away, and as he persisted in coming nearer, she hit him courageously with her umbrella over the head, and, without once looking back, ran like the wind with the perambulator as far as the first house in the village. She stopped then, out of breath, and spoke to old Lewis, hammering there at a heap of stones; and the old chap, taking off his immense black wire goggles, got up on his shaky legs to look where she pointed. Together they followed with their eyes the figure of the man running over a field; they saw him fall down, pick himself up, and run on again, staggering and waving his long arms above his head, in the direction of the New Barns Farm. From that moment he is plainly in the toils of his obscure and touching destiny. There is no doubt after this of what happened to him. All is certain now: Mrs. Smith's intense terror; Amy Foster's stolid conviction held against the other's nervous attack, that the man "meant no harm"; Smith's exasperation (on his return from Darnford Market) at finding the dog barking himself into a fit, the back-door locked, his wife in hysterics; and all for an unfortunate dirty tramp, supposed to be even then lurking in his stackyard. Was he? He would teach him to frighten women.

'Smith is notoriously hot-tempered, but the sight of some nondescript and miry creature sitting cross-legged amongst a lot of loose straw, and swinging itself to and fro like a bear in a cage, made him pause. Then this tramp stood up silently before him, one mass of mud and filth from head to foot. Smith, alone amongst his stacks with this apparition, in the stormy twilight ringing with the infuriated barking of the dog, felt the dread of an inexplicable strangeness. But when that being, parting with his black hands the long matted locks that hung before his face, as you part the two halves of a curtain, looked out at him with glistening, wild, black-and-white eyes, the weirdness of this silent encounter fairly staggered him. He has admitted since (for the story has been a legitimate subject of conversation about here for years) that he made more than one step backwards. Then a sudden burst of rapid, senseless speech persuaded him at once that he had to do with an escaped lunatic. In fact, that impression never wore off completely. Smith has not in his heart given up his secret conviction of the man's essential insanity to this very day.

'As the creature approached him, jabbering in a most discomposing manner, Smith (unaware that he was being addressed as "gracious lord," and adjured in God's name to afford food and shelter) kept on speaking firmly but gently to it, and retreating all the time into the other yard. At last, watching his chance, by a sudden charge he bundled him headlong into the wood-lodge, and instantly shot the bolt. Thereupon he wiped his brow, though the day was cold. He had done his duty to the community by shutting up a wandering and probably dangerous maniac. Smith isn't a hard man at all, but he had room in his brain only for that one idea of lunacy. He was not imaginative enough to ask himself whether the man might not be perishing with cold and hunger. Meantime, at first, the maniac made a great deal of noise in the lodge. Mrs. Smith was screaming upstairs, where she had locked herself in her bedroom; but Amy Foster sobbed piteously at the kitchen-door, wringing her hands and muttering, "Don't! don't!" I daresay Smith had a rough time of it that evening with one noise and another, and this insane, disturbing voice crying obstinately through the door only added to his irritation. He couldn't possibly have connected this troublesome lunatic with the sinking of a ship in Eastbay, of which there had been a rumour in the Darnford market place. And I daresay the man inside had been very near to insanity on that night. Before his excitement collapsed and he became unconscious he was throwing himself violently about in the dark, rolling on some dirty sacks, and biting his fists with rage, cold, hunger, amazement, and despair.

'He was a mountaineer of the eastern range of the Carpathians, and the vessel sunk the night before in Eastbay was the Hamburg emigrant-ship *Herzogin Sophia-Dorothea*, of appalling memory.

'A few months later we could read in the papers the accounts of the bogus "Emigration Agencies" among the Sclavonian peasantry in the more remote provinces of Austria. The object of these scoundrels was to get hold of the poor ignorant people's homesteads, and they were in league with the local usurers. They exported their victims through Hamburg mostly. As to the ship, I had watched her out of this very window, reaching close-hauled under short canvas into the bay on a dark, threatening afternoon. She came to an anchor, correctly by the chart, off the Brenzett Coastguard station. I remember before the night fell looking out again at the outlines of her spars and rigging that stood out dark and pointed on a background of ragged, slaty clouds like another and a slighter spire to the left of the Brenzett church-tower. In the evening the wind rose. At midnight I could hear in my bed the terrific gusts and the sounds of a driving deluge.

'About that time the Coastguardmen thought they saw the lights of a steamer over the anchoring-ground. In a moment they vanished; but it is clear that another vessel of some sort had tried for shelter in the bay on that awful, blind night, had rammed the German ship amidships (a breach – as one of the divers told me afterwards – "that you could sail a Thames barge through"), and then had gone out either scathless or damaged, who shall say; but had gone out, unknown, unseen, and fatal, to perish mysteriously at sea.

Of her nothing ever came to light, and yet the hue and cry that was raised all over the world would have found her out if she had been in existence anywhere on the face of the waters.

'A completeness without a clue, and a stealthy silence as of a neatly executed crime, characterize this murderous disaster, which, as you may remember, had its gruesome celebrity. The wind would have prevented the loudest outcries from reaching the shore; there had been evidently no time for signals of distress. It was death without any sort of fuss. The Hamburg ship, filling all at once, capsized as she sank, and at daylight there was not even the end of a spar to be seen above water. She was missed, of course, and at first the Coastguardmen surmised that she had either dragged her anchor or parted her cable some time during the night, and had been blown out to sea. Then, after the tide turned, the wreck must have shifted a little and released some of the bodies, because a child – a little fair-haired child in a red frock – came ashore abreast of the Martello tower. By the afternoon you could see along three miles of beach dark figures with bare legs dashing in and out of the tumbling foam, and rough-looking men, women with hard faces, children, mostly fair-haired, were being carried, stiff and dripping, on stretchers, on wattles, on ladders, in a long procession past the door of the "Ship Inn," to be laid out in a row under the north wall of the Brenzett Church.

'Officially, the body of the little girl in the red frock is the first thing that came ashore from that ship. But I have patients amongst the seafaring population of West Colebrook, and, unofficially, I am informed that very early that morning two brothers, who went down to look after their cobble hauled up on the beach, found a good way from Brenzett, an ordinary ship's hen-coop, lying high and dry on the shore, with eleven drowned ducks inside. Their families ate the birds, and the hen-coop was split into firewood with a hatchet. It is possible that a man (supposing he happened to be on deck at the time of the accident) might have floated ashore on that hen-coop. He might. I admit it is improbable, but there was the man – and for days, nay, for weeks – it didn't enter our heads that we had amongst us the only living soul that had escaped from that disaster. The man himself, even when he learned to speak intelligibly, could tell us very little. He remembered he had felt better (after the ship had anchored, I suppose), and that the darkness, the wind, and the rain took his breath away. This looks as if he had been on deck some time during that night. But we mustn't forget he had been taken out of his knowledge, that he had been sea-sick and battened down below for four days, that he had no general notion of a ship or of the sea, and therefore could have no definite idea of what was happening to him. The rain, the wind, the darkness he knew; he understood the bleating of the sheep, and he remembered the pain of his wretchedness and misery, his heartbroken astonishment that it was neither seen nor understood, his dismay at finding all the men angry and all the women fierce. He had approached them as a beggar, it is true, he said; but in his country, even if they gave nothing, they spoke gently to beggars. The children in his country were not taught to throw stones at those who asked for compassion. Smith's strategy overcame him completely. The wood-lodge presented the horrible aspect of a dungeon. What would be done to him next? . . . No wonder that Amy Foster appeared to his eyes with the aureole of an angel of light. The girl had not been able to sleep for thinking of the poor man, and in the morning, before the Smiths were up, she slipped out across the back yard. Holding the door of the wood-lodge ajar, she looked in and extended to him half a loaf of white bread –

"such bread as the rich eat in my country," he used to say.

'At this he got up slowly from amongst all sorts of rubbish, stiff, hungry, trembling, miserable, and doubtful. "Can you eat this?" she asked in her soft and timid voice. He must have taken her for a "gracious lady." He devoured ferociously, and tears were falling on the crust. Suddenly he dropped the bread, seized her wrist, and imprinted a kiss on her hand. She was not frightened. Through his forlorn condition she had observed that he was good-looking. She shut the door and walked back slowly to the kitchen. Much later on, she told Mrs. Smith, who shuddered at the bare idea of being touched by that creature.

'Through this act of impulsive pity he was brought back again within the pale of human relations with his new sur-roundings. He never forgot it – never.

'That very same morning old Mr. Swaffer (Smith's nearest neighbour) came over to give his advice, and ended by carry-ing him off. He stood, unsteady on his legs, meek, and caked over in half-dried mud, while the two men talked around him in an incomprehensible tongue. Mrs. Smith had refused to come downstairs till the madman was off the premises; Amy Foster, far from within the dark kitchen, watched through the open back-door; and he obeyed the signs that were made to him to the best of his ability. But Smith was full of mistrust. "Mind, sir! It may be all his cunning," he cried repeatedly in a tone of warning. When Mr. Swaffer started the mare, the deplorable being sitting humbly by his side, through weakness, nearly fell out over the back of the high two-wheeled cart. Swaffer took him straight home. And it is then that I come upon the scene.

'I was called in by the simple process of the old man beck-oning to me with his forefinger over the gate of his house as I happened to be driving past. I got down, of course.

' "I've got something here," he mumbled, leading the way to an out-house at a little distance from his other farm-buildings.

'It was there that I saw him first, in a long, low room taken upon the space of that sort of coach-house. It was bare and whitewashed, with a small square aperture glazed with one cracked, dusty pane at its further end. He was lying on his back upon a straw pallet; they had given him a couple of horse-blankets, and he seemed to have spent the remainder of his strength in the exertion of cleaning himself. He was almost speechless; his quick breathing under the blankets pulled up to his chin, his glittering, restless black eyes reminded me of a wild bird caught in a snare. While I was examining him, old Swaffer stood silently by the door, passing the tips of his fingers along his shaven upper lip. I gave some directions, promised to send a bottle of medicine, and naturally made some inquiries.

' "Smith caught him in the stackyard at New Barns," said the old chap in his deliberate, unmoved manner, and as if the other had been indeed a sort of wild animal. "That's how I came by him. Quite a curiosity, isn't he? Now tell me, doctor – you've been all over the world – don't you think that's a bit of a Hindoo we've got hold of here?"

'I was greatly surprised. His long black hair scattered over the straw bolster contrasted with the olive pallor of his face. It occurred to me he might be a Basque. It didn't necessarily follow that he should understand Spanish; but I tried him with the few words I know, and also with some French. The whispered sounds I caught by bending my ear to his lips puzzled me utterly. That afternoon the young ladies from the Rectory (one of them read Goethe with a dictionary, and the other had struggled with Dante for years), coming to see Miss Swaffer, tried their German and Italian on him from

395

the doorway. They retreated, just the least bit scared by the flood of passionate speech which, turning on his pallet, he let out at them. They admitted that the sound was pleasant, soft, musical – but, in conjunction with his looks perhaps, it was startling – so excitable, so utterly unlike anything one had ever heard. The village boys climbed up the bank to have a peep through the little square aperture. Everybody was wondering what Mr. Swaffer would do with him.

'He simply kept him.

'Swaffer would be called eccentric were he not so much respected. They will tell you that Mr. Swaffer sits up as late as ten o'clock at night to read books, and they will tell you also that he can write a cheque for two hundred pounds without thinking twice about it. He himself would tell you that the Swaffers had owned land between this and Darnford for these three hundred years. He must be eighty-five to-day, but he does not look a bit older than when I first came here. He is a great breeder of sheep, and deals extensively in cattle. He attends market days for miles around in every sort of weather, and drives sitting bowed low over the reins, his lank gray hair curling over the collar of his warm coat, and with a green plaid rug round his legs. The calmness of advanced age gives a solemnity to his manner. He is clean-shaved; his lips are thin and sensitive; something rigid and monachal in the set of his features lends a certain elevation to the character of his face. He has been known to drive miles in the rain to see a new kind of rose in somebody's garden, or a monstrous cabbage grown by a cottager. He loves to hear tell of or to be shown something what he calls "outlandish." Perhaps it was just that outlandishness of the man which influenced old Swaffer. Perhaps it was only an inexplicable caprice. All I know is that at the end of three weeks I caught sight of Smith's lunatic digging in Swaffer's kitchen garden.

They had found out he could use a spade. He dug barefooted.

'His black hair flowed over his shoulders. I suppose it was Swaffer who had given him the striped old cotton shirt; but he wore still the national brown cloth trousers (in which he had been washed ashore) fitting to the leg almost like tights; was belted with a broad leathern belt studded with little brass discs; and had never yet ventured into the village. The land he looked upon seemed to him kept neatly, like the grounds round a landowner's house; the size of the cart-horses struck him with astonishment; the roads resembled garden walks, and the aspect of the people, especially on Sundays, spoke of opulence. He wondered what made them so hardhearted and their children so bold. He got his food at the back-door, carried it in both hands, carefully, to his out-house, and, sitting alone on his pallet, would make the sign of the cross before he began. Beside the same pallet, kneeling in the early darkness of the short days, he recited aloud the Lord's Prayer before he slept. Whenever he saw old Swaffer he would bow with veneration from the waist, and stand erect while the old man, with his fingers over his upper lip, surveyed him silently. He bowed also to Miss Swaffer, who kept house frugally for her father – a broad-shouldered, big-boned woman of forty-five, with the pocket of her dress full of keys, and a gray, steady eye. She was Church – as people said (while her father was one of the trustees of the Baptist Chapel) – and wore a little steel cross at her waist. She dressed severely in black, in memory of one of the innumerable Bradleys of the neighbourhood, to whom she had been engaged some twenty-five years ago – a young farmer who broke his neck out hunting on the eve of the wedding-day. She had the unmoved countenance of the deaf, spoke very seldom, and her lips, thin like her father's, astonished one sometimes by a mysteriously ironic curl.

'These were the people to whom he owed allegiance, and an overwhelming loneliness seemed to fall from the leaden sky of that winter without sunshine. All the faces were sad. He could talk to no one, and had no hope of ever understanding anybody. It was as if these had been the faces of people from the other world – dead people – he used to tell me years afterwards. Upon my word, I wonder he did not go mad. He didn't know where he was. Somewhere very far from his mountains – somewhere over the water. Was this America, he wondered?

'If it hadn't been for the steel cross at Miss Swaffer's belt he would not, he confessed, have known whether he was in a Christian country at all. He used to cast stealthy glances at it, and feel comforted. There was nothing here the same as in his country! The earth and the water were different; there were no images of the Redeemer by the roadside. The very grass was different, and the trees. All the trees but the three old Norway pines on the bit of lawn before Swaffer's house, and these reminded him of his country. He had been detected once, after dusk, with his forehead against the trunk of one of them, sobbing, and talking to himself. They had been like brothers to him at that time, he affirmed. Everything else was strange. Conceive you the kind of an existence overshadowed, oppressed, by the everyday material appearances, as if by the visions of a nightmare. At night, when he could not sleep, he kept on thinking of the girl who gave him the first piece of bread he had eaten in this foreign land. She had been neither fierce nor angry, nor frightened. Her face he remembered as the only comprehensible face amongst all these faces that were as closed, as mysterious, and as mute as the faces of the dead who are possessed of a knowledge beyond the comprehension of the living. I wondered whether the memory of her compassion prevented him from cutting his throat. But there! I suppose I am an old sentimentalist, and forget the instinctive love of life which it takes all the strength of an uncommon despair to overcome.

'He did the work which was given him with an intelligence which surprised old Swaffer. By-and-by it was discovered that he could help at the ploughing, could milk the cows, feed the bullocks in the cattle-yard, and was of some use with the sheep. He began to pick up words, too, very fast; and suddenly, one fine morning in spring, he rescued from an untimely death a grand-child of old Swaffer.

'Swaffer's younger daughter is married to Wilcox, a solicitor and the Town Clerk of Colebrook. Regularly twice a year they come to stay with the old man for a few days. Their only child, a little girl not three years old at the time, ran out of the house alone in her little white pinafore, and, toddling across the grass of a terraced garden, pitched herself over a low wall head first into the horsepond in the yard below.

'Our man was out with the waggoner and the plough in the field nearest to the house, and as he was leading the team round to begin a fresh furrow, he saw, through the gap of a gate, what for anybody else would have been a mere flutter of something white. But he had straight-glancing, quick, far-reaching eyes, that only seemed to flinch and lose their amazing power before the immensity of the sea. He was barefooted, and looking as outlandish as the heart of Swaffer could desire. Leaving the horses on the turn, to the inexpressible disgust of the waggoner he bounded off, going over the ploughed ground in long leaps, and suddenly appeared before the mother, thrust the child into her arms, and strode away.

'The pond was not very deep; but still, if he had not had such good eyes, the child would have perished – miserably suffocated in the foot or so of sticky mud at the bottom.

Old Swaffer walked out slowly into the field, waited till the plough came over to his side, had a good look at him, and without saying a word went back to the house. But from that time they laid out his meals on the kitchen table; and at first, Miss Swaffer, all in black and with an inscrutable face, would come and stand in the doorway of the living-room to see him make a big sign of the cross before he fell to. I believe that from that day, too, Swaffer began to pay him regular wages.

'I can't follow step by step his development. He cut his hair short, was seen in the village and along the road going to and fro to his work like any other man. Children ceased to shout after him. He became aware of social differences, but remained for a long time surprised at the bare poverty of the churches among so much wealth. He couldn't understand either why they were kept shut up on week-days. There was nothing to steal in them. Was it to keep people from praying too often? The rectory took much notice of him about that time, and I believe the young ladies attempted to prepare the ground for his conversion. They could not, however, break him of his habit of crossing himself, but he went so far as to take off the string with a couple of brass medals the size of a sixpence, a tiny metal cross, and a square sort of scapulary which he wore round his neck. He hung them on the wall by the side of his bed, and he was still to be heard every evening reciting the Lord's Prayer, in incomprehensible words and in a slow, fervent tone, as he had heard his old father do at the head of all the kneeling family, big and little, on every evening of his life. And though he wore corduroys at work, and a slop-made pepper-and-salt suit on Sundays, strangers would turn round to look after him on the road. His foreignness had a peculiar and indelible stamp. At last people became used to see him. But they never became used to him.

His rapid, skimming walk; his swarthy complexion; his hat cocked on the left ear; his habit, on warm evenings, of wearing his coat over one shoulder, like a hussar's dolman; his manner of leaping over the stiles, not as a feat of agility, but in the ordinary course of progression – all these peculiarities were, as one may say, so many causes of scorn and offence to the inhabitants of the village. *They* wouldn't in their dinner hour lie flat on their backs on the grass to stare at the sky. Neither did they go about the fields screaming dismal tunes. Many times have I heard his high-pitched voice from behind the ridge of some sloping sheep-walk, a voice light and soaring, like a lark's, but with a melancholy human note, over our fields that hear only the song of birds. And I would be startled myself. Ah! He was different; innocent of heart, and full of good will, which nobody wanted, this castaway, that, like a man transplanted into another planet, was separated by an immense space from his past and by an immense ignorance from his future. His quick, fervent utterance positively shocked everybody. "An excitable devil," they called him. One evening, in the tap-room of the Coach and Horses, (having drunk some whisky), he upset them all by singing a love-song of his country. They hooted him down, and he was pained; but Preble, the lame wheelwright, and Vincent, the fat blacksmith, and the other notables, too, wanted to drink their evening beer in peace. On another occasion he tried to show them how to dance. The dust rose in clouds from the sanded floor; he leaped straight up amongst the deal tables, struck his heels together, squatted on one heel in front of old Preble, shooting out the other leg, uttered wild and exulting cries, jumped up to whirl on one foot, snapping his fingers above his head – and a strange carter who was having a drink in there began to swear, and cleared out with his half-pint in his hand into the bar. But when suddenly he sprang upon a table and continued to dance among the glasses, the landlord interfered. He didn't want any "acrobat tricks in the tap-room." They laid their hands on him. Having had a glass or two, Mr. Swaffer's foreigner tried to expostulate: was ejected forcibly: got a black eye.

'I believe he felt the hostility of his human surroundings. But he was tough – tough in spirit, too, as well as in body. Only the memory of the sea frightened him, with that vague terror that is left by a bad dream. His home was far away; and he did not want now to go to America. I had often explained to him that there is no place on earth where true gold can be found lying ready and to be got for the trouble of the picking up. How, then, he asked, could he ever return home with empty hands when there had been sold a cow, two ponies, and a bit of land to pay for his going? His eyes would fill with tears, and, averting them from the immense shimmer of the sea, he would throw himself face down on the grass. But sometimes, cocking his hat with a little conquering air, he would defy my wisdom. He had found his bit of true gold. That was Amy Foster's heart; which was "a golden heart, and soft to people's misery," he would say in the accents of overwhelming conviction.

'He was called Yanko. He had explained that this meant Little John; but as he would also repeat very often that he was a mountaineer (some word sounding in the dialect of his country like Goorall) he got it for his surname. And this is the only trace of him that the succeeding ages may find in the marriage register of the parish. There it stands – Yanko Goorall – in the rector's handwriting. The crooked cross made by the castaway, a cross whose tracing no doubt seemed to him the most solemn part of the whole ceremony, is all that remains now to perpetuate the memory of his name.

'His courtship had lasted some time – ever since he got

his precarious footing in the community. It began by his buying for Amy Foster a green satin ribbon in Darnford. This was what you did in his country. You bought a ribbon at a Jew's stall on a fair-day. I don't suppose the girl knew what to do with it, but he seemed to think that his honourable intentions could not be mistaken.

'It was only when he declared his purpose to get married that I fully understood how, for a hundred futile and inappreciable reasons, how – shall I say odious? – he was to all the countryside. Every old woman in the village was up in arms. Smith, coming upon him near the farm, promised to break his head for him if he found him about again. But he twisted his little black moustache with such a bellicose air and rolled such big, black fierce eyes at Smith that this promise came to nothing. Smith, however, told the girl that she must be mad to take up with a man who was surely wrong in his head. All the same, when she heard him in the gloaming whistle from beyond the orchard a couple of bars of a weird and mournful tune, she would drop whatever she had in her hand – she would leave Mrs. Smith in the middle of a sentence – and she would run out to his call. Mrs. Smith called her a shameless hussy. She answered nothing. She said nothing at all to anybody, and went on her way as if she had been deaf. She and I alone in all the land, I fancy, could see his very real beauty. He was very good-looking, and most graceful in his bearing, with that something wild as of a woodland creature in his aspect. Her mother moaned over her dismally whenever the girl came to see her on her day out. The father was surly, but pretended not to know; and Mrs. Finn once told her plainly that "this man, my dear, will do you some harm some day yet." And so it went on. They could be seen on the roads, she tramping stolidly in her finery – gray dress, black feather, stout boots, prominent white cotton gloves that caught your eye a hundred yards away; and he, his coat slung picturesquely over one shoulder, pacing by her side, gallant of bearing and casting tender glances upon the girl with the golden heart. I wonder whether he saw how plain she was. Perhaps among types so different from what he had ever seen, he had not the power to judge; or perhaps he was seduced by the divine quality of her pity.

'Yanko was in great trouble meantime. In his country you get an old man for an ambassador in marriage affairs. He did not know how to proceed. However, one day in the midst of sheep in a field (he was now Swaffer's under-shepherd with Foster) he took off his hat to the father and declared himself humbly. "I daresay she's fool enough to marry you," was all Foster said. "And then," he used to relate, "he puts his hat on his head, looks black at me as if he wanted to cut my throat, whistles the dog, and off he goes, leaving me to do the work." The Fosters, of course, didn't like to lose the wages the girl earned: Amy used to give all her money to her mother. But there was in Foster a very genuine aversion to that match. He contended that the fellow was very good with sheep, but was not fit for any girl to marry. For one thing, he used to go along the hedges muttering to himself like a dam' fool; and then, these foreigners behave very queerly to women sometimes. And perhaps he would want to carry her off somewhere – or run off himself. It was not safe. He preached it to his daughter that the fellow might ill-use her in some way. She made no answer. It was, they said in the village, as if the man had done something to her. People discussed the matter. It was quite an excitement, and the two went on "walking out" together in the face of opposition. Then something unexpected happened.

'I don't know whether old Swaffer ever understood how much he was regarded in the light of a father by his foreign retainer. Anyway the relation was curiously feudal. So when Yanko asked formally for an interview – "and the Miss, too" (he called the severe, deaf Miss Swaffer simply *Miss*) – it was to obtain their permission to marry. Swaffer heard him unmoved, dismissed him by a nod, and then shouted the intelligence into Miss Swaffer's best ear. She showed no surprise, and only remarked grimly, in a veiled blank voice, "He certainly won't get any other girl to marry him."

'It is Miss Swaffer who has all the credit of the munificence: but in a very few days it came out that Mr. Swaffer had presented Yanko with a cottage (the cottage you've seen this morning) and something like an acre of ground – had made it over to him in absolute property. Wilcox expedited the deed, and I remember him telling me he had a great pleasure in making it ready. It recited: "In consideration of saving the life of my beloved grand-child, Bertha Wilcox."

'Of course, after that no power on earth could prevent them from getting married.

'Her infatuation endured. People saw her going out to meet him in the evening. She stared with unblinking, fascinated eyes up the road where he was expected to appear, walking freely, with a swing from the hip, and humming one of the love-tunes of his country. When the boy was born, he got elevated at the "Coach and Horses," essayed again a song and a dance, and was again ejected. People expressed their commiseration for a woman married to that Jack-in-the-box. He didn't care. There was a man now (he told me boastfully) to whom he could sing and talk in the language of his country, and show how to dance by-and-by.

'But I don't know. To me he appeared to have grown less springy of step, heavier in body, less keen of eye. Imagination, no doubt; but it seems to me now as if the net of fate had been drawn closer round him already.

'One day I met him on the footpath over the Talfourd Hill. He told me that "women were funny." I had heard already of domestic differences. People were saying that Amy Foster was beginning to find out what sort of man she had married. He looked upon the sea with indifferent, unseeing eyes. His wife had snatched the child out of his arms one day as he sat on the door-step crooning to it a song such as the mothers sing to babies in his mountains. She seemed to think he was doing it some harm. Women are funny. And she had objected to him praying aloud in the evening. Why? He expected the boy to repeat the prayer aloud after him by-and-by, as he used to do after his old father when he was a child – in his own country. And I discovered he longed for their boy to grow up so that he could have a man to talk with in that language that to our ears sounded so disturbing, so passionate, and so bizarre. Why his wife should dislike the idea he couldn't tell. But that would pass, he said. And tilting his head knowingly, he tapped his breastbone to indicate that she had a good heart: not hard, not fierce, open to compassion, charitable to the poor!

'I walked away thoughtfully; I wondered whether his difference, his strangeness, were not penetrating with repulsion that dull nature they had begun by irresistibly attracting. I wondered. . . .'

The Doctor came to the window and looked out at the frigid splendour of the sea, immense in the haze, as if enclosing all the earth with all the hearts lost among the passions of love and fear.

'Physiologically, now,' he said, turning away abruptly, 'it was possible. It was possible.'

He remained silent. Then went on –

'At all events, the next time I saw him he was ill – lung trouble. He was tough, but I daresay he was not acclimatized

406

as well as I had supposed. It was a bad winter; and, of course, these mountaineers do get fits of home sickness; and a state of depression would make him vulnerable. He was lying half dressed on a couch downstairs.

'A table covered with a dark oilcloth took up all the middle of the little room. There was a wicker cradle on the floor, a kettle spouting steam on the hob, and some child's linen lay drying on the fender. The room was warm, but the door opens right into the garden, as you noticed perhaps.

'He was very feverish, and kept on muttering to himself. She sat on a chair and looked at him fixedly across the table with her brown, blurred eyes, "Why don't you have him upstairs?" I asked. With a start and a confused stammer she said, "Oh! ah! I couldn't sit with him upstairs, sir."

'I gave her certain directions; and going outside, I said again that he ought to be in bed upstairs. She wrung her hands. "I couldn't. I couldn't. He keeps on saying something – I don't know what." With the memory of all the talk against the man that had been dinned into her ears, I looked at her narrowly. I looked into her short-sighted eyes, at her dumb eyes that once in her life had seen an enticing shape, but seemed, staring at me, to see nothing at all now. But I saw she was uneasy.

' "What's the matter with him?" she asked in a sort of vacant trepidation. "He doesn't look very ill. I never did see anybody look like this before. . . ."

' "Do you think," I asked indignantly, "he is shamming?"

' "I can't help it, sir," she said, stolidly. And suddenly she clapped her hands and looked right and left. "And there's the baby. I am so frightened. He wanted me just now to give him the baby. I can't understand what he says to it."

' "Can't you ask a neighbour to come in to-night?" I asked.

' "Please, sir, nobody seems to care to come," she muttered, dully resigned all at once.

'I impressed upon her the necessity of the greatest care, and then had to go. There was a good deal of sickness that winter. "Oh, I hope he won't talk!" she exclaimed softly just as I was going away.

'I don't know how it is I did not see – but I didn't. And yet, turning in my trap, I saw her lingering before the door, very still, and as if meditating a flight up the miry road.

'Towards the night his fever increased.

'He tossed, moaned, and now and then muttered a complaint. And she sat with the table between her and the couch, watching every movement and every sound, with the terror, the unreasonable terror, of that man she could not understand creeping over her. She had drawn the wicker cradle close to her feet. There was nothing in her now but the maternal instinct and that unaccountable fear.

'Suddenly coming to himself, parched, he demanded a drink of water. She did not move. She had not understood, though he may have thought he was speaking in English. He waited, looking at her, burning with fever, amazed at her silence and immobility, and then he shouted impatiently, "Water! Give me water!"

'She jumped to her feet, snatched up the child, and stood still. He spoke to her, and his passionate remonstrances only increased her fear of that strange man. I believe he spoke to her for a long time, entreating, wondering, pleading, ordering, I suppose. She says she bore it as long as she could. And then a gust of rage came over him.

'He sat up and called out terribly one word – some word. Then he got up as though he hadn't been ill at all, she says. And as in fevered dismay, indignation, and wonder he tried to get to her round the table, she simply opened the door

408

and ran out with the child in her arms. She heard him call twice after her down the road in a terrible voice – and fled. . . . Ah! but you should have seen stirring behind the dull, blurred glance of those eyes the spectre of the fear which had hunted her on that night three miles and a half to the door of Foster's cottage! I did the next day.

'And it was I who found him lying face down and his body in a puddle, just outside the little wicker-gate.

'I had been called out that night to an urgent case in the village, and on my way home at daybreak passed by the cottage. The door stood open. My man helped me to carry him in. We laid him on the couch. The lamp smoked, the fire was out, the chill of the stormy night oozed from the cheerless yellow paper on the wall. "Amy!" I called aloud, and my voice seemed to lose itself in the emptiness of this tiny house as if I had cried in a desert. He opened his eyes. "Gone!" he said, distinctly. "I had only asked for water – only for a little water. . . ."

'He was muddy. I covered him up and stood waiting in silence, catching a painfully gasped word now and then. They were no longer in his own language. The fever had left him, taking with it the heat of life. And with his panting breast and lustrous eyes he reminded me again of a wild creature under the net; of a bird caught in a snare. She had left him. She had left him – sick – helpless – thirsty. The spear of the hunter had entered his very soul. "Why?" he cried, in the penetrating and indignant voice of a man calling to a responsible Maker. A gust of wind and a swish of rain answered.

'And as I turned away to shut the door he pronounced the word "Merciful!" and expired.

'Eventually I certified heart-failure as the immediate cause of death. His heart must have indeed failed him, or

409

else he might have stood this night of storm and exposure, too. I closed his eyes and drove away. Not very far from the cottage I met Foster walking sturdily between the dripping hedges with his collie at his heels.

' "Do you know where your daughter is?" I asked.

' "Don't I!" he cried. "I am going to talk to him a bit. Frightening a poor woman like this."

' "He won't frighten her any more," I said. "He is dead."

'He struck with his stick at the mud.

' "And there's the child."

'Then, after thinking deeply for a while –

' "I don't know that it isn't for the best."

'That's what he said. And she says nothing at all now. Not a word of him. Never. Is his image as utterly gone from her mind as his lithe and striding figure, his carolling voice are gone from our fields? He is no longer before her eyes to excite her imagination into a passion of love or fear; and his memory seems to have vanished from her dull brain as a shadow passes away upon a white screen. She lives in the cottage and works for Miss Swaffer. She is Amy Foster for everybody, and the child is "Amy Foster's boy." She calls him Johnny – which means Little John.

'It is impossible to say whether this name recalls anything to her. Does she ever think of the past? I have seen her hanging over the boy's cot in a very passion of maternal tenderness. The little fellow was lying on his back, a little frightened at me, but very still, with his big black eyes, with his fluttered air of a bird in a snare. And looking at him I seemed to see again the other one – the father, cast out mysteriously by the sea to perish in the supreme disaster of loneliness and despair.'

DOROTHY PARKER

LADY WITH A LAMP

WELL, MONA! WELL, you poor sick thing, you! Ah, you look so little and white and *little*, you do, lying there in that great big bed. That's what you do – go and look so child-like and pitiful nobody'd have the heart to scold you. And I ought to scold you, Mona. Oh, yes, I should so, too. Never letting me know you were ill. Never a word to your oldest friend. Darling, you might have known I'd understand, no matter what you did. What do I mean? Well, what do you *mean* what do I mean, Mona? Of course, if you'd rather not talk about – Not even to your oldest friend. All I wanted to say was you might have known that I'm always for you, no matter what happens. I do admit, sometimes it's a little hard for me to understand how on earth you ever got into such – well. Goodness knows I don't want to nag you now, when you're so sick.

All right, Mona, then you're *not* sick. If that's what you want to say, even to me, why, all right, my dear. People who aren't sick have to stay in bed for nearly two weeks, I sup-pose; I suppose people who aren't sick look the way you do. Just your nerves? You were simply all tired out? I see. It's just your nerves. You were simply tired. Yes. Oh, Mona, Mona, why don't you feel you can trust me?

Well – if that's the way you want to be to me, that's the way you want to be. I won't say anything more about it. Only I do think you might have let me know that you had – well, that you were so *tired*, if that's what you want me to

413

say. Why, I'd never have known a word about it if I hadn't run bang into Alice Patterson and she told me she'd called you up and that maid of yours said you had been sick in bed for ten days. Of course, I'd thought it rather funny I hadn't heard from you, but you know how you are – you simply let people go, and weeks can go by like, well, like *weeks*, and never a sign from you. Why, I could have been dead over and over again, for all you'd know. Twenty times over. Now, I'm not going to scold you when you're sick, but frankly and honestly, Mona, I said to myself this time, 'Well, she'll have a good wait before I call her up. I've given in often enough, goodness knows. Now she can just call me first.' Frankly and honestly, that's what I said!

And then I saw Alice, and I did feel mean, I really did. And now to see you lying there – well, I feel like a complete *dog*. That's what you do to people even when you're in the wrong, the way you always are, you wicked little thing, you! Ah, the poor dear! Feels just so awful, doesn't it?

Oh, don't keep trying to be brave, child. Not with me. Just give in – it helps so much. Just tell me all about it. You know I'll never say a word. Or at least you ought to know. When Alice told me that maid of yours said you were all tired out and your nerves had gone bad, I naturally never said anything, but I thought to myself, 'Well, maybe that's the only thing Mona could say was the matter. That's probably about the best excuse she could think of.' And of course *I'll* never deny it – but perhaps it might have been better to have said you had influenza or ptomaine poisoning. After all, people don't stay in bed for ten whole days just because they're nervous. All right. Mona, then they *do*. Then they do. Yes, dear.

Ah, to think of you going through all this and crawling off here all alone like a little wounded animal or something.

And with only that colored Edie to take care of you. Darling, oughtn't you have a trained nurse, I mean really oughtn't you? There must be so many things that have to be done for you. Why, Mona! Mona, please! Dear, you don't have to get so excited. Very well, my dear, it's just as you say – there isn't a single thing to be done. I was mistaken, that's all. I simply thought that after – Oh, now, you don't have to do that. You never have to say you're sorry, to *me*. I understand. As a matter of fact, I was glad to hear you lose your temper. It's a good sign when sick people are cross. It means they're on the way to getting better. Oh, I know! You go right ahead and be cross all you want to.

Look, where shall I sit? I want to sit some place where you won't have to turn around, so you can talk to me. You stay right the way you're lying, and I'll – Because you shouldn't move around, I'm sure. It must be terribly bad for you. All right, dear, you can move around all you want to. All right, I must be crazy. I'm crazy, then. We'll leave it like that. Only please, please don't excite yourself that way.

I'll just get this chair and put it over – oops, I'm sorry I joggled the bed – put it over here, where you can see me. There. But first I want to fix your pillows before I get settled. Well they certainly are *not* all right, Mona. After the way you've been twisting them and pulling them, these last few minutes. Now look, honey, I'll help you raise yourself ve-ry, ve-ry slo-o-ow-ly. Oh. Of course you can sit up by yourself, dear. Of course you can. Nobody ever said you couldn't. Nobody ever thought of such a thing. There now, your pillows are all smooth and lovely, and you lie right down again, before you hurt yourself. Now, isn't that better? Well, I should think it was!

Just a minute, till I get my sewing. Oh, yes, I brought it along, so we'd be all cozy. Do you honestly, frankly and honestly, think it's pretty? I'm so glad. It's nothing but a tray-cloth, you know. But you simply can't have too many. They're a lot of fun to make, too, doing this edge – it goes so quickly. Oh, Mona dear, so often I think if you just had a home of your own, and could be all busy, making pretty little things like this for it, it would do so *much* for you. I worry so about you, living in a little furnished apartment, with nothing that belongs to you, no roots, no nothing. It's not right for a woman. It's all wrong for a woman like you. Oh, I wish you'd get over that Garry McVicker! If you could just meet some nice, sweet, considerate man, and get married to him, and have your own lovely place – and with your *taste*, Mona! – and maybe have a couple of children. You're so simply adorable with children. Why, Mona Morrison, are you crying? Oh, you've got a cold? You've got a cold, *too?* I thought you were crying, there for a second. Don't you want my handkerchief, lamb? Oh, you have yours. Wouldn't you have a pink chiffon handkerchief, you nut! Why on earth don't you use cleansing tissues, just lying there in bed with no one to see you? You little idiot, you! Extravagant little fool!

No, but really, I'm serious. I've said to Fred so often, 'Oh, if we could just get Mona married!' Honestly, you don't know the feeling it gives you, just to be all secure and safe with your own sweet home and your own blessed children, and your own nice husband coming back to you every night. That's a woman's *life*, Mona. What you've been doing is really horrible. Just drifting along, that's all. What's going to happen to you, dear, whatever is going to become of you? But no – you don't even think of it. You go, and go falling in love with that Garry. Well, my dear, you've got to give me credit – I said from the very first, 'He'll never marry her.' You know that. What? There was never any thought of marriage, with you and Garry? Oh, Mona, now listen! Every woman on earth thinks of marriage as soon as she's in love with a man. Every woman, I don't care who she is.

Oh, if you were only married! It would be all the difference in the world. I think a child would do everything for you, Mona. Goodness knows, I just can't speak *decently* to that Garry, after the way he's treated you – well, you know perfectly well, *none* of your friends can – but I can frankly and honestly say, if he married you, I'd absolutely let bygones be bygones, and I'd be just as happy as happy, for you. If he's what you want. And I will say, what with your lovely looks and what with good-looking as he is, you ought to have simply *gorgeous* children. Mona, baby, you really have got a rotten cold, haven't you? Don't you want me to get you another handkerchief? Really?

I'm simply sick that I didn't bring you any flowers. But I thought the place would be full of them. Well, I'll stop on the way home and send you some. It looks too dreary here, without a flower in the room. Didn't Garry send you any? Oh, he didn't know you were sick. Well, doesn't he send you flowers anyway? Listen, hasn't he called up, all this time, and found out whether you were sick or not? Not in ten days? Well, then, haven't you called him and told him? Ah now, Mona, there *is* such a thing as being too much of a heroine. Let him worry a little, dear. It would be a very good thing for him. Maybe that's the trouble – you've always taken all the worry for both of you. Hasn't sent any flowers! Hasn't even telephoned! Well, I'd just like to talk to that young man for a few minutes. After all, this is all *his* responsibility.

He's away? He's *what?* Oh, he went to Chicago two weeks ago. Well, it seems to me I'd always heard that there were telephone wires running between here and Chicago, but of

417

course – And you'd think since he's been back, the least he could do would be to do something. He's not back yet? He's not *back* yet? Mona, what are you trying to tell me? Why, just night before last – Said he'd let you know the minute he got home? Of all the rotten, low things I ever heard in my life, this is really the – Mona, dear, please lie down. Please. Why, I didn't mean anything. I don't know what I was going to say, honestly I don't, it couldn't have been anything. For goodness' sake, let's talk about something else.

Let's see. Oh, you really ought to see Julia Post's living-room, the way she's done it now. She has brown walls – not beige, you know, or tan or anything, but brown – and these cream-colored taffeta curtains and – Mona, I tell you I absolutely don't know what I was going to say, before. It's gone completely out of my head. So you see how unimportant it must have been. Dear, please just lie quiet and try to relax. Please forget about that man for a few minutes, anyway. No man's worth getting that worked up about. Catch me doing it! You know you can't expect to get well quickly, if you get yourself so excited. You know that.

What doctor did you have, darling? Or don't you want to say? Your own? Your own Doctor Britton? You don't mean it! Well, I certainly never thought he'd do a thing like – Yes, dear, of course he's a nerve specialist. Yes, dear. Yes, dear. Yes, dear, of course you have perfect confidence in him. I only wish you would in me, once in a while; after we went to school together and everything. You might know I absolutely sympathize with you. I don't see how you could possibly have done anything else. I know you've always talked about how you'd give anything to have a baby, but it would have been so terribly unfair to the child to bring it into the world without being married. You'd have had to go live abroad and never see anybody and – And even then, somebody would

418

have been sure to have told it sometime. They always do. You did the only possible thing, *I* think. Mona, for heaven's sake! Don't scream like that. I'm not deaf, you know. All right, dear, all right, all right, all right. All right, of course I believe you. Naturally I take your word for anything. Anything you say. Only please do try to be quiet Just lie back and rest, and have a nice talk.

Ah, now don't keep harping on that. I've told you a hundred times, if I've told you once, I wasn't going to say anything at all. I tell you I don't remember *what* I was going to say. 'Night before last'? When did I mention 'night before last'? I never said any such – Well. Maybe it's better this way, Mona. The more I think of it, the more I think it's much better for you to hear it from me. Because somebody's bound to tell you. These things always come out. And I know you'd rather hear it from your oldest friend, wouldn't you? And the good Lord knows, anything I could do to make you see what that man really is! Only do relax, darling. Just for me. Dear, Garry isn't in Chicago. Fred and I saw him night before last at the Comet Club, dancing. And Alice saw him Tuesday night at El Rhumba. And I don't know how many people have said they've seen him around at the theater and night clubs and things. Why, he couldn't have stayed in Chicago more than a day or so – if he went at all.

Well, he was with *her* when we saw him, honey. Apparently he's with her all the time; nobody ever sees him with anyone else. You really must make up your mind to it, dear; it's the only thing to do. I hear all over that he's just simply *pleading* with her to marry him, but I don't know how true that is. I'm sure I can't see why he'd want to, but then you never can tell what a man like that will do. It would be just good enough *for* him if he got her, that's what *I* say. Then he'd see. She'd never stand for any of his nonsense. She'd make him toe the mark. She's a smart woman.

But, oh, so *ordinary*. I thought, when we saw them the other night, 'Well, she just looks cheap, that's all she looks.' That must be what he likes, I suppose. I must admit he looked very well. I never saw him look better. Of course you know what I think of him, but I always had to say he's one of the handsomest men I ever saw in my life. I can understand how any woman would be attracted to him – at first. Until they found out what he's really like. Oh, if you could have seen him with that awful, common creature, never once taking his eyes off her, and hanging on every word she said, as if it was pearls! It made me just—

Mona, angel, are you *crying?* Now, darling, that's just plain silly. That man's not worth another thought. You've thought about him entirely too much, that's the trouble. Three years! Three of the best years of your life you've given him, and all the time he's been deceiving you with that woman. Just think back over what you've been through – all the times and times and times he promised you he'd give her up; and you, you poor little idiot, you'd believe him, and then he'd go right back to her again. And *everybody* knew about it. Think of that, and then try telling me that man's worth crying over! Really, Mona! I'd have more pride.

You know, I'm just glad this thing happened. I'm just glad you found out. This is a little too much, this time. In Chicago, indeed! Let you know the minute he came home! The kindest thing a person could possibly have done was to tell you, and bring you to your senses at last. I'm not sorry I did it, for a second. When I think of him out having the time of his life and you lying here deathly sick all on account of him, I could just – Yes, it is on account of him. Even if you didn't have an – well, even if I was mistaken about what

420

I naturally thought was the matter with you when you made such a secret of your illness, he's driven you into a nervous breakdown, and that's plenty bad enough. All for that man! The skunk! You just put him right out of your head.

Why, of course you can, Mona. All you need to do is to pull yourself together, child. Simply say to yourself, 'Well, I've wasted three years of my life, and that's that.' Never worry about *him* any more. The Lord knows, darling, he's not worrying about you.

It's just because you're weak and sick that you're worked up like this, dear. I know. But you're going to be all right. You can make something of your life. You've got to, Mona, you know. Because after all – well, of course, you never looked sweeter, I don't mean that; but you're – well, you're not getting any younger. And here you've been throwing away your time, never seeing your friends, never going out, never meeting anybody new, just sitting here waiting for Garry to telephone, or Garry to come in – if he didn't have anything better to do. For three years, you've never had a thought in your head but that man. Now you just forget him.

Ah, baby, it isn't good for you to cry like that. Please don't. He's not even worth talking about. Look at the woman he's in love with, and you'll see what kind he is. You were much too good for him. You were much too sweet to him. You gave in too easily. The minute he had you, he didn't want you any more. That's what he's like. Why, he no more loved you than—

Mona, don't! Mona, stop it! Please, Mona! You mustn't talk like that, you mustn't say such things. You've got to stop crying, you'll be terribly sick. Stop, oh, stop it, oh, please stop! Oh, what am I going to do with her? Mona, dear – Mona! Oh, where in heaven's name is that fool maid?

Edie. Oh, Edie! Edie, I think you'd better get Dr. Britton on the telephone, and tell him to come down and give Miss Morrison something to quiet her. I'm afraid she's got herself a little bit upset.

ROBERT A. HEINLEIN

LIFE-LINE

THE CHAIRMAN RAPPED loudly for order. Gradually the cat-calls and boos died away as several self-appointed serjeants-at-arms persuaded a few hot-headed individuals to sit down. The speaker on the rostrum by the chairman seemed unaware of the disturbance. His bland, faintly insolent face was impassive. The chairman turned to the speaker, and addressed him, in a voice in which anger and annoyance were barely restrained.

'Dr Pinero' – the Doctor was faintly stressed – 'I must apologize to you for the unseemly outburst during your remarks. I am surprised that my colleagues should so far forget the dignity proper to men of science as to interrupt a speaker, no matter' – he paused and set his mouth – 'no matter how great the provocation.' Pinero smiled in his face, a smile that was in some way an open insult. The chairman visibly controlled his temper and continued, 'I am anxious that the programme be concluded decently and in order. I want you to finish your remarks. Nevertheless, I must ask you to refrain from affronting our intelligence with ideas that any educated man knows to be fallacious. Please confine yourself to your discovery – if you have made one.'

Pinero spread his fat white hands, palms down. 'How can I possibly put a new idea into your heads if I do not first remove your delusions?'

The audience stirred and muttered. Someone shouted

from the rear of the hall: 'Throw the charlatan out! We've had enough.' The chairman pounded his gavel.

'Gentlemen! Please!' Then to Pinero, 'Must I remind you that you are not a member of this body, and that we did not invite you?'

Pinero's eyebrows lifted. 'So? I seemed to remember an invitation on the letterhead of the Academy?'

The chairman chewed his lower lip before replying. 'True. I wrote that invitation myself. But it was at the request of one of the trustees – a fine public-spirited gentleman, but not a scientist, not a member of the Academy.'

Pinero smiled his irritating smile. 'So? I should have guessed. Old Bidwell, not so, of Amalgamated Life Insurance? And he wanted his trained seals to expose me as a fraud, yes? For if I can tell a man the day of his own death, no one will buy his pretty policies. But how can you expose me if you will not listen to me first? Even supposing you had the wit to understand me? Bah! He has sent jackals to tear down a lion.' He deliberately turned his back on them. The muttering of the crowd swelled and took on a vicious tone. The chairman cried vainly for order. There arose a figure in the front row.

'Mr Chairman!'

The chairman grasped the opening and shouted, 'Gentlemen! Dr Van RheinSmitt has the floor.' The commotion died away.

The doctor cleared his throat, smoothed the forelock of his beautiful white hair, and thrust one hand into a side pocket of his smartly tailored trousers. He assumed his women's-club manner.

'Mr Chairman, fellow members of the Academy of Science, let us have tolerance. Even a murderer has the right to say his say before the State exacts its tribute. Shall we do

426

less? Even though one may be intellectually certain of the verdict? I grant Dr Pinero every consideration that should be given by this august body to any unaffiliated colleague, even though' – he bowed slightly in Pinero's direction – 'we may not be familiar with the university which bestowed his degree. If what he has to say is false, it cannot harm us. If what he has to say is true, we should know it.' His mellow, cultivated voice rolled on, soothing and calming. 'If the eminent doctor's manner appears a trifle inurbane for our tastes, we must bear in mind that the doctor may be from a place, or a stratum, not so meticulous in these little matters. Now our good friend and benefactor has asked us to hear this person and carefully assess the merit of his claims. Let us do so with dignity and decorum.'

He sat down to a rumble of applause, comfortably aware that he had enhanced his reputation as an intellectual leader. Tomorrow the papers would again mention the good sense and persuasive personality of 'America's Handsomest University President'. Who knew? Perhaps old Bidwell would come through with that swimming-pool donation.

When the applause had ceased, the chairman turned to where the centre of the disturbance sat, hands folded over his little round belly, face serene.

'Will you continue, Dr Pinero?'

'Why should I?'

The chairman shrugged his shoulders. 'You came for that purpose.'

Pinero arose. 'So true. So very true. But was I wise to come? Is there anyone here who has an open mind, who can stare a bare fact in the face without blushing? I think not. Even that so beautiful gentleman who asked you to hear me out has already judged me and condemned me. He seeks order, not truth. Suppose truth defies order, will he accept

427

it? Will you? I think not. Still, if I do not speak, you will win your point by default. The little man in the street will think that you little men have exposed me, Pinero, as a hoaxer, a pretender. That does not suit my plans. I will speak.

'I will repeat my discovery. In simple language, I have invented a technique to tell how long a man will live. I can give you advance billing of the Angel of Death. I can tell you when the Black Camel will kneel at your door. In five minutes' time with my apparatus I can tell any of you how many grains of sand are still left in your hour-glass.'

He paused and folded his arms across his chest. For a moment no one spoke. The audience grew restless. Finally the chairman intervened.

'You aren't finished, Dr Pinero?'

'What more is there to say?'

'You haven't told us how your discovery works.'

Pinero's eyebrows shot up. 'You suggest that I should turn over the fruits of my work for children to play with. This is dangerous knowledge, my friend. I keep it for the man who understands it, myself.' He tapped his chest.

'How are we to know that you have anything back of your wild claims?'

'So simple. You send a committee to watch me demonstrate. If it works, fine. You admit it and tell the world so. If it does not work, I am discredited, and will apologize. Even I, Pinero, will apologize.'

A slender, stoop-shouldered man stood up in the back of the hall. The chair recognized him and he spoke:

'Mr Chairman, how can the eminent doctor seriously propose such a course? Does he expect us to wait around for twenty or thirty years for someone to die and prove his claims?'

Pinero ignored the chair and answered directly:

'Pfui! Such nonsense! Are you so ignorant of statistics that you do not know that in any large group there is at least one who will die in the immediate future? I make you a proposition; let me test each one of you in this room and I will name the man who will die within the fortnight, yes, and the day and hour of his death.' He glanced fiercely around the room. 'Do you accept?'

Another figure got to his feet, a portly man who spoke in measured syllables. 'I, for one, cannot countenance such an experiment. As a medical man, I have noted with sorrow the plain marks of serious heart trouble in many of our elder colleagues. If Dr Pinero knows those symptoms, as he may, and were he to select as his victim one of their number, the man so selected would be likely to die on schedule, whether the distinguished speaker's mechanical egg-timer works or not.'

Another speaker backed him up at once. 'Dr Shepard is right. Why should we waste time on voodoo tricks? It is my belief that this person who calls himself *Dr* Pinero wants to use this body to give his statements authority. If we participate in this farce, we play into his hands. I don't know what his racket is, but you can bet that he has figured out some way to use us for advertising for his schemes. I move, Mr Chairman, that we proceed with our regular business.'

The motion was carried by acclamation, but Pinero did not sit down. Amidst cries of 'Order! order!' he shook his untidy head at them, and had his say:

'Barbarians! Imbeciles! Stupid dolts! Your kind have blocked the recognition of every great discovery since time began. Such ignorant canaille are enough to start Galileo spinning in his grave. That fat fool down there twiddling his elk's tooth calls himself a medical man. Witch doctor would be a better term! That little bald-headed runt over there – You! You style yourself a philosopher, and prate about life and time in your neat categories. What do you know of either one? How can you ever learn when you won't examine the truth when you have a chance? Bah!' He spat upon the stage. 'You call this an Academy of Science. I call it an undertakers' convention, interested only in embalming the ideas of your red-blooded predecessors.'

He paused for breath and was grasped on each side by two members of the platform committee and rushed out to the wings. Several reporters arose hastily from the Press table and followed him. The chairman declared the meeting adjourned.

The newspapermen caught up with him as he was going out by the stage door. He walked with a light, springy step, and whistled a little tune. There was no trace of the belligerence he had shown a moment before. They crowded about him. '– How about an interview, Doc?' 'What d'yu think of Modern Education?' 'You certainly told 'em. What are your views on Life after Death?' 'Take off your hat, Doc, and look at the birdie.'

He grinned at them all. 'One at a time, boys, and not so fast. I used to be a newspaperman myself. How about coming up to my place, and we'll talk about it?'

A few minutes later they were trying to find places to sit down in Pinero's messy bed-living-room, and lighting his cigars.

Pinero looked around and beamed. 'What'll it be, boys? Scotch, or Bourbon?' When that was taken care of he got down to business. 'Now, boys, what do you want to know?'

'Lay it on the line, Doc. Have you got something, or haven't you?'

'Most assuredly I have something, my young friend.'

'Then tell us how it works. That guff you handed the profs won't get you anywhere now.'

'Please, my dear fellow. It is my invention. I expect to make some money with it. Would you have me give it away to the first person who asks for it?'

'See here, Doc, you've got to give us something if you expect to get a break in the morning papers. What do you use? A crystal ball?'

'No, not quite. Would you like to see my apparatus?'

'Sure. Now we are getting somewhere.'

He ushered them into an adjoining room, and waved his hand. 'There it is, boys.'

The mass of equipment that met their eyes vaguely resembled a medico's office X-ray gear. Beyond the obvious fact that it used electrical power, and that some of the dials were calibrated in familiar terms, a casual inspection gave no clue to its actual use.

'What's the principle, Doc?'

Pinero pursed his lips and considered. 'No doubt you are all familiar with the truism that life is electrical in nature? Well, that truism isn't worth a damn, but it will help to give you an idea of the principle. You have also been told that time is a fourth dimension. Maybe you believe it, perhaps not. It has been said so many times that it has ceased to have any meaning. It is simply a cliché that windbags use to impress fools. But I want you to try to visualize it now and try to feel it emotionally.'

He stepped up to one of the reporters. 'Suppose we take you as an example. Your name is Rogers, is it not? Very well, Rogers, you are a space-time event having duration four ways. You are not quite six feet tall, you are about twenty inches wide and perhaps ten inches thick. In time, there stretches behind you more of this space-time event

431

reaching to perhaps nineteen-sixteen, of which we see a cross-section here at right angles to the time axis, and as thick as the present. At the far end is a baby, smelling of sour milk and drooling its breakfast on its bib. At the other end lies, perhaps, an old man someplace in the nineteen-eighties. Imagine this space-time event which we call Rogers as a long pink worm, continuous through the years, one end at his mother's womb, the other at the grave. It stretches past us here, and the cross-section we see appears as a single discrete body. But that is illusion. There is physical continuity to this pink worm, enduring through the years. As a matter of fact there is physical continuity in this concept to the entire race, for these pink worms branch off from other pink worms. In this fashion the race is like a vine whose branches intertwine and send out shoots. Only by taking a cross-section of the vine would we fall into the error of believing that the shoot-lets were discrete individuals.'

He paused and looked around at their faces. One of them, a dour, hard-bitten chap, put in a word.

'That's all very pretty, Pinero, if true; but where does that get you?'

Pinero favoured him with an unresentful smile. 'Patience, my friend. I asked you to think of life as electrical. Now think of our long pink worm as a conductor of electricity. You have heard, perhaps, of the fact that electrical engineers can, by certain measurements, predict the exact location of a break in a trans-Atlantic cable without ever leaving the shore. I do the same with our pink worms. By applying my instruments to the cross-section here in this room I can tell where the break occurs, that is to say, when death takes place. Or, if you like, I can reverse the connexions and tell you the date of your birth. But that is uninteresting; you already know it.'

The dour individual sneered. 'I've caught you, Doc. If what you said about the race being like a vine of pink worms is true, you can't tell birthdays because the connexion with the race is continuous at birth. Your electrical conductor reaches on back through the mother into a man's remotest ancestors.'

Pinero beamed. 'True, and clever, my friend. But you have pushed the analogy too far. It is not done in the precise manner in which one measures the length of an electrical conductor. In some ways it is more like measuring the length of a long corridor by bouncing an echo off the far end. At birth there is a sort of twist in the corridor, and, by proper calibration, I can detect the echo from that twist. There is just one case in which I can get no determinant reading; when a woman is actually carrying a child, I can't sort out her life-line from that of the unborn infant.'

'Let's see you prove it.'

'Certainly, my dear friend. Will you be a subject?'

One of the others spoke up. 'He's called your bluff, Luke. Put up, or shut up.'

'I'm game. What do I do?'

'First write the date of your birth on a sheet of paper, and hand it to one of your colleagues.'

Luke complied. 'Now what?'

'Remove your outer clothing and step upon these scales. Now tell me, were you ever very much thinner, or very much fatter, than you are now? No? What did you weigh at birth? Ten pounds? A fine bouncing baby boy. They don't come so big any more.'

'What is all this flubdubbery?'

'I am trying to approximate the average cross-section of our long pink conductor, my dear Luke. Now will you seat yourself here? Then place this electrode in your mouth. No,

433

it will not hurt you; the voltage is quite low, less than one micro-volt, but I must have a good connexion.'

The doctor left him and went behind his apparatus, where he lowered a hood over his head before touching his controls. Some of the exposed dials came to life and a low humming came from the machine. It stopped and the doctor popped out of his little hide-away.

'I get sometime in February, nineteen-twelve. Who has the piece of paper with the date?'

It was produced and unfolded. The custodian read, '22 February 1912.'

The stillness that followed was broken by a voice from the edge of the little group. 'Doc, can I have another drink?'

The tension relaxed, and several spoke at once. 'Try it on me, Doc.' 'Me first, Doc; I'm an orphan and really want to know.' 'How about it, Doc? Give us all a little loose play.'

He smilingly complied, ducking in and out of the hood like a gopher from its hole. When they all had twin slips of paper to prove the doctor's skill, Luke broke a long silence:

'How about showing how you predict death, Pinero?'

'If you wish. Who will try it?'

No one answered. Several of them nudged Luke forward. 'Go ahead, smart guy. You asked for it.' He allowed himself to be seated in the chair. Pinero changed some of the switches, then entered the hood. When the humming ceased, he came out, rubbing his hands briskly together.

'Well, that's all there is to see, boys. Got enough for a story?'

'Hey, what about the prediction? When does Luke get his "thirty"?'

Luke faced him. 'Yes, how about it? What's your answer?'

Pinero looked pained. 'Gentlemen, I am surprised at you. I give that information for a fee. Besides, it is a professional

confidence. I never tell anyone but the client who con-
sults me.'

'I don't mind. Go ahead and tell them.'

'I am very sorry. I really must refuse. I agreed only to show
you how, not to give the results.'

Luke ground the butt of his cigarette into the floor. 'It's a
hoax, boys. He probably looked up the age of every reporter
in town just to be ready to pull this. It won't wash, Pinero.'

Pinero gazed at him sadly. 'Are you married, my friend?'

'No.'

'Do you have anyone dependent on you? Any close
relatives?'

'No, why; do you want to adopt me?'

Pinero shook his head sadly. 'I am very sorry for you, my
dear Luke. You will die before tomorrow.'

'SCIENCE MEET ENDS IN RIOT'
'SAVANTS SAPS SAYS SEER'
'DEATH PUNCHES TIMECLOCK'
'SCRIBE DIES PER DOC'S DOPE'
'"HOAX" CLAIMS SCIENCE HEAD'

'. . . within twenty minutes of Pinero's strange prediction,
Timons was struck by a falling sign while walking down
Broadway towards the offices of the *Daily Herald* where he
was employed.

'Dr Pinero declined to comment but confirmed the
story that he had predicted Timons' death by means of his
so-called baronovitameter. Chief of Police Roy . . .'

Does the FUTURE worry You????????
Don't waste money on fortune-tellers – Consult
Dr Hugo Pinero, Bio-Consultant

to help you plan for the future by infallible
scientific methods.
No Hocus-Pocus
No 'Spirit' Messages
$10,000 Bond posted in forfeit to back
our predictions
Circular on request
SANDS of TIME, Inc.
Majestic Bldg., Suite 700
(adv.)

Legal Notice

To whom it may concern, greetings: I, John Cabot Winthrop III, of the firm Winthrop, Winthrop, Ditmars and Winthrop, Attorneys-at-Law, do affirm that Hugo Pinero of this city did hand to me ten thousand dollars in lawful money of the United States, and instruct me to place it in escrow with a chartered bank of my selection with escrow instructions as follows:

The entire bond shall be forfeit, and shall forthwith be paid to the first client of Hugo Pinero and/or Sands of Time, Inc. who shall exceed his life tenure as predicted by Hugo Pinero by one per centum, or to the estate of the first client who shall fail of such predicted tenure in a like amount, whichever occurs first in point of time.

I do further affirm that I have this day placed this bond in escrow with the above related instructions with the Equitable First National Bank of this city.

Subscribed and sworn,
John Cabot Winthrop III

Subscribed and sworn to before me
this 2nd day of April, 1951.

Albert M. Swanson

Notary Public in and for this county and state

My commission expires June 17, 1951.

'Good evening, Mr and Mrs Radio Audience. Let's go to Press! Flash! Hugo Pinero, the Miracle Man from Nowhere, has made his thousandth death prediction without a claimant for the reward he posted for anyone who catches him failing to call the turn. With thirteen of his clients already dead it is mathematically certain that he has a private line to the main office of the Old Man with the Scythe. That is one piece of news I don't want to know before it happens. Your Coast-to-Coast Correspondent will *not* be a client of Prophet Pinero. . . .'

The judge's watery baritone cut through the stale air of the courtroom. 'Please, Mr Weems, let us return to our muttons. This court granted your prayer for a temporary restraining order, and now you ask that it be made permanent. In rebuttal, Dr Pinero claims that you have presented no cause and asks that the injunction be lifted, and that I order your client to cease from attempts to interfere with what Pinero describes as a simple lawful business. As you are not addressing a jury, please omit the rhetoric and tell me in plain language why I should not grant his prayer.'

Mr Weems jerked his chin nervously, making his flabby grey dewlap drag across his high stiff collar, and resumed:

'May it please the honourable court, I represent the public—'

'Just a moment. I thought you were appearing for Amalgamated Life Insurance.'

'I am, Your Honour, in a formal sense. In a wider sense I represent several other of the major assurance, fiduciary, and financial institutions; their stockholders, and policy-holders, who constitute a majority of the citizenry. In addition, we feel that we protect the interests of the entire population; unorganized, inarticulate, and otherwise unprotected.'

'I thought that I represented the public,' observed the judge drily. 'I am afraid I must regard you as appearing for your client-of-record. But continue; what is your thesis?'

The elderly barrister attempted to swallow his Adam's apple, then began again: 'Your Honour, we contend that there are two separate reasons why this injunction should be made permanent, and, further, that each reason is sufficient alone. In the first place, this person is engaged in the practice of soothsaying, an occupation proscribed both in common law and statute. He is a common fortune-teller, a vagabond charlatan who preys on the gullibility of the public. He is cleverer than the ordinary gypsy palm-reader, astrologer, or table-tipper, and to the same extent more dangerous. He makes false claims of modern scientific methods to give a spurious dignity to his thaumaturgy. We have here in court leading representatives of the Academy of Science to give expert witness as to the absurdity of his claims.

'In the second place, even if this person's claims were true – granting for the sake of arguments such an absurdity' – Mr Weems permitted himself a thin-lipped smile – 'we contend that his activities are contrary to the public interest in gen-eral and unlawfully injurious to the interests of my client in particular. We are prepared to produce numerous exhibits with the legal custodians to prove that this person did pub-lish, or cause to have published, utterances urging the public to dispense with the priceless boon of life insurance to the

438

great detriment of their welfare and to the financial damage of my client.'

Pinero arose in his place. 'Your Honour, may I say a few words?'

'What is it?'

'I believe I can simplify the situation if permitted to make a brief analysis.'

'Your Honour,' cut in Weems, 'this is most irregular.'

'Patience, Mr Weems. Your interests will be protected. It seems to me that we need more light and less noise in this matter. If Dr Pinero can shorten the proceedings by speaking at this time, I am inclined to let him. Proceed, Dr Pinero.'

'Thank you, Your Honour. Taking the last of Mr Weems's points first, I am prepared to stipulate that I published the utterances he speaks of—'

'One moment, doctor. You have chosen to act as your own attorney. Are you sure you are competent to protect your own interests?'

'I am prepared to chance it, Your Honour. Our friends here can easily prove what I stipulate.'

'Very well. You may proceed.'

'I will stipulate that many persons have cancelled life insurance policies as a result thereof, but I challenge them to show that anyone so doing has suffered any loss or damage therefrom. It is true that the Amalgamated have lost business through my activities, but that is the natural result of my discovery, which has made their policies as obsolete as the bow and arrow. If an injunction is granted on that ground, I shall set up a coal-oil lamp factory, then ask for an injunction against the Edison and General Electric companies to forbid them to manufacture incandescent bulbs.

'I will stipulate that I am engaged in the business of making predictions of death, but I deny that I am practising magic, black, white, or rainbow coloured. If to make predictions by methods of scientific accuracy is illegal, then the actuaries of the Amalgamated have been guilty for years in that they predict the exact percentage that will die each year in any given large group. I predict death retail; the Amalgamated predicts it wholesale. If their actions are legal, how can mine be illegal?

'I admit that it makes a difference whether I can do what I claim, or not; and I will stipulate that the so-called expert witnesses from the Academy of Science will testify that I cannot. But they know nothing of my method and cannot give truly expert testimony on it—'

'Just a moment, doctor. Mr Weems, is it true that your expert witnesses are not conversant with Dr Pinero's theory and methods?'

Mr Weems looked worried. He drummed on the table-top, then answered, 'Will the Court grant me a few moments' indulgence?'

'Certainly.'

Mr Weems held a hurried whispered consultation with his cohorts, then faced the bench. 'We have a procedure to suggest, Your Honour. If Dr Pinero will take the stand and explain the theory and practice of his alleged method, then these distinguished scientists will be able to advise the Court as to the validity of his claims.'

The judge looked inquiringly at Pinero, who responded, 'I will not willingly agree to that. Whether my process is true or false, it would be dangerous to let it fall into the hands of fools and quacks' – he waved his hand at the group of professors seated in the front row, paused, and smiled maliciously – 'as these gentlemen know quite well. Furthermore, it is not necessary to know the process in order to prove that it will work. Is it necessary to understand the complex miracle of biological reproduction in order to observe that a hen lays eggs? Is it necessary for me to re-educate this entire body of self-appointed custodians of wisdom – cure them of their ingrown superstitions – in order to prove that my predictions are correct? There are but two ways of forming an opinion in science. One is the scientific method; the other, the scholastic. One can judge from experiment, or one can blindly accept authority. To the scientific mind, experimental proof is all important and theory is merely a convenience in description, to be junked when it no longer fits. To the academic mind, authority is everything and facts are junked when they do not fit theory laid down by authority.

'It is this point of view – academic minds clinging like oysters to disproved theories – that has blocked every advance of knowledge in history. I am prepared to prove my method by experiment, and, like Galileo in another court, I insist, "It still moves!"

'Once before I offered such proof to this same body of self-styled experts, and they rejected it. I renew my offer; let me measure the life-lengths of the members of the Academy of Science. Let them appoint a committee to judge the results. I will seal my findings in two sets of envelopes; on the outside of each envelope in one set will appear the name of a member, on the inside the date of his death. In the other envelopes I will place names, on the outside I will place dates. Let the committee place the envelopes in a vault, then meet from time to time to open the appropriate envelopes. In such a large body of men some deaths may be expected, if Amalgamated actuaries can be trusted, every week or two. In such a fashion they will accumulate data very rapidly to prove that Pinero is a liar, or not.'

He stopped, and pushed out his little chest until it almost

caught up with his little round belly. He glared at the sweating savants. 'Well?'

The judge raised his eyebrows, and caught Mr Weems's eye. 'Do you accept?'

'Your Honour, I think the proposal highly improper—'

The judge cut him short. 'I warn you that I shall rule against you if you do not accept, or propose an equally reasonable method of arriving at the truth.'

Weems opened his mouth, changed his mind, looked up and down the faces of learned witnesses, and faced the bench. 'We accept, Your Honour.'

'Very well. Arrange the details between you. The temporary injunction is lifted, and Dr Pinero must not be molested in the pursuit of his business. Decision on the petition for permanent injunction is reserved without prejudice pending the accumulation of evidence. Before we leave this matter I wish to comment on the theory implied by you, Mr Weems, when you claimed damage to your client. There has grown up in the minds of certain groups in this country the notion that because a man or corporation has made a profit out of the public for a number of years, the government and the courts are charged with the duty of guaranteeing such profit in the future, even in the face of changing circumstances and contrary public interest. This strange doctrine is supported neither by statute nor common law. Neither individuals nor corporations have any right to come into court and ask that the clock of history be stopped, or turned back, for their private benefit. That is all.'

Bidwell grunted in annoyance. 'Weems, if you can't think up anything better than that, Amalgamated is going to need a new chief attorney. It's been ten weeks since you lost the injunction, and that little wart is coining money hand over fist. Meantime every insurance firm in the country is going broke. Hoskins, what's our loss ratio?'

'It's hard to say, Mr Bidwell. It gets worse every day. We've paid off thirteen big policies this week; all of them taken out since Pinero started operations.'

A spare little man spoke up. 'I say, Bidwell, we aren't accepting any new applications for United until we have time to check and be sure that they have not consulted Pinero. Can't we afford to wait until the scientists show him up?'

Bidwell snorted. 'You blasted optimist! They won't show him up. Aldrich, can't you face a fact? The fat little blister has got something; how I don't know. This is a fight to the finish. If we wait, we're licked.' He threw his cigar into a spittoon, and bit savagely into a fresh one. 'Clear out of here, all of you! I'll handle this my own way. You too, Aldrich. United may wait, but Amalgamated won't.'

Weems cleared his throat apprehensively. 'Mr Bidwell, I trust you will consult with me before embarking on any major change in policy?'

Bidwell grunted. They filed out. When they were all gone and the door closed, Bidwell snapped the switch of the inter-office announcer. 'OK; send him in.'

The outer door opened; a slight dapper figure stood for a moment at the threshold. His small dark eyes glanced quickly about the room before he entered, then he moved up to Bidwell with a quick soft tread. He spoke to Bidwell in a flat emotionless voice. His face remained impassive except for the live animal eyes. 'You wanted to talk to me?'

'Yes.'

'What's the proposition?'

'Sit down, and we'll talk.'

* * *

443

Pinero met the young couple at the door of his inner office.

'Come in, my dears, come in. Sit down. Make yourselves at home. Now tell me, what do you want of Pinero? Surely such young people are not anxious about the final roll call?'

The boy's honest young face showed slight confusion. 'Well, you see, Dr Pinero, I'm Ed Hartley, and this is my wife, Betty. We're going to have – that is, Betty is expecting a baby and, well—'

Pinero smiled benignly. 'I understand. You want to know how long you will live in order to make the best possible provision for the youngster. Quite wise. Do you both want readings, or just yourself?'

The girl answered, 'Both of us, we think.'

Pinero beamed at her. 'Quite so. I agree. Your reading presents certain technical difficulties at this time, but I can give you some information now, and more later, after your baby arrives. Now come into my laboratory, my dears, and we'll commence.' He rang for their case histories, then showed them into his workshop. 'Mrs Hartley first, please. If you will go behind that screen and remove your shoes and your outer clothing, please. Remember, I am an old man, whom you are consulting as you would a physician.'

He turned away and made some minor adjustments of his apparatus. Ed nodded to his wife, who slipped behind the screen and reappeared almost at once, clothed in two wisps of silk. Pinero glanced up, noted her fresh young prettiness and her touching shyness.

'This way, my dear. First we must weigh you. There. Now take your place on the stand. This electrode in your mouth. No, Ed, you mustn't touch her while she is in the circuit. It won't take a minute. Remain quiet.'

He dived under the machine's hood and the dials sprang

into life. Very shortly he came out with a perturbed look on his face. 'Ed, did you touch her?'

'No, doctor.' Pinero ducked back again, remained a little longer. When he came out this time he told the girl to get down and dress. He turned to her husband.

'Ed, make yourself ready.'

'What's Betty's reading, doctor?'

'There is a little difficulty. I want to test you first.'

When he came out from taking the youth's reading his face was more troubled than ever. Ed inquired as to his trouble. Pinero shrugged his shoulders, and brought a smile to his lips.

'Nothing to concern you, my boy. A little mechanical misadjustment, I think. But I shan't be able to give you two your readings today. I shall need to overhaul my machine. Can you come back tomorrow?'

'Why, I think so. Say, I'm sorry about your machine. I hope it isn't serious.'

'It isn't, I'm sure. Will you come back into my office and visit for a bit?'

'Thank you, doctor. You are very kind.'

'But Ed, I've got to meet Ellen.'

Pinero turned the full force of his personality on her. 'Won't you grant me a few moments, my dear young lady? I am old and like the sparkle of young folks' company. I get very little of it. Please.' He nudged them gently into his office, and seated them. Then he ordered lemonade and cookies sent in, offered them cigarettes, and lit a cigar.

Forty minutes later Ed listened entranced, while Betty was quite evidently acutely nervous and anxious to leave, as the doctor spun out a story concerning his adventures as a young man in Tierra del Fuego. When the doctor stopped to relight his cigar, she stood up.

'Doctor, we really must leave. Couldn't we hear the rest tomorrow?'

'Tomorrow? There will not be time tomorrow.'

'But you haven't time today either. Your secretary has rung five times.'

'Couldn't you spare me just a few more minutes?'

'I really can't today, doctor. I have an appointment. There is someone waiting for me.'

'There is no way to induce you?'

'I'm afraid not. Come, Ed.'

After they had gone, the doctor stepped to the window and stared out over the city. Presently he picked out two tiny figures as they left the office building. He watched them hurry to the corner, wait for the lights to change, then start across the street. When they were part way across there came the scream of a siren. The two little figures hesitated, started back, stopped, and turned. Then the car was upon them. As the car slammed to a stop they showed up from beneath it, no longer two figures, but simply a limp unorganized heap of clothing.

'Cancel my appointments for the rest of the day . . . No . . . No one . . . I don't care; cancel them.'

Then he sat down in his chair. His cigar went out. Long after dark he held it, still unlighted.

Pinero sat down at his dining-table and contemplated the gourmet's luncheon spread before him. He had ordered this meal with particular care, and had come home a little early in order to enjoy it fully.

Somewhat later he let a few drops of *fiori d'Alpini* roll round his tongue and trickle down his throat. The heavy, fragrant syrup warmed his mouth, and reminded him of the little mountain flowers for which it was named. He sighed. It had been a good meal, an exquisite meal, and had justified the exotic liqueur. His musing was interrupted by a disturbance at the front door. The voice of his elderly maidservant was raised in remonstrance. A heavy male voice interrupted her. The commotion moved down the hall and the dining-room door was pushed open.

'*Madonna! Non si puo entrare!* The Master is eating!'

'Never mind, Angela. I have time to see these gentlemen. You may go.' Pinero faced the surly-faced spokesman of the intruders. 'You have business with me; yes?'

'You bet we have. Decent people have had enough of your damned nonsense.'

'And so?'

The caller did not answer at once. A smaller, dapper individual moved out from behind him and faced Pinero.

'We might as well begin.' The chairman of the committee placed a key in the lock-box and opened it. 'Wenzell, will you help me pick out today's envelopes?' He was interrupted by a touch on his arm.

'Dr Baird, you are wanted on the telephone.'

'Very well. Bring the instrument here.'

When it was fetched he placed the receiver to his ear. 'Hello. . . . Yes; speaking. . . . What? . . . No, we have heard nothing. . . . Destroyed the machine, you say. . . . Dead! How? . . . No! No statement. None at all. . . . Call me later. . . .'

He slammed the instrument down and pushed it from him.

'What's up?' – 'Who's dead now?'

Baird held up one hand. 'Quiet, gentlemen, please! Pinero was murdered a few moments ago at his home.'

'Murdered?'

'That isn't all. About the same time vandals broke into his office and smashed his apparatus.'

447

No one spoke at first. The committee members glanced round at each other. No one seemed anxious to be the first to comment.

Finally one spoke up. 'Get it out.'

'Get what out?'

'Pinero's envelope. It's in there too. I've seen it.'

Baird located it and slowly tore it open. He unfolded the single sheet of paper, and scanned it.

'Well? Out with it!'

'One thirteen P M – today.'

They took this in silence.

Their dynamic calm was broken by a member across the table from Baird reaching for the lock-box. Baird interposed a hand.

'What do you want?'

'My prediction – it's in there – we're all in there.'

'Yes, yes. We're all in here. Let's have them.'

Baird placed both hands over the box. He held the eye of the man opposite him but did not speak. He licked his lips. The corner of his mouth twitched. His hands shook. Still he did not speak. The man opposite relaxed back into his chair.

'You're right, of course,' he said.

'Bring me that waste basket.' Baird's voice was low and strained but steady.

He accepted it and dumped the litter on the rug. He placed the tin basket on the table before him. He tore a half-dozen envelopes across, set a match to them, and dropped them in the basket. Then he started tearing a double handful at a time, and fed the fire steadily. The smoke made him cough, and tears ran out of his smarting eyes. Someone got up and opened a window. When he was through, he pushed the basket away from him, looked down, and spoke.

'I'm afraid I've ruined this table-top.'

RHYS DAVIES

I WILL KEEP HER COMPANY

WHEN HE ACHIEVED the feat of getting down the stairs to the icy living room, it was the peculiar silence there that impressed him. It had not been so noticeable upstairs, where all night he had had company, of a kind. Down in this room, the familiar morning sounds he had known for sixty years – all the crockery, pots and pans, and fire-grate noises of married life at break of day, his wife's brisk soprano not least among them – were abolished as though they had never existed.

It was the snow had brought this silence, of course. How many days had it been falling – four, five? He couldn't remember. Still dazed and stiff from his long vigil in a chair upstairs, he hobbled slowly to the window. Sight of the magnificent white spread brought, as always, astonishment. Who would have thought such a vast quantity waited above? Almighty in its power to obliterate the known works of man, especially his carefully mapped highways and byways, the weight of odourless substance was like a reminder that he was of no more account than an ant. But only a few last flakes were falling now, the small aster shapes drifting with dry languor on the hefty waves covering the long front garden.

'They'll be here today,' he said aloud, wakened a little more by the dazzle. The sound of his voice was strange to him, like an echo of it coming back from a chasm. His head turning automatically towards the open door leading to the hallway, he broke the silence again, unwilling to let it settle. 'Been snowing again all night, Maria. But it's stopping now. They'll come today. The roads have been blocked. Hasn't been a fall like it for years.'

His frosting breath plumed the air. He turned back to the window and continued to peer out for a while. A drift swelled to above the sill, and there was no imprint of the robins and tits that regularly landed before the window in the mornings, for breakfast crumbs. Neither was there a sign of the garden gate into the lane, nor a glimpse of the village, two miles distant down the valley, which could be seen from this height on green days. But the mountains, ramparts against howling Atlantic gales, were visible in glitteringly bleached outline against a pale-blue sky. Savage guardians of interior Wales, even their lowering black clouds and whipping rains were vanquished today. They looked innocent in their unbroken white.

His mind woke still more. The manacled landscape gave him, for the moment, a feeling of security. This snow was a protection, not a catastrophe. He did not want the overdue visitors to arrive, did not want to exercise himself again in resistance to their arguments for his future welfare. Not yet. He thought of his six damson trees, which he had introduced into the orchard a few years before and reared with such care. Last summer, there had been a nice little profit from the baskets of downy fruit. Was he to be forced away from his grown-up darlings now? Just one more season of gathering, and, afterwards, he would be ready to decide about the future . . .

Then, remembering something else, he lamented, 'They'll come, they'll come!' They had such a special reason for making the journey. And this marooning snow would give even more urgency to their arguments regarding himself. He

452

strained his keen old countryman's eyes down the anonymous white distances. *Could* they come? Could anyone break a way through those miles of deep snow, where nothing shuffled, crawled, or even flew? The whole world had halted. They would not come today. There would be one more day of peace.

Mesmerized at the window, he recalled another supreme time of snow, long ago, before he was married. He and two other farm workers had gone in search of Ambrose Owen's sheep. An old ram was found in a drift, stiff and upright on his legs, glassy eyes staring at nothing, curls of wool turned to a cockleshell hardness that could be chipped from the fleece. Farther away in the drift, nine wise ewes lay huddled against each other, and these were carried upside down by the legs to the farmhouse kitchen, where they thawed into life. But Ambrose, like that man in the Bible with a prodigal son, had broken down and shed tears over his lost ram that had foolishly wandered from the herd. The elderly farmer was in a low condition himself at the time, refusing to be taken to hospital, wanting to kick the bucket not only in his own home but downstairs in his fireside chair. Quite right too.

He returned from the window at last, drew a crimson flannel shawl from his sparsely-haired head, and rearranged it carefully over his narrow shoulders. He wore two cardigans and trousers of thick homespun, but the cold penetrated to his bones. Still unwilling to begin the day's ritual of living down in this room, he stood gazing vaguely from the cinder-strewn fireplace to the furniture, his eyes lingering on the beautifully polished rosewood table at which, with seldom a cross word exchanged (so it seemed now), he had shared good breakfasts for a lifetime. Was it because of the unnatural silence, with not the whirr of a single bird outside, that all

453

the familiar contents of the room seemed withdrawn from ownership? They looked stranded.

Remembrance came to him of the room having this same hush of unbelonging when he and Maria had first walked into it, with the idea of buying the place, a freehold stone cottage and its four acres, for ninety-five sovereigns, cash down. They were courting at the time, and the property was cheap because of its isolation; no one had lived there for years. The orchard, still well-stocked, had decided him, and Maria, who could depend on herself and a husband for all the talking company she needed, agreed because of the tremendous views of mountain range and sky from this closed end of the valley. What a walker she had been! Never wanted even a bike, did not want to keep livestock, and was content with the one child that came very soon after the rushed purchase of the cottage. But, disregarding gossip, she had liked to go down to church in the village, where she sang psalms louder than any other woman there.

He had huddled closer into the shawl. Since he would not be staying long down here, was it worth while lighting a fire? Then he realized that if the visitors found means of coming, it would be prudent to let them see he could cope with the household jobs. First, the grate to be raked and a fire laid; wood and coal to be fetched from outside. But he couldn't hurry. His scalp was beginning to prickle and contract, and he drew the shawl over his head again. Feeling was already gone from his feet when he reached the shadowy kitchen lying off the living room, fumblingly pulled the back door open, and faced a wall of pure white.

The entire door space was blocked, sealing access to the shed in which, besides wood and coal, oil for the cooking stove was stored. He had forgotten that the wall had been there the day before. Snow had drifted down the mountain slope and piled as far as the back window upstairs even then; it came back to him that he had drawn the kitchen window curtains to hide that weight of tombstone white against the panes. 'Marble,' he said now, curiously running a finger over the crisply hardened surface. He shut the door, relieved that one item in the morning jobs was settled; it would be impossible to reach the shed from the front of the cottage.

Pondering in the dowdy light of the kitchen, he looked at the empty glass oil-feeder of the cooking stove, at the empty kettle, at an earthenware pitcher, which he knew was empty, too. He remembered that the water butt against the outside front wall had been frozen solid for days before the snow began. And even if he had the strength to dig a path to the well in the orchard, very likely that would be frozen. Would snow melt inside the house? But a little water remained in an ewer upstairs. And wasn't there still some of the milk that the district nurse had brought? He found the jug in the slate-shelved larder, and tilted it; the inch-deep, semi-congealed liquid moved. He replaced the jug with a wrinkling nose, and peered at three tins of soup that also had been brought by Nurse Baldock.

Sight of the tins gave him a feeling of nausea. The last time the nurse had come – *which* day was it? – a smell like ammonia had hung about her. And her pink rubber gloves, her apron with its row of safety pins and a tape measure dangling over it, had badly depressed him. A kind woman, though, except for her deciding what was the best way for a man to live. The sort that treated all men as little boys. She had a voice that wouldn't let go of a person, but being a woman, a soft wheedling could come into it when she chose. Thank God the snow had bogged her down.

He reached for a flat box, opened it, and saw a few biscuits. Maria always liked the lid picture of Caernarvon

Castle, which they'd visited one summer day; he looked at it now with a reminiscent chuckle. His movements became automatically exact, yet vague and random. He found a tin tray inscribed 'Ringer's Tobacco' and placed on it the box, a plate and, forgetting there was no milk left upstairs, a clean cup and saucer. This done, he suddenly sat down on a hard chair and closed his eyes.

He did not know how long he remained there. Tapping sounds roused him; he jerked from the chair with galvanized strength. Agitation gave his shouts an unreasonable cantankerousness as he reached the living room. 'They've come! Open the door, can't you? It's not locked.'

He opened the front door. There was nobody. The snow reached up to his waist, and the stretch of it down the garden slope bore not a mark. Only an elephant could come to this door. Had he dreamed the arrival? Or had a starving bird tapped its beak on the window? The dread eased. He shut the door with both his shaking hands, and stood listening in the small hallway. 'They haven't come!' he shouted up the stairs, wanting to hear his voice smashing the silence. 'But they will, they will! They are bringing my pension money from the post office. Dr Howells took my book with him.' Self-reminder of this ordinary matter helped to banish the dread, and the pain in his chest dwindled.

Pausing in the living room, he remembered that it was actually Nurse Baldock who had taken his book and put it in that important black bag of hers. She had arrived that day with Dr Howells in his car, instead of on her bike. The snow had begun to fall, but she said it wouldn't be much – only a sprinkling. And Dr Howells had told him not to worry and that everything would be put in hand. But even the doctor, who should have had a man's understanding, had argued about the future, and coaxed like Nurse Baldock. Then *she* had said she'd bring Vicar Pryce on her next visit. People fussing! But he couldn't lock the door against them yet. It was necessary for them to come just once again. He would pretend to listen to them, especially the vicar, and when they had gone he would lock the door, light a fire, and sit down to think of the future in his own way.

His eyes strayed about the room again. He looked at the table with its green-shaded oil lamp, at the dresser with its display of brilliant plates and lustre jugs, at the comfortable low chairs, the bright rugs, the scroll-backed sofa from which Maria had directed his activities for the week before she was obliged to take to her bed at last. After the shock of the fancied arrival, the objects in the room no longer seemed withdrawn from ownership. They would yield him security and ease, for a long while yet. And the cooking stove in the kitchen, the pans, brooms, and brushes – they had belonged solely to Maria's energetic hands, but after a lifetime with her he knew exactly how she dealt with them. Any man with three-penn'orth of sense could live here independently as a lord. Resolve lay tucked away in his mind. Today, with this cold stunning his senses, not much could be done. He must wait. His eyes reached the mantelpiece clock; lifting the shawl from his ears, he stared closer at the age-yellowed face. *That* was why the silence had been so strange! Was even a clock affected by the cold? Surely he had wound it last night, as usual; surely he had come downstairs? The old-fashioned clopping sound, steady as horse hoofs ambling on a quiet country road, had never stopped before. The defection bothering him more than the lack of means for a fire and oil for the stove, he reached for the mahogany-framed clock, his numb fingers moving over it to take a firm grip. It fell into the stoneflagged hearth. There was a tinkle of broken glass.

'Ah,' he shouted guiltily, 'the clock's broken, Maria! Slipped out of my hand!'

He gazed at it in a stupor. But the accident finally decided him. Down in this room the last bits of feeling were ebbing from him. There was warmth and company upstairs. He stumbled into the kitchen, lifted the tin tray in both hands without feeling its substance, and reached the hallway. Negotiation of the stairs took even more time than his descent had. As in the kitchen, it was the propulsion of old habit that got him up the flight he had climbed thousands of times. The tray fell out of his hands when he reached a squeaking stair just below the landing. This did not matter; he even liked the lively explosion of noise. 'It's only that advertisement tray the shop gave you one Christmas!' he called out, not mentioning the crocks and biscuit box which had crashed to the bottom. He did not attempt to retrieve anything. All he wanted was warmth.

In the clear white light of a front room he stood for some moments looking intently at the weather-browned face of the small woman lying on a four-poster bed. Her eyes were compactly shut. Yet her face bore an expression of prim vigour; still she looked alert in her withdrawal. No harsh glitter of light from the window reached her, but he drew a stiff fold of the gay-patterned linen bed curtains that, as if in readiness for this immurement, had been washed, starched, and ironed by her three weeks before. Then he set about his own task. The crimson shawl still bonneted his head.

His hands plucked at the flannel blankets and larger shawls lying scattered on the floor around a wheelbacked armchair close to the bed. Forcing grip into his fingers, he draped these coverings methodically over the sides and back of the chair, sat down, and swathed his legs and body in the overlapping folds. It all took a long time, and for a while it brought back the pain in his chest, compelling him to stop. Finally, he succeeded in drawing portions of two other shawls over his head and shoulders, so that he was completely encased in draperies. There had been good warmth in this cocoon last night. The everlasting flannel was woven in a mill down the valley, from the prized wool of local mountain sheep. Properly washed in rain water, it yielded warmth for a hundred years or more. There were old valley people who had been born and had gone in the same pair of handed-down family blankets.

Secure in the shelter, he waited patiently for warmth to come. When it began to arrive, and the pain went, his mind flickered into activity again. It was of the prancing mountain ponies he thought first, the wild auburn ponies that were so resentful of capture. He had always admired them. But what did their lucky freedom mean now? *They* had no roof over their heads, and where could they find victuals? Had they lost their bearings up in their fastnesses? Were they charging in demented panic through the endless snow, plunging into crevices, starvation robbing them of instinct and sense? Then there were the foxes. He remembered hearing that during that drastic time of snow when he rescued Ambrose Owen's sheep, a maddened fox had dashed into the vicarage kitchen when a servant opened the back door. It snatched in its teeth a valuable Abyssinian cat lying fast asleep on the hearth rug, and streaked out before the petrified woman could scream.

A little more warmth came. He crouched into it with a sigh. Soon it brought a sense of summer pleasures. A long meadow dotted with buttercups and daisies shimmered before him, and a golden-haired boy ran excitedly over the bright grass to a young white goat tied to an iron stake. Part of the meadow was filled with booths of striped canvas, and a roundabout of painted horses galloped to barrel-organ music. It was that Whitsuntide fête when he had won the raffled goat on a sixpenny ticket – the only time he had won anything all his life. Maria had no feeling for goats, especially rams, but she had let their boy lead the snowy-haired beast home. Richard had looked after it all its sturdy years and, at its hiring, got for himself the fees of its natural purpose in life – five shillings a time, in those far-off days.

The father chuckled. He relaxed further in the dark chair. His hands resting lightly on his knees, he prepared for sleep. It was slow in taking him, and when, drowsily, he heard a whirring sound he gave it no particular attention. But he stirred slightly and opened his eyes. The noise approached closer. It began to circle, now faint, then loud, now dwindling. He did not recognize it. It made him think of a swarm of chirping grasshoppers, then of the harsh clonking of roused geese. Neutral towards all disturbance from outside, he nestled deeper into the warmth bred of the last thin heat of his blood, and when a louder noise shattered the peace of his cocoon he still did not move, though his eyes jerked wide open once more.

The helicopter circled twice above the half-buried cottage. Its clacking sounded more urgent as it descended and began to pass as low as the upstairs windows at the front and back. The noise became a rasp of impatience, as if the machine were annoyed that no reply came to this equivalent of a knocking on the door, that no attention was paid to the victory of this arrival. A face peered down from a curved grey pane; the head of another figure dodged behind, moving to both the side panels.

Indecision seemed to govern this hovering above the massed billows of snow. After the cottage had been circled three times, the machine edged nearer the front wall, and a square box wrapped in orange-coloured oilskin tumbled out, fell accurately before the door, and lay visible in a hole of snow. The machine rose; its rotor blades whirled for seconds above the cottage before it mounted higher. It diminished into the pale afternoon light, flying down the valley towards immaculate mountains that had never known a visit from such a strange bird.

Evening brought an unearthly blue to the sculptured distances. Night scarcely thickened the darkness; the whiteness could be seen for miles. Only the flashing of clear-cut stars broke the long stillness of the valley. No more snow fell. But the cold hardened during the low hours, and at dawn, though a red glow lay in the sun's disc on Moelwyn's crest, light came with grudging slowness, and there was no promise of thaw all morning. But, soon after the sun had passed the zenith, another noise smashed into the keep of silence at the valley's closed end.

Grinding and snorting, a vehicle slowly burrowed into the snow. It left in its wake, like a gigantic horned snail, a silvery track, on which crawled a plain grey motor van. Ahead, the climbing plough was not once defeated by its pioneering work, thrusting past shrouded hedges on either side of it, its grunting front mechanism churning up the snow and shooting it out of a curved-over horn on to bushes at the left. The attendant grey van stopped now and then, allowing a measure of distance to accumulate on the smooth track.

The van had three occupants. Two of them, sitting on the driver's cushioned bench, were philosophically patient of this laborious journeying. The third, who was Nurse Baldock, squatted on the floor inside the small van, her legs stretched towards the driver's seat and her shoulders against the back door. She was a substantial woman, and the ungainly fur

461

coat she wore gave her the dimensions of a mature bear. She tried not to be restless. But as the instigator of this rescuing operation, she kept looking at her watch, and she failed to curb herself all the time. The two men in front had not been disposed for talk.

'I hope that thing up there won't break down,' she said presently. 'It's a Canadian snowplough – so I was told on the phone. The Council bought it only last year.'

'It took them a deuce of a time to get one after we had that nasty snowfall in 1947,' remarked the driver, a middle-aged man in a sombre vicuna overcoat and a bowler hat. 'A chap and his young lady were found buried in their car halfway up Moelwyn when we had *that* lot – been there a week, if you remember, Vicar. Thank God these bad falls don't come often.'

'Councils seldom look far outside their town hall chamber after election,' mumbled Vicar Pryce, who had been picked up in Ogwen village twenty minutes earlier. Under his round black hat only his eyes and bleak nose were visible from wrappings of scarves. It was very cold in the utilitarian van, lent for this emergency expedition by a tradesman of the market town at the valley's mouth; the road from there to Ogwen had been cleared the day before.

'Well, our Council has got hold of a helicopter this time, too,' Nurse Baldock reminded them, not approving of criticism of her employers from anyone. 'Soon as I heard they had hired one to drop bundles of hay to stranded cattle and mountain ponies, I said to myself, "Man first, then the beasts," and flew to my phone. I'm fond of old John Evans, though he's so wilful. I arranged to have tins of food, fruit juice, milk, a small bottle of brandy, fresh pork sausages, and bread put in the box, besides a plastic container of cooker oil and a message from me.'

'Couldn't you have gone in the helicopter?' the driver asked, rather inattentively.

'What, and got dropped out into the snow with the box?' The nurse's bulk wobbled with impatience. 'If the machine couldn't land anywhere on those deep slopes of snow, how could I get down, I ask you?'

'I thought they could drop a person on a rope.' The driver sounded propitiatory now. For him, as for most people, the district nurse was less a woman than a portent of inescapable forces lying in wait for everybody.

'Delivery of necessities was the point,' she said dismissingly, and, really for Vicar Pryce's wrapped ears, continued, 'After getting the helicopter man's report yesterday, I was on the phone to the Town Hall for half an hour. I insisted that they let me have the snowplough today – I *fought* for it. It was booked for this and that, they said, but I had my way in the end.'

'Last night was bitter,' Vicar Pryce said, following a silence. 'I got up at 3 A.M. and piled a sheepskin floor rug on my bed.'

'Bitter it *was*,' agreed Nurse Baldock. 'We single people feel it the more.' Neither of the men offered a comment, and, with another look at her watch, she pursued, 'Of course, the helicopter man's report needn't mean a lot. Who could blame Evans if he stayed snuggled in bed all day? And at his age, he could sleep through any noise.'

'One would think a helicopter's clatter would bring him out of any sleep, Nurse,' the Vicar remarked.

'I think he's a bit deaf,' she replied, rejecting the doubt. 'In any case, I don't suppose he'd know what the noise meant.' The van stopped, and she decided, 'We'll have our coffee now.'

She managed to spread quite a picnic snack on the flat top

463

of a long, calico-covered object lying beside her, on which she wouldn't sit. There were cheese and egg sandwiches, pieces of sultana cake, plates, mugs, sugar and a large Thermos flask. A heavy can of paraffin propped her back, and, in addition to the satchel of picnic stuff, she had brought her official leather bag, well known in the valley. Nurse Baldock's thoroughness was as dreaded by many as was sight of her black bag. After determined efforts over several years, she had recently been awarded a social science diploma, and now, at forty-five, she hoped for a more important position than that of a bicycle-borne district nurse. This rescuing mission today would help prove her mettle, and Vicar Pryce, to whom she had insisted on yielding the seat in front, would be a valuable witness of her zeal.

'I'll keep enough for the young man in the snowplough,' she said, pouring coffee. 'He ought not to stop now. The quicker we get there the better.'

'Makes one think of places in the moon,' the driver remarked, gazing out at the waxen countryside.

Sipping coffee, she resumed, 'I have eight patients in Ogwen just now, and really I ought not to be spending all this time on a man who's got nothing the matter with him except old age and obstinacy. Two confinements due any day now.' The men drank and ate, and she added, 'What a time for births! There's Mavis Thomas, for instance – she's not exactly entitled to one, is she, Vicar? But at least that man she lives with keeps her house on Sheep's Gap warm, and her water hasn't frozen.'

'Nobody except a choirboy turned up for matins last Sunday,' the meditative vicar said. 'So I cancelled all services that day.'

Nurse Baldock finished a piece of cake. 'I heard yesterday that a married woman living up on Sheep's Gap was chased by two starving ponies that found a way down from the mountains. You know how they won't go near human beings as a rule, but when this woman came out of her farmhouse in her gumboots they stampeded from behind a barn; with their teeth grinding and eyes flaring. She ran back screaming into the house just in time.'

'Perhaps she was carrying a bucket of pig feed and they smelt it,' the driver suggested, handing back his mug.

Undeterred, Nurse Baldock gave a feminine shiver. 'I keep an eye open for them on my rounds. We might be back in the days of wolves.' The van resumed its amble on the pearly track as she proceeded. 'But these are modern times. Old Evans would never dream he would get a helicopter for his benefit, to say nothing of that great ugly thing in front, *and* us. There's real Christianity for you! This affair will cost the Council quite a sum. It will go on the rates, of course.'

'John and Maria Evans', Vicar Pryce said, rewrapping his ears in the scarves, 'were always faithful parishioners of mine when they were able to get down to the village. I remember their son Richard, too. A good tenor in the choir. Emigrated to New Zealand and has children of his own there, I understand.'

'Well, Vicar,' Nurse Baldock said, packing the crocks into the satchel between her knees, 'I hope you'll do your very best to persuade Evans to leave with us today and go to Pistyll Mawr Home. Heaven knows, I did all I could to coax him when I was at the cottage with Dr Howells the other day.'

'It will be a business,' he mumbled.

She pursed her lips. 'He told me it was healthy up there in his cottage, and that he and his wife had always liked the views. "Views!" I said, "Views won't feed and nurse you if you fall ill. Come now, facts must be faced." Then he said something about his damson trees. I told him Pistyll Mawr had fruit trees in plenty.'

The driver, who lived in the market town, spoke. 'Don't the new cases take offence at being forced to have a bath as soon as they enter the doors of Pistyll Mawr?'

'So you've heard that one, have you? Why, what's wrong with a bath? Is it a crime?' Nurse Baldock had bridled. 'I am able to tell you there's a woman in Pistyll Mawr who *brags* about her baths there – says that for the first time in her life she feels like a well-off lady, with a maid to sponge her back and hand her a towel. You're out of date, sir, with your "take offence".'

'Aren't there separate quarters for men and women, even if they're married?' he persisted.

'As if very elderly people are bothered by what you mean! Besides, they can flirt in the garden if they want. But old people have too much dignity for such nonsense.'

'I dare say there are one or two exceptions.'

'Ah, I agree there.' Nurse Baldock pulled gauntlet gloves over her mittens. 'The aged! They're our biggest problem. The things that come my way from some of them! One has to have nerves of iron, and it doesn't do to let one's eyes fill. Why must people trouble themselves so much about the young? My blood boils when I see all the rubbishy fuss made about the youngsters by newspapers and busybodies of the lay public. Sight of the word "teenagers" makes me want to throw up. Leave the young alone, I say! They've got all the treasures of the world on their backs, and once they're out of school they don't put much expense on the rates.'

After this tirade no one spoke for a time. As the van crawled nearer the valley's majestic closure, Nurse Baldock herself seemed to become oppressed by the solemn deso-lation outside. Not a boulder or streak of path showed on

Moelwyn's swollen heights. Yet, close at hand, there were charming snow effects. The van rounded a turn of the lane, and breaks in the hedges on either side revealed birch glades, their spectral depths glittering as though from the light of ceremonial chandeliers. All the crystalline birches were struck into eternal stillness – fragile, rime-heavy boughs sweeping downward, white hairs of mourning. Not a bird, rabbit, or beetle could stir in those frozen grottoes, and the blue harebell or the pink convolvulus never ring out in them again.

'Up here doesn't seem to belong to us,' Vicar Pryce said, when the van halted again. 'It's the white. If only we could see just one little robin hopping about the branches! The last time I came this way, I saw pheasants crossing the road, and then they rose. Such colour! It was soon after Easter, and the windflowers and primroses were out.'

'We might be travelling in a wheelbarrow,' sighed Nurse Baldock, as the van moved. She looked at her watch, then into her official bag, and said, 'I've got Evans's old-age pension money. Because of his wife's taking to her bed, he worried about not being able to leave the cottage. I told him, "You're lucky you've got someone like me to look after you, but it's not my bounden task to collect your pension money, Council-employed though I am. Things can't go on like this, my dear sir, come now." '

'You've been kind to him,' the Vicar acknowledged at last.

'It's the State that is kind,' she said stoutly. 'We can say there's no such thing as neglect or old-fashioned poverty for the elderly now. But in my opinion the lay public has begun to take our welfare schemes too much for granted. The other day, I was able to get a wig free of charge for a certain madam living not a hundred miles from this spot, and when I turned

467

up with it on my bike she complained it wasn't the right brown shade and she couldn't wear it – a woman who is not able to step outside her door and is seventy-eight!'

'The aged tend to cling to their little cussednesses,' Vicar Pryce mumbled, in a lacklustre way.

'Yes, indeed.' They were nearing their destination now, and Nurse Baldock, tenacity unabated, seized her last opportunity. 'But do press the real advantages of Pistyll Mawr Home to Evans, Vicar. We are grateful when the Church does its share in these cases. After all, my concern is with the body.' This earned no reply, and she said, 'Germs! It's too icy for them to be active just now, but with the thaw there'll be a fine crop of bronchials and influenzas, mark my words! And I don't relish coming all this way to attend to Evans if he's struck down, probably through not taking proper nourishment.' There was a further silence, and she added, 'On the other hand, these outlying cases ought to convince the Health Department that I must be given a car – don't you agree, Vicar?'

'I wonder you have not had one already. Dr Howells should—'

A few yards ahead, the plough had stopped. Its driver leaned out of his cabin and yelled, 'Can't see a gate!'

'I'll find it,' Nurse Baldock declared.

The vicar and van driver helped to ease her out of the back doors. She shook her glut of warm skirts down, and clumped forward in her gumboots. A snow-caked roof and chimney could be seen above a billowing white slope. Scanning the contours of a buried hedge, the nurse pointed. 'The gate is there. I used to lean my bike against that tree.' It was another lamenting birch, the crystal-entwined branches drooped to the snow.

468

The plough driver, an amiable-looking young man in an elegant alpine sweater, brought out three shovels. Nurse Baldock scolded him for not having four. Valiantly, when he stopped for coffee and sandwiches, she did a stint, and also used the Vicar's shovel while he rested. They had shouted towards the cottage. There was no response, and, gradually, they ceased to talk. It took them half an hour to clear a way up the garden. They saw the oilskin-wrapped box as they neared the door. The nurse, her square face professionally rid of comment now, had already fetched her bag.

It was even colder in the stone house than outside. Nurse Baldock, the first to enter, returned from a swift trot into the living room and kitchen to the men clustered in the little hallway. She stepped to the staircase. All-seeing as an investigating policewoman, she was nevertheless respecting the social decencies. Also, despite the sight of broken crockery, a biscuit box, and a tray scattered below the stairs, she was refusing to face defeat yet. 'John Ormond Evans,' she called up, 'are you there?' Her voice had the challenging ring sometimes used for encouraging the declining back to the world of health, and after a moment of silence, she added, with an unexpected note of entreaty, 'The vicar is here!' The three men, like awkward intruders in a private place, stood listening. Nurse Baldock braced herself. 'Come up with me,' she whispered.

Even the plough driver followed her. But when the flannel wrappings were stripped away, John Ormond Evans sat gazing out at them from his chair as though in mild surprise at this intrusion into his comfortable retreat. His deep-sunk blue eyes were frostily clear under arched white brows. He looked like one awakened from restorative slumber, an expression of judicious independence fixed on his spare face. His hands rested on his knees, like a Pharaoh's.

Nurse Baldock caught in her breath with a hissing sound. The two older men, who had remained hatted and gloved in the icy room, stood dumbly arrested. It was the ruddy-cheeked young man who suddenly put out a bare, instinctive hand and, with a movement of extraordinary delicacy, tried to close the blue eyes. He failed.

'I closed my father's eyes,' he stammered, drawing away in bashful apology for his strange temerity.

'Frozen,' pronounced Vicar Pryce, removing his round black hat. He seemed about to offer a few valedictory words.

Nurse Baldock pulled herself together. She swallowed, and said, 'Lack of nourishment, too!' She took off a gauntlet glove, thrust fingers round one of the thin wrists for a token feel, and then stepped back. 'Well, here's a problem! Are we to take him back with us?'

Vicar Pryce turned to look at the woman lying on the curtain-hung bed. Perhaps because his senses were blurred by the cold, he murmured, 'She's very small – smaller than I remember her. Couldn't he go in the coffin with her for the journey back?'

'No,' said Nurse Baldock promptly. 'He couldn't be straightened here.'

The van driver, an auxiliary assistant in busy times to Messrs Eccles, the market-town undertakers, confirmed, 'Set, set.'

'As he was in his ways!' burst from Nurse Baldock in her chagrin. 'This needn't have happened if he had come with me, as I wanted six days ago! Did he sit there all night deliberately?'

It was decided to take him. The coffin, three days late in delivery, was fetched from the van by the driver and the young man. Maria Evans, aged eighty-three, and prepared for this journey by the nurse six days before, by no means filled its depth and length. Gone naturally, of old age, and kept fresh by the cold, she looked ready to rise punctiliously to meet the face of the Almighty with the same hale energy as she had met each washing day on earth. Her shawl-draped husband, almost equally small, was borne out after her in his sitting posture. Nurse Baldock, with the Vicar for witness, locked up the house. Already it had an air of not belonging to anyone. 'We must tell the police we found the clock lying broken in the hearth,' she said. 'There'll be an inquest, of course.'

John Evans, head resting against the van's side, travelled sitting on his wife's coffin; Vicar Pryce considered it unseemly for him to be laid on the floor. The helicopter box of necessities and the heavy can of oil, placed on either side of him, held him secure. Nurse Baldock chose to travel with the young man in the draughty cabin of his plough. Huddled in her fur coat, and looking badly in need of her own hearth, she remained sunk in morose silence now.

The plough, no longer spouting snow, trundled in the van's rear. 'Pretty in there!' the driver ventured to say, in due course. They were passing the spectral birch glades. A bluish shade had come to the depths.

Nurse Baldock stirred. Peering out, she all but spat. 'Damned, damned snow! All my work wasted! Arguments on the phone, a helicopter, and this plough! The cost! I shall have to appear before the Health Committee.'

'I expect they'll give you credit for all you've done for the old fellow,' said the driver, also a Council employee.

She was beyond comforting just then. 'Old people won't *listen!* When I said to him six days ago, "Come with me, there's nothing you can do for her now," he answered, "Not yet. I will keep her company." I could have taken him at once to Pistyll Mawr Home. It was plain he couldn't look after himself. One of those unwise men who let themselves be spoilt by their wives.'

'Well, they're not parted now,' the young man said.

'The point is, if he had come with me he would be enjoying a round of buttered toast in Pistyll Mawr at this very moment. I blame myself for not trying hard enough. But how was I to know all this damn snow was coming?'

'A lot of old people don't like going into Pistyll Mawr Home, do they?'

'What's wrong with Pistyll Mawr? Hetty Jarvis, the matron, has a heart of gold. What's more, now I've got my social science diploma, I'm applying for her position when she retires next year.'

'Good luck to you.' The driver blew on his hands. Already, the speedier van had disappeared into the whiteness.

'The lay public,' Nurse Baldock sighed, looking mollified, '*will* cling to its prejudices.' And half to herself, she went on, 'Hetty Jarvis complained to me that she hasn't got anything like enough inmates to keep her staff occupied. "Baldock," she said to me, "I'm depending on you," and I phoned her only this week to say I had found someone for her, a sober and clean man I would gamble had many years before him if he was properly cared for.'

'Ah,' murmured the driver. He lit a cigarette, at which his preoccupied passenger – after all, they were in a kind of funeral – frowned.

'People should see the beeswaxed parquet floors in Pistyll Mawr,' she pursued. 'When the hydrangeas are in bloom along the drive, our Queen herself couldn't wish for a better approach to her home. The Bishop called it a noble sanctuary in his opening-day speech. And so it is!'

'I've heard the Kingdom of Heaven is like that,' the young man remarked idly. 'People have got to be pushed in.'

Nurse Baldock turned to look at his round face, to which had come, perhaps because of the day's rigours, the faint purple hue of a ripening fig. 'You might think differently later on, my boy,' she commented in a measured way. 'I can tell you there comes a time when few of us are able to stand alone. You saw today what resulted for one who made the wrong choice.'

'Oh, I don't know. I expect he knew what he was doing, down inside him.'

She sighed again, apparently patient of ignorance and youthful lack of feeling. 'I was fond of old Evans,' she said.

'Anyone can see it,' he allowed.

She remained silent for a long while. The costly defeat continued to weigh on her until the plough had lumbered on to the flat of the valley's bed. There, she looked at her watch and began to bustle up from melancholy. 'Five hours on this one case!' she fidgeted. 'I ought to have gone back in the van. I'm due at a case up on Sheep's Gap.'

'Another old one?'

'No, thank God. An illegitimate maternity. Not the first one for her either! And I've got another in the row of cottages down by the little waterfall – a legitimate.' The satisfaction of a life-giving smack on the bottom seemed to resound in her perked-up voice. 'We need them more than ever in nasty times like these, don't we? Providing a house is warm and well stocked for the welcome. Can't you make this thing go faster?'

'I'm at top speed. It's not built for maternities of any kind.'

Nurse Baldock sniffed. She sat more benevolently, however, and offered from the official black bag a packet of barley-sugar sweets. The village lay less than a mile distant. But it was some time before there was a sign of natural life out in the white purity. The smudged outline of a church tower and clustering houses had come into view when the delighted young man exclaimed, 'Look!' Arriving from nowhere, a hare had jumped on to the smooth track. His jump lacked a hare's usual celerity. He seemed bewildered, and sat up for an instant, ears tensed to the noise breaking the silence of these chaotic acres, a palpitating eye cast back in assessment of the oncoming plough. Then his forepaws gave a quick play of movement, like shadowboxing, and he sprang forward on the track with renewed vitality. Twice he stopped to look, as though in need of affiliation with the plough's motion. But, beyond a bridge over the frozen river, he took a flying leap and, paws barely touching the hardened snow and scut whisking, escaped out of sight.

ALICE MUNRO

THE MOONS OF JUPITER

I FOUND MY father in the heart wing, on the eighth floor of Toronto General Hospital. He was in a semi-private room. The other bed was empty. He said that his hospital insurance covered only a bed in the ward, and he was worried that he might be charged extra.

'I never asked for a semi-private,' he said.

I said the wards were probably full.

'No. I saw some empty beds when they were wheeling me by.'

'Then it was because you had to be hooked up to that thing,' I said. 'Don't worry. If they're going to charge you extra, they tell you about it.'

'That's likely it,' he said. 'They wouldn't want those doohickeys set up in the wards. I guess I'm covered for that kind of thing.'

I said I was sure he was.

He had wires taped to his chest. A small screen hung over his head. On the screen a bright jagged line was continually being written. The writing was accompanied by a nervous electronic beeping. The behavior of his heart was on display. I tried to ignore it. It seemed to me that paying such close attention – in fact, dramatizing what ought to be a most secret activity – was asking for trouble. Anything exposed that way was apt to flare up and go crazy.

My father did not seem to mind. He said they had him

on tranquillizers. You know, he said, the happy pills. He did seem calm and optimistic.

It had been a different story the night before. When I brought him into the hospital, to the emergency room, he had been pale and close-mouthed. He had opened the car door and stood up and said quietly, 'Maybe you better get me one of those wheelchairs.' He used the voice he always used in a crisis. Once, our chimney caught on fire; it was on a Sunday afternoon and I was in the dining room pinning together a dress I was making. He came in and said in that same matter-of-fact, warning voice, 'Janet. Do you know where there's some baking powder?' He wanted it to throw on the fire. Afterwards he said, 'I guess it was your fault – sewing on Sunday.'

I had to wait for over an hour in the emergency waiting room. They summoned a heart specialist who was in the hospital, a young man. He called me out into the hall and explained to me that one of the valves of my father's heart had deteriorated so badly that there ought to be an immediate operation.

I asked him what would happen otherwise.

'He'd have to stay in bed,' the doctor said.

'How long?'

'Maybe three months.'

'I meant, how long would he live?'

'That's what I meant too,' the doctor said.

I went to see my father. He was sitting up in bed in a curtained-off corner. 'It's bad, isn't it?' he said. 'Did he tell you about the valve?'

'It's not as bad as it could be,' I said. Then I repeated, even exaggerated, anything hopeful the doctor had said. 'You're not in any immediate danger. Your physical condition is good, otherwise.'

478

'Otherwise,' said my father gloomily.

I was tired from the drive – all the way up to Dalgleish, to get him, and back to Toronto since noon – and worried about getting the rented car back on time, and irritated by an article I had been reading in a magazine in the waiting room. It was about another writer, a woman younger, better-looking, probably more talented than I am. I had been in England for two months and so I had not seen this article before, but it crossed my mind while I was reading that my father would have. I could hear him saying, Well, I didn't see anything about you in *Maclean's*. And if he had read something about me he would say, Well, I didn't think too much of that write-up. His tone would be humorous and indulgent but would produce in me a familiar dreariness of spirit. The message I got from him was simple: Fame must be striven for, then apologized for. Getting or not getting it, you will be to blame.

I was not surprised by the doctor's news. I was prepared to hear something of the sort and was pleased with my-self for taking it calmly, just as I would be pleased with myself for dressing a wound or looking down from the frail balcony of a high building. I thought, Yes, it's time; there has to be something, here it is. I did not feel any of the protest I would have felt twenty, even ten, years before. When I saw from my father's face that he felt it – that refusal leapt up in him as readily as if he had been thirty or forty years younger – my heart hardened, and I spoke with a kind of badgering cheerfulness. 'Otherwise is plenty,' I said.

The next day he was himself again.

That was how I would have put it. He said it appeared to him now that the young fellow, the doctor, might have been a bit too eager to operate. 'A bit knife-happy,' he said. He was both mocking and showing off the hospital slang. He said that another doctor had examined him, an older man, and had given it as his opinion that rest and medication might do the trick.

I didn't ask what trick.

'He says I've got a defective valve, all right. There's certainly some damage. They wanted to know if I had rheumatic fever when I was a kid. I said I didn't think so. But half the time then you weren't diagnosed what you had. My father was not one for getting the doctor.'

The thought of my father's childhood, which I always pictured as bleak and dangerous – the poor farm, the scared sisters, the harsh father – made me less resigned to his dying. I thought of him running away to work on the lake boats, running along the railway tracks, toward Goderich, in the evening light. He used to tell about that trip. Somewhere along the track he found a quince tree. Quince trees are rare in our part of the country; in fact, I have never seen one. Not even the one my father found, though he once took us on an expedition to look for it. He thought he knew the crossroad it was near, but we could not find it. He had not been able to eat the fruit, of course, but he had been impressed by its existence. It made him think he had got into a new part of the world.

The escaped child, the survivor, an old man trapped here by his leaky heart. I didn't pursue these thoughts. I didn't care to think of his younger selves. Even his bare torso, thick and white – he had the body of a working-man of his generation, seldom exposed to the sun – was a danger to me; it looked so strong and young. The wrinkled neck, the age-freckled hands and arms, the narrow, courteous head, with its thin gray hair and mustache, were more what I was used to.

'Now, why would I want to get myself operated on?' said

480

my father reasonably. 'Think of the risk at my age, and what for? A few years at the outside. I think the best thing for me to do is go home and take it easy. Give in gracefully. That's all you can do, at my age. Your attitude changes, you know. You go through some mental changes. It seems more natural.'

'What does?' I said.

'Well, death does. You can't get more natural than that. No, what I mean, specifically, is not having the operation.'

'That seems more natural?'

'Yes.'

'It's up to you,' I said, but I did approve. This was what I would have expected of him. Whenever I told people about my father I stressed his independence, his self-sufficiency, his forbearance. He worked in a factory, he worked in his garden, he read history books. He could tell you about the Roman emperors or the Balkan wars. He never made a fuss.

Judith, my younger daughter, had come to meet me at Toronto Airport two days before. She had brought the boy she was living with, whose name was Don. They were driving to Mexico in the morning, and while I was in Toronto I was to stay in their apartment. For the time being, I live in Vancouver. I sometimes say I have my headquarters in Vancouver.

'Where's Nichola?' I said, thinking at once of an accident or an overdose. Nichola is my older daughter. She used to be a student at the Conservatory, then she became a cocktail waitress, then she was out of work. If she had been at the airport, I would probably have said something wrong. I would have asked her what her plans were, and she would have gracefully brushed back her hair and said, 'Plans?' – as if that was a word I had invented.

'I knew the first thing you'd say would be about Nichola,' Judith said.

'It wasn't. I said hello and I—'

'We'll get your bag,' Don said neutrally.

'Is she all right?'

'I'm sure she is,' said Judith, with a fabricated air of amusement. 'You wouldn't look like that if I was the one who wasn't here.'

'Of course I would.'

'You wouldn't. Nichola is the baby of the family. You know, she's four years older than I am.'

'I ought to know.'

Judith said she did not know where Nichola was exactly. She said Nichola had moved out of her apartment (that dump!) and had actually telephoned (which is quite a deal, you might say, Nichola phoning) to say she wanted to be incommunicado for a while but she was fine.

'I told her you would worry,' said Judith more kindly on the way to their van. Don walked ahead carrying my suitcase. 'But don't. She's all right, believe me.'

Don's presence made me uncomfortable. I did not like him to hear these things. I thought of the conversations they must have had, Don and Judith. Or Don and Judith and Nichola, for Nichola and Judith were sometimes on good terms. Or Don and Judith and Nichola and others whose names I did not even know. They would have talked about me. Judith and Nichola comparing notes, relating anecdotes; analyzing, regretting, blaming, forgiving. I wished I'd had a boy and a girl. Or two boys. They wouldn't have done that. Boys couldn't possibly know so much about you.

I did the same thing at that age. When I was the age Judith is now I talked with my friends in the college cafeteria or, late at night, over coffee in our cheap rooms. When I was the age Nichola is now I had Nichola herself in a carry-cot or squirming in my lap, and I was drinking coffee again all the rainy Vancouver afternoons with my one neighborhood friend, Ruth Boudreau, who read a lot and was bewildered by her situation, as I was. We talked about our parents, our childhoods, though for some time we kept clear of our marriages. How thoroughly we dealt with our fathers and mothers, deplored their marriages, their mistaken ambitions or fear of ambition, how competently we filed them away, defined them beyond any possibility of change. What presumption.

I looked at Don walking ahead. A tall ascetic-looking boy, with a St. Francis cap of black hair, a precise fringe of beard. What right did he have to hear about me, to know things I myself had probably forgotten? I decided that his beard and hairstyle were affected.

Once, when my children were little, my father said to me, 'You know those years you were growing up – well, that's all just a kind of a blur to me. I can't sort out one year from another.' I was offended. I remembered each separate year with pain and clarity. I could have told how old I was when I went to look at the evening dresses in the window of Benbow's Ladies' Wear. Every week through the winter a new dress, spotlit – the sequins and tulle, the rose and lilac, sapphire, daffodil – and me a cold worshipper on the slushy sidewalk. I could have told how old I was when I forged my mother's signature on a bad report card, when I had measles, when we papered the front room. But the years when Judith and Nichola were little, when I lived with their father – yes, *blur* is the word for it. I remember hanging out diapers, bringing in and folding diapers; I can recall the kitchen counters of two houses and where the clothesbasket sat. I remember the television programs – *Popeye the Sailor*, *The Three Stooges*,

483

Funorama. When *Funorama* came on it was time to turn on the lights and cook supper. But I couldn't tell the years apart. We lived outside Vancouver in a dormitory suburb: Dormir, Dormer, Dormouse – something like that. I was sleepy all the time then; pregnancy made me sleepy, and the night feedings, and the west coast rain falling. Dark dripping cedars, shiny dripping laurel; wives yawning, napping, visiting, drinking coffee, and folding diapers; husbands coming home at night from the city across the water. Every night I kissed my homecoming husband in his wet Burberry and hoped he might wake me up; I served up meat and potatoes and one of the four vegetables he permitted. He ate with a violent appetite, then fell asleep on the living-room sofa. We had become a cartoon couple, more middle-aged in our twenties than we would be in middle age.

Those bumbling years are the years our children will remember all their lives. Corners of the yards I never visited will stay in their heads.

'Did Nichola not want to see me?' I said to Judith.

'She doesn't want to see anybody, half the time,' she said. Judith moved ahead and touched Don's arm. I knew that touch – an apology, an anxious reassurance. You touch a man that way to remind him that you are grateful, that you realize he is doing for your sake something that bores him or slightly endangers his dignity. It made me feel older than grandchildren would to see my daughter touch a man – a boy – this way. I felt her sad jitters, could predict her supple attentions. My blunt and stocky, blond and candid child. Why should I think she wouldn't be susceptible, that she would always be straightforward, heavy-footed, self-reliant? Just as I go around saying that Nichola is sly and solitary, cold, seductive. Many people must know things that would contradict what I say.

In the morning Don and Judith left for Mexico. I decided I wanted to see somebody who wasn't related to me, and who didn't expect anything in particular from me. I called an old lover of mine, but his phone was answered by a machine: 'This is Tom Shepherd speaking. I will be out of town for the month of September. Please record your message, name, and phone number.'

Tom's voice sounded so pleasant and familiar that I opened my mouth to ask him the meaning of this foolishness. Then I hung up. I felt as if he had deliberately let me down, as if we had planned to meet in a public place and then he hadn't shown up. Once, he had done that, I remembered.

I got myself a glass of vermouth, though it was not yet noon, and I phoned my father.

'Well, of all things,' he said. 'Fifteen more minutes and you would have missed me.'

'Were you going downtown?'

'Downtown Toronto.'

He explained that he was going to the hospital. His doctor in Dalgleish wanted the doctors in Toronto to take a look at him, and had given him a letter to show them in the emergency room.

'Emergency room?' I said.

'It's not an emergency. He just seems to think this is the best way to handle it. He knows the name of a fellow there. If he was to make me an appointment, it might take weeks.'

'Does your doctor know you're driving to Toronto?' I said.

'Well, he didn't say I couldn't.'

The upshot of this was that I rented a car, drove to Dalgleish, brought my father back to Toronto, and had him in the emergency room by seven o'clock that evening.

Before Judith left I said to her, 'You're sure Nichola knows I'm staying here?'

485

'Well, I told her,' she said.

Sometimes the phone rang, but it was always a friend of Judith's.

'Well, it looks like I'm going to have it,' my father said. This was on the fourth day. He had done a complete turnaround overnight. 'It looks like I might as well.'

I didn't know what he wanted me to say. I thought perhaps he looked to me for a protest, an attempt to dissuade him.

'When will they do it?' I said.

'Day after tomorrow.'

I said I was going to the washroom. I went to the nurses' station and found a woman there who I thought was the head nurse. At any rate, she was gray-haired, kind, and serious-looking.

'My father's having an operation the day after tomorrow?' I said.

'Oh, yes.'

'I just wanted to talk to somebody about it. I thought there'd been a sort of decision reached that he'd be better not to. I thought because of his age.'

'Well, it's his decision and the doctor's.' She smiled at me without condescension. 'It's hard to make these decisions.'

'How were his tests?'

'Well, I haven't seen them all.'

I was sure she had. After a moment she said, 'We have to be realistic. But the doctors here are very good.'

When I went back into the room my father said, in a surprised voice, '*Shore*-less seas.'

'What?' I said. I wondered if he had found out how much, or how little, time he could hope for. I wondered if the pills had brought on an untrustworthy euphoria. Or if he had wanted to gamble. Once, when he was talking to me about his life, he said, 'The trouble was I was always afraid to take chances.'

I used to tell people that he never spoke regretfully about his life, but that was not true. It was just that I didn't listen to it. He said that he should have gone into the Army as a tradesman – he would have been better off. He said he should have gone on his own, as a carpenter, after the war. He should have got out of Dalgleish. Once, he said, 'A wasted life, eh?' But he was making fun of himself, saying that, because it was such a dramatic thing to say. When he quoted poetry too, he always had a scoffing note in his voice, to excuse the showing-off and the pleasure.

'Shoreless seas,' he said again. ' "Behind him lay the gray Azores, / Behind the Gates of Hercules; / Before him not the ghost of shores, / Before him only shoreless seas." That's what was going through my head last night. But do you think I could remember what kind of seas? I could not. Lonely seas? Empty seas? I was on the right track but I couldn't get it. But there now when you came into the room and I wasn't thinking about it at all, the word popped into my head. That's always the way, isn't it? It's not all that surprising. I ask my mind a question. The answer's there, but I can't see all the connections my mind's making to get it. Like a computer. Nothing out of the way. You know, in my situation the thing is, if there's anything you can't explain right away, there's a great temptation to – well, to make a mystery out of it. There's a great temptation to believe in – You know.'

'The soul?' I said, speaking lightly, feeling an appalling rush of love and recognition.

'Oh, I guess you could call it that. You know, when I first came into this room there was a pile of papers here by the bed. Somebody had left them here – one of those tabloid sort of things I never looked at. I started reading them. I'll read anything handy. There was a series running in them on personal experiences of people who had died, medically speaking – heart arrest, mostly – and had been brought back to life. It was what they remembered of the time when they were dead. Their experiences.'

'Pleasant or un-?' I said.

'Oh, pleasant. Oh, yes. They'd float up to the ceiling and look down on themselves and see the doctors working on them, on their bodies. Then float on further and recognize some people they knew who had died before them. Not see them exactly but sort of sense them. Sometimes there would be a humming and sometimes a sort of – what's that light that there is or color around a person?'

'Aura?'

'Yes. But without the person. That's about all they'd get time for; then they found themselves back in the body and feeling all the mortal pain and so on – brought back to life.'

'Did it seem – convincing?'

'Oh, I don't know. It's all in whether you want to believe that kind of thing or not. And if you are going to believe it, take it seriously, I figure you've got to take everything else seriously that they print in those papers.'

'What else do they?'

'Rubbish – cancer cures, baldness cures, bellyaching about the younger generation and the welfare bums. Tripe about movie stars.'

'Oh, yes. I know.'

'In my situation you have to keep a watch,' he said, 'or you'll start playing tricks on yourself.' Then he said, 'There's a few practical details we ought to get straight on,' and he told me about his will, the house, the cemetery plot. Everything was simple.

'Do you want me to phone Peggy?' I said. Peggy is my

sister. She is married to an astronomer and lives in Victoria.

He thought about it. 'I guess we ought to tell them,' he said finally. 'But tell them not to get alarmed.'

'All right.'

'No, wait a minute. Sam is supposed to be going to a conference the end of this week, and Peggy was planning to go along with him. I don't want them wondering about changing their plans.'

'Where is the conference?'

'Amsterdam,' he said proudly. He did take pride in Sam, and kept track of his books and articles. He would pick one up and say, 'Look at that, will you? And I can't understand a word of it!' in a marvelling voice that managed nevertheless to have a trace of ridicule.

'Professor Sam,' he would say. 'And the three little Sams.' This is what he called his grandsons, who did resemble their father in braininess and in an almost endearing pushiness – an innocent energetic showing-off. They went to a private school that favored old-fashioned discipline and started calculus in Grade 5. 'And the dogs,' he might enumerate further, 'who have been to obedience school. And Peggy . . .'

But if I said, 'Do you suppose she has been to obedience school too?' he would play the game no further. I imagine that when he was with Sam and Peggy he spoke of me in the same way – hinted at my flightiness just as he hinted at their stodginess, made mild jokes at my expense, did not quite conceal his amazement (or pretended not to conceal his amazement) that people paid money for things I had written. He had to do this so that he might never seem to brag, but he would put up the gates when the joking got too rough. And of course I found later, in the house, things of mine he had kept – a few magazines, clippings, things I had never bothered about.

Now his thoughts travelled from Peggy's family to mine. 'Have you heard from Judith?' he said.

'Not yet.'

'Well, it's pretty soon. Were they going to sleep in the van?'

'Yes.'

'I guess it's safe enough, if they stop in the right places.'

I knew he would have to say something more and I knew it would come as a joke.

'I guess they put a board down the middle, like the pioneers?'

I smiled but did not answer.

'I take it you have no objections?'

'No,' I said.

'Well, I always believed that too. Keep out of your children's business. I tried not to say anything. I never said anything when you left Richard.'

'What do you mean, "said anything"? Criticize?'

'It wasn't any of my business.'

'No.'

'But that doesn't mean I was pleased.'

I was surprised – not just at what he said but at his feeling that he had any right, even now, to say it. I had to look out the window and down at the traffic to control myself.

'I just wanted you to know,' he added.

A long time ago, he said to me in his mild way, 'It's funny. Richard when I first saw him reminded me of what my father used to say. He'd say if that fellow was half as smart as he thinks he is, he'd be twice as smart as he really is.'

I turned to remind him of this, but found myself looking at the line his heart was writing. Not that there seemed to be anything wrong, any difference in the beeps and points. But it was there.

He saw where I was looking. 'Unfair advantage,' he said.

'It is,' I said. 'I'm going to have to get hooked up too.'

We laughed, we kissed formally; I left. At least he hadn't asked me about Nichola, I thought.

The next afternoon I didn't go to the hospital, because my father was having some more tests done, to prepare for the operation. I was to see him in the evening instead. I found myself wandering through the Bloor Street dress shops, trying on clothes. A preoccupation with fashion and my own appearance had descended on me like a raging headache. I looked at the women in the street, at the clothes in the shops, trying to discover how a transformation might be made, what I would have to buy. I recognized this obsession for what it was but had trouble shaking it. I've had people tell me that waiting for life-or-death news they've stood in front of an open refrigerator eating anything in sight – cold boiled potatoes, chili sauce, bowls of whipped cream. Or have been unable to stop doing crossword puzzles. Attention narrows in on something – some distraction – grabs on, becomes fanatically serious. I shuffled clothes on the racks, pulled them on in hot little changing rooms in front of cruel mirrors. I was sweating; once or twice I thought I might faint. Out on the street again, I thought I must remove myself from Bloor Street, and decided to go to the museum.

I remembered another time, in Vancouver. It was when Nichola was going to kindergarten and Judith was a baby. Nichola had been to the doctor about a cold, or maybe for a routine examination, and the blood test revealed something about her white blood cells – either that there were too many of them or that they were enlarged. The doctor ordered further tests, and I took Nichola to the

491

hospital for them. Nobody mentioned leukemia but I knew, of course, what they were looking for. When I took Nichola home I asked the babysitter who had been with Judith to stay for the afternoon and I went shopping. I bought the most daring dress I ever owned, a black silk sheath with some laced-up arrangement in front. I remembered that bright spring afternoon, the spike-heeled shoes in the department store, the underwear printed with leopard spots.

I also remembered going home from St. Paul's Hospital over the Lions Gate Bridge on the crowded bus and holding Nichola on my knee. She suddenly recalled her baby name for *bridge* and whispered to me, 'Whee – over the whee.' I did not avoid touching my child – Nichola was slender and graceful even then, with a pretty back and fine dark hair – but realized I was touching her with a difference, though I did not think it could ever be detected. There was a care – not a withdrawal exactly but a care – not to feel anything much. I saw how the forms of love might be maintained with a condemned person but with the love in fact measured and disciplined, because you have to survive. It could be done so discreetly that the object of such care would not suspect, any more than she would suspect the sentence of death itself. Nichola did not know, would not know. Toys and kisses and jokes would come tumbling over her; she would never know, though I worried that she would feel the wind between the cracks of the manufactured holidays, the manufactured normal days. But all was well. Nichola did not have leukemia. She grew up – was still alive, and possibly happy. Incommunicado.

I could not think of anything in the museum I really wanted to see, so I walked past it to the planetarium. I had never been to a planetarium. The show was due to start in ten minutes. I went inside, bought a ticket, got in line.

There was a whole class of schoolchildren, maybe a couple of classes, with teachers and volunteer mothers riding herd on them. I looked around to see if there were any other unattached adults. Only one – a man with a red face and puffy eyes, who looked as if he might be here to keep himself from going to a bar.

Inside, we sat on wonderfully comfortable seats that were tilted back so that you lay in a sort of hammock, attention directed to the bowl of the ceiling, which soon turned dark blue, with a faint rim of light all around the edge. There was some splendid, commanding music. The adults all around were shushing the children, trying to make them stop crackling their potato-chip bags. Then a man's voice, an eloquent professional voice, began to speak slowly, out of the walls. The voice reminded me a little of the way radio announcers used to introduce a piece of classical music or describe the progress of the Royal Family to Westminster Abbey on one of their royal occasions. There was a faint echo-chamber effect.

The dark ceiling was filling with stars. They came out not all at once but one after another, the way the stars really do come out at night, though more quickly. The Milky Way appeared, was moving closer; stars swam into brilliance and kept on going, disappearing beyond the edges of the sky-screen or behind my head. While the flow of light continued, the voice presented the stunning facts. A few light-years away, it announced, the sun appears as a bright star, and the planets are not visible. A few dozen light-years away, the sun is not visible, either, to the naked eye. And that distance – a few dozen light-years – is only about a thousandth part of the distance from the sun to the center of our galaxy, one galaxy, which itself contains about two hundred billion suns. And is, in turn, one of millions, perhaps billions, of galaxies.

Innumerable repetitions, innumerable variations. All this rolled past my head too, like balls of lightning.

Now realism was abandoned, for familiar artifice. A model of the solar system was spinning away in its elegant style. A bright bug took off from the earth, heading for Jupiter. I set my dodging and shrinking mind sternly to recording facts. The mass of Jupiter two and a half times that of all the other planets put together. The Great Red Spot. The thirteen moons. Past Jupiter, a glance at the eccentric orbit of Pluto, the icy rings of Saturn. Back to Earth and moving in to hot and dazzling Venus. Atmospheric pressure ninety times ours. Moonless Mercury rotating three times while circling the sun twice; an odd arrangement, not as satisfying as what they used to tell us – that it rotated once as it circled the sun. No perpetual darkness after all. Why did they give out such confident information, only to announce later that it was quite wrong? Finally, the picture already familiar from magazines: the red soil of Mars, the blooming pink sky.

When the show was over I sat in my seat while the children clambered across me, making no comments on anything they had just seen or heard. They were pestering their keepers for eatables and further entertainments. An effort had been made to get their attention, to take it away from canned pop and potato chips and fix it on various knowns and unknowns and horrible immensities, and it seemed to have failed. A good thing too, I thought. Children have a natural immunity, most of them, and it shouldn't be tampered with. As for the adults who would deplore it, the ones who promoted this show, weren't they immune them-selves to the extent that they could put in the echo-chamber effects, the music, the churchlike solemnity, simulating the awe that they supposed they ought to feel? Awe – what was that supposed to be? A fit of the shivers when you looked

494

out the window? Once you know what it was, you wouldn't be courting it.

Two men came with brooms to sweep up the debris the audience had left behind. They told me that the next show would start in forty minutes. In the meantime, I had to get out.

'I went to the show at the planetarium,' I said to my father. 'It was very exciting – about the solar system.' I thought what a silly word I had used: *exciting*. 'It's like a slightly phony temple,' I added.

He was already talking. 'I remember when they found Pluto. Right where they thought it had to be. Mercury, Venus, Earth, Mars,' he recited. 'Jupiter, Saturn, Nept – no, Uranus, Neptune, Pluto. Is that right?'

'Yes,' I said. I was just as glad he hadn't heard what I said about the phony temple. I had meant that to be truthful, but it sounded slick and superior. 'Tell me the moons of Jupiter.'

'Well, I don't know the new ones. There's a bunch of new ones, isn't there?'

'Two. But they're not new.'

'New to us,' said my father. 'You've turned pretty cheeky now I'm going under the knife.'

' "Under the knife." What an expression.'

He was not in bed tonight, his last night. He had been detached from his apparatus, and was sitting in a chair by the window. He was bare-legged, wearing a hospital dressing gown, but he did not look self-conscious or out of place. He looked thoughtful but good-humored, an affable host.

'You haven't even named the old ones,' I said.

'Give me time. Galileo named them. Io.'

'That's a start.'

'The moons of Jupiter were the first heavenly bodies

495

discovered with the telescope.' He said this gravely, as if he could see the sentence in an old book. 'It wasn't Galileo named them, either; it was some German. Io, Europa, Ganymede, Callisto. There you are.'

'Yes.'

'Io and Europa, they were girlfriends of Jupiter's, weren't they? Ganymede was a boy. A shepherd? I don't know who Callisto was.'

'I think she was a girlfriend too,' I said. 'Jupiter's wife – Jove's wife – changed her into a bear and stuck her up in the sky. Great Bear and Little Bear. Little Bear was her baby.'

The loudspeaker said that it was time for visitors to go.

'I'll see you when you come out of the anesthetic,' I said.

'Yes.'

When I was at the door, he called to me, 'Ganymede wasn't any shepherd. He was Jove's cupbearer.'

When I left the planetarium that afternoon, I had walked through the museum to the Chinese garden. I saw the stone camels again, the warriors, the tomb. I sat on a bench looking toward Bloor Street. Through the evergreen bushes and the high grilled iron fence I watched people going by in the late-afternoon sunlight. The planetarium show had done what I wanted it to after all – calmed me down, drained me. I saw a girl who reminded me of Nichola. She wore a trenchcoat and carried a bag of groceries. She was shorter than Nichola – not really much like her at all – but I thought that I might see Nichola. She would be walking along some street maybe not far from here – burdened, preoccupied, alone. She was one of the grown-up people in the world now, one of the shoppers going home.

If I did see her, I might just sit and watch, I decided. I felt like one of those people who have floated up to the ceiling,

496

enjoying a brief death. A relief, while it lasts. My father had chosen and Nichola had chosen. Someday, probably soon, I would hear from her, but it came to the same thing.

I meant to get up and go over to the tomb, to look at the relief carvings, the stone pictures, that go all the way around it. I always mean to look at them and I never do. Not this time, either. It was getting cold out, so I went inside to have coffee and something to eat before I went back to the hospital.

ACKNOWLEDGMENTS

J. G. BALLARD: 'Minus One' by J. G. Ballard. Copyright © 2001, J. G. Ballard, used by permission of The Wylie Agency (UK) Limited. 'Minus One'. Copyright © 1967 by J. G. Ballard, from *The Complete Stories of J. G. Ballard* by J. G. Ballard. Used by permission of W. W. Norton & Company, Inc.

ELIZABETH BERRIDGE: 'The Hard and the Human' by Elizabeth Berridge, from *Selected Stories*, Maurice Fridberg, publishers, reprinted with permission from David Higham Associates.

MIKHAIL BULGAKOV: 'The Embroidered Towel' from *A Country Doctor's Notebook*, trans. Michael Glenny. © Collins and Harvill, 1975, © 1975 in the English translation by Michael Glenny. Reprinted with permission of The Random House Group Limited. 'The Embroidered Towel' by Mikhail Bulgakov from *A Country Doctor's Notebook* translated by Michael Glenny. Published by Collins, 1975. Copyright © Michael Glenny. Reproduced by permission of the estate c/o Rogers, Coleridge & White Ltd, 20 Powis Mews, London W11 1JN.

RHYS DAVIES: 'I Will Keep Her Company' from *The Chosen One*, Heinemann, 1967, copyright © 1960, 1962, 1964, 1966, 1967 by Rhys Davies. First published in *The New Yorker*, 1964. Mr A. L. Davies.

GRAHAM GREENE: 'Doctor Crombie' from *May We Borrow Your Husband?*, Bodley Head, 1967. Copyright ©

Graham Greene, 1967. Reprinted with permission from David Higham Associates.

ROBERT A. HEINLEIN: 'Life-Line' from *The Man Who Sold the Moon*, Shasta Publishers, 1950. First published in Great Britain by Sidgwick and Jackson, 1953. Copyright © by Robert Heinlein. Spectrum Literary Agency.

ANNA KAVAN: 'Airing a Grievance' from *Asylum Piece*, Peter Owen Publishers. Reprinted with permission from David Higham Associates.

JHUMPA LAHIRI: 'Interpreter of Maladies' from *Interpreter of Maladies* by Jhumpa Lahiri. Copyright © 1999 by Jhumpa Lahiri. Reprinted by permission of Houghton Mifflin Harcourt Publishing Company. All rights reserved. 'Interpreter of Maladies' from *Interpreter of Maladies*, 4th Estate, an imprint of HarperCollins Publishers, 2019. First published in Great Britain in 1999 by Flamingo. Copyright © Jhumpa Lahiri, 1999.

JULIAN MACLAREN-ROSS: 'I Had to Go Sick' from *The Stuff to Give the Troops*, Jonathan Cape, 1944. Estate of Julian Maclaren-Ross/Andrew Lownie Literary Agency.

W. SOMERSET MAUGHAM: 'Lord Mountdrago' from *The Mixture as Before*, Heinemann, 1940. Copyright © by The Royal Literary Fund. Reprinted with the permission of United Agents LLP on behalf of The Royal Literary Fund.

GUY DE MAUPASSANT: 'A Coup d'État' from *The Complete Short Stories, Vol. 1*, Cassell, 1970. Translation: Anonymous.

LORRIE MOORE: 'People Like That Are the Only People Here: Canonical Babbling in Peed Onk' from *Birds of America: Stories* by Lorrie Moore, copyright © 1998 by Lorrie Moore. Used by permission of Alfred A. Knopf, an imprint of the Knopf Doubleday Publishing Group, a division of Penguin Random House LLC. All rights reserved. 'People Like That Are the Only People Here: Canonical Babbling in